"The Tribune does for [?] Name of the Rose did for medie [?] Europe and Gorky Park did for the corrupt Soviet Union. A terrific, well-researched thriller."
—Kevin J. Anderson, New York Times bestselling author of Dune: The Butlerian Jihad

Praise for the novels of Patrick Larkin written with Larry Bond

Red Phoenix

"A big, big book . . . *Red Phoenix* is wonderfully entertaining and deserves to be the bestseller that it is."
—*The New York Times Book Review*

"Harrowingly real and persuasive."   —*Newsday*

"Gripping . . . masterfully accurate."
—*The Baltimore Sun*

Cauldron

"Dazzling. . . . A sprawling turbulent epic."
—*Chicago Tribune*

"An epic saga of tremendous scope."   —Stephen Coonts

continued . . .

THE TRIBUNE

A NOVEL OF ANCIENT ROME

Patrick Larkin

A SIGNET BOOK

SIGNET
Published by New American Library, a division of
Penguin Putnam Inc., 375 Hudson Street,
New York, New York 10014, U.S.A.
Penguin Books Ltd, 80 Strand,
London WC2R 0RL, England
Penguin Books Australia Ltd, 250 Camberwell Road,
Camberwell, Victoria 3124, Australia
Penguin Books Canada Ltd, 10 Alcorn Avenue,
Toronto, Ontario, Canada M4V 3B2
Penguin Books (N.Z.) Ltd, Cnr Rosedale and Airborne Roads,
Albany, Auckland 1310, New Zealand

Penguin Books Ltd, Registered Offices:
Harmondsworth, Middlesex, England

First published by Signet, an imprint of New American Library, a division of
Penguin Putnam Inc.

First Printing, June 2003
10 9 8 7 6 5 4 3 2 1

Ⓟ REGISTERED TRADEMARK—MARCA REGISTRADA

Printed in the United States of America

PUBLISHER'S NOTE
This is a work of fiction. Names, characters, places, and incidents either are the
product of the author's imagination or are used fictitiously, and any resemblance to
actual persons, living or dead, business establishments, events, or locales is entirely
coincidental.

BOOKS ARE AVAILABLE AT QUANTITY DISCOUNTS WHEN USED TO PROMOTE PRODUCTS OR
SERVICES. FOR INFORMATION PLEASE WRITE TO PREMIUM MARKETING DIVISION, PENGUIN
PUTNAM INC., 375 HUDSON STREET, NEW YORK, NEW YORK 10014.

To Mennette, Olivia, and Rhys,
with all my love forever

Prologue

A man's life may end and yet begin again, even from one breath to the next. My name is Lucius Aurelius Valens, and I am a soldier in the service of Rome. I know what I say is true.

For it happened to me.

Not so long ago, if anyone else had made such a claim I would have dismissed it as a tavern tale told after drinking too much unwatered wine — or as the product of a disordered mind.

But now . . .

Now I see the world in a different light. What I once held certain seems more shadow than substance. And what I once would have laughed at as mere superstition has stepped from the heavens into our own mortal world.

I can only tell you what I saw and heard and felt and learned. You must judge for yourselves whether I speak the truth — or whether I have simply lost all sense and reason.

* * *

But first, you must know something of who I am.

I was born in Rome during the twenty-fourth year after Octavian, the adopted son of Julius Caesar, took the title Augustus and became ruler of the entire civilized world. The long and bloody civil wars that had destroyed the old Republic were over. Augustus was still slowly and shrewdly building a new order on the ashes of the old. And my father, a member of the knightly class, was a rising man in that new order.

He had great ambitions for himself and for me, his only son.

To fulfill those aspirations, he saw to my education and used his influence to secure my first military posting—the necessary first step on the road to greater glory. In this, he acted honorably and justly, as any father would.

This I acknowledge.

But I confess that my father and I had little else in common. His life was consumed with business, with profits and investments—and with trading favors to advance our family's interests. He spent his days in pursuit of wealth and the power that comes from wealth.

I did not share his passions.

Even as a boy, I coveted one thing only.

Honor.

Even now, even after everything I have lived through, there is still something in that single, short word that speeds my pulse.

From my youth, I longed to be known as a man of honor—to be respected by friend and foe alike as a man who would do what was right at all times and in all places.

My father considered this sheer folly and fought hard to turn my mind toward more practical and sensible aims. He blamed my mother's father for filling my head with what he called "idle dreams of profitless distinction."

He was right.

My grandfather was already old when he married. He had no sons, and only one daughter—my mother. As a child, I spent part of every summer on his farm, helping with the harvest and listening to his stories of war and the legions.

He was a veteran soldier who had risen through the ranks to become a senior centurion before finally retiring to the farm he had earned with his service. He bore many scars and had earned many awards for bravery.

But his most valued possession was a plain gold ring—a ring given to him by Augustus himself.

"Look at it, Lucius," my grandfather would say on some evenings as we sat eating together at a table in his simple kitchen. Then he'd hold his hand up to the lamp, letting the flickering light glint off the aureate circle on a finger of his left hand. "It seems such a little thing, doesn't it? Someone like your father would call it just a piece of common jewelry. But it is more than that. Much more. You know that, don't you?"

I would nod, waiting eagerly as always for the old and familiar tale.

Forty years before I was born, my grandfather was a centurion in a legion commanded by Octavian, who was then only nineteen years old. The assassination of Caesar had just thrown Rome and all the provinces into chaos. Most men shifted their allegiances with the prevailing winds, but not my grandfather. He had served Caesar, and he decided to keep faith by obeying the orders of his beloved general's adopted son.

At the time, Octavian had allied himself with the Senate against Marcus Antonius, Caesar's old lieutenant. Antonius had angered him by denying him his inheritance and opposing his political plans.

Their two armies clashed in a fierce battle around the city of Mutina in northern Italy.

At one point in the fray, Antonius' troops tore a gap in the legion's line. The standard-bearer went down, pierced by a javelin. Octavian, seeing his legionaries wavering and beginning to panic, snatched up the Eagle himself and held it aloft. My grandfather rallied those closest to him and led them back to the Eagle's defense—arriving just in time to fend off a ferocious attack by enemy soldiers. During the frantic melee, he protected Octavian with his own shield, despite taking several wounds himself.

The next day, as he lay in the hospital tent, Octavian came to see him.

"Well, Marcus Valerius," said the young man who would one day rule all of Rome, "I've come to thank you for saving my life. What can I give you as a sign of my gratitude?"

But my grandfather just shook his head. "There's no need, sir. You owe me nothing."

Octavian chuckled. "I hardly think so. Like any man of sense, I put a high value on my own skin. Tell me what I can do to repay you."

Again my grandfather shook his head. "You're under a misapprehension, sir. I didn't fight to save your life. I fought to save the Eagle—and the honor of our legion."

Clearly startled, Octavian stared down at him in silence for a few moments; then he turned on his heel and left without saying another word.

A week later, though, he sent his gift. It was a plain gold ring and it bore a simple inscription engraved on the inner surface: Honor and Truth.

From that day forward, my grandfather wore that ring with pride.

And now I wear it.

It came to me on the day I came of age. My grandfather, though already in his eighties, traveled to Rome for the occasion. He was thinner than when I'd last seen him, but he still moved spryly and had the same fierce gaze that could cow even my father into silence. After the feasting was over, he called me to his side. Before I could say anything, he slipped the ring off his own finger and placed it on mine.

"This is yours now, Lucius," he said simply, looking straight into my eyes. "My honor is now your honor. Uphold it. Act always in honor and in truth. Never shame me."

I nodded dumbly, too overcome with emotion to speak.

Then my grandfather smiled. "You are my true heir, Lucius. You will be worthy. I have seen it."

He died later that same year—carried off by a fever that took hold in one of his old wounds.

In all the years since, in everything that I have done and refused to do, I have tried to keep my grandfather's last commandment. It has never been easy. And I am sure that I have failed far more often than I would like to admit.

Still, I have always tried to do what is right. I have always tried to speak the truth.

Listen to me now, then, as I tell you a strange and frightening and marvelous story.

Listen.

And, if you can, believe.

Chapter I

I had been on the road from Apamea since before dawn—riding hard to see the aftermath of a massacre.

Sweat prickled under my armor, trickling down my ribs. Though it was still morning, the heat was already intense. Smoke stained the sky above me as I turned my horse off the main road and trotted up a narrow, tree-lined track. Ahead, I could see the walled farm compound that had once been the heart of a large country estate. The black shapes of carrion birds circled low overhead.

It was August in the fifth year of Tiberius Caesar, and it was the height of the summer. Eight years had passed since my grandfather gave me his blessing and his ring. I was a tribune of the Sixth Legion. This was my second assignment since taking the military oath. I'd spent the first four years of my army career along the Rhine, commanding a cohort of light infantry in the endless wars against the German barbarians. Now, I'd been promoted and transferred to the Sixth—one of four legions garrisoning the province of Syria against any attack by our old Parthian enemies.

The confidential reports I'd studied before arriving

had described the province as peaceful and prosperous. Our treaty with Parthia still held firm. The nomad tribes along the desert frontier were quiet. The Syrians themselves were said to be placid and happy under our rule. Under those circumstances, I'd expected to spend a restful time wrestling with the details of legionary administration and army law, acquiring more of the skills and knowledge—and influential friends—I would need to advance to higher command.

I was wrong.

Syria was not at peace. It was at war with itself.

The main gate of the farmstead hung loose, battered off its hinges by a ram. The smoke was thicker now.

I urged my mount forward through the open gate. A raven shrieked and soared into the sky as I rode past.

The dead were everywhere.

Mutilated bodies were strewn across the hard-packed earth. Others lay crumpled in and around the adjoining barns, granaries, and slave quarters. Soldiers stripped to their tunics were hauling more corpses out of the splendid stone villa standing at the center of the compound.

Ahead of me, an officer in armor and a scarlet cloak sat on a horse, issuing clipped, angry orders to the men at work.

Smoke from burning outbuildings hung heavy in the still, stagnant air. Its acrid stench burned my throat and stung my eyes. Beneath the pall, clouds of swollen black flies droned lazily above the corpses of both men and beasts—feasting on the torn flesh and dried blood.

I swallowed hard against the sour taste of bile rising into my mouth. My horse—a sprightly Spanish mare I'd named Dancer—whinnied uneasily, unnerved by the grotesque sights and smells all around us. I leaned forward and calmed her with a soft pat. When she was steadier I rode slowly on toward the officer in command, picking a careful path through the scattered dead.

A young woman, probably a serving girl, lay huddled off to one side. She would have been pretty, if it weren't for the cruel sword slash across her face. Close by, an older man, a steward perhaps, sat propped up against a wall. His dead eyes were still full of horror. He'd been stabbed in the stomach by a spear and left to die in agony. A few yards farther on, the bodies of two small children—a little olive-skinned girl and a younger boy who could only have just left his mother's arms—were heaped one on top of the other. Their skulls had been smashed in.

Olive oil from shattered jars pooled on the ground nearby, already turning rancid in the hot sun. Sacks of dried figs and other staples had been slashed open and tossed aside. I could see shards of broken glass glinting in the sun amid heaps of broken pottery and splintered furniture.

It was the same everywhere I looked. More corpses. More wreckage. More senseless slaughter. The villains who'd done this hadn't shown mercy to anyone, not to a single man, woman, or child. They'd even butchered the animals, the pigs, sheep, and goats.

I felt sick.

Death is a soldier's trade. When you go into battle, you either kill or you get killed. Anyone who picks up a sword without admitting that to himself is a fool or a liar. I hope that I am neither.

But this hadn't been a battle. This had been a massacre of innocents. These deaths were without meaning. There was no honor or glory here, only waste and cruelty and pointless destruction.

My jaw tightened. I wanted to find the men responsible for this butchery. I wanted them to know that their crimes would cost them their lives.

I reined in beside the stern-faced officer watching the legionaries at their grim work. He grunted in disgust and yanked the red-crested helmet off his head in one swift motion, cradling it under his arm. Then he ran a weary hand through his close-cropped graying hair.

"By the gods, Valens," he muttered angrily to me. "What a cursed shambles!"

I nodded silently. There wasn't anything I could say.

The legate, Titus Petronius Faustus, commander of the Sixth Legion, had every right to be furious.

The ravaged estate before us had belonged to a wealthy Syrian landowner, a man of Greek descent named Demetrius. It lay within the territory allotted to our legion, and Demetrius had expected us to defend his property, his life, and the lives of his family and his slaves.

We had failed.

A burly soldier in the red tunic of a centurion sauntered up to Faustus and saluted. "My lads have found a survivor, Legate. One of the house slaves legged it out in time and spent the night hiding up there." He jerked a thumb east toward a steep ridge rising beyond the sun-baked fields. A thick grove of gnarled olive trees covered the slope right up to its crest.

Faustus nodded impatiently. "Well?"

The centurion, a big, bull-necked man named Domitius Capito, shrugged. "The usual story. He says a band of armed men wearing masks and hoods visited his master last night, demanding money for 'protection.'"

Listening, I gritted my teeth in frustration. It was a tale I'd heard all too often since arriving in Syria. Gangs of marauders were pillaging their way through the

cities, towns, and countryside of the entire province—
apparently at will. They were preying on all the richest
merchants and farmers. Their victims were approached
quietly with demands for large sums of money. Those
who refused were murdered, along with their wives,
children, and servants, and their holdings were torched.

Demetrius had refused.

Faustus snorted. "This Greek farmer was a fool!"

"Sir?" I asked.

The legate pointed to the carnage all around us.
"Where was the sense in inviting this, Valens? Better to
lose a little money than your life. Until we run these
criminals to ground, this sort of defiance gains nothing
for anyone!"

I frowned. I couldn't deny the sense of what the
legate said, but I couldn't find it in my heart to defame
a man who'd died because we had failed to keep the
peace. Rome had ruled Syria for more than eighty years.
The locals paid their taxes peaceably, and they had a
right to expect our protection.

For a moment longer, Faustus stared down at the
dead scattered across the ransacked farm. Then he
straightened up. "I'll have no more of this wasteful folly
in the area under *my* authority." He turned in his saddle.
"Caelius!"

His scribe, a weedy little man with a pallid face and
perpetually ink-stained fingers, trotted up. He was already pulling a waxed tablet and stylus out of his
satchel. "Yes, Legate?"

"Take this down," Faustus commanded. He pursed
his lips, pondering briefly, and then began. "Titus
Petronius Faustus, commander of the Sixth Legion,
sends his warmest greetings to all leading men of the

district. While this unfortunate state of emergency persists, I offer you the following counsel . . ."

I held my tongue while the legate dictated his letter, but I confess that it was difficult.

Faustus was practically ordering the local landowners and merchants to comply with the bandits' demands. Oh, he couched his instructions in the most favorable light—promising full restitution once our legion had captured or killed the marauders—but no one hearing this missive could mistake his real message: Give in or be killed. The legion cannot protect you.

I could scarcely believe what I was hearing. Allowing these bandit gangs to run rings around us was dishonor enough. But how could the legate admit our failure so openly? It was humiliating. More than that, it was shameful.

If we failed to keep the peace for which we taxed the Syrians, we would be nothing more than bandits ourselves.

My hand curled around the pommel of the sword slung at my left side. I was a Roman officer and a member of the knightly class, the equestrian order. I had *not* come to Syria to witness a feeble surrender to mere robbers and thieves, I thought bitterly. Not after spending four long years fighting against real warriors in the wilds of Germany.

When he finished his dictation, Faustus ordered, "Have that copied and sent out as soon as we get back to camp."

The scribe nodded and then faded back into the gaggle of orderlies and bodyguards waiting a few yards behind us.

Satisfied, the legate swung back toward the big centurion still standing in front of him. "Very well, Capito.

Have your troops build a pyre, then burn the bodies. No sense in leaving anything for the scavengers to pick over."

"Right, Legate." The centurion tilted his helmet back a bit and scratched at his forehead. "What do you want done with the slave we found?"

Faustus shrugged. "Bring him back with you. I know a broker who'll take him off our hands. The proceeds can go to the legion social fund."

Capito grinned. "Yes, sir. At least that'll make the lads a bit happier while they're stacking up corpses."

The impatience I'd been feeling boiled over. I edged Dancer closer to the two of them so that I could speak without being overheard by the soldiers around us. A good officer may disagree with his commander's decisions, but he should never do so in front of the troops.

"What about this massacre?" I asked. "Shouldn't we pursue the men who've done this?"

Faustus eyed me grimly. "To what end, Valens? How many times have we sent troops trudging off into the hills? A dozen times? Two dozen? And what do we have to show for it?"

"Broken boots. Sore feet. Sun sickness. And nothing else," the centurion answered quickly—cutting in before I could speak.

The legate nodded. "Well said, Capito." He frowned at me. "Chasing these bandits would be a race that was lost before it even began. They have at least half a day's head start on us. They'll be deep in the wild lands and out of reach before sunset."

That was true enough, I realized reluctantly. But there were other options.

"Then give me the troops I need, and I'll hit them when they move on the next farm," I said flatly.

Faustus stared at me. "And just how will you do that, Tribune?" His lip curled. "Have the gods granted you a vision denied to us lesser mortals?"

I flushed. "They have not, Legate."

"Well?"

Dancer shifted uneasily beneath me—agitated by my anger and embarrassment. Her head tossed. I calmed her again, this time with pressure from my knees. Then I looked back at Faustus. "I've read all the reports for our district. There's a pattern to this brigandage, at least out here in the countryside."

The legate's frown grew deeper. "Go on."

"Last night, the marauders slaughtered Demetrius and all his people. We know that they collected tribute from two landowners north of here a few days before that. A month earlier, they burned out an estate even farther north—and robbed another four or five farms in the same area."

I waited for Faustus to see what I was driving at, but he just sat silently on his horse, still frowning. Strange, I thought. Surely even a blind man could see it.

"These bandits aren't striking at random, Legate," I said at last. "They're working steadily, almost methodically, up the river toward Apamea, toward the city. They move at night—using the waxing moon for light. Knowing that, I'll wager any amount that their next target is a rich landowner somewhere just south of here. And that they will move within the week."

I noticed the legate's eyes flicker toward Capito. The centurion stood rigid, watching me closely with a strange expression on his face. Was it contempt? Anger? Or surprise? I couldn't decide.

"Petronius Faustus," I went on earnestly, "we can use

this knowledge against them. Give me a cohort of your best troops, and I'll smash these marauders for you."

The legate just stared at me. Then he blinked.

The silence dragged on.

At last he said, "Your self-confidence is remarkable, Lucius Aurelius." He smiled, but it was a brittle, false smile. "Before you assume the mantle of my authority completely, however, I think you should consider something."

"Sir?"

He leaned closer. The smile slipped entirely off his face. "This legion—and everyone in it—is under my orders. Not yours."

I stiffened in the saddle. "I have never doubted that, Legate."

"You do remember that you are a junior tribune, an officer of the narrow stripe?" Faustus asked, referring to the slender purple strip on my tunic that marked me as a member of the middle-ranked equestrian order. His own tunic, like that of the senior tribune in the legion, bore the wide purple of a member of the more elite senatorial class.

"Yes, sir." I forced the words out through my teeth.

"And you know that your chief duties are administrative?"

I nodded abruptly.

"Good. Then bear this in mind, Tribune," Faustus snapped. "I do *not* rely on you for military advice. Of *any* kind. Ever. Is that clear?"

My face felt hot.

Strictly speaking, the legate was right. Each legion had six tribunes—one of senatorial rank, the rest of us from the equestrian class. Though technically we ranked above the centurions, we were all aware that they were supposed to be the real professionals. In practical terms, however, Faustus was wrong. Other commanders, especially in the legions along the Rhine, gave their junior officers more latitude and military responsibility.

But I was now painfully aware that whether I was right or wrong didn't matter. I'd seen something important that Faustus had missed. And then, carried away by the power of my own reasoning, I'd wounded the legate's pride by rubbing it in his face.

Domitius Capito sniggered.

I felt a flash of sudden anger at the big centurion.

Capito and others like him were responsible for many of the Sixth Legion's failed attempts to trap the bandits. The patrols they led never managed to find the marauders' camps. The ambushes they set were never in the right place. And when the local landowners called for help, the relief columns they commanded always arrived too late to do more than sift the ashes and bury the bodies.

Just like here.

My eyes narrowed as I studied the centurion more closely. He stood lazily at his ease in front of the legate and me—looking up at me with a smirk on his unshaven face.

Capito was the *Primus Pilus*, the First Spear, the senior centurion in the whole Sixth Legion. Along the Rhine frontier and elsewhere in the empire, a legion's top-ranking centurion was always a veteran—the best of the best. He was the tough professional soldier every other man in the ranks admired and took as a model. I knew very well what a real *Primus Pilus* should look like. My grandfather had held that rank himself.

Alas for the Sixth, Capito set a bad example. He was a great, grumbling oaf of a man—sometimes drunk on duty, often dirty, and always riding on the edge of insubordination. He was also a bully who played favorites and abused the perks of his position.

Custom allowed centurions to accept small gratuities from soldiers who wanted to avoid the more unpleasant camp duties: cleaning the latrines, night guard duty, and the like. But Capito pushed his demands for bribes far beyond what was customary. I'd heard rumors that he'd squeezed the men in his cohort so hard that many of them had to borrow from Syrian moneylenders just to make ends meet.

The corners of my mouth turned down as I stared at him. I wouldn't have trusted a man like that to lace his own boots, let alone made him the senior soldier of a legion. Try as I might, I could not understand why Petronius Faustus tolerated him.

Of course, I must admit that I didn't like the legate much either.

Faustus was often petty. He loved nothing better than finding fault with his subordinates whenever anything went wrong. He was also fond of boasting about his personal wealth and his close ties to Tiberius Caesar. And nothing I'd seen since joining the legion had given me a lot of confidence in his leadership abilities. Before he sweet-talked Tiberius into giving him a legion, the legate's only military experience had come years before—as senior tribune with the Third Legion in Egypt. Supervising grain harvests and prying taxes out of the poor Egyptian peasants hadn't done much to prepare him for higher command. But I didn't think he was so blind that he couldn't see what a hash Capito and others like him were making of the Sixth.

At least I was beginning to realize why so many of us—all veteran officers and centurions—had been transferred to Syria from the Rhine frontier. Someone high up pretty clearly knew that the eastern legions were dangerously slack and needed sharpening.

The legate's voice broke in on my thoughts. "Since you seem bored with your ordinary duties, Tribune, I'll find you something a bit more challenging." He smiled thinly. "It's time to relieve one of the outpost garrisons along the *harra*. I'm sending a century under Quintus Rufus out there for a month's duty. You will be in overall command. Do we understand each other, Lucius Aurelius?"

"Sir." I met his gaze squarely, trying hard to hide my own anger. I would not give the legate the pleasure of seeing that he'd scored a solid blow. Not if I could help it.

The *harra*, a rugged wilderness of black basalt boulders, marked the southeast edge of the Sixth Legion's territory. We maintained a few small watchtowers and fortified posts along the frontier to keep an eye on the nomads who wandered the *harra* and the desert wastes beyond. But the tribes were at peace with Rome just now—barring a little harmless sheep stealing here and there. Duty at those outposts in the summer was a mind-numbing daily grind of scorching heat and utter tedium.

Petronius Faustus must have believed that he'd picked the perfect way to punish me for daring to criticize his leadership, even if only implicitly. No doubt he thought I'd come staggering back from the frontier so grateful to be back among the taverns and bathhouses of Apamea that I would keep my mouth shut in the future.

If so, he would be disappointed.

Even as a boy, I'd often spoken plainly without much thought for the consequences. My father and a succession of tutors had tried hard to teach me the civilized art of sheltering the truth inside a web of honeyed flattery. They had failed. I knew the forms, the twists and tricks of subtle rhetoric well enough. But I could rarely bring myself to use them. My grandfather, that blunt, honest old man, would have scoffed at the smooth-talking orators and courtiers of the present age.

So I would march out into the sun-baked desolation of the *harra* as ordered, but I'd be damned if I'd go without trying to do my best for the provincials we were supposed to be protecting.

"I have just one request, Legate," I said as calmly as I could.

Faustus eyed me warily. "Well?"

"Set ambushes on the roads and tracks running south up the river valley from here. That's where the marauders will strike next. I'm sure of it."

The legate forced a short, sharp laugh. "By the gods, Valens! You're like a rutting bull sometimes—just one thought in your mind and no quarter for anyone who gets in your way."

He glanced at Capito, who stood frowning up at me. "You've heard the tribune's suggestion, Centurion. What do you think?"

"It won't work." The big man hawked noisily and then spat on the ground, right at Dancer's feet.

Startled, the Spanish mare tossed her head, but I held her firmly, fighting down a fresh wave of anger.

"Go on," Faustus said.

Capito snorted. "It's typical book-learned tactics. The fancy sort that sound good in camp, and then turn to shit in the field." He grinned nastily at me. "No offense meant, of course, Tribune."

I stared coldly down at him. At eighteen, I'd led my first patrol deep into the dark, dank German forests—

slogging through rain-soaked underbrush amid tall trees
that seemed to run all the way to the ends of the earth.
At nineteen, my cohort of auxiliary light infantry had
cut a bigger Chatti raiding party to pieces. At twenty, I'd
been the first man over the stockade of a fortified Cher-
usci village — and I had the scar across my ribs to prove
it. All in all, I'd crammed more real fighting into the last
four years than Capito had in a twenty-year career devoted mostly to idleness, debauchery, and bootlicking.

Faustus spread his hands. "You've heard the *Primus
Pilus*, Valens. I'm afraid I have to agree with him. I
won't deploy detachments willy-nilly up and down the
Orontes. The Sixth will handle these bandit gangs in the
time-tested manner."

By doing nothing, I thought bitterly, again running
my eyes over the burned-out, bloodstained ruins of
Demetrius' farm. An ugly suspicion began taking root in
the back of my mind.

The legate settled his helmet back on his head and
took up the reins of his horse. Then he turned to me. "I
want you on your way to the outpost line by first light
tomorrow, Tribune. I suggest you focus your attention
on that and leave the marauders to me."

I had one throw of the dice left.

"Do I have your permission to conduct field training
with Rufus and his troops?" I asked quietly. "Both on
the march and once we've reached the frontier?"

"Field training?" Faustus repeated. He chuckled.
"My dear Valens! By all means. For all I care, you can
have Quintus Rufus and his men recite Greek poetry
and run naked in circles."

He kicked his horse into a walk and rode away, still
laughing softly to himself.

I watched the legate go — saying nothing and still

wondering whether or not I dared use the freedom he'd unwittingly given me.

Shadows rippled across moonlit fields, cast by clouds drifting across the vast, black night sky. The land all around lay quiet. The farmers, their slaves, and the beasts of the fields were abed—drowsing after a long day of toil. The rutted track of the local road running south to Apamea stretched empty below me, plainly visible in the light of the full moon.

I moved cautiously a little farther down the slope and dropped to one knee beside the twisted trunk of an ancient olive tree. Low murmurs and the muffled clank and rattle of armor and weapons reached my ears as the soldiers I led spread out along the edge of the grove.

Quintus Rufus joined me, cat-quiet despite his heavy mail corselet and bronze greaves. The tall, red-haired centurion was another veteran of the Rhine frontier. The deadly war of vengeance raids and murderous ambushes waged in the sunless German forests had taught us both a hard lesson: You were quiet. Or you were dead.

I was very glad to have him with me. Unlike Capito, he was a real professional—and I could count on his courage and good sense. Even his speech was a reminder of home. Like my grandfather, he came from the north of Italy, from the region known as Cisalpine Gaul. Both of us counted some of the wild, warlike Celts who'd once ruled there among our ancestors. They'd given the centurion his imposing height and his red hair. I was shorter and darker, but I'd inherited the fierce, pale blue eyes of my own Celtic forebears.

"We're ready, Tribune," he murmured.

"Good." I turned toward him. "The men know their orders?"

"They do." Rufus hesitated. "But they're a bit edgy."

I nodded. That was understandable.

Like all the legions in Syria, the Sixth was under-manned and had more than its fair share of raw recruits. But it wasn't just the recruits who were nervous. There hadn't been any serious fighting in the East for decades and very few of the older troops knew much about real war. Year in and year out, their lives had followed the comfortable, dull, predictable rhythms of peacetime sol-diering. They'd grown used to an unvarying round of guard duty, camp chores, ceremonial parades, training marches, and all the rest.

Now, in the blink of an eye, the sixty legionaries of Rufus' century had been yanked away from their cozy routine.

By me.

I'd harried, chivied, and driven them all the way to the little fort on the very edge of the *harra*—covering three days' worth of ground in two grueling days of hard marching. I'd detached the *optio*, the century's second-in-command, and twenty men to garrison the outpost. And then I'd marched the rest of them back again, though taking care to circle around Apamea. We'd spent another two days moving cautiously north through the rough hill country rising east of the river.

I'd chosen to interpret the phrase "field training" with far more latitude than Petronius Faustus could pos-sibly have expected.

Now, exactly seven nights after the bandit gang had slaughtered the Greek landowner Demetrius, I'd brought Rufus and the rest of his men to the base of an olive tree–crowned hill overlooking one of the roads to Apamea. We were right on the edge of a country estate owned by a wealthy provincial named Eumenes.

According to the tax records I'd studied, Eumenes was one of the richest landlords of the local district. So far, he'd been left alone by the marauders plaguing the province.

I expected that to change. Tonight.

I said as much aloud.

"You're sure, Tribune?" Rufus said softly, pitching his voice low enough to make sure no one else could hear him.

I forced myself to nod confidently. "They'll come, Centurion. They have to. This moon is the only thing that makes travel at night possible. Once it wanes, it'll be too damned dark for them to find their way along these miserable tracks."

Rufus grunted, pulled his military cloak tighter against the growing cold, and turned his gaze back toward the road.

Left to my own thoughts, I swallowed hard, wishing suddenly that I wasn't so stubborn and desperately hoping that my reasoning was sound. The array of facts and logic that had seemed so solid and self-evident in daylight seemed far less imposing and persuasive amid the darkness and shadows. I had staked my honor—my life, perhaps—on what now seemed a patchwork of guesses.

If I were wrong, if the bandits never showed up or if they chose someone else as their victim, the centurion and his men were in for nothing worse than another long, uncomfortable night spent out in the open. But nothing short of complete success would save me from disgrace if Faustus accused me of disobeying his orders.

If I were broken and stripped of my rank, what then? Could I live with that shame? Could I expect my family to bear it, too? Even in these degenerate times, we Romans are a proud people. I knew what would be expected of me. My mouth felt dry. If I failed here, would I have the courage to fall on my own sword?

For what seemed an eternity, I wrestled with my innermost fears, determined to master them. The Greeks who had tutored me claimed that our fates were predestined, already woven into the fabric of the universe. Since this was so, they argued, a man's measure was in the courage and calm with which he met the twists and turns of fortune.

I snorted softly. Stoicism was a philosophy that offered more consolation in the schoolroom than it did on a lonely, windswept hill in Syria. I decided wryly that I would probably have found more comfort in a whole-hearted belief in the gods and goddesses of my childhood. Instead, here I was, caught between two contending beliefs—and wholly allied to neither.

The sudden crunch of hobnailed boots on rocks and gravel—faint at first, then louder—snapped me back to the present. My hearing has always been good.

The centurion started slightly at the feel of my hand on his arm.

"They're close," I whispered, checking to make sure my sword slid easily in and out of the scabbard slung at my left side. Despite the cool night air, I could feel the sweat starting to roll down from under my helmet. I picked up the infantryman's shield I'd borrowed and slipped my left arm through the grip. "Pass the word: Wait for my command, then hit them hard!"

Quintus Rufus nodded.

I ignored the low murmur spreading through the shadowed olive grove as my orders were repeated down the waiting line, focusing instead on the empty, moonlit road just a few yards away. A droplet of sweat fell into my right eye, harsh and stinging. I shook it off, feeling the pulse beating time in my temple, pounding faster and faster.

Suddenly, the road wasn't empty. It was filled with men. Most of them were marching on foot, but a few were on horseback. I leaned forward, straining to see more clearly in the dim half-light cast by the moon and by the guttering torches some of them held aloft. My lips moved as I counted under my breath. Ten. Twenty. Several more. Perhaps thirty men in all. All were armed with swords, clubs, or spears. I could hear the jingle of armor. All wore black masks or hoods to hide their faces.

We had them.

The first sauntering, swaggering marauders passed the boundary stone that marked the edge of Eumenes' land. A low guttural laugh ghosted above the bandit column. The sound raised the hairs on the back of my neck. It was akin to the growl of a wolf—not that of a man.

I shoved my fear aside. Whether they were wolves or men, they were my prey now.

I jumped to my feet, shouting, "Up! Up! Ready javelins!"

With a roar that echoed through the night, Quintus Rufus and his legionaries came pouring out from under the trees. Each soldier held a javelin secure in his right hand, ready to throw.

Our sudden appearance caught the masked raiders by complete surprise. They stood frozen on the rough, moonlit road.

It was perfect.

I felt a sudden burst of wild, fierce pride surging through my veins. There's almost nothing more exhilarating than seeing a carefully laid plan unfold in every detail. It must be something akin to the experience of a god looking down from Olympus.

Still exulting, I filled my lungs and yelled, "Javelins! Loose!"

Forty iron-tipped spears whirred through the air and tore into the bandit column caught motionless on the road. Men went down in heaps as javelins found their mark, punching through clothing and armor with ease. Horrified screams and shrieks rose from the wounded and the dying. A horse reared, whinnying in fear and pain, and then bolted off into the barren field on the other side of the road.

Now.

I rapped out my next orders, already moving toward the road—crowding my way into the fighting line. "Swords out! Forward!"

"Forward!" the centurion's deep voice roared out, repeating my order.

More voices up and down the line took up the shout. "Forward!"

We surged down the slope and charged into the bandits before they could recover from the shock of our javelin volley.

As I ran onto the road, one of them swung around to face me with a broad-bladed hunting spear gripped in both hands. I slammed the spear aside with my shield and thrust home with my long sword. He groaned, staggered, and then fell onto his face. Blood spilled across the dirt, black in the dim light. The legionary on my left stabbed downward with his shorter Spanish blade, making sure the bandit was dead. We moved on together.

I caught more blows on my shield and thrust back. All around me, men were dying—almost all of them marauders. I bared my teeth in a tight, savage grin. My men and I were the wolves now, not these bandits. Their masks, worn to sow terror in hapless farmers and tradesmen, were no match for our armor and discipline.

An angry bellow rose above the iron clang of sword on sword, the clatter of shields, moans, curses, and the dull meaty thud of blades driving home into flesh. "Rally! Rally, damn you! Stand and fight!"

I turned toward the voice and saw a burly man on a dappled horse flailing away at the panicked bandits with the flat of his own sword. One of their leaders had kept his nerve.

That was bad. If he succeeded in stiffening their resistance, more of my own men might be killed. The brigands might even be able to break off the fight and escape into the surrounding blackness. I couldn't risk that.

I drove through the press of the melee—fighting my way toward the horseman. He saw me coming and swung his sword down in a vicious, overhand arc aimed at my head. The blade skidded off my upraised shield in a shower of wood splinters and sparks, but the force of the blow knocked me to one knee.

I struggled to stand up, to regain my footing.

The bandit leader forced his foaming horse into my chest, shoving me backward and off balance. I fell sprawling in the dirt. He pulled his mount sideways and leaned far over, his sword arm rising for another lightning-fast slash . . .

Gods!

I threw my shield up again. Another blow hammered down, driving the shield hard into my shoulder. A wave of pain tore the breath from my lungs.

Panting, I staggered to my feet, levering myself upright with my sword.

Momentum had carried the hooded bandit's horse a few feet beyond me. He sawed frantically at the reins, urging his mount around again for another attack.

I lunged desperately, driving the point of my blade straight into the horse's hindquarters. It screamed and reared, kicking and bucking in agony. Caught off balance, the bandit flew out of the saddle and crashed to the ground right at my feet. Freed of its master, his mount whirled and galloped off into the night.

Still breathing heavily, I leaned forward and rested the bloodied tip of my sword on the fallen brigand's neck. Though he was still dazed, the bandit's eyes widened.

Around us, the surviving marauders began throwing away their weapons—holding their arms outstretched while begging, "Mercy! Mercy, comrades! We yield!"

My men moved in cautiously, swords out and ready to strike if there was any more resistance. There wasn't any. The bandits huddled together like sheep, still pleading for their lives.

"Strip them," I ordered harshly. I indicated the burly man I'd bested. "This one, too."

Two of my soldiers grabbed the bandit leader, yanked him to his feet, and hustled him off toward the other prisoners. I turned away, looking for Quintus Rufus. "Centurion!"

The tall, red-haired man came forward. "Yes, Tribune?"

"Get the doctor down here to treat the wounded. Ours first. The brigands after."

"Sir."

"Then form a detail and have them search the dead. Tell the men to collect every weapon they can find. I don't want to leave so much as a paring knife behind. Understand?"

Rufus nodded and moved off to set my orders in motion. I stood still briefly, fighting off a sudden wave of fatigue. I had too much work to do to rest for very long. Our fight with the marauders had lasted only moments. But I knew from bitter experience that clearing up the mess the skirmish had left behind would take hours.

"Tribune!" The shout came from the soldiers guarding the prisoners.

I hurried over, all my aches and pains forgotten. "What is it?"

They dragged one of the bandits forward. It was the man I'd captured. The hood he'd worn to hide his identity had been stripped off and now the moonlight fell on him—revealing a rough, scarred, broken-nosed face.

It was a face I knew only too well.

The bandit leader standing before me was Domitius Capito, the *Primus Pilus* of our own legion.

I stared at him, feeling sick inside as my own worst fears were confirmed. The brigands and marauders who'd been ravaging this region of Syria were fellow soldiers—soldiers who'd sworn allegiance to Rome and to Tiberius Caesar. Those who should have been shepherds for Rome's subjects had become ravenous wolves instead.

Chapter II

Night had faded into sweltering day before I had a chance to rest.

Now I was filthy. And hot. And weary.

I was sitting on the ground with my back against the trunk of an old olive tree. Flies buzzed in and around its branches, flitting busily between blinding sunshine and the small patch of shade.

To the west, the fields and fruit orchards shimmered, pounded by the merciless rays of the midday sun. Off in the distance I could just make out the brown trace of the Orontes meandering from south to north. Everything beyond the river was swallowed up in a gray haze of heat and humidity.

Nothing moved—except the insects.

A column of ants crawled up and over the bronze cuirass I'd taken off and laid on the ground next to me. Others, either bolder or lost, explored the horsehair-crested helmet I'd set beside the body armor.

My scalp itched suddenly, and I scratched vigorously at my head. Sweat and grime matted the short brown curls my mother had loved to rumple when I was a small boy.

I wanted a bath. Or a cup of cool wine. Or a woman. Preferably all three, come to think of it—and in that order.

I let my eyes close, trying to ignore the dull throb from my bruised left shoulder.

"Lucius."

I looked up.

A man stood there, peering down at me with tired brown eyes. He was about my own height, but stockier, and powerfully muscled. His black hair, short beard, and carefully trimmed mustache were streaked with gray. His belted tunic, once white, was spattered and stained with dried blood.

His name was Aristides. He was a Hellene, a native of the city of Philippi. He was my personal physician. And also my friend.

"I've done what I can for the wounded," he said simply. "The rest is up to time and nature—or the gods, if one believes in that sort of thing."

I nodded. Like many Greek doctors, Aristides turned a somewhat skeptical eye on many of the claims of divine healing made by other physicians and temple priests.

You can lance a boil or pray to Asklepios, he'd often say sardonically, but the wise man prefers seeing a bit of pus on a surgical probe to smelling incense.

Aristides wasn't an atheist, and he acknowledged the power of the gods over hopeless cases. But he also believed that the gods expected mortals to solve most of their own problems. Like any man of sense, though, he was careful to keep such sentiments private. Most men, whether illiterate or educated, are prey to superstition—and quick to blame any setback or catastrophe on those who don't share their beliefs.

"What's the final tally?" I asked quietly.

The exultation I'd felt in my victory had faded quickly once I'd seen the bodies littering the road and heard the groans and sobs of the wounded and dying. Winning a battle is infinitely better than losing it, but military glory carries a fearful price. I've known soldiers who can walk through the blood and gore left behind on a battlefield without blinking an eye. I am not one of them.

"Two of Rufus' men are dead. Four more were badly hurt." Aristides shrugged. "They may live, if a fever doesn't kill them."

I nodded again. Even the slightest injury could turn deadly if a fever took hold. Washing a wound with wine or vinegar seemed to help. So did various ointments of copper, pitch, pine resin, or alum. But once a sword, javelin, or arrow tore your flesh there was never any certainty of survival.

"Can they be moved?" I asked.

Aristides shook his head. "Not with any safety. At least not far."

"Then we'll leave them in Eumenes' care."

The doctor considered that briefly, then nodded. "It will serve. I'll prepare a kit of bandages and medicines and instruct his steward in their use."

"Good."

Eumenes, the rich Syrian landowner, owed his fortune and possibly his life to the legionaries under my command. Looking after our seriously wounded would be a small price to pay for that protection. He knew what Capito's bandits had done to his neighbor Demetrius, so I didn't expect him to squawk. At least not much.

"What about the prisoners?" I asked Aristides. We'd

killed half the marauders outright. Of the rest, several had wounds that would kill them soon enough. But we'd still taken a good dozen or so of Capito's scum alive.

He frowned. "They're cut and bruised, but they should be able to stumble along on their own two feet."

He swayed abruptly and only stopped himself from falling by grabbing on to an olive branch.

I sat up straight, concerned. "Are you all right?"

Aristides waved me back with his other hand. Then he chuckled and squatted down beside me, resting on his haunches. "Don't worry, Lucius. I'm not ill or struck by the sun . . . just worn-out." He stifled a yawn. "Going without sleep isn't so easy anymore."

Relieved, I grinned. "I seem to remember a certain Greek doctor who could spend all day treating the sick and still have the energy to chase women all night long. You're not as young as you used to be, old man."

"No one is as young as they used to be," Aristides said dryly. "Not even you."

I couldn't deny that. Aristides had been hired as my doctor when I was just a small boy of six and very ill. My family had business interests in the region around his home city, and he'd come to Rome armed with recommendations from some of Philippi's most prominent citizens. I think my father—who kept a firm grip on every brass sesterce—would have been happier if he could have found a slave or a cheaper freedman to treat me. My mother, though, stood firm, insisting that I needed the best possible care.

She had been right. I owed Aristides my life.

He'd stayed on after the first crisis passed. At first, only a few new patients had come to him, mostly on my family's recommendation. But his reputation as a healer and surgeon soon spread, and before long he was earning a tidy living to supplement the retainer my father rather grudgingly paid out.

He'd earned another reputation, too. This one as a lover of beautiful women of all classes, from the lowest to the highest. If any single man could have changed the average Roman's view of all Greeks as effeminate, boy-loving aesthetes, Aristides was that man. There were even rumors that a number of the rich but bored senators' wives who swore by his ointments and salves were equally enamored of his prowess in the bedchamber. After seeing the quality of the gifts they pressed on him—precious jewelry and rings, carved ivory spice boxes and silks from India, and fine decorated pottery from the best workshops in Italy and Gaul—I tended to believe the rumors.

In twelve years, the doctor had made himself a reasonably wealthy man with a growing circle of grateful and prominent patients.

But when I left Rome to join the legions on the Rhine, Aristides came with me. When I'd asked him why, he'd only smiled and said simply, "I'm your physician, Lucius. I have been since you were a boy. Where you go, I go."

A cynic might have suspected that some powerful senator had finally tumbled to the fact that Aristides had made him a cuckold. But I am no cynic, at least not completely. I was glad of his company and his counsel, and I'd taken him at his word.

I felt I knew Aristides better than I knew my own father. Certainly, I liked him more.

"When do we march?" he asked. "I'll need some time to settle the wounded we're leaving behind."

I squinted at the sun. It hung close to the zenith.

"We'll wait a bit. There's no sense in broiling the troops in this midday heat. But I want to cover as much ground as we can this evening, camp overnight, and then move on before first light."

Aristides arched an eyebrow in surprise. "Why the hurry? Surely we can be back in Apamea in a single day's easy march."

"True enough," I said quietly. "But I'm not taking Capito and the other prisoners back to the Sixth Legion. We're heading north instead—to Antioch."

Antioch, fifty miles down the Orontes from where we sat, was the third largest city in all the empire. More important for my purposes, it was the capital of all Roman Syria.

The doctor stared closely at me for a few moments and then shook his head in disbelief. "You don't look as though you're suffering from a brain fever. But I can't think of what else it could be."

I met his gaze squarely. "I'm perfectly well. And I meant what I said. I'm taking Capito and the others to Antioch. I won't hand them over to Petronius Faustus."

Aristides looked troubled. "Don't let anger cloud your judgment, Lucius. Yes, the legate is a pompous fool. And yes, you disobeyed the spirit of his orders so you could smash this gang of marauders. But he can't argue with success."

I only wished that were true.

The doctor leaned closer and lowered his voice. "If you take this matter over his head, though, he can't turn a blind eye to your disobedience. Humiliate Faustus so openly and he'll do his best to break you."

"I know that," I said softly, staring down at the plain gold ring on my left hand. It felt heavier than I remembered. I looked up. "I don't have a choice, Aristides."

The Greek grimaced. "Of course you have a choice, Lucius! Drag Capito right up to the headquarters building instead and watch the legate squirm. Faustus named that piece of filth the *Primus Pilus* of his legion. So make him handle Capito's disgrace and punishment himself."

I sighed. This was an argument I'd known was coming. Aristides saw himself as a pragmatic man and often sought to temper what he considered my stubborn pride and misplaced idealism. There were moments when he was probably right to do so. This was not one of them.

"If you caught a fox raiding your chickens, would you take him back to his den and let him go?" I asked him quietly.

The doctor whistled in sudden understanding. "You think the legate had some idea of what Capito and his men were doing?"

"More than that," I said grimly. "I think they were acting under his orders."

"Gods!" Aristides swore. He looked even more troubled. "Do you have any proof of that?"

I hesitated, knowing that I didn't have hard evidence of the legate's involvement—at least not the kind that would persuade a magistrate in a formal trial. But I was sure that my suspicions were correct. Nothing else made sense. Nothing else explained Capito's behavior when I'd questioned him.

Quintus Rufus and I had spent half the night interrogating the bandits we'd captured alive. All of them were legionaries from Capito's own First Cohort. All of them insisted they were just following the senior centurion's orders. All of them claimed that they'd received only a small share of the loot, and swore that Capito had handled the rest.

I believed them.

Every centurion carries a heavy vine wood cane as a badge of his rank. This cane is also used to punish disobedience and enforce discipline. Ten years of service had made Rufus a master of its use. He could strike any number of blows that could paralyze a man with pain—and yet leave him without any lasting injury.

By the time he was through with them, Capito's men were only too glad to answer all our questions and too afraid to tell us any lies.

Capito himself was another matter. Marauder or not, he was still the Sixth Legion's highest-ranking centurion. We couldn't use force while questioning him—not without breaking every rule and regulation governing the legions. I was willing to bend my orders to do what I thought right, but I wasn't willing to abandon everything I'd been taught about discipline and good order. At least not yet.

Given those restrictions, I didn't really expect the bastard to talk.

He didn't disappoint me.

As we hammered him with our questions, Capito just sat silent, arms bound behind him, staring up at us with red-rimmed eyes filled with rage and hatred.

It was what I didn't see in his eyes that worried me.

I didn't see any fear.

And he should have been afraid.

Few commanders in this day and age inflicted the death penalty traditionally prescribed for the more serious military offenses. Most preferred finding other punishments, even for crimes like desertion and gross insubordination. But no legionary legate worth his post could possibly avoid ordering Capito's head cut off—not if he were convicted of murder and banditry.

The *Primus Pilus* was a bully, not a hero. I didn't think he was the sort who could sneer at his own approaching death.

So why wasn't he frightened?

I was afraid I knew the answer to that question. And to all the other questions that had robbed me of so much sleep over the past seven nights. How could so many troops on active service pillage Apamea and its environs without being caught? Why had every other attempt to intercept the "marauders" failed so completely? How could the Sixth Legion's senior centurion spend so many days and nights outside the fortress masquerading as a brigand without his superiors suspecting something?

Only one answer made any sense at all, no matter how hard I tried to find some other way to make the pieces fit.

I was now convinced that Petronius Faustus, the legate of the Sixth Legion, the officer charged with maintaining law and order in this part of the province, had instead set his own soldiers to work as robbers, thieves, rapists, and murderers.

Aristides was still troubled when I finished explaining my reasoning to him. He took a deep breath and stared down at the ground for a few moments before sighing. "I think you're right, Lucius. I wish I could prove your theory wrong, and yet I can't. Still, if Faustus hears of your suspicions, and you can't produce solid evidence against him . . ."

His voice trailed off into silence.

"I know," I said softly. "But I've learned too much to pretend ignorance now. My hope is that Capito will break his silence when he realizes the legate can't protect him."

"Will you bring him to trial before the governor?" Aristides asked.

I shook my head. I didn't know Gnaeus Piso, the governor of Syria, but I didn't like what I had heard of him. Though he was said to be a close ally of Tiberius Caesar, the emperor, his record wasn't very impressive. Before I was born, Augustus, the old emperor, had named Piso the governor of Spain, but his tax collectors had squeezed the locals so hard and behaved so arrogantly that he'd been recalled to Rome in some disgrace. He hadn't held a significant post since, and nobody I knew could understand why Tiberius had dropped Syria—a highly prized appointment—right into his aging lap.

"Who then?" Aristides asked. "You need to convince Capito that Faustus can't save him from the executioner's sword. And no one else on the governor's staff wields that much power."

"I'm going straight to the top," I said flatly.

A little of the worry left Aristides' eyes. He nodded approvingly. "Germanicus. A wise decision."

Germanicus Julius Caesar, the nephew and now the adopted son of Tiberius, had been given full authority over all the eastern provinces two years before. He had his headquarters at Antioch.

I knew Germanicus. And he knew me.

I'd held my first command during the last two years of his punitive campaigns against the German tribes. And I'd acquitted myself honorably enough to earn his approval. Like the other officers and men who'd served under him on that dismal and bloody frontier, I valued his plain, firmly spoken "well done" higher than any other award or decoration.

Like most young men of my class, I viewed Germanicus as the ideal Roman. Though only in his early thirties, he'd already proven himself an outstanding soldier, scholar, and playwright. He embodied all the traditional virtues that had made Rome great. He was gifted with enormous physical and moral courage. He was also generous, kindhearted, and most surprising of all in a man who could expect to rule the whole empire one day, genuinely modest.

Now I hoped to use my ties to him to crack Domitius Capito open like an egg. If the centurion had any intelligence at all, he'd know that Germanicus Caesar loathed military corruption and indiscipline above all other crimes. Kindhearted or not, he'd come down hard on any officer who'd turned his own soldiers into murderous thieves and night raiders. With the very real prospect of an ignominious execution dangling before his eyes, Capito should be eager to confess the crimes of his patron, Petronius Faustus, the legate of the Sixth Legion.

Or so I prayed.

Because I knew that if the centurion kept his silence, I couldn't expect Germanicus to act against Faustus. Whether or not he privately believed the legate to be guilty, he would never condemn him without solid proof.

Two hours later, I led my Spanish mare, Dancer, down the sun-baked slope toward the road paralleling the Orontes. Aristides followed me, pulling a mule piled high with his kit and medical supplies. Quintus Rufus and his legionaries came trudging along behind us. Each man had his shield slung across his back and carried a pole with his pack and mess gear lashed to it. Our prisoners plodded along in the middle of the column, with their heads hanging in shame and despair, and with their arms bound behind them.

The sun still hung high overhead, blinding bright. But the heat was somewhat less intense and it was time we were on the march.

I reached the road and stood for just a moment, deliberating with myself.

Every schoolboy knows the story of Julius Caesar crossing the Rubicon. That river was his moment of decision. Leading his army across it marked an irrevocable declaration of war against his enemies in the Senate.

This dry and dusty dirt road was my Rubicon.

If I turned south, I could limp back to Apamea, hand Capito and the others over to Faustus—and then watch in shamed silence as the legate found a way to cover up their crimes. Then, if I did nothing further, I could probably serve out my remaining time with the Sixth Legion, or find a quiet way to transfer to another unit in some distant province.

But if I turned north, I would be declaring war against Faustus and the corruption he represented. I would be tossing the dice in a game with only two possible outcomes: triumph or death.

I took a deep breath. The sunlight gleamed off my grandfather's ring.

So be it.

I squared my shoulders, gave Dancer a gentle pat, and then swung north, marching toward Antioch with an easy stride.

Chapter III

The trial of Domitius Capito began just two days after I marched my captives through Antioch's Eastern Gate.

The court convened in a colonnade along the west wing of the governor's praetorium — an ancient palace once used by the city's old Seleucid kings. It was late in the afternoon and the day's heat was slowly fading. A cool breeze blew off the nearby river. The sun slanted in between tall, sculpted columns, slicing the stone paving into narrow bands of light and shadow.

I stood in one of the patches of sunlight. As the accuser and prosecutor my appointed place was just yards away from my prisoner.

I glanced at Capito out of the corner of my eye and frowned.

Someone had cleaned the bastard up. They'd shaved him, let him use the baths, and given him a freshly laundered regulation red tunic. He even had a brand-new centurion's staff tucked carelessly under one arm.

He looked the very model of a veteran legionary soldier.

That was a bad omen.

And when he'd been summoned to face the charges

I'd brought against him, Capito had marched up the steps with most of his old swagger. The fear I'd seen slowly building in him as we drew nearer to Antioch was gone.

That was worse.

Now the Sixth Legion's corrupt *Primus Pilus* stood confidently, almost at ease, in front of the man who would judge his guilt or innocence.

Gnaeus Calpurnius Piso, the governor of Syria.

My plan to bring Capito and his gang of marauders to trial before Germanicus Caesar had foundered on one damnable detail: He was not in Antioch when we arrived. He'd been called away to the frontier by reports of serious trouble among the Armenian mountain tribes there.

No one at his headquarters could predict when he would be back. The situation on the border was dangerous, and Germanicus didn't intend to let some petty tribal feud drag us into an unwanted war with Parthia.

In his absence, Piso had asserted the right as governor to try Capito and my other prisoners.

Unwilling to fully trust his judgment, I'd requested a delay, pending Germanicus' return.

That was a mistake.

One of Piso's aides had haughtily rejected my request, coldly informing me that "the governor will uphold the law in his own province in his own way."

Without intending it, I'd stepped headlong into the middle of a public vendetta.

In the legionary camp at Apamea, I'd heard rumors that Piso and Germanicus were quarreling over power and authority in Syria. Some even spoke of rival edicts, of heated private arguments, and of hastily countermanded orders. But the rumors were behind the times.

The situation at Antioch was much worse than I'd imagined.

Piso and Germanicus and their respective followers were now openly at odds with one another. Early disagreements over minor issues had boiled over into conflicts over serious policy—the conduct of the legions, our relations with Parthia, tax collection, and even the way in which the laws were administered.

The result was growing confusion.

The officials in Germanicus' faction followed his orders. Those who sided with Piso ignored them. And vice versa. Officials at the lowest levels of the provincial bureaucracy—local magistrates, district tax collectors, and the like—were caught between the two rival camps. They swayed back and forth like reeds caught in a windstorm, meekly obeying one set of laws one day and disregarding them the next.

It was madness.

Our authority in Syria rested on the stability we imposed. Now that peace was threatened—both by the marauders ravaging the countryside and by the escalating administrative chaos in Antioch. If someone didn't restore order soon, the provincials might tire of Roman rule and rise against us. And a revolt in Syria could set the whole of the eastern empire afire.

I stood straighter, trying to push those larger worries aside for the time being.

Stick to the job at hand, Lucius, my grandfather always used to say. "Life is like a battle, boy," he'd rasp. "When you're in a fight, the man who's worrying about where he'll pitch his tent that night is the man who goes down with a spear in his guts."

And right now, I had a fight on my hands.

Somehow I had to persuade Gnaeus Piso to convict

Capito. With an execution order hanging over his head, there was still a chance that the centurion would testify against Faustus to save his own life. That, in turn, would give Germanicus a chance to root out the corruption at the heart of the Sixth Legion.

Unfortunately, my first real look at the governor of Syria didn't inspire much confidence—either in his judgment or in his willingness to do justice.

Piso sat in the shade, lounging carelessly on a cushioned bench. A flagon of wine stood on a small table at his elbow, along with a richly decorated silver cup. A dark-complexioned slave, probably a Spaniard, stood close by—ready to attend to his master's wishes.

As a small boy in Rome, I'd once seen a python in a traveling menagerie. The snake had just eaten an entire lamb. It lay motionless in its cage, with its great, glistening scales bulging in the middle. Despite the enormous serpent's apparent torpor, I was sure that I saw an evil, hungry gleam in its eyes as it stared back at me through the iron bars.

Piso reminded me of that snake.

The governor was bald, save for a few dyed strands of hair combed over the dome of his head. Beneath that expanse of pallid, wrinkled skin, his black eyes glittered. A vast paunch dwarfed his spindly arms and legs.

He took a deep gulp of wine and then waved a languid hand in my direction. "Whenever you are ready, Tribune."

I risked a quick glance around the colonnade. It was almost deserted. Except for Piso, his slave, a small knot of bodyguards off to one side, and a single bored-looking scribe, no one else was in sight. There were no other witnesses, no spectators.

This was more like a private audience than a formal

court of law, I realized. I was prosecuting some of
Rome's own soldiers for banditry and murder. Who
could blame the governor for wanting to keep such a
scandal within a tightly controlled circle?

Not good, Lucius, I told myself silently. Not good at
all.

Enough. It was time to speak—to unleash the carefully chosen phrases I'd silently rehearsed every step of
the long, dusty march to Antioch.

I took a step forward and nodded toward Capito. "My
case against this prisoner is simple and straightforward,
sir. In brief, I accuse him of extortion, theft, the viola-
tion of his military oath, and mass murder. I will prove
those accusations beyond doubt. And once I have done
that, I ask that you find him guilty and sentence him to
death."

Piso arched a single thin eyebrow. "So you charge the
Primus Pilus of your own legion with a catalogue of
horrific crimes and then ask me for his head?" He
smiled tightly. "You have a curious definition of the
word *simple,* Tribune."

I held my temper in check. It was not easy.

Like every Roman youth of my class, I'd observed a
number of criminal and civil trials as part of my schooling. The best magistrates let the advocates on each side
present their arguments without unnecessary interruption. Others were more interested in showing off their
own cleverness than in hearing the facts of the case.

Gnaeus Piso was plainly one of the latter.

I shook my head. "I don't claim the political or military consequences of this case are uncomplicated, sir.
The crimes involved are vile. And they raise serious
questions about the discipline and reliability of the Sixth

Legion. But the evidence of Capito's guilt is clear and convincing."

The governor shrugged. "I'll be the judge of that—not you." He took another drink and eyed me over the rim of his embossed cup. "You prosecute. I decide. Try to remember that, young man."

I swallowed hard—angry with myself for having given him the opening.

Piso gulped more wine and then held out his cup for the slave to refill it. "Well? Get on with it, Tribune. Convince me."

I breathed out slowly. Men I respected had warned me that the governor was a sour-tempered old goat. Now that I'd seen him in action, I was beginning to wonder whether such a comparison was really fair to old goats.

I decided to charge straight to the heart of the matter. "Six nights ago, soldiers under my command ambushed a gang of masked bandits on their way to pillage an estate outside Apamea. We killed half the gang and captured the rest—including their chief. The man who had led them on a spree of murder, rape, and robbery."

I turned and pointed again at Domitius Capito. "That man."

Capito stood still, apparently unfazed by my words, but I could see the hatred in his eyes.

I swung back to face Piso. "While questioning the prisoners, I discovered that these bandits were in fact soldiers from the centurion's own cohort. For months they've been extorting large sums from local landowners—and slaughtering those who refused their demands. I have written summaries of those interrogations with me—"

The governor stopped me in midsentence. "A moment, Tribune." Slowly, he sat up straighter on the bench. "I have a few questions of my own first."

"Sir."

Piso smiled pleasantly, but his eyes were cold and unwavering. "I find this ambush of yours . . . interesting. You see, I've been informed that the legionaries you commanded had orders to garrison a border outpost— not to go wandering about the countryside at night hunting brigands."

Damn. Just who had been whispering in the governor's ear? I wondered grimly. Was it Capito? Or Petronius Faustus himself?

"My orders included permission to conduct field exercises, sir," I said levelly. "I considered the chance to smash a bandit gang an effective form of training."

Piso ignored my riposte. "Tell me, Tribune. How far from your assigned post were you when you attacked the *Primus Pilus* and his men?"

For a heartbeat, I stared at him in silence—suddenly aware that the ground had just shifted beneath my feet. I was the one on trial here, not Domitius Capito.

"Answer my question," Piso snapped.

"Fifty miles," I said quietly.

"Fifty miles. Three full days' march." He let the distance hang in the air for a long moment before continuing. "Did anyone at the Sixth's headquarters know you were operating so far from your duty station?"

I gritted my teeth. "No, sir."

Piso smiled tightly again. "Let me see if I understand you properly, Tribune. First, you abandoned the fort placed in your care. Then you took your men on a long march across the back of the beyond. And you did all this without taking the time or trouble to inform any of the senior officers at Apamea of your intentions or your whereabouts?"

That was too much. My temper flared. "I had reason to suspect that some of those so-called senior officers were in league with the bandits, sir. There's no other way—"

"Silence!" Piso slammed the cup down on the table beside him. Red wine sloshed out over the rim onto his hand. His slave hurried over and knelt before him, offering a fresh linen towel.

The governor glared at me over the slave's head. "Let me be clear, Tribune. I'm not here to listen to your wild speculations. Or to indulge your idle fantasies. I am here to ferret out the facts surrounding this appalling disaster."

Calmer now, he turned toward Capito. "What were you doing when you were ambushed that night, Centurion?"

Capito drew himself up to his full height. "Leading a patrol, sir."

"I see." Piso finished wiping his hand and waved the slave away with an idle gesture. He looked back at Capito. "And was that a routine patrol?"

"Routine? No, sir." The centurion flashed a nasty grin in my direction. "We were out hunting the marauders who've been making so much trouble in the district."

"Commendable," the governor said dryly. "And was it your own idea to march out after these marauders in the dark?"

"My idea? Not exactly, sir." Capito smirked at me again and then looked back at Piso. "As a matter of fact, it was something the tribune himself suggested. He wanted troops posted on all the roads around Apamea.

Well, once he was gone—marching toward the frontier, we all thought—the legate decided there was something to the notion, after all."

Piso showed his teeth. "How ironic." He studied me coldly. "You've heard the *Primus Pilus*, Tribune. What is your response?"

"Capito is lying," I said grimly. "His own men have admitted their guilt under my interrogation and in front of witnesses."

The governor shook his head. "I'm very much afraid those precious confessions of yours count for nothing in this matter."

I stared at him, stunned. "What?"

Piso smiled. "I've received a dispatch from Petronius Faustus himself. In it, he confirms the centurion's story." He shrugged. "When I have the word of a legate, a fellow senator, and a friend of Caesar, why should I listen to the frightened babbling of common legionaries?"

Cunning, I thought, feeling sick at heart. I'd been outmaneuvered—first by Faustus and now by this serpent wearing human form. As the magistrate hearing the case, Piso had the power to consider—or dismiss—any of the evidence before him. No one in Rome would fault him for accepting the oath of a fellow senator.

His smile grew wider as he watched the full realization of my failure sink in.

Then he turned to the scribe sitting off to one side of the colonnade. "Hear my judgment in this case. Make three copies—one for the archives here, one for the Sixth Legion, and one for Rome."

He cleared his throat. "It seems quite clear that this was nothing more than a tragic accident—a confused clash between two units of friendly troops in the dark. It is also clear, however, that this tragedy was greatly compounded by reckless action taken by the tribune Lucius Aurelius Valens."

Piso shook his head in mock sorrow. "This young officer's intentions, though perhaps good, cannot justify the pointless waste of so many brave Roman soldiers. Nor can they justify the false accusations heaped on Domitius Capito, the brave and honorable *Primus Pilus* of the Sixth Legion. Therefore, I hereby dismiss all charges against Capito and restore him to full rank and responsibility."

He paused briefly, then he put the knife in. "I also strongly encourage the legate of the Sixth Legion to consider taking stern disciplinary action against the said Lucius Aurelius Valens."

Piso signaled the end of his dictation with an abrupt gesture to his scribe. "That's all." He turned his attention back to me. "For now, Tribune, consider yourself temporarily relieved of duty. I want Faustus to have plenty of time to decide just what to do with you."

And with that, the governor of Syria rose to his feet, moving lightly despite his great bulk. "This court is closed."

He spun on his heel and strode out, followed by his slave, bodyguards, and the scribe.

Capito stopped at my side. "You're finished, boy," he sneered. "Once Faustus is done with you, you'll be happy to swallow your own sword. And I'll be there to dance on your corpse."

Then he spat on the paving stones at my feet and hurried off in Piso's wake.

After they had gone, I stood alone for a time, shivering as the shadows grew around me.

I had failed. And in failing, I had lost everything of value—both my honor and my good name.

The shadows looming over me began to lift at a dinner party.

I reclined at table on the central couch—in the place reserved for the guest of honor. The poor, barbarians, and troops in the field may sit or stand to eat, but the wealthy of Rome take their formal meals lying down.

I raised myself higher on my left elbow, took a sip of cool white wine from the cup before me, and eyed my surroundings.

The dining room was one of the most elegant I'd seen outside of Rome itself. Intricate mosaics covered the floor—foremost among them a rendition of the god Apollo chasing a lovely and startled nymph. Beyond the mosaics, the room opened out into a beautiful garden. Clear, clean water gushed from the mouth of a statue of a winged, boyish god and splashed into a small pond surrounded by a profusion of flowers. A single laurel tree stood in one corner of the garden, shading a bench and patio.

I found myself nodding in approval. The man who'd designed this room and its surroundings had a fine artistic sense and a keen wit. Everything before me told a single story. Long ago, it was said, Apollo—pierced by one of Cupid's arrows—fell in love with the daughter of the river god Peneus. Frightened, the nymph fled his amorous advances. Still, he pursued her. At last, her prayers for help were answered, and she was transformed into a laurel tree, ever green and ever flourishing.

The nymph's name was Daphne.

And that was the name of this town—a wealthy suburb of Antioch. Villas covered the terraced hillsides, surrounded by fresh streams, waterfalls, and verdant groves of laurel. An ancient temple and spring sacred to Apollo were close by.

Soothed by what I saw, I leaned forward and took a bite from the dish set in front of me—artichoke leaves bathed in a garlic and pepper sauce. For the first time in two days, I felt hungry.

A pleasant contralto interrupted my musings. "Is that a smile I see, Aurelius Valens? This is improvement indeed! I take it, then, that you approve of my cook? Or is it my architect whose work you admire?"

I turned to the woman on my left, my hostess. "Both, my lady. If I could afford it, I'd hire them both away from you."

The lady Agrippina, the wife of Germanicus Caesar, laughed softly. She wasn't especially beautiful—not in the conventional sense, at least. But she was striking, with thick dark hair, bright brown eyes, clear, olive-toned skin, and a wide, generous mouth. She was also highly intelligent and fiercely devoted to her husband and their nine children. The daughter of Marcus Agrippa (Augustus' chief general) and the granddaughter of Augustus himself, she'd followed Germanicus from post to post—even staying at his side in the crude, damp legionary camps along the Rhine. Their marriage was much more a meeting of equals than most.

Some who'd caught the rough side of her tongue grumbled that she was far too outspoken to be a proper Roman matriarch. Germanicus, though, laughed off any complaints. He'd just chuckle and say, "Anyone who expects modest reticence from the offshoot of those two old bulls, Agrippa and Augustus, is more of a fool than I am!"

Like most of the officers and men who'd met her in
the Rhine camps, though, I greatly admired the lady
Agrippina. Her presence and her radiant smile had been
a living reminder of the warm Italian sun during what
had otherwise been a dreary and bloody tour of duty.
She and Germanicus entertained their friends and supporters whenever they could—and I'd spent many
happy hours in their company.

What I wondered about was why I'd been invited to
their house *now*, after my disgrace at Piso's hands and
in Germanicus' absence. I could tell that my presence
was making some of her other guests, all of them high
officials or members of rich Antiochene families, uneasy. I'd caught a number of raised eyebrows, disgusted
sniffs, and haughty looks aimed in my direction.

I shifted uncomfortably. Some of the peace I'd just
begun to feel drained away.

Agrippina read my thoughts and leaned closer to me.
"Relax, Aurelius. You are welcome in our house—now
more than ever."

"But Piso's judgment against me—" I began.

"Was flawed, corrupt, and foolish," she said firmly.
She smiled at the look of surprise on my face. "I've
heard the gist of the case and that is my considered
opinion. In fact, that is precisely *why* you are here
tonight."

"My lady?" I kept a tight rein on my expression,
scarcely willing to let myself hope that she'd invited me
for any reason beyond the courtesy owed one of her
husband's loyal officers.

Agrippina tore a piece of bread from a round loaf,
nibbled it daintily, and then brushed a few crumbs from
her fingers. She eyed me calmly. "Don't play the naïve
fool with me, Aurelius Valens. You may prize that blunt

old Roman manner of yours, but we both know you've got a crafty head on your shoulders. Though I must say there seem to be distressingly few occasions when you choose to use it."

I stifled a grin.

"I want that fat slug Gnaeus Piso to realize that his decision won't stand up to scrutiny," she continued. "I want him sweating over the fact that my husband will overrule him at the first opportunity."

"And that is why I'm your guest of honor . . . as a warning to the governor," I murmured.

"Of course." Agrippina nodded. "I expect Piso will know you were here before the night is out." She smiled icily. "For that matter, he'll probably have a detailed report of what you ate and which wines you enjoyed the most."

I glanced cautiously round the table at the other seven guests, most of whom seemed to be trying very hard to ignore what they were overhearing.

Agrippina noticed. She lowered her voice so that only I could catch her next words. "Half the men in this room would kiss our esteemed governor's dirty sandals if he asked them to. One or two of them would do it without even being asked."

Her expression darkened. "Oh, they bow, and they scrape, and they simper before me. It's 'yes, my lady' this, and 'of course, my lady' that. But only my husband can really bring them to heel. Until he's back, Piso holds power—and these men flock to power the way vultures flock to a new-dead corpse."

"Is there any word from Germanicus?" I asked quietly. "Will he return to Antioch soon?"

"I pray that he will," Agrippina said simply. She shrugged. "His most recent letter was optimistic. In it, he writes that the Armenian clans seem agreeable and willing to accept his mediation. With luck, he might be on his way home even now."

I frowned. "Or not for another week or more. And that's a disaster."

Agrippina watched me closely. "Go on."

I took another sip of wine, buying time to put my racing thoughts in some order. "Every passing day gives Piso more time to cover his tracks. To 'lose' the confessions of the soldiers who turned bandit. To 'persuade' some of my witnesses to change their stories. To transfer others to distant posts beyond my reach . . ."

"Or to kill them," Agrippina said flatly.

I nodded. There were ugly rumors abroad in Antioch. Some weeks ago, a group of Syrian landowners and merchants had confronted the governor in person, demanding that he put an end to the marauder rampage. He'd listened sympathetically, thanked them for their efforts, and then sent them home.

A day later, those hapless provincials had been found heaped by the side of the road—beaten to death.

A tragedy, Piso had said sorrowfully. A cruel fate must have carried them into the clutches of one of the wandering bandit gangs.

Some had even believed him.

I knew better now.

But what could I do about it? Until Germanicus got back, Piso controlled the levers of authority in the province. My head throbbed.

"There may be an alternative," Agrippina said, with some reluctance.

I turned toward her. "Yes, my lady?"

She hesitated briefly and then went on, speaking even more quietly than before. "There is a man in Anti-

och now. A powerful man. A senator and former consul."

"Who?" I asked.

"His name is Decimus Junius Silanus."

The name meant little to me. I'd been out of Rome
too long to follow all the twists and turns of politics.

"Silanus leads a potent faction in the Senate," Agrippina said. "But more importantly, he is a staunch friend
of Tiberius Caesar."

I stared at her. "What is such a man doing in Antioch?
Especially at this moment?"

She shrugged uneasily. "No one knows. Some say
this senator is on a private mission for Caesar, and that
he is only stopping here on his way to Judea. Others
claim he is investigating Piso's misdeeds. A few believe
he is spying on my husband and me. The only thing certain is that he and his bodyguards have commandeered
a house in the city."

"And you think I should approach him about this
case?"

Agrippina looked back at me in silence. I could understand her reluctance to advise me. She herself had no
great reason to love any friend of the new emperor.
Years before her own mother, Julia, though married to
Tiberius, had been exiled after a great scandal. Shortly
after Augustus died, Julia, too, had died. Some whispered that Tiberius, still angry with her, had ordered her
starved to death in her island prison.

I thought quickly. Germanicus could overrule the
court judgment against me—but he wouldn't go further
than that without real proof against Capito, Faustus, and
the others. Yet if there were even the slightest chance that
I could persuade this Silanus to act against the governor
and his cronies *now*, wasn't it worth trying?

Yes, I decided. It was.

Germanicus could give me back my official standing. My honor was another matter entirely. Standing idly by while Capito and the rest walked away from their murderous crimes was not an option. Not if I wanted to take any pride in the name and reputation I carried.

I nodded. "Very well. I'll speak to this senator as soon as I can."

Agrippina touched my arm gently. The hairs rose on the back of my neck. "You are a brave man, Aurelius. I honor you for it. Tread carefully, though. Silanus is said to be a man of integrity. Perhaps that is so. But not all such sayings are true. Some of those closest to Tiberius are capable of great evil. Even those with the fairest words and most pleasing countenance. Remember that."

Decimus Junius Silanus granted me an audience the next afternoon.

An elderly, white-haired slave led me into a large, sunlit chamber at the back of the house the senator had rented, announced me, and then scurried out.

Silanus sat upright in a straight-backed chair made of fragrant cedar. Several scrolls, a pot of ink, and a few pens were precisely aligned on the marble top of the small writing table at his side.

We were alone.

He was older than I'd first thought. From a distance, the senator's erect posture, trim figure, and lean, aristocratic face conveyed the impression of early middle age. As I drew nearer, I could see the deep-etched lines around his eyes and mouth. He was closer to sixty than forty, I realized. That made him a contemporary of Tiberius'—perhaps a boyhood acquaintance—and not just some jumped-up politician who'd recently caught the eye of the emperor.

His greeting was formal. "You are welcome in this house, Tribune. May the gods grant you their favor."

I stopped a few paces away from him and inclined my head briefly. "Thank you for agreeing to see me on such short notice, sir."

The senator's formality extended to his garments. He sat draped in a heavy white woolen toga, complete with the broad purple stripe of his rank. Despite the heat, he seemed perfectly at ease.

In contrast, I wore only my military tunic and a cloak. The city's streets were too crowded and dusty to go far in a toga—unless one hired a litter and the slaves to carry it. Too impatient to waste the time dickering over the price of a fare, I'd decided to walk.

If Silanus considered me underdressed for the occasion, he concealed his thoughts. Instead, he looked me up and down with a slight smile. "Your family name strikes a familiar note, Tribune. I believe I've heard it connected with several very lucrative mining contracts and franchises in Greece and Thrace. A close relative of yours, perhaps?"

"My father, sir," I said grimly.

The senator looked impressed. "You are fortunate."

I let that pass without comment.

On my way from Germany to Syria, I'd inspected one of the silver mines my father leased. No one expected a slave's lot in life to be a happy one. Nor did I have any great love for the brutish German tribesmen we'd captured in raids and battles. We sold them as slaves to wealthy entrepreneurs like my father, but at least they were alive. The Germans themselves took heads—not prisoners. But the pointless cruelty I'd seen inflicted in those cramped, hellish tunnels surpassed all bounds of reason and decency.

Silanus reached in among the scrolls on his table and held up the letter that Agrippina had written to introduce me. "The wife of Germanicus Caesar speaks highly of you, Tribune." He scanned it quickly again. His right eyebrow went up. "Very highly. Only her husband seems to warrant greater praise."

I blushed. "She is very kind."

Silanus nodded. "Yes. She is." He tapped the scroll gently with one bony finger. "But I fear that her note still leaves me at a loss as to exactly why you've come to see me today."

I explained the whole matter in as few words as possible—the bandit gangs, my arrest of Capito and his men, and Piso's attempt to conceal their crimes. The senator listened intently, but his expression remained impassive, wholly unreadable. He might have been listening to a tedious accounting of the year's Egyptian grain exports instead of a sordid tale of banditry, murder, and massive official corruption.

When I finished, he smiled thinly. "You place me in a difficult position, young man."

"That was not my intent, sir," I said quickly.

He held up a hand. "I realize that. Nevertheless, the difficulty remains. What if I told you that I'm only visiting this province on my own whim? As a simple private citizen?"

Despite my best efforts, I couldn't hide a slight smile of my own.

Silanus frowned. "I wasn't aware I'd told a joke, Tribune."

I shook my head. "No, sir. You haven't." I shrugged. "But tourists—even former consuls—don't usually rate a detachment of Praetorian guardsmen as an escort. If you're traveling incognito, you might tell the boys minding the front door to cover their shields."

There'd been two armed sentries on duty when I'd entered the senator's house. Both were big, hard-faced men. I'd seen their shields propped up in an alcove near the door. The gold scorpions emblazoned on them were a dead giveaway. Tiberius was a Scorpio. To honor him, his personal troops, the Praetorian Guards, had adopted his birth sign as their insignia.

To his credit, Silanus chuckled softly. "A solid thrust, Tribune. I confess it." Then the humor left his voice. "But even if I were here with a commission to investigate the governor of Syria, I'd scarcely admit as much to the first junior officer to come sniffing around my heels."

I started to speak, but he waved me to silence.

"My mission here — if I have any mission — is a matter between Caesar and myself. And, as it happens, I'm leaving Antioch within the week," the senator said. "Therefore, I will say . . . nothing. And I will do . . . nothing."

I stared at him in shock. "Nothing?"

Silanus nodded coolly. "You heard me plainly enough."

I couldn't believe it. "Then you'll just sit back and watch while Piso rapes this province for his own profit?"

The senator's gaze turned ice cold. "I will do my duty to Rome and to Tiberius Caesar," he snapped. "And I will follow my orders. I recommend the same course to you, boy!"

My jaw tightened. With an effort, I held my tongue. I'd already said too much — and all for nothing.

Silanus studied me carefully for a few moments. The anger in his face faded. Instead, he donned the sort of mild, reasonable "let's all be friends" look that must have come in handy during heated debate in the Senate.

I suppose some people might have found his new expression reassuring. It merely set my teeth on edge.

The senator sighed. "Let me offer you some advice, Aurelius Valens. For the sake of your father and your family name, if not for yourself."

"If you wish," I said flatly.

"You're a military tribune. Act like one," he said. "Go back to your post, obey your legate, and concentrate on your assigned duties."

Silanus sighed again. "But whatever else you do, Valens, stop meddling in the private feuds of those above your rank! The governor is a respected man, the choice of Caesar and of the Senate. You gain nothing by making him an enemy—not for yourself and not for Rome."

I kept my mouth shut. It wasn't easy. But hitting a senator—especially one with several Praetorian bully boys at his disposal—seemed unwise. Even to me.

Exasperated, the senator held up Agrippina's letter. "Open your eyes, boy. The lady is no fool. She's using you. First, to lash out at her husband's rival. And second, to pry into my business here."

He tossed the letter back onto his writing table. "Well, I will not dance to her tune. Neither should you."

I couldn't deny some of what Silanus had said. The lady Agrippina had every reason to despise Piso. She also had every reason to question the senator's presence in Antioch. But his belief that she was only manipulating me for petty private ends told me a great deal about Silanus himself. So did his effort to play down Piso's crimes as just another part of some personal dispute with Germanicus.

Tiring of my continued silence, the senator leaned forward in his chair. "Do you understand me, Tribune?" he demanded.

I looked him straight in the eye. "I understand you perfectly, Senator."

Silanus wasn't fooled by the even tone I'd forced. He must have seen the contempt in my eyes. He turned beet red. "Tiro!"

The slave who'd ushered me in appeared. "Sir?"

The senator picked up a pen and a blank piece of parchment. He swung away from me, bent over his writing table, and began scribbling something with short, sharp, slashing strokes. "The tribune Lucius Aurelius Valens is leaving. *Now*. See that he finds his way out to the street."

I stalked out after the slave. If nothing else, I thought with bitter amusement, I was developing a talent for angering powerful men. First Petronius Faustus. Then Piso. And now Silanus.

My grandfather had prided himself on his refusal to fawn over those above him. I suspected, however, that even he might have drawn the line at infuriating a legionary legate, a provincial governor, and a high-ranking member of the Roman Senate—at least all in the short space of a single fortnight.

I followed the old slave Tiro out through a maze of connecting corridors, rooms, and courtyards. Neither of us spoke. I didn't have anything to say. And Tiro was shrewd enough to realize that he didn't need to make polite small talk.

We were near the front entrance when a flaxen-haired girl wearing a drab brown tunic and a slave collar burst out of an adjoining room. Whimpering quietly, she rushed past me, hurrying deeper into the house. I had just enough time to notice the raw, red mark left by a fist on her cheek.

Surprised, I stared after her. She couldn't have been more than ten or twelve. Who would hit such a slip of a girl, even if she were just a slave?

I peered through a half-open door into the chamber from which she'd fled.

What I saw was strange. Very strange.

The room was small and dimly lit. Oil lamps on stands flickered in the corners. Grotesque symbols in scarlet, green, and black were daubed across the white-washed walls. I recognized several of them as signs of the zodiac. The other twisted and mystical shapes meant nothing—at least to me. A massive, flat-topped table took up most of the room. Scrolls, clay inkpots, and stacks of waxed writing tablets were heaped across the table's surface.

A man wearing a red silk robe with full-length, black sleeves stood behind the table, peering at one of the scrolls. As I watched, he tossed the manuscript aside and looked up.

Our eyes met.

Now there's a real bastard, I decided.

The other man was taller than I was—perhaps by half a head. Hooded dark eyes stared coldly back at me above a hooked nose. His thin, cruel lips twisted into a sneer.

Almost without thought, my hand dropped to the sword belted at my waist.

I felt Tiro's wrinkled fingers brush the hem of my cloak. "Tribune? If you please?"

I glanced at the old slave. "Yes?"

He nodded down the hall, toward the front door. "This way, sir."

When I looked back into the room, the red-robed man was leaning over the table again, studying yet another of the scrolls piled in front of him.

I turned away slowly, thinking hard.

Just a few steps from the outer door, I stopped and looked down at Tiro. "Who's that sour-faced lad? The one in the robes?"

The elderly slave stared back at me, his face carefully blank. "Sir?"

I slipped a silver coin out of the pouch on my belt and pressed it into his palm.

Tiro closed his fingers around the denarius and looked both ways, making sure the corridor was clear. He swallowed hard. "He is called Araneus, sir. They say he is a magus of great power and wisdom."

Araneus. "Spider." The nickname suited the robed bastard perfectly. And he was said to be a magus. That was interesting. And puzzling, too.

Shortly after taking power, Tiberius had banished all professional astrologers, ordering them out of Rome on pain of death. He'd also outlawed the use of magic, declaring it a wicked and vile practice unworthy of any true Roman. I'd read the decrees myself.

So why would Decimus Junius Silanus, member of the Senate and a friend of the emperor himself, bring a seer or sorcerer with him to Antioch?

The street outside the mansion rented by Silanus wound downhill past other large houses. Several were still under construction. This area was mostly new. As wealth flooded in from the surrounding countryside and from the trade routes to the east, Antioch's rich mer-

chant families were pouring money into huge new
homes on the lower slopes of Mount Silpius, which towers above the whole city. The view from there was spectacular—the red tile rooftops of old Antioch, the
Orontes, and the fertile fields and thick orchards beyond
the river all in sight at once.

On almost any other day, I would have spent at least
some time taking it all in. But not now. I was still furious—both with the senator for refusing to act against
Piso, and with myself for letting my temper get the best
of me.

Tread carefully, the lady Agrippina had warned me. I
should have paid more attention to her good advice.

My anger carried me down the hill and into the city's
crowded main thoroughfare.

The Great Street of Antioch ran north and south, cutting a straight line through the heart of the city. The road
was wide enough for several carts and wagons to drive
abreast. Colonnades running the length of the street created covered porticos filled with shops and stalls of
every size and description. Jars of wheat, wine, and
olive oil, stacks of pots and plates, rolls of cloth and
silk, spices, amulets, jewelry, and dozens of other com-
modities were being hawked and haggled over at every
turn.

Still seething inside, I pushed through the milling
crowds. I was heading south, toward the Daphne Gate.
There were people from every corner of the empire—
Syrians, Greeks, Egyptians, Jews, dark-skinned Numid-
ians, Arabs, and Armenians. At every step, I waved
aside bellowed sales pitches made in garbled Greek,
Aramaic, and languages I didn't even recognize.

"Fine wines from Chios and Rhodes! Vintages from
the gods themselves! Drink deep and live a long life!"

"Buy the best garments! Tunics! Robes! Cloth of all colors! Fit for a king! Feel their softness, sir. Test their strength!"

I moved on.

"Astonish women with the size and power of your manhood, sir!" A wizened creature with a wispy beard hung at my side, shoving a tray filled with jars of foul-smelling ointments and salves into my face. "See!" he wheedled. "A precious compound of rhinoceros horn, myrrh, and hair from the head of mighty Herakles himself!"

My head began to ache. I elbowed him out of my way and quickened my pace.

Suddenly, the shrill piping notes of a flute rose above the din.

A solid phalanx of weirdly dressed people blocked the street ahead of me — shouting and dancing and shrieking and whirling in all directions. Some wore caps and robes of lemon yellow. Others capered about in flowing white tunics striped with crimson. Clay and paint stained their faces and outlined bulging, staring eyes.

Wild, wavering yells echoed off the surrounding columns. "Atargatis! Atargatis! I give my life to the Goddess!"

"The Goddess comes! She comes!"

Others in the crowd echoed the cry, brandishing swords and axes as they wailed. Some bit themselves, grinning madly through bloodied teeth. A few sliced their own arms with their weapons, laughing at each cut. Spit and blood flew in all directions.

The sound of the flute grew louder.

A donkey emerged from the frenzied mob, carrying a gilded statue of a woman topped by the image of a crescent moon. A band of dirty-faced acolytes trotted beside the statue, holding open empty bags. They broke ranks and fanned out through the surrounding porticos.

"Alms for Atargatis! Feed the Goddess! Gain Her favor!"

I backed up, with my hand on my money pouch. I'd run straight into a procession honoring the *Dea Syria*, the Syrian Goddess. Her crazed devotees, the nomadic *galli*, roamed the villages and cities of Syria — gathering food, clothing, and coinage for themselves and for their deity.

I frowned. Rome doesn't interfere with most local religious practices, but I disliked the wild, irrational fervor and self-mutilation I saw before me. Even the nearest shopkeepers were caught up by the frenzy. Many of them were already pushing forward with offerings for the Goddess.

An alley opened off the nearest portico and I slid through the crowd in that direction.

It was dark and quiet in the alley and I was grateful for that. I walked on — moving past rows of jars, bales, and sacks waiting their turn in the shops lining the Great Street. Narrow doorways led off into shadowed, private houses.

I felt myself relaxing. I was well out of the madness, chaos, and deafening noise, I thought gratefully.

I was wrong.

Several small wicker cages were stacked against the closest wall. The cages were filled with white doves. They were probably intended for use as temple sacrifices. Something—perhaps all the clamor in the street behind me—had stirred them up. They were fluttering back and forth, beating their wings against the wicker bars.

Suddenly, one of the cages flew open. A dove broke loose, and it sped straight past my face, so close that its wingtips brushed my forehead.

Startled, I spun round.

And then I saw them.

There were two men close behind me—one much taller and broader-shouldered than the other. Both wore tattered, sand-colored robes. Loose hoods concealed most of their faces. Both carried long knives.

Stunned, I stepped back just as the big man lunged at me. I threw my left arm up in a desperate bid to knock the dagger away. The blade tore a line of fire across my forearm and then skidded off the bone.

Panting, I fell back. I needed time. Time to get my sword out. Time to defend myself.

The big man flicked my blood from his knife, grinned nastily at me, and waved his comrade forward.

I spun round and pulled the stack of cages over, spilling birds and broken wicker across the alley. The frightened doves whirled up in a cloud of beating wings.

Caught off guard, the smaller man backed off with his hands shielding his face, swearing loudly.

In Latin.

I yanked my sword out of its scabbard and thrust it into his stomach in the same smooth motion. I could feel it bite deep. He screamed and folded over the blade. I tore the sword loose as he went down.

Before I could bring my blade back into position, the big man attacked again. He leaped straight over the body of his dying comrade and threw himself into me.

I slammed into the stone wall at my back, gasping as the impact knocked the air out of my lungs. My sword spun away. His dagger grated along my ribs, ripping more flesh and muscle.

Gods!

I hooked my right foot around his heel and shoved hard. He fell backward, dragging me down with him. We rolled on the ground, punching, kicking, and clawing at each other.

I got the worst of it. Blows rattled my teeth. Hooked fingernails tore my left cheek.

He was bigger, heavier, and stronger than I was, I realized in dismay. I had to get out of this, now!

I let go of his arm just long enough to scrabble around in the dust as he slammed his elbow sideways into my collarbone. The bone didn't break, but agony racked my left side. Finally, my fingers closed on a stone. I hurled it into his face as hard as I could. Swearing, he snapped his head back.

I broke loose and rolled away—frantically searching the ground around me for my sword.

There it was! I grabbed the hilt as the big man roared like a lion and threw himself at me again.

I whirled round with the sword in my hand.

The point took him squarely in the throat. His eyes opened wide in horror as the blade drove deep—almost tearing his head off his shoulders. Blood sprayed across me, drenching my tunic and face.

He flopped backward, shuddered once, and lay still.

Still gasping and panting, I wiped some of the blood out of my eyes with the torn edge of my cloak. Then slowly and painfully, I got to my knees and leaned over the corpse.

It was Domitius Capito.

The senior centurion lay on his back in the dust. His money pouch had torn loose in the struggle, its contents spilled across the alley. Silver gleamed in the dim half-light.

I spat more blood out of my mouth and picked up one of the denarii. The blunt profile of Tiberius Caesar stared back at me. It was untarnished. These coins were freshly minted.

And I knew exactly who had tried to use them to buy my death.

Gnaeus Calpurnius Piso, the governor of Syria.

Chapter IV

Aristides carefully unwound the blood-soaked scrap of cloak from my left forearm, revealing the gash left by Capito's dagger. He dropped the makeshift bandage into a plain terra-cotta basin set between us on the stone-paved floor. Then he pulled my arm into a shaft of sunlight streaming through the narrow window and examined the wound more closely. Squinting, he poked and prodded at it with a pair of bronze tweezers, looking for any piece of torn cloth or filth left inside.

I stiffened.

Aristides raised an eyebrow. "Painful?"

I nodded. There wasn't any point in denying it. The Greek doctor knew me too well.

"It'll hurt worse in a moment," he said flatly. "Hold your arm out over the basin."

Sighing, I obeyed.

In one smooth motion, Aristides gripped my arm with his own left hand and then, with his right, poured the contents of a small beaker over the wound. Clear liquid splashed across the long, gaping cut, washing away dirt and dried blood.

For an instant, everything turned red and the room

spun around me. My arm felt as though it were on fire. I gasped, took a deep breath, and then wished I hadn't. My eyes watered—stung by strong, sour fumes.

"Zeus!" I forced out through gritted teeth. "Pure vinegar?"

Aristides nodded calmly. "It cleans best." One corner of his mouth lifted in a slight smile. "At least, for those who can bear its strength."

He set the beaker aside and used a vinegar-soaked sponge to finish swabbing the gash. I took several more deep, shuddering breaths to fend off some of the pain.

The doctor looked down again. "The wound bleeds again," he said in satisfaction. "But no more than is desirable."

I was glad to hear that. Aristides and his fellow physicians believed that bleeding was one of the body's defenses against decay and a killing fever. If the new rivulet of red trickling down my arm hadn't satisfied him, he'd already be fingering one of his scalpels and looking for a fresh vein to slit open. I didn't doubt his expertise, but I couldn't help feeling that I'd already left enough of my own blood spattered around Antioch's streets today.

I turned my head away when Aristides began closing the wound, drawing its edges together with small bronze pins called *fibulae*. The sharp jabs as each fibula went in were bearable—especially after the searing vinegar. Still, I didn't like seeing my flesh so painstakingly and deliberately punctured.

Battles, at least, are fought in a numbing cauldron of fury and fear and exhilaration. Swords and spears stab or are parried in the blink of an eye. There's no time to think deeply—only to act and react. But surgery has always seemed to me a very calculating and cold-blooded business. I'd said as much to Aristides once. "Of course, it is," he'd said caustically. "Healing is always more difficult than killing." Then he'd looked down the broad beak of his nose at me. "Perhaps you would-be heroes should remember that before you next rush off to war."

Abashed, I'd let the subject drop.

Satisfied at last, Aristides bandaged my arm with a new length of clean, cool linen. Then he moved on to the knife wound over my ribs.

His treatment there was just the same and just as painful. I was sweating and light-headed by the time he finished.

The doctor used the last of the vinegar to sluice my blood off his own hands. He sat back and eyed me appraisingly. "You'll live, I think. Both injuries should heal without complication."

I felt a surge of relief. I'd hoped that my wounds weren't serious, but hearing Aristides issue the same prognosis was enormously reassuring. "I was fortunate."

He frowned. "Yes, Lucius. You were." He lowered his voice. "But I'm not sure you deserved such luck— not after indulging in so much folly."

I bit back a sharp retort. Part of me wanted to bristle at the accusation. Another part had to admit he was right. I was still alive, and Capito and the other assassin were dead. But only by the narrowest of margins.

"You were already in trouble enough with the governor and his faction," the doctor went on. "You should have waited for Germanicus to come back from Armenia before you went plowing ahead."

It was an old argument. After Piso tossed out the criminal case I'd brought against Capito and his bandit gang, Aristides had tried hard to persuade me to let the matter rest for a time, pointing out that I couldn't hope to accomplish anything without direct backing from Germanicus. As so often before, he'd counseled patience and prudence. And, as usual, I'd listened respectfully and then gone my own way.

"What was the sense of fanning the flames by trying to drag this pet senator of Tiberius into the middle of things?" he asked again.

"My meeting with Silanus was a gamble worth taking," I said stubbornly. "The emperor has always demanded strict discipline and order in his legions. No real friend of his should have been willing to turn a blind eye to the corruption and rot among our troops here."

"And yet Piso is also a crony of this same Tiberius," Aristides pointed out skeptically, "which should have told you that the emperor's friends don't feel much need to measure up to those famous standards of his."

Again, I didn't say anything, but again I had to struggle against the urge to snap back. There's almost nothing more irritating than listening to someone point out the mistakes you've made. Especially after you've already admitted them to yourself.

Aristides shook his head in exasperation. "Well, if you had to go wandering about Antioch like some kind of sacrificial lamb, why in Hades' name didn't you at least take Quintus Rufus and one or two of his legionaries with you?"

"Visiting the senator was a private act, not an official call," I said, knowing even as I spoke how unconvincing that sounded. "I didn't have the right to bring troops along as an escort."

The doctor snorted. "That's a rather subtle point of military etiquette, Lucius. And it might sound more credible coming from a young officer who didn't have a habit of bending rules to suit his own views of right and wrong."

I shrugged. The truth was that I hadn't wanted to drag Rufus and his soldiers any deeper into the mess I'd created. Unless I could somehow find a way to oust Petronius Faustus from his post as commander of the Sixth Legion, the centurion and his men would be in serious trouble when they returned to Apamea. I didn't have any illusions. The legate was a notoriously vindictive man. He'd be glad to punish soldiers whose only mistake was that they'd obeyed my orders to ambush Capito and his gang.

"At the very least, you should have taken me with you," Aristides said tightly.

I stared at him for a moment, surprised. As far as I knew, the doctor had never so much as picked up a sword in all his life. I was sure that he'd learned to wrestle as a boy, but it must have been the sort of formal sparring better suited to the gymnasium than real combat. If he'd thrown himself into the fray against Capito and his comrade, he'd only have gotten himself killed—and probably me as well.

He read my expression and shook his head. "Not to guard your back. I know that I'm no warrior." He lowered his voice still further. "But I have a good pair of eyes, Lucius."

I saw what he was driving at. "You would have been a witness."

He nodded. "And you need one—very badly."

I knew that. But I'd been hoping that Aristides was so busy worrying about my injuries that he'd missed the bigger danger I was facing. I should have known better.

I kept my tone light. "So you don't think Piso will accept my account? Even on my honor as a Roman knight?"

The doctor looked pointedly around the small, cramped room I'd been assigned by one of the governor's officials. The rickety bed we were both sitting on was the only piece of furniture. One narrow window offered a little light and air, but not enough to clear away the musty smell of dirt and sweat. He didn't say anything. He didn't have to.

I held up a hand. "All right, I admit it. This is the closest thing to a prison cell I've ever been in. But at least there's no guard at the door."

Aristides scowled. "No. But some of the governor's hired killers are lounging about just down the corridor. Somehow I doubt they're on duty to protect you."

"I've seen them," I said flatly. There were four of them—all openly armed with swords and daggers. Piso's men were already on watch by the time I'd been politely, but firmly, escorted to this small, squalid chamber. They'd sneered at me, but at least they'd stepped aside to let me pass.

Most high-ranking officials who were entitled to bodyguards assigned the job to legionary soldiers on detached duty. Gnaeus Piso was no exception. Regular troops were posted as sentries at several points around the palace.

The governor, though, also kept a band of armed men as his private retainers. Officially, they were simply loyal clients and freedmen drawn from his vast estates in Italy and Spain. At best, that was a polite fiction. At worst, it was an outrageous lie.

Some of Piso's bodyguards were ex-gladiators attracted by the high wages he offered. I suspected that most of the others were bandits who'd chosen the security of paid service over the perilous freedom of their former way of life. All of them looked ready to do anything for money—no matter how vile, illegal, or depraved.

Despite that, I didn't think I was in immediate danger. Not even the governor could expect to get away with ordering the murder of a legionary officer held under his own roof. At the same time, I couldn't ignore the fact that I was treading on very dangerous ground.

And I was there largely by my own choice.

I could have just walked away from the bodies of the two men I'd killed in that narrow alley off the Great Street. No one had seen my desperate, vicious fight against Capito and his friend. Amid all the chaos and frenzy of the Syrian Goddess' religious procession, I doubt that anyone would even have noticed my torn and bloodied tunic and cloak.

What's more, if I'd stayed silent, it wasn't likely that anyone would ever have connected me with the dead men—except, of course, for Piso. At sunset, the city's law-abiding inhabitants retreated to their homes. Once it was dark, the streets and winding alleys were left to criminals, the destitute, and the depraved. Detachments from the legions were stationed in the city to maintain order, but there were never enough men to go around. By the time the bodies were found, Antioch's beggars and thieves would have stripped them of anything that might identify them as Roman soldiers. Even if someone in authority recognized Capito, his death would have been considered a routine killing, probably the result of a botched mugging.

No one would ever have known what I'd done.

But I couldn't do it. I couldn't skulk away as though I were nothing more than a common criminal ashamed of my own deeds. I was a Roman knight and an officer of the legions. More important to me, I was the heir of my grandfather's stern sense of duty.

So I'd reported the attempt on my life to the first legionary guard post I'd come across.

The young, fresh-faced *optio* who'd followed me back to the alley had stared down at the gory mess my sword thrust had made of Capito's neck, swallowed hard, and then said faintly, "Jupiter! This fellow was senior centurion of the Sixth Legion? This is well over my head, Tribune. I'll have to fetch someone with enough rank to investigate this . . . this . . ." He trailed off, unable to find the right word to describe what he saw.

I'd nodded wearily and then found myself sliding down the wall I'd been leaning against, overcome at last by the wounds I'd taken in the fight.

I was still too dizzy to stand when the centurion commanding the district arrived. An older, more experienced, and cynical soldier than his subordinate, he'd prodded the corpses with his sandal, scooped up and studied the coins from Capito's money pouch, and then squatted down to ask for my version of events.

I gave it to him straight—holding back only my belief that the governor was involved. I didn't have any hard evidence to back my suspicions, and I didn't know which faction, if any, the centurion supported.

After I finished my tale, the centurion rubbed his jaw for a moment or two in silence. Then he examined the bodies again. Finally, he sighed. "Right, Tribune. Well, this is as big a mess as I've seen in my time, but I don't see any point in holding you here longer. You'll stay in the city until this is sorted out?"

I nodded.

"Good," he said heavily. "Look, I'll have to file a report. Once some jumped-up scribe on the governor's staff bothers reading it, I'm sure somebody will want to ask you more questions." The centurion shrugged. "But the gods only know when that might be. Maybe tomorrow. Maybe not until sometime next week. Everything's fouled up just now."

I nodded again. The feud between Germanicus and Piso was sowing confusion at every level of provincial administration.

In fact, though, the centurion was completely wrong about how long it would take for his report to filter up through the bureaucracy. Someone, either Piso himself or one of his top aides, must have been waiting for the news that the military tribune Lucius Aurelius Valens had been found dead in Antioch's labyrinth of streets. Whoever it was must have been sadly disappointed to learn that I was still alive. I grinned at that thought and then felt the smile slip off my face. Disappointed or not, they had reacted swiftly to the unwelcome news.

By the time I reached the house I'd rented near the Daphne Gate, soldiers from the governor's guard detachment were already waiting outside the front door. I'd been allowed barely enough time to pack a spare tunic and cloak and give Aristides the gist of what had happened. I wasn't exactly under arrest, but I certainly wasn't free to go where I wished. The official version was that I was "in protective custody, pending further investigation." My personal physician, Aristides, had been allowed in to see me, but I had the distinct impression that other visitors would have been turned away.

I sighed and leaned back against the wall, trying to ignore the throbbing ache from my wounds and bruises. The situation was uncomfortable, and so was I.

Aristides stood up and prowled over to the door. He poked his head out into the corridor to make sure no one was in earshot. Then he came back to sit beside me. "The lady Agrippina sent a message for you," he muttered. "It arrived right after they marched you off."

I sat upright again. "Tell me."

"She just received a dispatch from Germanicus. He's on his way back to Antioch. The Armenian tribes have agreed to his proposals. There'll be no war on that frontier—at least this year."

That was good news. With Germanicus back at his own headquarters, Piso's authority would be greatly diminished. But Armenia was a long way off, and it would take weeks for him to return. I said as much to Aristides.

The doctor shook his head. "He'll be here much sooner than that, Lucius. This dispatch was sent four days ago—from Samosata."

I closed my eyes briefly, trying to call to mind the maps I'd studied. Soon enough the geography fell into place. Samosata was a city to the east and north of Antioch. Sited on the western bank of the Euphrates River, it was the capital of Commagene, one of the several small client kingdoms we used as buffers against the Parthians.

I whistled softly in surprise. "That's more than halfway here!"

Aristides nodded.

"But why didn't Germanicus send word as soon as he left Armenia?" I wondered aloud.

The doctor frowned. "The lady Agrippina is quite sure that he did."

That seemed likely enough. Germanicus would have wanted his wife and supporters to know that all was well.

And yet, no dispatch had arrived.

I didn't believe that was an accident.

True, decades of scrimping by successive money-grubbing governors had left the roads in Syria in pretty poor condition. But one of Germanicus' first priorities upon taking command in the East had been to improve communications all along the frontier. Now, most of the major routes from Antioch toward the Parthian border were lined with relay stations, inns, and guard posts. Each kept a string of fresh horses ready for use by those traveling on imperial business.

No, the odds were very much against any important message simply going astray. The roads were well traveled and this wasn't a season of storms. Nor was it likely that the courier had fallen prey to robbers or thieves. Ordinary bandits rarely troubled imperial messengers. The pickings were too slim, and the chances of serious retribution too high.

My jaw tightened. Piso must be responsible.

The governor had every incentive to conceal the news of Germanicus' imminent return. The longer men looked to him as the sole power in Antioch, the more secure he could make himself against the day when his superior reappeared.

I shook my head angrily. The thought that Piso had his dirty fingers all over the *cursus publicus*, the imperial postal service, shouldn't have surprised me. He'd already shown himself willing to do whatever he could to interfere with Germanicus' exercise of civil and military authority. The more important question now was when we could expect Germanicus himself.

I knew that he usually traveled with only a modest escort—one or two trusted aides, a secretary to handle correspondence, two or three slaves, and just a few handpicked bodyguards. Still, small or not, any band of travelers would move far more slowly than would a single rider.

I summoned up what I'd learned about the road to Samosata again, trying to recall the distances shown between the various stopping places. It seemed to me that if a courier riding hard could cover the ground in four days, Germanicus and his companions could certainly make the journey in eight.

I glanced around the small, squalid chamber that had become my unofficial prison. Four more nights to spend in this fleapit, I thought grimly. Four more days until I could lay my case against Petronius Faustus and Piso before a man I trusted and respected.

I sighed and slumped back against the wall again. The hours and days would pass slowly. But they would pass. And then I would be free to act against those who had made themselves my enemies—against those willing to misuse their power and position to rob, maim, and murder.

I should have realized that I wasn't the only one in Antioch who could reckon travel times. Piso's cutthroats came for me near the evening of the next day.

With two of them close at my back and two more swaggering just ahead, they marched me through a labyrinth of connecting hallways and corridors, and then into a large chamber somewhere deep within the palace. The walls and floor were bare stone, without any ornamentation or decoration at all. Only a row of narrow, arched windows set high on one wall and a pair of oil lamps on bronze stands provided a small measure of light. Most of the room was still cloaked in a mass of shadows. It was a cold, sterile place—one that struck me as intended for the secret exercise of raw power.

Against my will, I shivered.

Gnaeus Piso himself sat behind a long table at the far end of the room, idly reading a scroll. Another pair of bodyguards stood beside him, watching me closely.

Despite my growing anxiety, I stifled a sudden urge to laugh. If he still felt the need to confront me with six heavily armed men close at hand, the governor must consider me quite a dangerous character. I only wished his assessment were accurate. In truth, I was beginning to feel very foolish as well as very worried. I'd acted lawfully and honorably by reporting Domitius Capito's attempt on my life, but by doing so I'd put myself squarely into Piso's power. Living up to my grandfather's standards was proving harder than I'd ever imagined.

"The tribune Lucius Aurelius Valens," one of the guards who'd marched me in announced in a rough, guttural voice.

The governor looked up from the scroll. He studied me placidly for a moment, then frowned. "I see that your negligence extends even to your personal appearance, Tribune." He pushed the scroll aside and sniffed contemptuously. "You may think it fitting to appear before me clad in filth and rags. I do not."

I stood silent.

He knew very well that I hadn't been given the courtesy of a visit to the baths or even the chance to shave. In Rome, defendants sometimes tear their clothes and pour ashes over their heads in a bid to win sympathy from a judge or jury. I had no such illusions where Piso was concerned. Nothing I did or said was likely to have the slightest effect on him.

One side of the governor's mouth curled upward in amusement. "No excuses, then? Nothing to say?" He shrugged. "Perhaps that is wise. After all, the disrespect you show me is the least of your several crimes."

"I've committed no crimes!" I replied hotly. I knew that he must be trying to shake my confidence, but my self-respect wouldn't let me leave his false accusation unchallenged.

"Really?" He raised an eyebrow. "If we could call it back from the underworld, the shade of Domitius Capito, once *Primus Pilus* of the Sixth Legion, might find your assertion of innocence surprising."

I did my best to speak calmly. If nothing else, pride demanded that I deny Piso the satisfaction of seeing my fear. "Capito and his comrade attacked me without warning. I defended myself. No more and no less."

"So you claim." The governor nodded toward the scroll he'd been perusing when his bodyguards brought me in. "I've read the investigating centurion's report."

His countenance, amused a moment before, now hardened. "But I see the matter quite differently. I think you bore a grudge against Capito because I dismissed your absurd accusations against him. This grudge then turned to hatred when you realized how much shame you had brought on yourself."

I felt the blood rush to my face.

Piso smiled icily. "That is why I believe you murdered him, Tribune."

I said nothing.

"What? No outraged denial?" the governor said, feigning surprise. "No anguished plea of innocence?"

This time I held my tongue and tried to think before I replied.

"Is this a formal trial?" I asked through clenched

teeth. "Or just a meaningless show? I see no prosecutor, no scribe, and no witnesses."

"This is whatever I wish it to be, boy," Piso said flatly. "I have the power to convict you of any crime I choose. And I have the power to order your execution. You should remember that."

"As a Roman citizen, I have the right to appeal directly to the emperor," I reminded him. "No sentence you pass on me is final."

"That is certainly true." The governor seemed unmoved by the possibility that Tiberius Caesar would have the final say over my fate. He changed tack abruptly. "Tell me something, Lucius Aurelius Valens. Do you consider yourself a man of honor?"

"I try to act honorably," I said slowly, wondering why Piso asked this question.

He smiled broadly. "Splendid! So you stand before me as a shining example of young Roman nobility and virtue! As a living rebuke to all those who prate about the growing decadence and depravity of our age."

I bit back an angry retort. He was goading me, I decided, trying to shatter the calm demeanor I was struggling so desperately to preserve. No doubt the exercise gave him pleasure.

Piso stopped smiling. His eyes glittered. "Now do you seriously suppose that the emperor—or anyone of consequence in Rome, for that matter—would be surprised to learn that such an exemplar, overcome by the disgrace of being found guilty of murder, had decided to take his own life?"

I saw what he intended in the blink of an eye. It would only take a single, brutal order. Two of his henchmen could pinion my arms, while a third thrust a dagger deep into my stomach and up under my ribs. To all outward appearances, my death would be a sui-cide—the expected end for any true Roman facing an intolerable future. For an instant, I felt despair, the sheer icy certainty that I stood on the brink of oblivion.

Gnaeus Piso must have seen that. He chuckled, plainly delighted by the effect his threat had on me.

Though gripped by hopelessness, I felt the begin-nings of a great fury building deep within me. Whatever happened, I swore to myself and to the memory of my grandfather's name that I would not give him the satis-faction of seeing me beg for my life. I swayed slightly, thrown off balance by the flood of conflicting emotions I was trying to restrain.

Piso nodded to the guards behind me. They stepped forward and gripped my forearms with callused hands, holding me tight.

I shook them off angrily and stood up straight. If he planned to have me killed now, I would at least meet death on my own two feet.

Then, to my surprise, Piso waved his ruffians back.

Before I could say anything, the governor changed his tone yet again, this time adopting a somber, serious manner. "There's really no need for so distressing a con-clusion to this hearing, Tribune. No need at all." He spread his hands. "Who knows? Perhaps my suspicions are unjust. Perhaps you can convince me that you acted in self-defense after all."

The bastard was toying with me.

I swallowed hard, fighting nausea provoked by the rage and fear churning inside me. Gain control, Lucius, I told myself. Remember your beliefs. Accept fate and meet it with dignity. Stay calm.

"What do you want?" I asked harshly.

"Only the truth, Tribune, I assure you," Piso said

mildly. "Nothing but the truth. Your complete candor would greatly assist me. There are several aspects of your account that require some clarification." He raised a quizzical eyebrow.

"Go on."

"The centurion who first investigated this regrettable incident is an admirably direct man, but his report overlooks certain matters that might be considered crucial." He picked up the scroll again, unrolled it, and tapped a fleshy finger against one section. "For instance, it says here that you claim you were attacked by Capito and this other man on your way back from an interview with the senator Decimus Junius Silanus."

"That's true."

"And this interview was arranged by the lady Agrippina?"

I caught the sound of something odd in his tone. A note of suppressed anxiety, perhaps? I nodded. "The lady wrote a letter of introduction for me."

"I see." Piso mulled that over for a few moments.

I said nothing more.

"And what was the subject of this meeting?" he asked at last, this time unable to conceal the anticipation in his voice.

Well, well, well, I thought. Now we get down to it. So this was why he'd run me through the gauntlet of threats and false hope: to extract information about Silanus and his purpose in Antioch. Which meant that he, too, didn't know what the senator, another close ally of Tiberius', was doing here. Both he and the lady Agrippina were in the dark. And maybe that meant I could make him sweat a bit.

After all, I didn't really have anything to lose. Piso's plans for me were clear. Once he'd squeezed me for everything he could, he'd have his bodyguards finish me off. If he let me live, I could still make things very awkward for him once Germanicus returned.

I fixed my eyes on him and spoke bluntly. "I gave Junius Silanus a full account of your corrupt and ruinous administration of this province—and of my strong suspicions that the brigands ravaging Syria are carrying out your orders."

Piso's composure slipped. His hands curled into fists and he turned red with anger. For the space of a heartbeat I thought he might snap out the order for my execution then and there. Slowly, though, he mastered himself. At last, he gave me a wintry smile. "And how did the good senator react to these rather extravagant claims?"

"He listened quite intently."

Piso's right eye twitched. "Nothing more?"

I matched his cold smile with one of my own. I wouldn't lie to him, but I'd be damned if I'd offer him the reassurance of hearing that Silanus had dismissed my complaints out of hand. Let him stew over the possibility that another of the emperor's confidants might be here sniffing around for evidence of his crimes. "I don't think the further details of my conversation with Silanus have any real bearing on Capito's attempt to murder me, do you?"

"You insolent young pup!" Piso glared back at me. He rose ponderously to his feet. "I'll have you . . ."

The sudden clatter of hobnailed sandals and the jingle of armor in the corridor outside cut short whatever new threat he planned to make.

A tall, handsome man wearing a travel-stained scarlet cloak over his tunic strode confidently into the room.

A dozen legionaries in full battle gear followed him in, shields up and ready for trouble.

Piso stood frozen in shock. His hirelings edged backward, uneasily trying to put as much distance as they could between themselves and the hard-eyed soldiers who accompanied the newcomer. Piso's thugs were careful to keep their hands well away from their swords and belt knives.

I couldn't stop a smile from spreading across my face. The despair I'd been fighting against began draining away.

Germanicus Julius Caesar stopped at my side, flashed a quick grin of his own at me, and then turned his full attention to the governor. "Hail, Gnaeus Calpurnius! I'm glad to see you looking so well."

Piso's mouth fluttered open and shut without making any sound, reminding me of a newly landed fish thrashing frantically at the bottom of a boat. He sat down heavily. Then he rallied enough to make a faint reply. "Most noble Germanicus! This is a surprise . . . though a most welcome one, of course. I had not thought to see you for several more days."

Germanicus smiled broadly. "So I understand. But a dispatch I finally received at Samosata convinced me that I'd been away from Antioch for far too long. I rode ahead, leaving most of my escort to follow at a slower pace. For four days I've stayed in the saddle from dawn to the last flicker of light—changing horses at every way station. And from the way my backside feels right now, I can assure you I've got more respect for the work of the imperial post!"

Piso scowled, but kept his mouth shut.

I stayed quiet myself. I had every hope that Germanicus would intervene on my behalf, but I also knew that

he intensely disliked playing favorites in the administration of justice.

He surveyed the scene before him with his hands on
his hips. Though plainly tired, he was also clearly
amused by what he saw. The legionaries he'd brought
with him had formed a hollow square along the walls,
with the rest of us in the middle. The governor's bodyguards huddled near the far corner of the chamber.

Germanicus swung back toward Piso. "This room appears a bit crowded, Gnaeus Calpurnius. With so many
sharp edges about, somebody could get hurt. It might be
safer for us all if you ask your lads to wait outside."

The governor's lips tightened, but he wasn't prepared
to press the issue. "You may be right. Scurra!"

"Sir?" One of the guards, a villainous-looking
Spaniard, looked nervously toward his master.

"Take the others and get out!"

The rest of Piso's men didn't even wait for the
Spaniard's order. They were already hurrying toward
the door.

Once they were gone, Germanicus came straight to
the point. "My wife informs me that Aurelius Valens
here is in some small bit of trouble. Is that true, Piso?"

"Your wife has the gift of remarkable understatement," the governor said grimly. "At the moment, I'm
investigating charges that the tribune murdered both the
Primus Pilus and another soldier from his own legion."

"Serious charges, to be sure," Germanicus agreed. He
turned to me. "And what do you say to these allegations,
Valens?"

Now I looked him straight in the eye. "They are false,
sir. I fought only to defend myself against a murderous
assault. I will swear that by the honor of my name—
and by all the gods and spirits of this place."

"Do you have anyone who can confirm your story?"

"No, sir," I admitted.

Germanicus nodded. He turned back to the governor. "A difficult case on the surface, Piso. There aren't any witnesses and the accused assailant is the only one left alive. Perhaps I should take over this investigation of yours?"

Piso pursed his lips and then shook his head. "I think that would be a mistake. As you say, the matter is complicated. It's best left to me—as one with direct knowledge of the facts involved."

Germanicus laughed. "Oh, I think I can cope. Agrippina has already apprised me of the important details."

Piso clouded up. He said thickly, "With all due respect, the lady, for all her admitted virtues, is only a woman—and therefore lacks any real knowledge of the law."

Germanicus ignored him. He moved forward and picked up the scroll in front of the governor. He read through it quickly and then looked up at Piso. "Interesting. You've considered the centurion's testimony about the wounds he found on Capito and the other dead man, I suppose."

"What about them?" Piso asked peevishly.

"Both the tribune's thrusts were delivered from the front, not from the back—one into the stomach of the soldier and the other into Capito's neck," Germanicus pointed out.

The governor shrugged. "That doesn't seem very significant to me."

"No?" Germanicus arched an eyebrow in surprise. "Then I assume you don't see the significance of the injuries suffered by Valens himself?"

"I do not," Piso said flatly.

"Look at them," Germanicus said. He nodded toward the bandages wrapped around my left arm and the others around my rib cage. "Those wounds were inflicted at close quarters. They're the sort you take when trying to block a blade that's already too close to parry."

The governor snorted. "There's no mystery there. The tribune found Capito and his comrade in that alley. He attacked them with his sword. No doubt they did their best to defend themselves, but he had the edge in weapons."

Germanicus slowly shook his head, clearly amused. "You think a man with a sword has the better part of the bargain in such cramped surroundings? You've never really been in battle, have you, Piso?"

The governor flushed, but said nothing in reply.

I held my rising hopes in check, but only with difficulty. How far would Germanicus go in my favor?

"In my view, what little physical evidence there is confirms the story told by Aurelius," Germanicus commented. "Two men, both—according to the centurion's report—wearing clothing that could have concealed their identity, jumped him in that alley and tried to kill him. He fought back, took wounds—and won."

"What about motive? I can tell you why this young blunderer would want Capito dead!" Piso said angrily, pointing at me. "But what reason can you find for the *Primus Pilus* of his own legion to attack him?"

Germanicus looked at him for a time, letting the silence drag on. Then he asked softly, "Do you really want me to begin looking closely into questions of motive in this case, Gnaeus Calpurnius Piso? Have you forgotten the bag of coins found on Domitius Capito? Shall I try to discover how he laid his hands on such a large sum of money?"

Piso stared back. I watched the color drain slowly from his face. His shoulders drooped. At last he shook his head wearily. "That is not necessary. I yield to your judgment in this matter."

Germanicus nodded, satisfied. "Very well."

He turned to me and I stood straighter, waiting.

"Lucius Aurelius Valens, hear my ruling," he said. "I find you innocent of any wrongdoing in the deaths of Capito and his comrade. Your actions were fully justified. You are free to go."

A feeling of enormous relief flooded through me, washing away every trace of the fear I'd felt so short a time before. Almost overcome by emotion, I was only able to offer him an awkward, strangled, "Sir . . . I want to thank you for . . ."

Germanicus clapped me gently on the shoulder. "No thanks are needed, Aurelius. I simply did what was right." He glanced coolly at Piso before turning his back on the governor. "I find that acting justly is the best way to live life. Others might profit from that lesson."

Then he moved toward the door, motioning me to accompany him. "Agrippina insists that you come and stay with us for a few days. You need a real rest—and the chance to let those wounds of yours heal properly."

Germanicus dropped his voice. "We also have a lot to discuss. The Sixth Legion. This plague of brigands. And I want to hear more about this strange, unheralded visit to Antioch by one of my uncle's closest cronies."

We left Piso sitting alone in that empty room, staring after us with eyes full of cold, implacable hatred.

Chapter V

For the first time in four days I sat at peace, on a marble bench in the gardens of Germanicus' house, reading a scroll borrowed from the lady Agrippina. The warm sun soaked into my shoulders—helping to ease knots that had been there for weeks, perhaps even months.

A shadow fell across the scroll.

I looked up.

Germanicus stood close at hand, gazing down at me. He waved me back when I started to stand. "Sit, Aurelius, sit. I'll have no ceremony in my own gardens. Not for a guest, and especially not for a guest recovering from illness."

He sat down beside me. "Convalescent or not, though, you do seem much better."

I nodded. "I am better, sir. Aristides assures me the worst is over."

"The gods make it so," Germanicus said seriously. "Wound fever can be a terrible and vicious thing."

I nodded again. When he was a boy of six, just such a fever had killed his own father, Drusus. My own illness, though far less dangerous, had been bad enough. Shortly after reaching the safety of Germanicus' villa,

I'd been racked by alternating bouts of chills and sweating—compounded by spells of dizziness so severe that
I found it difficult to stand without feeling sick. Though
he professed confidence that I would live, Aristides had
ordered me to bed and kept me isolated from everyone
else of rank in the household. For three full days, I'd
been confined to my room—allowed out only for a
short visit to the villa's bathhouse in an effort to break
the fever's hold over me.

At last, his medicines and purges and treatments had
worked. The fever and nausea abated, and my appetite
and strength returned.

This morning I'd finally been well enough to satisfy
even Aristides. After issuing yet another stern warning
not to overexert myself, he'd sent me out into the gardens to rest and refresh myself. I'd already spent half
the day just sitting in the sun.

Germanicus glanced at the scroll in my hands. "What
are you reading, Aurelius? Caesar's *Commentaries*
again?"

I reddened. "No, sir."

"What then?" he asked with some amusement. "Another treatise on strategy or tactics—or is it something
on logistics this time?"

"Nothing that useful," I admitted reluctantly. "It's a
play. In Greek."

"Ah. A tragedy, I expect."

I shook my head ruefully. "A comedy."

"A comedy?" Germanicus chuckled. "I'm shocked,
Aurelius. I'd always thought you were the practical,
hardheaded sort—not one to spend your time reading
old jokes about licentious Athenian wives or greedy Tar-
entine merchants. Who wrote this witty work? Aristo-
phanes?"

I couldn't help grinning. "No one quite so famous, sir." I handed him the scroll. "You did."

Germanicus laughed out loud. "Ha! Caught in my own net!" He unrolled it, scanned a few lines in silence, and then looked up with a twinkle in his eye. "*A Night in Corinth!* I remember this one well. Not exactly a play for the ages, but how it made old Augustus chortle and sputter when I read it to him after a banquet one night."

He laughed again. "Of course, he'd had quite a lot to drink during dinner, too — which couldn't have hurt." He looked at me. "Perhaps that's the real secret of successful comedy. Make sure there's plenty of wine for the audience!"

I smiled. "It's certainly worth trying."

Germanicus laid the scroll aside. "Well, I'm afraid it will be some time before I have the chance to test my theory." His expression turned serious. "You heard that Junius Silanus came to call on me while you were ill?"

I nodded. "Aristides mentioned it. Did you learn anything from the visit, sir?"

Germanicus shook his head. "Nothing more than an admiration for his ability to talk endlessly — without conveying any real information. I see now why they prize him so highly in the Senate!"

"Do you think the emperor sent Silanus here as a spy?" I asked quietly. "To examine your conduct in command here?"

"It's possible. Perhaps even likely. My uncle has the unfortunate habit of distrusting those closest to him." He shrugged. "But whatever the senator's hidden purpose, he's gone now. He and his followers sailed for Judea yesterday."

"Judea?" I couldn't keep the surprise out of my

voice. That region, ruled by a procurator answerable to the governor of Syria, had been under our direct control for just thirteen years. It was a troublesome land, full of stubborn, stiff-necked Jews, and, from what I'd heard, scarcely worth the cost and effort needed to govern it. Why would Silanus want to tour such a backwater?

"An odd choice," Germanicus agreed. He shrugged again. "But I haven't the time to waste worrying about what he might be up to. Frankly, I'm just as happy to see the back of Decimus Junius Silanus. The situation is difficult enough now without yet another of my uncle's favorites breathing down my neck."

"Yes, sir," I agreed.

"A situation made somewhat more difficult by your recent actions, Lucius Aurelius Valens," Germanicus continued calmly.

I swallowed hard. "Yes, sir."

"Walk with me," he said. He stood up and began to pace along a path that wound between carefully tended beds of flowering plants and tall shade trees. I followed him.

Germanicus stopped beside a fountain topped by a statue of Cupid. He dipped his fingers in the cool, clean water for a moment, then looked over his shoulder at me. "First, there's the problem of the Sixth Legion. You've wiped out the nest of bandits led by Capito, but we both know that the principal source of the corruption is still rooted in place." He grimaced. "The legate Titus Petronius Faustus."

I nodded. As long as Faustus commanded the Sixth, he would be able to use its soldiers to line his own pockets—either by recruiting another band of legionaries to masquerade as brigands, or by some new scheme to extort money from the Syrian landowners and merchants within his jurisdiction.

"But without Capito as a witness, I can't charge the legate with any of the crimes we suspect he ordered," Germanicus said. "The Senate would dismiss the case out of hand, and I wouldn't blame them."

"No, sir," I sighed. More than ever I wished that I could have checked that final sword thrust, the one that had practically torn the senior centurion's head off his shoulders. If only I could have taken Capito alive . . .

Germanicus smiled tightly. "Don't look so glum, Aurelius. I said I couldn't put Faustus under arrest. That doesn't mean I can't get rid of him."

He splashed more water out of the fountain with a quick flick of his fingers. "I've reversed Piso's earlier finding—making it clear that Capito and his men were acting as brigands when you ambushed them."

"Thank you, sir," I said, greatly relieved. Piso's attempt to smear my judgment and my conduct had weighed heavily on my mind for days—no matter how hard I'd tried to persuade myself that it would be ignored or overturned.

Germanicus shook his head sternly. "There's no need for that. The evidence you presented for their guilt was overwhelming." He showed his teeth. "And you've given me the opening I need to strip Petronius Faustus of his rank and boot him all the way to Rome. After all, what's the best thing you could possibly say about a legate who's allowed his senior centurion to run wild behind his back?"

"That he's either blind, or a complete idiot," I answered swiftly.

Germanicus nodded. "Exactly. Faustus can complain all he wants to Tiberius or to the Senate, but no one can deny my right to ensure the competence of the officers under my authority." He turned away from the fountain and walked farther along the path. I kept pace with him.

"When will you act against him?" I asked.

"Today," he said quietly. "I've already written the dispatch relieving him of command."

"And who will you appoint in his place?"

"My chief military aide, Saturninus," he said.

I was delighted. I'd seen Gnaeus Saturninus in action in Germany. He was a tough veteran soldier and a man well suited to bringing the wayward soldiers of the Sixth Legion to heel.

I stood up straighter. "With your permission, sir, I'll have my gear packed and my horse made ready. Aristides may carp and complain a bit, but I'm fit enough to ride."

Germanicus turned to face me squarely. He laid a hand gently on my shoulder. "I'm afraid you won't be returning to the Sixth Legion, Aurelius. In fact, I have to ask you to leave Syria—and the sooner the better."

I was stunned. "But, sir . . ."

He shook his head slowly. "It can't be helped. You've made too great an enemy of Piso."

"Piso?" I was aghast. "But the governor is your enemy, too. Right now you need every reliable officer you can muster—"

He cut me off with an abrupt gesture. "Enough! I don't like Piso. I don't trust him. But he is not my public enemy, and I cannot risk an open break with him. Not yet, at least." He eyed me coldly. "You know better. You know the dangers of rebellion and invasion we face in this province. The Parthians would like nothing more than to see our hold over Syria dissolve in senseless squabbling. I won't put the security of the empire in jeopardy to pursue a private feud against Piso, no matter how much I despise his incompetence and corruption."

I lowered my eyes, knowing full well that he was right—and yet hating to admit it.

"Gnaeus Calpurnius Piso is a vengeful man. You, more than anyone else, should realize that. He's already orchestrated one attempt on your life. He'll try again."

"I'll take that chance," I said desperately.

"Well, I won't," he replied. "If Piso succeeds, Rome will have lost the services of a good officer. If he fails, he may leave so much evidence against himself that I'll have to take action. It's not worth the risk."

Germanicus looked directly into my eyes. "And so I ask you to leave, Aurelius. For your own good and the good of Rome."

"I see, sir," I said grimly, through clenched teeth. "Then I assume I have your permission to return home to my father?"

And the gods alone knew what I would do there, I thought to myself in despair. I could face my father's rage and disappointment. I'd seen it often enough as a child. Confronting the reality of my own failure would be far more difficult.

To my surprise, Germanicus laughed. "To your father's house? To Rome? Of course not!" He clapped me on the shoulder. "Aurelius, you proud idiot! I'm not punishing you! I'm promoting you!"

I wasn't sure I'd heard him right. "Promoting me?"

He nodded. "I want you to take over the Third Gallic Cavalry Regiment. The regiment's old prefect died of a wasting sickness several weeks ago. His ranking decurion isn't ready to assume command. I think you are."

I couldn't hide my amazement. Such a post was the pinnacle of any military career for a man of my social rank. Rising higher, to the command of a legion, required admission to the senatorial class. I'd served as a military tribune of the Sixth Legion for only a few months. By rights I should expect to spend at least another three or four years in administrative and staff work before even thinking about the chance to lead a cavalry unit.

Germanicus' eyes twinkled. "I suggest you close your mouth just a bit, Aurelius. Otherwise you'll find yourself swallowing flies." Then he turned serious. "I'm not offering you a soft, safe billet. Nor the chance for easy glory. The Third Cavalry is stationed in Judea. Most of its work is policing. You know what that means."

I nodded somberly. It meant long, boring patrols along the frontier to keep sheep-stealing nomads at bay. It meant endless sweeps through rugged countryside to discourage banditry and unrest. And it meant countless days and nights spent escorting obnoxious minor officials from village to village and town to town—just to make sure the locals paid their taxes on time and stayed loyal to Rome. In other words, all the dull, drab routine common to soldiering in any imperial province not threatened by open war.

I smiled thinly to myself. Service in Judea.

Many of the young men I'd counted as my friends in childhood would have been horrified at the prospect. Even those willing to leave the pleasures of Rome to advance their military and political careers tried to wangle assignments that would yield the most renown for the smallest possible amount of discomfort. A posting to Judea failed on both counts.

My father would be appalled, too, I realized. Promotion or not, he'd complain that patrol duty in the back of beyond wouldn't help me make the political connections he was counting on to smooth our family's path to greater prominence. And he would be right.

But I didn't care about the difficulties I would face. I didn't care about the fact that I'd be serving in one of the empire's least-prized possessions. And I didn't care a fig whether or not my father approved.

I would have a command.

I straightened to attention before Germanicus. "I accept. When do you want me to leave?"

He nodded approvingly. "That's the Roman spirit, Aurelius. Duty first. Personal considerations last." He turned toward the villa. "One of my secretaries will arrange passage on the next suitable ship headed south. By good fortune, one of the Third Cavalry's officers is in Antioch right now, meeting a new draft of recruits from Gaul. He and his men will form your escort on the voyage."

"Yes, sir." I was suddenly aware that all the lingering weakness left by my fever had vanished. In its place I felt only the urge to move, to take up my new responsibilities. "With your permission, I'll ride to Antioch straightaway. I'd like to introduce myself to this officer and inspect those new recruits."

Germanicus smiled at the eagerness in my voice. He squinted up at the sun and then shook his head. "It'll be dark in a few hours. Tomorrow will come soon enough. And when you go to the city, Aurelius, I want you to take a detachment of my personal troops with you." He frowned. "I don't really think our vindictive friend Piso will strike at you again so soon. Still, I don't see any point in giving him another easy opening."

I started to protest, but he motioned me to silence. "Not another word. I need you in command of the Third Gallic Cavalry, not as a corpse tumbled into a ditch somewhere between here and Antioch. Besides, neither Agrippina nor your physician would ever forgive me if I let anything happen to you." He grinned. "I might chance your doctor's anger. But I wouldn't want to be the man who found himself on the wrong side of my wife's temper!"

I spread my hands in mock surrender. "In that case, sir, I accept your generous offer. And I promise to act more prudently in the future. You have my word that I'll be as meek and mild as a newborn lamb."

Germanicus snorted. "And pigs may fly. I've heard many words used to describe you, Aurelius Valens. Meek, mild, and prudent have never been among them." He shook his head. "Well, come along, then. We'll drink some wine, have a bite to eat, and give Agrippina the chance to discern these remarkable new qualities in your character."

The Third Gallic Cavalry Regiment's new recruits were temporarily quartered in barracks just outside Antioch's Eastern Gate.

Early the next morning, I found the man I was seeking in the stables there, helping his servant groom his horse.

"I'm looking for a decurion of the Third Cavalry, a man named Aedan, the son of Dubis," I said tentatively.

He turned his head, still rubbing his hands briskly over the animal's back. "That would be me. And who might you be, if you please?"

"My name is Lucius Aurelius Valens." I watched him work for a moment longer, cleaning off the sweat and dirt left by a vigorous ride. "I am the new prefect of the regiment."

That stopped him. He swung away from his horse. "What was that?"

"I'm taking command of the regiment," I repeated patiently. I offered him a small writing tablet. "Here are my orders from Germanicus Caesar. You and the recruits you've gathered will sail with me to Caesarea Maritima in Judea."

Frowning, he wiped his hands off on a piece of cloth, took the tablet, and began reading.

As a decurion, Aedan commanded a *turma*, or troop, of thirty-two cavalrymen—one of sixteen in the regiment. In practice, his seniority made him the third highest-ranking officer in the Third Cavalry. He was taller than I was, lean, and wiry. He was also older, by at least ten years. Blond hair cropped short to fit under his helmet and eyes that were more green than blue testified to his race. Like all of the unit's officers and men, he was a Celt, a member of one of the many tribes inhabiting the Gallic provinces first conquered by Julius Caesar seventy years or so before.

The decurion made a good first impression on me. He had the air of quiet confidence and patience I'd seen in most veteran soldiers I respected. I felt inclined to trust his judgment and advice.

But I could also tell that his first look at me didn't inspire the same confidence. And who could blame him?

The Third, like most of our auxiliary cavalry units, had first been raised and commanded by a Celtic tribal noble, a chieftain who'd taken the Roman name Sextus Julius Gallus. The reports I'd read the night before told me that Gallus had been noted for both his fighting skill and his openhanded generosity to the warriors who followed him. He'd led the regiment for more than twenty years before falling victim to disease. And now here I was, an unknown stripling, and a Roman one at that, stepping into his shoes.

I didn't have any illusions that I would find this an easy assignment. Oh, I knew how to ride and I'd even studied some of the basics of cavalry leadership—the standard tactics and formations, the words of command, and the various administrative requirements. But I knew nothing of the day-to-day realities involved in commanding a formation containing hundreds of men and horses. Until I learned those things, I would be forced to rely heavily on the expertise and goodwill of my officers and their subordinates.

Earning that goodwill would be up to me.

Aedan finished reading the orders I'd brought with me. He handed the tablet back. "The lord Germanicus Caesar praises you."

I nodded. "Yes."

The Gaul rubbed his chin slowly. "They say he doesn't flatter men lightly or without justice."

"That's true," I said. Then I grinned. "So let's hope that I'm the rule—and not the exception."

A quick answering smile flitted across Aedan's face. "That will be my prayer also." The smile faded. He looked me up and down. "You've led men in battle before, have you?"

I nodded again, pushing down the flash of irritation his question prompted. The decurion had every right to probe my background. For all he knew, I was just a raw young Roman knight with influence and a taste for glory won at someone else's expense. "I commanded a cohort of light infantry in the German campaigns," I said calmly.

"A nasty war, that," Aedan said. "Or so I've heard."

"Yes," I agreed.

There was a long moment when neither of us said anything.

"And what was it like, then?" he asked at last.

"Germany? Or the campaign?"

"The fighting, of course," Aedan growled.

I hid a grin. "We won. The Germans lost."

The Gaul chuckled. "By the Great Lord of the Sun, I see that you must have been born to be a soldier."

I raised an eyebrow. "Oh? Why?"

"Because it's sure that you'd have starved as a teller of tales," Aedan retorted. He straightened up to his full height. "Well, then, I suppose you will want to take a good hard look at these new fellows I'm taking back to the regiment."

"I will." Then I held up a hand. "But not just yet."

The decurion stopped, plainly puzzled.

"First I want to see their horses," I explained.

A wide smile appeared on Aedan's face. "Do you indeed?" He laughed out loud. "By the Goddess, I begin to think that you, Lucius Aurelius Valens, may do very well as a commander of cavalry."

The decurion and I spent the rest of the morning examining the mounts assigned to the Third Cavalry's new recruits. They hadn't been allowed to bring their own horses from Gaul. The expense and difficulty involved in transporting animals so far made that impractical. Instead, provincial officials were responsible for procuring horses for local military use. Given Piso's proclivity for squeezing an illicit profit out of every official duty,

I wouldn't have been surprised to learn that his minions had tried to foist an assortment of useless, broken-down hacks on my regiment's inexperienced troopers.

I was relieved to discover that my fears weren't justified. Every mount appeared in perfect condition. I said as much to Aedan.

"They'll serve. And very nicely, too," he agreed. "Look at this fine tall lad here," he said, affectionately patting the shoulder of the big gray stallion beside him. "Nesaean blood, with a bit of Armenian or Cappadocian breeding in him, perhaps. Fast. Spirited. And bold as a lion, too, I shouldn't wonder."

I nodded my own approval. I'd match my own mare, Dancer, against this big brute any day, but no one could deny that he was a splendid-looking animal. Nesaean horses were a marvel, the finest of our age. They were swift, sturdy, quick-witted, and brave. They formed the backbone of the Parthian cavalry, and we had been quick to acquire our own breeding stock after suffering one or two humiliating defeats at their hands. Though we Romans are often a hardheaded lot, we do learn from our mistakes.

I watched the small band of horses ambling about, grazing placidly on clumps of tall grass. "Their breeding is good," I said. "But what about their schooling?"

"They need a good deal more work," Aedan admitted. "They're fit for daily riding, but I wouldn't want to see them caught up in a battle just yet."

Nor would I. Without intensive training, horses couldn't stand the shock of combat—the shrill noise of blaring trumpets, the clash of swords on shields, the shouts and screams, or the surging fury of a breakneck charge. Green horses would toss their riders and bolt, wreaking havoc on any unit luckless enough to have them in the ranks.

But cavalry horses need to do more than avoid panic in a fight. They must react promptly and properly to the faintest touch on the reins — moving smoothly and skillfully through every maneuver demanded of them. Troopers and their mounts need to act in concert, fighting as a perfect team. In a melee, the cavalryman who spends too much time worrying about keeping his horse under control is as good as dead.

We swung away from the paddock and strode toward the barracks where the recruits were quartered.

I glanced at Aedan. "You like the horses. But what do you think of the new men?"

He shrugged. "They're a decent bunch. Raw, bull-headed, and full of themselves, of course. But we can make soldiers of them. Mind you, right now I'd take any man who can stay on a horse without falling off, no matter how lazy or shiftless or stupid."

I nodded. I'd studied the most recent regimental returns the night before, the ones the decurion had brought with him to Antioch. Not counting this draft of twenty recruits from Gaul, the Third Cavalry was down to just over three hundred troopers — little more than half its original strength. That wasn't uncommon, especially among units stationed so far from their home province. Unless new soldiers were recruited from the local population, enlistments couldn't hope to keep pace with losses from illness, accidents, age, and the occasional clash with bandits or raiding nomads.

The Third Gallic Cavalry had been sent east more than fifteen years before, and it had been stationed in Judea for nearly a decade — shrinking slowl steadily, with each passing year. No one wanted the regiment evaporate. But no one wanted to chance bringing Jews or Greeks or Syrians into the ranks. It was a problem without an easy solution.

"Is there any hope that we'll be transferred soon?" Aedan asked quietly.

I looked at him. "Not that I know of, unless there's a new war with Parthia."

"Then I'll pray for war." The decurion said it lightly, but I could hear the undercurrent of seriousness in his voice.

I stopped and turned toward him. "Duty in Judea is that bad?"

Aedan frowned. "It's not dangerous often enough to be interesting. And it's not peaceful enough to be restful. The Greeks are all right, but the Jews don't like us one little bit—or so it seems. They don't have much to do with us, and we don't have much to do with them." He grimaced. "It's worth your life to so much as stare at a pretty girl in some of their villages."

He shrugged. "Gallus, the prefect, kept us busy with drills and hunts and feasts and games. If the lads weren't happy all the time, at least they weren't miserable all the time. But now . . ." He hesitated.

"But now Gallus is dead, and you've been saddled with some young Roman pup who looks as though he's barely out of his mother's arms," I finished for him.

Aedan nodded wryly. "That's about the size of it, sir. No offense intended, of course."

I matched his thin, tight smile. "None taken, Decurion."

"And there's the problem of language, too," he added.

I stared hard at him. "Go on."

"The veterans have enough Latin to understand orders and enough Greek to buy trinkets or chat up the whores in Caesarea, but if you try to speechify at them, sir, all the fine phrases in the world will fly right over their heads."

I snorted. "The men of my first command were Celts, Aedan. I may not know all the right words in your native tongue, but I think I can get my points across, and swear at them, too—when that's needed."

The decurion looked slightly relieved. "Ah, well, that's good, then." He cleared his throat, still plainly somewhat uncomfortable. "Look, Aurelius Valens, I hope you do not believe I've said these things to cast doubt on your right to command. I only—"

I stopped him abruptly. "Aedan, son of Dubis," I said. "You've said nothing that I haven't already thought myself. You are a warrior and a veteran officer. You have the right, even a duty, to speak your mind."

I paused briefly and then looked him straight in the eye. "I *am* young. I *am* a Roman—and not a man of your own tribe. But I give you my oath, as a knight, as a soldier, and as a man of honor, that I will do my best for the regiment and for every trooper in it." I took a step closer, coming right up to him. "And I can assure you that my best is *damned* good. Fair enough?"

Aedan stood silent for a moment. Then he nodded firmly. "Yes. That is more than fair enough. You command the Third. I will not gainsay your right to do so."

"Good." I swung round again. "Now let's go meet these recruits. I want to see how much work it will take to make them a real credit to the regiment—and not some shambling band of idle layabouts."

"Sir." Aedan led the way toward the barracks. Then he glanced over his shoulder at me. For an instant, merriment danced in his green eyes. "One thing's for sure. You have the boastfulness of a true Celt in you."

"I assume that's a compliment," I said dryly.

"Oh, it is, sir," the decurion said virtuously. "A very grand compliment, indeed."

The parade ground, an open area used for military training and martial displays, lay beyond the city wall—out in the fertile, well-tilled countryside surrounding Antioch. A rail fence surrounded the field, separating it from the Beroea Road and rugged hills rising to the east and the wide, rolling Orontes River on the west.

Mounted on my Spanish mare, Dancer, I waited near an open gate at the southern end of the parade ground. A row of wooden target posts lay straight ahead of me, stretching toward the distant end of the hard-packed enclosure.

I took a deep breath and settled the bronze-sheathed iron helmet more firmly on my head. The wide cheek guards pressed against both sides of my face. Dancer caught my own sense of anticipation and whinnied, loud in the early morning air. I settled her down with a quick pat. "Soon, girl. Soon."

I checked the grip of the tall oval shield I held in my left hand, making sure I still had full control over the reins. Satisfied, I slowly drew the long sword slung at my right side.

"Whenever you're ready, sir," Aedan muttered from his position beside the gate. I caught a glimpse of some of the Third Cavalry's recruits clustered along the fence, plainly curious to see how their new commander would perform. My palms felt sweaty. Failure now would not only humiliate me in front of them: It would also destroy any hope I had of gaining the whole regiment's confidence.

I took another deep breath in, then breathed out again, reminding myself to stay calm, to focus, and not worry about things beyond my control. My eyes settled on the first post, a tall spike of wood already well scarred by sword strokes. My pulse steadied. It was time.

"Hah!" I kicked Dancer into a gallop—accelerating through the opening and out onto the parade ground. Clumps of dirt flew from beneath her hooves, spattering high into the air behind us.

We raced forward, heading straight toward the line of posts. Dancer's stride was smooth, perfectly controlled in every sense. I bared my teeth, exulting in the sensation of speed and power.

A charge from concealment is one of the most practiced and crucial maneuvers for any cavalry formation. It is also one of the most difficult. Any horse thrown suddenly into a gallop from a standing start can easily become overexcited—tossing its head, trying to snatch the reins away from its master, or shortening its stride into a choppy, unsteady mess.

The first post loomed up to my left and I leaned forward over Dancer's neck, cutting down hard with my sword.

Thunk.

Chips flew off the target.

A touch on the reins and my horse wheeled slightly, crossing through the line of posts to bring the next one up on my right. I leaned back in the saddle and slashed up into it. More splinters flew.

We veered right again, crossing back through the target line. Another sword cut lopped off the top of the next post as we galloped past it. Then we swung back to the left. And right again. Dancer curved in and out between the targets with a grace that did justice to the name I'd given her.

Then, almost before I had time to think, we were done.

We wheeled back the way we'd come, and I reined her in—slowing to a brisk walk.

Another horseman cantered through the gate and out onto the parade ground. His polished armor gleamed in the sunlight and a cloak of imperial purple billowed behind him. It was Germanicus Caesar.

I brought Dancer to a halt in front of him.

"Well done, Aurelius!" Germanicus said loudly. "It appears that service in the cavalry suits you!"

I sheathed my sword, saluted him, and then pulled off my helmet, grateful for the gentle river breeze that whispered through my sweat-soaked hair. "Thank you, sir. That it does."

He drew nearer and stopped his own mount close beside me. "A nice little piece of theater," he said quietly. "A few of those young Celtic hotheads over there may still resent you for your race. But now none of them can deny your skills as a horseman and a soldier."

I nodded. "That was my hope, sir." I grinned. "Of course, there was always the chance that I might have been tossed onto my rear end before reaching the first post."

"Not likely, I think," Germanicus said, shaking his head. "You forget. I've seen you ride before." He changed tack abruptly. "I have a favor to ask of you, Aurelius."

"Anything, sir," I said flatly.

"I'd like you to take someone with you to Judea," Germanicus said. "The twelve-year-old son of a fairly prominent Roman citizen from Tarsus. I've just had a letter from the city assembly there asking me to arrange his safe passage south. They say the boy is already here in Antioch."

I was surprised. Tarsus was more than two hundred miles away from Antioch. "A boy, traveling on his own? Without his family?"

Germanicus nodded. "They're sending him to Jerusalem. For some sort of priestly education, according to the letter."

"The boy's a Jew?" I asked, even more surprised. "And yet a citizen?"

"Something of an odd combination, I agree," Germanicus said. He pursed his lips in mild disapproval. "The family trades in leather goods. They've been supplying a sizable portion of the tents, saddles, and other gear used by our troops here in Syria for a long time. It seems old Julius Caesar granted his great-grandfather citizenship as a reward."

He looked closely at me. "Anyway, Aurelius, I'd appreciate your taking the lad in hand."

I shrugged. "Of course, sir. Provided he's quiet and keeps well out of the way, I'll manage very well. After all, how much trouble can one twelve-year-old be?"

Germanicus chuckled. "How much trouble? You'll soon find out."

Too late, I remembered that one of his own sons, Drusus, had just passed his twelfth birthday the year before. I did my best to bury my sudden misgivings. "Where's this boy staying, sir?"

"In the city's Jewish Quarter," Germanicus answered. "At the house of a merchant named Theodoros."

"And the boy's name?" I asked.

Germanicus wheeled his horse about, then looked back at me. "His name is Paulus."

Chapter VI

"Form up! Form up! Move! Move! Move!"

The sound of Aedan's shouted commands drew me to the outer door of the room I was using as an office. I leaned against the doorpost with my arms folded, and watched the twenty recruits of my new regiment pour out of their quarters onto an open, sun-baked patch of ground. Whitewashed barracks, stables, storehouses, and fenced-in horse enclosures lined three sides of that central square.

I ran my eye over the troopers as they dashed past and formed up in two lines, facing each other. Despite the sun high overhead, each man wore a helmet, a waist-length mail shirt with shoulder reinforcements, a sleeved tunic underneath the armor, knee-length breeches, and studded leather sandals. Their faces, still unaccustomed to the fiery Syrian climate, were uniformly burned. Droplets of sweat glistened in the long, bushy mustaches that were the pride of every young Celtic warrior. I wondered idly how long it would take before pride gave way to common sense and they shaved them off.

"On my command," Aedan shouted. He took a last,

quick look around the drill ground, making sure everyone was ready. Then he bellowed, "Fight!"

With a guttural roar, the ten pairs of young men went after each other—attacking and defending in turn, slashing and thrusting with heavy wooden practice swords, dodging, and parrying with shields. Dust swirled high into the air, drifting slowly away on the wind.

I watched the sword and shield bout closely. I liked what I saw. The recruits made up in enthusiasm what some of them lacked in skill, and Aedan moved nimbly in and out of the melee, stopping a man here or there to point out a faulty attack or defense or, less often, offering praise for a well-executed maneuver.

"That Gaul knows his business, then?" Aristides asked.

I turned my head. The doctor was sitting on a bench close by. Though the colonnade provided shade, he was fanning himself with a battered, broad-brimmed hat. I hid a smile at the sight. Despite all the years he'd spent in Rome, I'd never been able to persuade Aristides to discard that horribly provincial hat. "It's comfortable, and it keeps rain and sun and flies off my face," he would argue. "With all that in its favor, why should I care about fashion?"

"The decurion knows what he's doing," I agreed.

"That's good," Aristides said sourly. "I'm glad that at least one man around here does."

"Oh?" I said, surprised by his evident ill humor. "And what exactly is that supposed to mean?"

The Greek shrugged. "I can't shake the feeling that Germanicus Caesar is making a mistake."

"By transferring me out of Syria?" I asked. "I thought you were in a hurry for us to leave this province."

"I still am," Aristides said. "The sooner you're safely out of the reach of Piso's paid killers, the better."

"Then you must think his mistake was in promoting me. That I'm not ready for the command I've been given," I said, trying to hide the anger and dismay I suddenly felt. The doctor had never hesitated to point out my faults, but I'd always counted him as my closest friend and supporter. The thought that he might not believe I was up to the job cut deeper than I would have believed.

Aristides shook his head. "That's not what I mean, Lucius." He looked up at me. "I don't question your military ability. You should know that."

"What then?"

"I only fear that this promotion is too much, too soon," the doctor said quietly. "Especially now. Piso and Faustus already hate you. They will see Germanicus' decision as a deliberate insult—as salt poured on their already wounded pride."

I shrugged. "Let them."

Aristides frowned. "Don't treat this so lightly! Those two may not be able to touch Germanicus, but they can certainly seek revenge on you. They both have the ear of Tiberius. And they both have allies in the Senate. How many friends do you have there? While Germanicus is here in the East, who will defend you in Rome?"

"Politics, Doctor?" I forced a harsh laugh. "Now you sound more and more like my father."

"Your father is many things, Lucius, but he is not a fool," he said coolly. "Nor am I."

The rebuke hit home like a spear point. I felt my face grow red-hot. Yet after all his years of friendship and devoted service, Aristides deserved better from me than an ill-tempered jibe.

"What would you have me do?" I asked quietly. "I can't go running to Germanicus and beg to be relieved of the position he's just given me. Not now. Should I resign from the army and slink off home in disgrace? Do you really think that would keep me safe from the malice of Gnaeus Piso or Petronius Faustus?"

For a moment, he just sat there in silence, clutching his disreputable old hat in both hands. At last he sighed heavily. "No, Lucius. I suppose not. I only wish I did have an answer for you. For now, all I see are the dangers that surround you—and no sure way through them."

The sorrow and worry in his voice shook me to the core. "I'll be more careful in the future, Aristides," I pledged. Then I shook my head. "But what's done is done—at least where Piso and Faustus are concerned. And I can't go through life paralyzed by a fear of events beyond my control. The Fates will deal with me as they choose."

"I don't want you paralyzed, boy," the doctor said testily. "Just a little less stubborn when it comes to dealing with those above you."

That was more like him. Some of the tension in me eased.

A soldier striding toward us caught my eye. As he drew nearer, I recognized the fellow as an orderly from headquarters.

I returned his salute. "Yes?"

"Orders from Germanicus, sir," he said crisply, presenting a sealed tablet.

I broke the seal and read the message aloud, for Aristides' benefit:

Germanicus Julius Caesar sends his warmest greetings to Lucius Aurelius Valens, Prefect of the Third Gallic Cavalry Regiment.

At dawn tomorrow, you will proceed with the troops under your command to the port of Seleucia Pieria. Two ships there, the Pride of Tyre *and the* Star of Sidon, *have been hired to ferry your soldiers, servants, animals, and all necessary supplies to Caesarea Maritima in Judea. You will consult with the two merchant captains, but you will sail only at your own discretion. Fair winds and a safe voyage!*

I looked at the doctor. "Well, that should meet with your approval."

He nodded.

I sent the messenger back to Germanicus with a hastily scrawled acknowledgment that his order had been received. Then I turned my mind to the task at hand—readying Aedan's recruits for the journey ahead. Making sure the troops, their equipment, and their horses were prepared for a day's hard march, with a sea voyage at the end of it, would take a lot of work and close attention to detail.

But first I decided to leave one small but annoying detail to Aristides.

I wrote another quick note and handed it to him.

"What's this?" he asked, surprised.

"A letter to the merchant Theodoros, telling him to send that boy Paulus back here with you." I shook my head in disgust. "If I have to play nursemaid on this trip, I want him under my wing as soon as possible—tonight, in fact. When the sun rises in the morning, we're going to be riding for Seleucia, not sitting on our backsides waiting for some young brat to make his appearance!"

Aristides laughed, a welcome sound. He rose from the bench and plopped that awful old hat onto his head. "Don't worry, Lucius. I'll fetch him for you. And who knows? Perhaps young Paulus won't be as much trouble as you fear."

"That would not be difficult," I said darkly.

Later that day I met Paulus for the first time. I have to admit that my first impression of him was not very favorable. Even for a boy his age, he was remarkably short, with a large head, bright brown eyes, a mop of unruly black hair, and an awkward, ungainly gait. In repose, his face bore a knowing, amused expression that seemed far too old for someone who was only twelve. It set my teeth on edge.

Despite that, I did my best to be polite. I wasn't happy about being pressed into service this way, but I'd already decided it couldn't hurt to treat the boy with common courtesy. Though they were only merchants, the letter Germanicus had received made it plain that his family wielded significant influence in their native city of Tarsus. And they were citizens, after all—worth as much, in theory, as anyone born within the bounds of Rome itself.

As the doctor ushered him into my quarters, I put down the stylus I'd been using to double-check a list of supplies and stood to greet them.

"This is Gaius Julius Paulus of Tarsus," Aristides announced. He urged the boy forward with a gentle pat on the shoulder. "Go on. Introduce yourself to the prefect, lad."

"Lucius Aurelius Valens, prefect of the Third Gallic

Cavalry Regiment," he began, plainly reciting by rote, but in flawless Greek. "On behalf of my father, I gratefully accept the kind and generous offer you have made to escort me to Judea. You have the everlasting appreciation of my family and of my city."

I fought a desperate battle to keep my face straight. This boy sounded as determinedly serious as did a consul addressing the Senate, or as an orator delivering a high-flown paean of praise to some fallen hero.

"I'm glad I can be of help to you," I answered, still trying hard not to laugh. "I understand you're being sent to Jerusalem to further your education?"

"Yes," Paulus said proudly. "I have been accepted as a student by the great Rabbi Gamliel."

"Rabbi?" I asked. There were a few Jews living in Rome, mostly craftsmen and traders, but I'd never had any reason to associate with them—and certainly no cause to learn the strange titles they awarded themselves.

"*Rabbi* means teacher," Paulus replied loftily. "Gamliel is a scholar famous for his knowledge and mastery of the Law. He is a man of remarkable wisdom and learning."

Now I really was puzzled. "The law? This Gamliel is a jurist? For some reason, I had the impression that he was a kind of priest of your god."

"Our Law comes directly from the Most High," the boy said, sniffing. "Any man who understands and interprets it is a man of great holiness—whether he conducts sacrifices at the Temple or not."

So the Jews claimed their laws were of divine origin? A foreign people indeed—even stranger in some ways than the Celts who handed over so much power to their holy men, the Druids. In Rome, we know that our laws are made by and for men. Why any rational people would believe that the gods would trouble themselves with crafting civil or criminal codes was beyond my understanding.

But there seemed little point in saying as much to Paulus. Challenging his people's odd religious beliefs was no concern of mine.

Instead, I just said, "Well, I'm sure you'll do very well under this learned fellow's instruction. In the meantime, my soldiers and I will do our best to make sure you get to Jerusalem safely and swiftly."

I nodded toward Aristides. "For now, Paulus, the doctor there will show you where you'll sleep. We leave at first light, so I suggest you get plenty of rest—"

"Excuse me, sir," the boy broke in. "I have one request."

I narrowed my eyes. I didn't find being interrupted by a mere stripling a pleasant experience. "Yes?"

"You have called me Paulus—and that is one of the names I have been given," he said hurriedly. "But since I am the oldest son of my father, of the people Israel, and of the tribe of Benjamin, I prefer to use my birth name, Saul."

I gritted my teeth, holding my temper in check. "Saul?"

"The first king of Israel was named Saul. He was a bold and brave warrior," the boy explained. He shrugged his shoulders awkwardly. "I'm small and short enough without being reminded of that fact every time someone calls my name."

Despite my irritation, I understood what he meant. I even felt somewhat sorry for him. The word *Paulus* means "little"— something other boys his age undoubtedly rubbed in his face from the moment one of them learned a bit of Latin. Children are often like wolves, savagely ready to fall on their playmates at the first hint of weakness.

There were some things, however, that I could not, or would not, allow. This was one of them.

I folded my arms. "I'm afraid I can't do that. You'll use your Roman name while under my authority, or none at all."

"But . . ."

I shook my head firmly. "No, Paulus. You've been given a place in my company because you and your family are citizens of Rome. Citizenship is a privilege—one rarely bestowed so far from the city. The very name you seem to dislike so much—Gaius Julius Paulus—is a symbol of that privilege." I looked him in the eye. "And when you trade on the value of your citizenship, you'd better be prepared to accept the consequences, both the good and the bad. Do you understand me?"

For an instant I thought he would snap back at me. His lips thinned and I saw his chin go up stubbornly. But the moment passed. His shoulders slumped.

"Well?" I asked pointedly.

Paulus swallowed hard, then forced out a reluctant assent. "Yes, Aurelius Valens. I understand you."

I relaxed. "Good. Now go with Aristides and put your head down. The dawn will come sooner than any of us like."

After they left, I went back to my table, shaking my head in frustration. I'd won a single small victory over that intelligent, arrogant boy from Tarsus. Somehow, though, I very much doubted this would be the last time Paulus tested my patience and my will.

I could only hope for a fast passage to Caesarea Maritima. Once we arrived there, I would find someone to take him off my hands—even if I had to assign a troop of cavalry to take him all the way to Jerusalem.

Later that evening, when I complained about Paulus to Aristides over a last cup of wine, the physician simply smiled wryly. "He is certainly a far cry from your Roman ideal of the dutiful and silent child. But in truth, Lucius, he reminds me of you as a small boy in almost every particular. Is it so uncomfortable to look into the mirror of Time and see oneself reflected?"

I stared at him. "I was that annoying?"

"Oh, no," Aristides answered.

"Well, that's a relief."

"You were much worse," the doctor said with a damnable grin.

We arrived at the port city of Seleucia Piera late the next afternoon. I left Aedan in charge of securing lodging for the troops and animals and walked down to the water. I wanted to look over the ships chartered for our use and confer with their captains.

Vessels of every size and kind crowded the crescent-shaped harbor and lined the quay. Stevedores, mostly slaves, bustled up and down gangplanks—handling cargo on the bigger merchant ships. All along the waterfront, clay jars full of wine, olive oil, figs, and other foodstuffs were piled high. There were bales of wool from Cappadocia and bundles of silk from India. Exotic smells wafted out of warehouses crammed with boxes of precious spices—camphor, cinnamon, sandalwood, balsam, ginger, and pepper. Hard-faced watchmen carrying cudgels patrolled everywhere to prevent pilferage.

Farther south along the curving shoreline, dozens of

small fishing boats were drawn up on the sand, unloading the day's catch. Seabirds circled overhead, shrieking loudly as they squabbled over fragments of fish snatched from cursing fishermen. In the distance, the rugged peak of Mount Thronos jutted through a low-hanging layer of haze and cloud.

I found the two hired ships, the *Pride of Tyre* and the *Star of Sidon*, moored side by side at the far end of the quay. They were large, broad-beamed, single-masted vessels with deep holds and ample deck space. Though I was no sailor, both appeared well suited to the task of transporting my soldiers and our horses and supplies.

The *Pride*'s master, a hawk-nosed Phoenician named Hanno, met me at the aft gangplank leading to his ship. With an oily grin, he invited me aboard and encouraged me to tour her every nook and cranny. I took him up on the offer. First, I inspected the straw laid down in the holds for the horses and mules. It seemed fresh and free of vermin. Next I used my dagger to prod gently at a few of the wood planks below the waterline. They appeared sound and strong, apparently untouched by rot or worms.

Satisfied for the moment, I followed the Phoenician shipmaster back up a narrow ladder to the deck. As I stood blinking in the red-tinged afternoon light, he showed me his teeth again. "You see, Prefect? All is in order. Everything aboard is ready. As I assured your officials, my crew and I will give you a fine, fast passage south."

I nodded briefly, running a wary eye over those sailors of his. Those in sight were a ragged, villainous-looking band—scarred, tattooed, and bronzed by long service on the sea. There were at least twenty men, more than I would have expected. Merchant ships usually make do with far smaller crews than war vessels.

"What about the *Star*?" I asked. "Is she ready to sail, too?"

The captain nodded rapidly. "Oh, yes, I promise you that. Her master is one of my younger cousins." He shrugged his shoulders elaborately. "But, of course, you are welcome to inspect her as well."

"I intend to," I said.

Try as I might, I could not bring myself to like or trust this man Hanno.

I knew that was irrational. The Phoenicians were a famed seafaring people. Their ships had plied the oceans for ages. They were said to have roamed far and wide across the whole of the known world when Rome itself was nothing more than a collection of huts and frightened shepherds.

So why did I feel so uneasy? Perhaps it was because, as a boy, I'd heard so many chilling tales of Phoenician cunning, cruelty, and treachery. After all, it was the Phoenicians who had breathed life into Carthage—for centuries our most bitter, dangerous, and deadly enemy. Time and again, Rome had come close to defeat and utter annihilation at Carthaginian hands. But we had destroyed that evil city more than a hundred and fifty years before I was even born. And now men like Hanno and his fellow sea captains were subjects of the empire. Their skills were ours to command, not to fear.

"Assuming your cousin's ship meets with my approval, when can we leave?" I asked brusquely, pushing my doubts and prejudices aside for the moment.

The Phoenician rubbed his chin reflectively. "Two days hence, I think. It will take some time to stow your beasts safely tomorrow—perhaps most of the day. And I do not like to sail too close to nightfall."

I nodded my understanding. Then I looked out to sea, shading my eyes against the setting sun. "What about the weather? Will it hold?"

The shipmaster's fingers curled tightly round an amulet of the goddess Astarte hung at his neck. "With the Lady of the Waves' blessing, I believe it will," he said. His eyes narrowed. "But you must bring your soldiers and their mounts aboard tomorrow. The season of storms draws nearer, and I do not care to waste the time we have left for safe voyaging."

Exhausted beyond all measure, I drifted with a slow current on the calm surface of the sea, clinging to a piece of wreckage. I winced as I ran my swollen tongue over lips left cracked and bleeding by the sun and salt water. The thirst that gripped me burned like a fire in my parched throat.

A raven flew low over my head, cawing wildly. Its great black wings almost brushed the water as it flapped past.

Slowly, in great pain, I turned my head to stare after it.

In that instant, in the blink of an eye, the storm that had been chasing me swallowed me whole.

A wall of wind and rain howled down out of a sky grown pitch-black, roaring across the sea. Driven by the shrieking, maddening tempest, the waves rose ever higher, growing fast into rolling monsters that tossed me helpless from one to the other. Salt-laden spray lashed my face.

Dimly, through stinging eyes, I saw the dark, jagged mass of an island ahead, looming up out of the gale-

whipped water. The wind and waves swept me closer
with frightening speed—driving me headlong toward a
narrow cave set in the midst of a sheer cliff.

I yelled in horror as I saw at last what lay before me.
Massive, sharp-edged rocks rose out of the foaming surf
at the cave mouth—ready to tear me to shreds. Frantically, I kicked away from the piece of wreckage.

A bright, blinding light flashed into the sky above
me. And from that light, I heard a soft but clear voice
utter a single word: "Beware."

At that moment, to my astonishment, the cave was
transformed—melting into a narrow, cruel, sneering
face that I recognized. It was the face of the Phoenician
ship captain, the master of the *Pride of Tyre*.

I jolted awake—gasping for air and drenched in
sweat.

I stared about me in shock. I was still on land. Still in
Seleucia Piera. Still in my room at the inn Aedan had
commandeered the day before.

Aristides hurried in, with a wide-eyed Paulus tagging
along close behind. They shared the chamber next to
mine. The doctor held a small oil lamp aloft. Its tiny
flame sent strange shadows flickering across the room's
whitewashed walls.

"Lucius, what's wrong?" Aristides asked urgently.
"We heard you cry out!"

I sat upright, my heart pounding. "A dream. It was
only a terrible dream," I stammered.

The doctor pursed his lips. "Tell me everything you
saw and heard in this dream," he ordered.

Still staggered by the vivid, terrifying images that
had flashed before my sleeping mind, I fumbled for the
right words to recount the nightmare. By the time I finished, my heart was beating more normally, but the

muscles of my neck and shoulders were still tense and drawn.

Paulus seemed plainly skeptical of what he'd heard. But Aristides' expression was somber. He sat in silence for a few moments, evidently gathering his thoughts. "Lucius," he said at last, almost hesitantly. "You know that I'm not the sort of gullible fool who interprets every passing flock of birds or puff of wind as some new message from the gods."

Despite the turmoil I felt inside, the doctor's deliberate understatement almost raised a smile on my face. His comments on the results of most auguries and other divinations were usually far more scathing—and scandalous. "I know that," I confirmed.

"But this dream—this nightmare—of yours seems so powerful, so clear . . ." His voice trailed off.

"Go on," I urged him. "What do you make of it?"

"I think it may be real," Aristides said quietly.

Paulus looked surprised. "What do you mean 'real'?" he demanded. "How can the grotesque imaginings of a sleeping mind be real?"

"I believe this dream may very well be a vision, a warning sent by one of the gods—perhaps divine Apollo himself," the doctor explained. He took a deep breath. "If so, its meaning seems plain enough."

Paulus snorted.

I silenced him with a sharp look. "Then you think I'm being warned that this Hanno and his crew might try to murder me once we're at sea and beyond help?" I asked Aristides.

"Maybe," the doctor said. He shrugged. "You have enemies enough who would reward them handsomely for such a deed."

I nodded. Gnaeus Piso had a long reach and a deep purse.

"Or it might be simpler than that," Aristides continued. "The dream may be an omen that the ships themselves are doomed—either by storm or wreck. In either case, it would be folly to set sail with this Phoenician and his men. We should find another way to Judea."

"This is nonsense," Paulus burst out, clearly unable to restrain himself any longer. "How can any man of sense or reason propose acting on a dream? It's ridiculous."

"Then how do you explain what the prefect saw?" Aristides asked calmly.

"Explain it?" The boy was incredulous. "Why should I have to explain it? Aurelius Valens had a nightmare, nothing more. If you want the reason for that, you'd be better off looking for the spoiled fig or bit of rotten fish he may have eaten at dinner."

The doctor eyed him with grudging approval. "Your skepticism does you credit, Paulus," he said gently. "But hasn't your own god spoken in dreams?"

The boy nodded slowly, almost reluctantly. "Yes. There are such accounts in our holy writings."

"Knowing that, how can you dismiss this vision so easily?" Aristides asked.

"The Most High has spoken to some of His prophets in their dreams," Paulus said stiffly. "But Aurelius Valens is no prophet. He is not even a Jew."

I forced a ragged smile. "Well, that's true enough."

I used a corner of a blanket to wipe away some of the sweat from my forehead. To my irritation, my hand was still trembling slightly. The sight of such weakness troubled me. I forced myself out of bed, stalked to the open window, and stood there in silence for a short time—

taking deep breaths of the cool, crisp night air in an effort to regain some measure of self-control.

It was still full dark, without even the faintest hint of light along the eastern horizon. I glanced back at Aristides and Paulus. "Whatever this was, divine vision or simple nightmare, it's over now. I suggest you both try to get some sleep during what is left of the night."

They nodded reluctantly and moved toward the door.

"Bide a moment, Aristides," I said. "I have one or two more questions for you."

"Oh?" The doctor looked at me curiously, and then motioned Paulus out the door ahead of him. "Go on, lad. Get to your cot."

The boy left, still shaking his head at the absurd notion that my dream might have real significance.

I confess I had the same doubts. My own reason was at war with what I had seen and heard in my sleep. Logic told me that the boy from Tarsus was right. No matter how vivid, how real, and how disturbing, this dream was surely nothing more than a simple nightmare.

And yet . . . those terrifying images still dazzled my waking mind. Were they really a warning sent from on high, from the very gods whose interest and even existence I had so often doubted?

One other horrible possibility haunted me and that was why I had asked the doctor to stay behind. I was afraid that this dream marked the return of an illness I thought I had conquered many years before.

When I was just six years old, Aristides had been hired into my family's service to treat a terrible brain fever that nearly killed me. Though the disease left no physical scars, I had been plagued for nearly a year afterward by recurring seizures. One moment I would be running, or playing, or reading. The next I would be stretched out on the ground or on a floor somewhere—almost always without any memory of what had just happened.

Aristides had diagnosed a mild form of the so-called divine sickness—epilepsy. The diagnosis sent my father into a towering paroxysm of rage and panic. Though it was said that Julius Caesar himself had suffered from that same illness, epilepsy was widely regarded as a disqualification from military and political service. My father could not bear the thought that I might not be allowed to advance his ambitions for our family. And so the doctor and I were exiled to my grandfather's distant farm in a bid to conceal my sickness until it was either cured or vanished of its own accord.

In the end, my epilepsy did abate, diminishing slowly, almost imperceptibly, over a period of several months. The seizures dwindled, both in frequency and in duration. At last, they faded away entirely.

I returned to Rome and resumed my schooling. My father pretended that nothing had ever happened. So did I. But I had long worried that my epilepsy might someday return.

Once the door shut behind Paulus, I told Aristides of my fear.

To my enormous relief, he shook his head immediately. "There's no connection. None at all. I'm sure of it. When you were a boy, your seizures wiped away memory—they didn't produce visions of such power and clarity."

The doctor looked intently at me. "You know what I believe this dream represents, Lucius. When Apollo speaks clearly, the wise man pays heed."

"I know," I said softly. "But Paulus, too, speaks a

measure of sense. Should I cast away all logic and learning? Should I follow what may be only a wisp of nonsense — a phantasm summoned into being by my dislike of this Phoenician ship captain?"

"A hard choice," Aristides acknowledged. "What will you do?"

"Do?" I repeated. I shrugged. "I don't know yet, Doctor."

I moved back to the window and looked up, hunting for familiar stars in the clear, cloudless black sky. When I was a boy, my grandfather had named them for me — and taught me to use their patterns as beacons when traveling by night. Were there signs out there now that would help guide me to the right path?

I let my mind drift briefly. Whose voice had spoken to me in my dream? Was it only the whispering of my own disordered senses? Was it the prophecy of a god? Or was it a warning from someone much closer to me in spirit?

My decision took shape.

I looked back over my shoulder at Aristides' anxious face. "Go and wake Aedan for me, if you please. The decurion and I have work to do before the sun comes up."

Chapter VII

I rode over the lip of a long rise and reined in. The road ran on ahead through a fertile plain stretching as far as the eye could see. Small villages dotted the countryside—each surrounded by walled vineyards, orchards, and fields. The local peasants were out in force harvesting grapes, figs, olives, onions, and dates. Soon the autumn rains would come, softening their wheat and barley fields for the plow. Flocks of sheep and herds of goats drifted through land set aside for pasture, grazing on the last of the summer grass.

Antioch lay behind us now, far to the north. My men and I had been on the move for six full days—usually riding from sunrise to near sunset. We'd passed some nights in modest comfort, stopping at inns along the way. Others were spent out in the rough, sleeping in tents erected beside campfires.

I pulled the itinerary I'd prepared from my travel pouch and studied my notes. We should be drawing closer to the city of Emesa. Our goal, Caesarea Maritima, was still at least fourteen days' journey away.

I shook my head, still wondering whether I'd shown folly or wisdom in allowing my dream to guide me.

My decision to turn away from the sea and ride to
Judea by land met with less official resistance than I had
first anticipated. A few bureaucrats on Piso's financial
staff complained about the costs involved in breaking
our contract with the two Phoenician ship captains. Fortunately, Germanicus agreed with Aristides that my
dream must have been a warning from the god Apollo.
Though temporarily laid low by a stomach sickness, he
sent word through the lady Agrippina overruling their
objections. The officials were ordered to approve my
requisitions for additional supplies and travel docu-
ments without further delay.

Two main roads ran south from Antioch. One paralleled the sea. It was the shortest and most direct route to
Judea, but the coastal plain was very narrow, densely
populated, and often broken by jagged spurs of rock jutting westward from the mountains of Lebanon.

I chose the inland road instead. The countryside was
more open and less settled—and that offered more
scope for training our new recruits on the march. It also
reduced the burden this movement imposed on the
provincial treasury. Much of the road ran through various petty client kingdoms and city-states. They were ob-
ligated to provide food and fodder for any troops
moving through their territory. Taking the coast road
would have meant requisitioning all our supplies from
towns under direct Roman control.

Dancer flicked her ears. Then she whinnied softly,
catching the sound of more hooves clip-clopping on the
road's hard-packed surface. The column had caught up.
I swung round in the saddle, watching the long line of
horsemen and pack animals plodding up the slope behind me.

Aedan and his twenty cavalrymen came first. Each

trooper wore a sword and had a quiver with three
javelins slung from one of his saddle horns, but no man
was in armor or carried a shield. We were moving in
friendly territory, so I didn't see any point in forcing our
mounts to carry the extra weight. Almost nothing cripples a horse faster than carrying a fully armed cavalryman too far for too long. The soldiers' servants came
next, each leading a pack mule piled high with supplies
and equipment. Every recruit brought a poor free man
from his own tribe along with him—paying him to tend
his horse, cook his food, and care for his equipment.
That freed him to spend more time honing his fighting
skills.

Aristides and Paulus brought up the rear, lagging behind as always.

I smiled at the sight. The two of them were riding
close to each other, carrying on their usual animated
conversation. From the way their fingers jabbed the
air while they talked, I guessed they were engaged in
yet another vehement argument—probably about
some small, remarkably obscure point of Greek philosophy.

My attitude toward Paulus had softened over the past
several days. Though he plainly disagreed with the decision I'd made to heed my dream, he hadn't complained or fussed—at least not in my hearing. In fact, it
quickly became clear that the boy from Tarsus saw our
extended travels as a grand adventure. He found something to excite or interest him in every new stretch of
road, whether in the changing landscape or in the dif-
fering customs of the cities, towns, and villages through
which we passed.

In many ways, I decided, Paulus was a study in con-
trasts.

For a boy of only twelve, he was extremely well educated. He also possessed an astonishingly active and agile mind. I'd given up expecting him to play the part of a typical dutiful and silent youth. Ideas, observations, and opinions poured out of him in a constant stream. And yet this bright, inventive boy seemed willingly confined inside a dizzying set of religious strictures, rituals, rules, and commandments.

I found some of his beliefs and behavior admirable. Paulus never passed a wandering beggar or blind man without giving him a coin or two from his own purse. "The Most High has blessed my family greatly," he would explain. "It is my duty to share our blessings with those less fortunate."

But he never expected thanks or praise from those he helped. That would have perplexed a man like my father. In Rome, the rich dole out food or money or advice to the poor, but they do so only in return for service and submission. Those granted favors become clients, at the beck and call of their patrons at all times and places.

Other things Paulus believed struck me as absurdly rigid and narrow. For example, he never ate anything at an inn without minutely interrogating the landlord about the ingredients contained in every dish. Often, he would push away food without tasting it, going hungry rather than risking ritual impurity.

When I asked Aristides what the boy was doing, he shrugged. "The Jews obey strict rules about what they can and cannot eat. Some animals are said to be clean. Others are impure. They even have laws that govern the preparation of food and the slaughter of beasts destined for the table."

Paulus tried explaining those rules to me one evening

when we were camped by the side of the road. The firelight flickered across his face as he eagerly lectured me on the intricacies involved—of ruminants, cloven hoofs, scales and fins, crawling beasts, winged insects, and half a dozen other categories of animals, fish, insects, and birds. I'm afraid I fell asleep sometime during his discourse. Certainly I never quite understood why his people's god would impose so many complex restrictions on what they could and could not eat.

Another time I asked him why he always referred to his god as the "Most High." "Doesn't he have a proper name?"

The boy nodded. "He does, but we do not use it in common practice."

"Why not?"

"To avoid its misuse or profanation," Paulus explained. "You Gentiles flaunt the names of those you worship as freely as a fishmonger shouts his wares in the marketplace. We Jews treat the Most High with more respect."

I found other customs he followed impressive, but also strange and utterly alien.

Before leaving Antioch the second time, we had spent a day preparing for the long journey south. All that day Paulus refused to eat or drink. Early in the morning he took off his sandals and walked barefoot through the streets of the city to the Jewish Quarter— to spend the day with his people in prayer, he told Aristides. I saw him come back to the cavalry barracks as the sun set. His feet were so sore that he was limping badly. When I asked him why he was tormenting himself to such an extent, he explained that this was a great festival of his people, their *Yom Kippur*, the Day of Atonement.

"Atonement?" I asked, puzzled. Though clearly still determined, his face was pale and drawn. Exhaustion, hunger, and thirst were taking a heavy toll on the boy. "What evil have you done that requires so much self-sacrifice?"

"This day gives us the chance to purify ourselves," Paulus said quietly, "to wash away the faults and failings of the past year—whether they are great or small. The Most High demands much of us, but he offers much in return. There are important sacrifices and ceremonies at the Temple in Jerusalem, but all Jews have an obligation to honor this day as best they can."

I eyed his cut and bleeding feet curiously. "And do all your people go to such lengths to fulfill this obligation?"

"Many, though not all," Paulus told me proudly. "My family and I are among those who follow the laws and commandments most faithfully. Others respect us for this—and seek our guidance in understanding and interpreting the true meaning of the law."

With that, the proud, limping boy walked off to his room. I watched him go in silence, still thinking over what I had learned.

Now I was more and more convinced that the Jews were perhaps the strangest race in all the empire. Religious festivals in Rome were important to the priests and temples involved in them. They took great care to conduct the prescribed sacrifices properly, to say the correct prayers, and to conduct the ancient ceremonies with careful precision. But for most citizens, these feast days were a holiday time, a time when they were free from work—a time to indulge and enjoy themselves. Any Roman who needed something from a god or goddess would certainly pay for a temple sacrifice, but I couldn't imagine anyone willing to walk their bare feet bloody as a sign of repentance for past wrongs.

I shook my head in wonder, still watching Paulus debating with Aristides as they rode uphill toward me. The East was a cauldron of alien cults and weird rituals, but even the crazed antics of the followers of the Syrian Goddess paled beside the steady, deadly serious conviction I saw in Paulus. He and his people believed in their single god with a passion that I found both commendable and deeply troubling. I was beginning to understand why so many of my countrymen found duty in Judea so unnerving.

Trouble erupted the morning after we reached Emesa.

We had passed the night at an inn outside the city's walls. And Aristides brought me the bad news while I was shaving in my room.

I stared back at him, still holding the bronze razor poised in my hand. "He said what?"

"Paulus says he won't travel today," the doctor repeated patiently.

"Why in Hades' name not?" I demanded.

"It's something called the Sabbath, a Jewish holy day. Every seventh day is supposed to be a day of rest," Aristides explained. "The boy says he's not allowed to walk more than half a mile while the sun is up."

"Another damned holy day," I muttered. I tossed the razor back into the bowl of water one of the inn's Arab slaves had brought me, mopped my face dry, and began buckling the sword over my tunic.

"What do you plan to do?" Aristides asked.

I glared at him. "I plan to put that little brat on his mule—whether he likes it or not."

"That may not be easy," the doctor warned. "Paulus is a remarkably stubborn young man."

"So am I."

Aristides nodded. "I know." He donned a grave expression. "I think I'll come watch this, Lucius. It should prove interesting—at least from the standpoint of natural philosophy."

"In what sense?" I asked suspiciously.

The doctor grinned cheerfully. "I've often wondered what happens when an irresistible force meets an immovable object. Now I'll find out."

I snorted and marched outside. Aristides followed me.

Paulus was in the stable, feeding his mule handfuls of barley and hay. He had his back to me. Aedan was there, too, saddling his horse while his groom, Commius, a stout, cheerful redhead, finished packing their gear.

The tall, blond-haired decurion raised an eyebrow when he saw me storm in. "You've come to reason with the lad, then?"

"Reason may have very little to do with it," I said grimly.

Paulus jumped at the sound of my voice. He looked around as I drew nearer. For an instant, he looked abashed, even a bit guilty, but then I saw that stubborn chin of his go up in the air. He wasn't going to give in—not easily anyway.

"I'm sorry, Valens. But I meant what I said to the doctor." The boy shook his head. "I will not travel on the Sabbath."

I forced myself to speak calmly. "Do you seriously expect the rest of us to sit around on our backsides all through the day, waiting for this Sabbath of yours to end?"

Paulus bit his lip. "The column can go on ahead." He stood straighter. "I could catch up with you later."

"Oh?" I nodded toward his mule. "On that?"

"Old Amon is really quite fast. Faster than you might think," the boy said quickly.

I heard Aristides stifle a laugh and shook my head. "If we rode off and left you on your own, you'd end up with your throat cut or shackled into slavery in no time at all. Some bandit gang or crooked innkeeper would see to that." I eyed him coolly. "And since I promised Germanicus Caesar I would look after you, there isn't any chance that I'm going to let that happen."

"But . . ." Paulus stammered.

"You don't have an option here," I told him. "Sabbath or not, my troops and I are leaving within the hour. And you're coming with us."

That chin of his went still higher. "No."

I gritted my teeth. "You're traveling with a military unit in the service of the emperor and of Rome. I am not making a request, boy. I'm giving you an order!"

"And I'm not one of your soldiers," Paulus shot back angrily.

"No," I said grimly. "But you're still a child and you're under my care and protection. That means you'll do as I say, or suffer the consequences. You know very well I could have you thrashed and tied to your ridiculous mule."

To his credit, Paulus didn't flinch. "Do what you will, Prefect. I won't break the Sabbath—not for you or any man."

I took a deep breath. Blast the boy! He wasn't leaving me any alternative. I swung round to give an order I knew I'd regret even before I finished issuing it.

Aedan intervened. "Can I speak to you for a moment, sir?" he said quietly. "Just off to ourselves, you see?"

I nodded stiffly, glad of the interruption. Together, we moved off to the far corner of the stable, leaving Paulus alone to face Aristides. "What is it, Decurion?" I asked.

The tall Celtic cavalry officer flashed a quick grin. "That little lad's big trouble, but at least he's a brave, bold fellow."

I sighed. "No argument there."

"And it seems a shame to whip the boy for trying to honor his people's customs, strange as they are."

"What choice do I have?" I asked flatly. "You heard him."

The decurion nodded. "So I did."

"Then what's your suggestion?"

"A compromise," Aedan replied.

Compromise? With that brat? My jaw tightened. "Go on."

"The horses need rest," Aedan said seriously. "If we push them too hard now, they'll die or fall sick on the march and most of these new soldiers of ours will be walking long before we reach Judea."

I nodded. That was true enough.

"The troops could use more drill, too," the decurion went on. "Oh, they handle their weapons well enough, but they're still too eager to break ranks and go racing off to glory for my comfort."

I nodded again. The empire recruited its auxiliary soldiers from the most warlike tribes. Without training, they were brave but impulsive and uncontrolled in battle. They lacked the discipline to fight as a cohesive force and not as just a wild mob.

"Well, then," Aedan said. "Why don't we use this Jewish Sabbath to our own advantage? The horses get a rest, and we use the time to pound more discipline into a few thick young skulls."

I frowned. What he said made sense, but it still meant yielding to Paulus' whims. I said as much out loud.

"Ah, well," Aedan replied, with just the hint of a smile hovering on his lips. "I've read what your man Julius Caesar wrote about his battles in my country. I know for a fact that we beat that bald old bugger a time or two, but you'd never know it from that book of his. So it seems to me that what's considered a victory or a defeat often lies entirely in how you define it."

I couldn't help but laugh. I shook my head reluctantly. "All right, all right! You make your point. I'll let the boy win. This time."

I'd lost a battle of wills with the boy from Tarsus, but it was a battle I shouldn't have fought. Much of the anger I'd felt had come from within—from my own unease at having surrendered to that dream of mine, my own irrational superstition. Fortunately for my self-respect, Paulus, coaxed no doubt by Aristides, later offered me a forced but sincere apology for his own rude behavior.

Early the next morning, we rode south toward the Coele-Syria, the great valley that would lead us closer to Judea and our journey's end.

Day in and day out we traveled, usually covering twenty miles or more before settling in for the night. We reached the mouth of the Coele-Syria near noon on the second day after leaving Emesa.

To the west, the mountains of Lebanon brushed against the heavens—a never-ending succession of white limestone cliffs topped by snowcapped peaks. Large forests of cedar and oak spilled across the sheer slopes below those cliffs. To the east, the Anti-Lebanon Range ran southwest—a long, rugged ridge of bleak gray slopes and eroded summits. Thin patches of scrub oak and juniper stood out here and there along those parched and barren precipices, the last barrier before the vast, lifeless desert beyond.

Sheltered between those two mountain ranges, the valley itself was a pleasant, settled region, a peaceful landscape of well-watered woods, orchards, and prosperous fields. We kept moving on, riding along roads that weren't particularly well maintained, but weren't utterly neglected either. The locals told us they rarely saw soldiers or large bands of travelers. Most armies and merchants took the coast road or went farther east, using the caravan routes across the wastelands.

At intervals during each day's march, Aedan and I pushed our recruits and their mounts through a series of drills and maneuvers—deploying scouts, detaching skirmishers, and forming for attacks on infantry or cavalry. "Your swordplay's fine and your javelin work's not bad," I told them after one bout. "But until you learn to hunt down a hidden enemy, you won't be cavalrymen. And until you learn to move and fight as one, you won't be soldiers worthy of the name."

"Let us do more than drill, drill, drill!" one of the bolder troopers retorted. "Put us in the field against more than shadows and we'll show you a thing or two!"

I grinned back at him. "You're sure of that, Durix?"

"That I am!" he said confidently. His comrades growled their agreement.

"Very well," I said, putting my hands on my hips and surveying the lot of them. "We'll put those proud mouths of yours to the test tomorrow. I'll take six men and ride on ahead. We'll find a good spot and go to ground. The rest—all fourteen of you—will seek us out."

"And when we find you?" Durix asked. "What then?"

"You attack us," I said simply. I grinned even wider. "But you won't find us. We'll hit you first, and so hard and fast you'll be scattered from here to the sea."

"Ha! Listen to the man!" they crowed. "It's to be two-to-one against him and yet he's as boastful as the storm god himself."

They settled themselves around the campfires that night with a great deal of chuckling and pleasurable anticipation at the thought of rubbing their Roman officer's proud face in the dirt.

I listened to them for a while, hiding my own smile, and then rolled over and drifted off to sleep.

I heard the muffled sound of horses close by and crawled quietly up the steep slope. At the top, I raised my head just high enough to peer over the edge of the ravine—careful to stay hidden among the shadows of the bracken, tall grass, and scrub oaks that lined the road here.

Two young Celtic troopers ambled past. They were acting as scouts for the main body. I dropped flat when they rode by, but their eyes and ears were focused on the high ground on the other side of the road. They weren't paying any heed to the boulder-strewn, brush-choked gully falling away to their right.

I laughed inside.

They were looking for places where enemy horsemen could conceal themselves before charging from ambush. It hadn't occurred to them that I might lead an attack on foot.

The scouts disappeared around a bend.

I slid back down the gully just far enough to signal the recruits waiting at the bottom. There were five of them. The sixth was a quarter mile away, holding our horses deep in the cover of a convenient copse of trees. He was disappointed to miss out on all the fun, but I'd consoled him with the promise of a double wine ration if the "battle" went our way.

We were in position, crouching just below the lip of the ravine, when the column rode into sight. The twelve young troopers wore their armor and had their shields out, but they were too busy talking and joking among themselves to pay much attention to their surroundings.

I shook my head. The poor fools — they were relying on their scouts.

Aedan, acting as judge for the contest, rode fifty paces behind them, nonchalantly surveying the terrain. I saw him notice the gully, fight down a quick grin, and then walk his horse innocently onward.

I hefted a practice javelin, waiting for the right moment. The men around me did the same.

The first pair of horsemen rode past.

"Now!" I shouted and threw my javelin as hard as I could. It whirred through the air and slammed squarely into the chest of the trooper I'd chosen as a target. He reeled in the saddle and dropped his shield. Practice javelins don't have sharpened iron heads like the real thing, but they're heavy enough to knock the wind out of any man struck by one at close range.

Our volley hit troopers and mounts down the whole

length of the column. Two horses bolted, tearing off uphill while their riders tried frantically to regain control. Another reared and tossed a young Celt right out of the saddle. The rest milled around in confusion, locked in a kicking, biting mass.

I'm not sure Durix and his boastful comrades even knew what had hit them as we poured out onto the road to encircle them and claim the victory.

It took Aedan and me quite a while to sort out the chaos my ambush caused, but no one was seriously hurt. And I thought the hard lessons learned were well worth every bruise and scrape—especially, I admitted to myself, since none of them were my own.

Halfway down the valley we turned southeast, following a well-worn track that climbed up the steep, barren foothills of the Anti-Lebanon. Our path dropped into the rugged gorge of the river Bardines, and then crossed into Abilene, another tiny kingdom subject to imperial authority.

Ahead of us, the massive peak of Mount Hermon dominated the whole southern skyline. Traces of snow were visible among the mountain's great crags and boulder fields. Thick pine forests and terraced vineyards blanketed the lower slopes.

Paulus turned his mule off the track and sat staring at the mountain in wonder. He intoned softly:

> Come from Lebanon, my promised bride,
> Come from Lebanon, come on your way.
> Lower your gaze, from the heights of Amana,
> From the crests of Senir and Hermon,
> The haunt of lions,
> The mountains of leopards . . .

I reined in beside him. "A love poem?" I asked with a smile. "It seems your education has been broader than I first supposed."

The boy blushed. He shook his head. "It is not what you think, not exactly anyway. The passage is from the Song of Songs, and it is a story of love. But it is a story of the love between the Most High and the people of Israel. It was written by Solomon, one of the mightiest of all our ancient kings."

I couldn't hide my surprise. "You claim this is a love song between Jews and this god of yours?"

Paulus nodded eagerly. "Yes. It is meant as a reflection of the love in which He holds us and of the love we are to give Him in return."

I glanced toward the looming presence of Mount Hermon, pondering the sacred poetry Paulus had recited. If the Jews really saw their relationship with their god as a kind of marriage, I could see trouble brewing.

In an effort to unify the disparate peoples under our rule, first Augustus and now Tiberius made serious efforts to encourage the worship of the divine spirits of Rome and of the emperor. For most of those we governed, this was not a matter of much importance. What was one more god or spirit among so many? The Jews, however, were certain to see our demands in a more menacing light. After all, what husband or wife would welcome the presence of a foreign mistress or lover under the same roof?

After leaving Abilene, our path wound back and forth along the sheer banks of the fast-flowing Bardines, tracing its main course down off the dry upland plateau and into the lush, fertile oasis surrounding Damascus. Olive trees and rich, irrigated fields already planted in wheat and barley surrounded the city, said to be the oldest in all the world. Its strong stone walls and tall towers gleamed in the late-afternoon light.

Damascus was the center of several major trade routes and a city of great wealth and power. Caravans from Parthia, Roman Syria, Egypt, and the mysterious lands across the Arabian Sea brought merchants and traders by the thousands, all trying to buy and sell goods in its crowded agoras and bustling streets.

We stayed on the outskirts for only a single night and then moved on. There was some grumbling from the troops—who'd been looking forward to a more extended spree through the city's taverns and brothels. For a day or so, they muttered and fretted and threw dark looks in my direction, but Aedan told me not to worry about it.

"A cavalryman who's bored is bound to kick up his heels from time to time," the decurion said with a grin. "Leave it to me, Valens. By the time we're through with these fine fellows, they'll be too tired to brood over all the drinks and whores they never had."

Aedan was as good as his word. He organized an even more intensive set of battle drills and a series of competitions—horse races, wrestling, javelin tosses, and the like—wherever we camped. The recruits threw themselves into these competitions with a will, whooping with glee at every victory and shrugging off every defeat with extravagant excuses. As their commander, I awarded small prizes to the winners and ribbed the losers. By the time we crossed into the territory ruled by the tetrarch Herod Philip, their naturally high spirits were largely restored.

This Herod Philip was one of the sons of Herod the Great, the last real king of the Jews. When Herod the

Great died, Augustus split his kingdom into pieces and awarded them to Philip and his brothers. Philip held the lands around Caesarea Philippi, a city he modestly renamed after himself.

From Caesarea Philippi we moved south to the shore of the Sea of Galilee — a large, freshwater lake shaped something like a harp. We were near the dividing line between Philip's territory and the Galilean domain of his brother Herod Antipas.

We reached the lake near evening and camped on a hillside overlooking a small fishing town the locals called Bethsaida. It was the seventeenth day since we had left Antioch. There were more clouds in the sky and the winds were freshening — a sign that the first real rains of the season might soon be on us.

After setting up our camp and making sure that the horses were cared for, Aedan took a small party of soldiers and their servants and went off to town to requisition supplies. Paulus went with them as an interpreter. Few people in the local villages spoke much Greek, but he'd grown up speaking Aramaic in his own household, and he had a surprising knack for making himself understood despite the differences in dialect.

When the decurion and his men returned just before sunset, they brought with them a fine suckling pig. Since I thought that Jews shunned pork, I was surprised at first, but Aedan explained that there were a large number of Greek-settled cities and towns east of the lake. He had procured his prized young pig from a Greek merchant who traded wares from those cities for fish from the lake.

Paulus trailed behind them with a face like a small dark storm cloud. He stood off at a distance, watching us with his arms folded angrily across his chest.

"Now that we've got a proper beast in hand, we'd like to offer a sacrifice to Epona," Aedan explained, "in thanks for our safe passage."

I nodded my understanding. Epona was the Celtic goddess of horses, the patroness of all riders and horses. She was usually depicted as a beautiful woman riding sidesaddle on a mare. "Tonight?" I asked. I looked up at the sky. "It may rain."

"The Lady won't mind a little rain if it comes," the decurion assured me. "She's not a bit fussy about the small matters."

He hesitated briefly and then plunged ahead. "We were wondering, sir, whether you would be willing to perform the sacrifice for us."

"I would be greatly honored," I said quickly.

I fully understood the gift Aedan and his fellow countrymen were offering me. It was customary for a commander to officiate at the sacrifices made for his unit, but I was Roman, not a Celtic tribal chief. Their request was another sign that they accepted my right to lead them in peace or in war, in the secular and in the spiritual.

Paulus came up to me after Aedan went off to make the necessary preparations. "You're going to join in this nonsense?" he asked, clearly surprised.

"Of course I am," I answered. "Why do you ask? Don't tell me the thought of this ceremony frightens you in some fashion."

"Not the ceremony," he replied stoutly. "I am from Tarsus. My city is a mixture of many different peoples. I've seen the temples, rituals, and processions of a dozen false gods and goddesses. They don't scare me!"

"What, then?"

"I've listened to you talk, Aurelius Valens," Paulus said. "You claim to be a man of reason."

I nodded, wondering where the boy was going with this. "I try to be."

"Then how can you lead this sacrifice to a wisp of nothing? To a bare-breasted phantasm conjured up by ignorant barbarians? You don't believe in this ridiculous horse goddess any more than I do," Paulus said hotly.

I checked to make sure no one else could hear us and then said quietly, "What I believe or don't believe is of no importance. My soldiers worship the Queen of Horses, and I respect their right to do so. And they have a right to see me join them in honoring her. More to the point, I won't insult them by denying their beliefs or ridiculing them."

The boy scowled up at me. "That's not the point!"

I shook my head. "There's where you're wrong. That is exactly the point. Unless the worship of a god or cult subverts the order imposed by the empire, Rome does not forbid it. No one is harmed by the offer of one small pig to Epona—whether she exists or not."

"A blood offering will profane this ground," Paulus said angrily.

I ran my eye over the barren hillside and then turned back to him. "I don't see any temple or sacred boundary stone."

"All this land is sacred to the Most High," the boy retorted. "His Law knows no bounds."

I looked at him coolly. "This place falls under the law of the tetrarch Philip. But he holds sway here only at the pleasure of Tiberius Caesar. Do you seriously claim your god has dominion over the emperor himself?"

Paulus didn't reply. He just stared back at me in silence. Suddenly, I understood that was exactly what he did believe. The realization shocked me. I'd listened to all the various stories he'd told about the overwhelming power of his god, but I'd thought of them mostly as legends designed to soothe the wounded pride of a subject people. Now, for the first time, I began to fully comprehend the magnitude of the challenge posed by this Jewish creed of a single all-powerful deity.

It was fully dark.

The fires around our camp blazed brighter, leaping higher in the rising wind. Clouds scudded across the sky, blotting out the stars.

Clad in my best tunic, I stood before the rough pile of stones Aedan and his men had built as an altar. The cavalry troopers formed a circle around me, their faces ruddy in the flickering firelight. Aristides stood with them, watching intently. He caught my eye and winked quickly. I kept my face still.

Paulus was not there. Shortly before the ceremony began, he'd stalked off into the surrounding darkness, angrily muttering that he wouldn't waste his time or risk impurity by observing our folly. I'd let him go. Our fires should keep any nearby bandits or other predators at a safe distance.

Aedan strode into the circle, carrying the suckling pig in his arms. He'd already stunned the poor creature with a sharp blow from the hilt of his sword. "Lady of the White Mare, Queen of Horses, Protector of Horsemen," he cried. "Behold! Behold! Your gift comes."

He handed the pig to me and stepped back a pace.

"Epona! Divine Lady! Keeper of the keys of life, of death, and of rebirth," I said solemnly, running through the tongue-twisting Celtic phrases the decurion had helped me memorize earlier. "Accept this sacrifice in thanks and praise for your protection and guidance!"

I glanced at Aedan. He nodded in approval.

The soldiers repeated my words, chanting them louder.

The throaty roar of a leopard prowling somewhere in the surrounding hills startled us all into silence. Then, in the sudden stillness, one of the horses neighed shrilly, answering the leopard with its own fierce challenge.

"The Lady answers!" I said instantly. "Hear her!"

"We hear her," Aedan declared loudly. The others echoed him, tentatively at first and then with greater confidence.

The decurion showed his teeth, plainly relieved that a bad omen had been averted.

Out of the corner of my eye, I saw Paulus slip swiftly out of the darkness and into the safer circle of the light thrown by our campfires. His face was deathly pale.

I held the unconscious animal out over the altar, drew my knife, and slashed its throat with one smooth motion. The blood poured out into a bronze bowl set atop the pile of stones, glistening black in the dim light.

One by one, the troopers came forward, solemnly bringing amulets of Epona to dip in the sacrificial blood. When they were done, Aedan signaled the servants forward to carry away the carcass of the pig. They would roast it and distribute the meat as part of the evening meal.

The ceremony was over.

Later that night, I had the chance to ask Paulus to explain his speedy return.

Abashed, he insisted that he had simply decided to

confront our ignorance head-on, rather than flee it. Gravely, I nodded my understanding, and then, grinning, sent Paulus off to bed.

In the morning we would enter Galilee.

Chapter VIII

It rained the next day.

We crossed into Galilee and pushed on south along the western shore of the great lake, riding through intermittent showers that left the road passable, but gradually soaked us to the skin. After several miles, the road swung away from the lake, heading west through a notch between steep hills and ridges. We sheltered for the night at a village just beyond this narrow pass.

The sky was clear the next morning.

By the time we saddled our horses and mules, the road and surrounding fields and hillsides were already dry. All the rain had soaked swiftly into soil parched by the long hot summer.

We rode on, moving west in a haze of dust past villages and towns. Most were built on the slopes or on the tops of hills. A few were walled. Fields, fruit and olive orchards, terraced vineyards, and grazing land surrounded all of them. It was clear that this land of Galilee was remarkably fertile, but the individual fields, orchards, and pastures looked barely big enough to support the families I could see busily harvesting the last of their summer crops and preparing for the autumn planting.

A few of the villagers paused in their labors to watch us ride past, but most went on working, blind to our presence. I found their lack of interest startling, very different from our experiences on the way through Syria and other client kingdoms. There the townspeople and farmers had often lined the side of the road, curious to know who we were and where we were going. These Galileans seemed content to ignore us entirely. Was the sight of a column of cavalry so commonplace in this land?

Aedan shrugged his shoulders when I asked him about it. "They've certainly seen soldiers enough before," he said. "Your man Herod Antipas has a fair-sized army of his own to keep the local people in line."

"Are they good troops?" I asked, curious to hear the Gaul's appraisal. We didn't exercise direct control over Galilee, but there was bound to be some overlap of jurisdictions along the border. In case of war or rebellion, the tetrarch would also be expected to provide soldiers to fight under Roman command.

"A few are," the decurion admitted. Then he snorted. "Most of the others, though, are useless. Oh, they're tough enough when it comes to menacing farmers who haven't paid their taxes on time. But I wouldn't want any of them guarding my flank in a real battle." He listed a few of the several different contingents in the tetrarch's service, counting them off on his fingertips. There were Idumaean archers and infantry from farther south, Arab nomads, and hired troops from Thrace, Germany, and half a dozen other distant lands.

"No locals?"

Aedan shook his head. "There's not many Antipas

would trust—and fewer still who would shoulder a spear for him. The peasants hate this tetrarch of yours because they don't think he's a proper Jew. The Greeks from the cities despise him precisely because he *is* a Jew, whether the proper sort or not. And both complain bitterly about the taxes he imposes. But they distrust each other too much to join hands against him.

"To these Galileans," Aedan went on, "Herod's soldiers are no more than handsomely clad bandits feeding off the farmers' own hard labor."

"But we're not his men," I pointed out stubbornly.

"No," the decurion said quietly. For an instant, he looked sadder and far older than his thirty-odd years. "To them, we're worse. We're the bloody-handed lads in the shadows behind their tetrarch's golden throne. We're the hard men who'll come killing and burning if there's ever any real trouble here. They know that—and so do we."

He shrugged. "I don't imagine there are many in Rome unhappy about that sad state of affairs."

I nodded reluctantly, conceding the point. There was truth in what Aedan said. This was exactly the sort of political situation preferred first by Augustus and now by Tiberius. Exercising authority through local dynasties wherever possible saved Rome a great deal of money and trouble. We exacted our tribute off the top. The rulers paid for their own troops and handled their own internal affairs with whatever monies were left over. In return, we kept the barbarian tribes beyond the frontier at bay and maintained law and order in the lands under our rule.

The system worked best when these petty kings realized their hold on power depended on backing from the emperor and our legions, and not on the affection of their own people. Knowing that kept them loyal to Rome and attentive to our demands.

Herod Antipas had good reasons of his own to know that he ruled at our sufferance. His older brother, Archelaus, had been given the regions of Judea, Idumea, and Samaria. But Archelaus botched things up so badly that Augustus had banished him thirteen years before and placed those lands under our direct control. Roman troops had been stationed in Judea ever since.

In theory, the peace we provided guaranteed prosperity for both subjects and citizens alike. But the sullen faces I saw in the fields and vineyards we passed showed only too clearly that many in Galilee held a very different view of our dominion.

I rode on in silence, wrestling with a growing unease. The valley was narrowing, angling toward another pass through the rough country rising ahead. Sepphoris, the administrative capital of Herod Antipas' realm, lay a few miles farther on. I hoped to reach the city by late afternoon. After that, one more day's hard march would take us to my new regiment's headquarters in Caesarea Maritima. The end of our long overland trek was almost in sight.

But try as I might, I couldn't shake the feeling that we were under close watch from the terraced ridges and rolling hills to the north and south. From time to time, I found my hand straying near the hilt of my sword. If Aedan noticed, he kept quiet. Perhaps he shared my sense of foreboding.

Near midday, we met a man striding fast along the road toward us. He was a shepherd, evidently just down from the hills, brown as a nut and with teeth that showed white through a thick beard. He bore a six-month-old lamb on his broad shoulders without the slightest sign of strain.

Alone of all the people we had seen so far that day, the shepherd greeted us with a wave and a wide, friendly smile. "You are well met," he called out in rough, accented Greek. "Come! Rejoice with me!"

Surprised, I stopped before him. The column halted behind me.

"Well met, indeed," I replied politely. "But tell me, why do you rejoice?"

"For the best of reasons, sir." He nodded toward the lamb on his shoulders. "This little one strayed from my flock yesterday. She was lost, and now is found."

I understood something of his joy and relief. The flocks I'd seen grazing these slopes were small, usually no more than a dozen animals at most. The loss of even one small lamb to a jackal or wolf would mean more to this shepherd and his family than would the collapse of a mine or the loss of a ship to my father.

"That is good news," I agreed. "You were fortunate."

"The Most High has been kind to me," the shepherd said firmly. "In thanks, I offer His blessings to all I meet."

"Even to foreigners like us?" I asked, even more surprised.

He shrugged. "Why not? If the Most High is lord of all the world as I believe, shouldn't His gifts be offered to all who need them?"

I had no reply. His words echoed what Paulus had said after giving alms to beggars and blind men. Could it be that this simple shepherd, with his tattered, stained tunic and his drab cloak, regarded us in much the same light? As nothing more than beggars and cripples? I shook my head in wonder. There was no knowing and nothing to be gained by asking him.

I took up the reins, preparing to ride on.

"You're bound for the villages over that way, I suppose," the Galilean said suddenly, indicating the high ground rising steeply to the south.

Puzzled, I shook my head. "Our route takes us to Sepphoris."

Now it was the shepherd's turn to appear surprised. "You're Roman soldiers, aren't you?" he asked. He pointed to my red military cloak. "The tetrarch's men don't wear that color."

I nodded. "We serve Caesar." I looked down at him. "But why should that have a bearing on where we march?"

"There are Roman troops posted in the hills," he replied. "Or so the gossip runs. I've heard it said these soldiers are guarding a powerful man, a great lord of some kind. I thought you must be on your way to join them."

"A great lord? From Rome?" I eyed the shepherd curiously. "Why would such a man spend time in your villages with the comforts of the city so close at hand?"

He shook his head with a quick grin. "That I can't tell you, sir. I know my sheep, and my sheep know me." He patted the lamb still lying placidly across his shoulders. "But this little one knows as much about the interests of the mighty as I do . . . and perhaps a bit more!"

Further questioning established that the shepherd believed these soldiers had been moving among the nearby villages for some time, perhaps ten days or more. From what he said, the other locals were as puzzled as he was by their presence. After satisfying myself that he was telling us the truth, at least as he understood it, I sent him on his way.

Once he was out of sight, I looked at Aedan. "What do you think? Why would we have troops stationed so deep in Galilee?"

The decurion frowned. "There's been no real trouble here that I know of. Not in the ten years the regiment's been stationed in Judea. Certainly nothing that would warrant our meddling in Herod's internal affairs. But then I've been away in Antioch picking up these recruits and much can happen in the blink of an eye."

I turned Dancer off the road a few paces and scanned the high ground to the south. Several rough but plainly well-traveled trails led up into the hills. I glanced back at Aedan. "What's on the far side?"

"A valley called Esdraelon," he said. "And another road from there to Caesarea."

I pondered that briefly. Cutting across this chain of ridges and hills would cost us time—perhaps as much as half a day. Was satisfying my curiosity worth the price?

I decided it was.

If there was trouble brewing in Galilee, the sooner I learned of it, the better. Besides, even if the soldiers and the "great lord" reported by the shepherd turned out to be nothing more than a party of surveyors working for a minor tax-gatherer, finding them would be good training for the new recruits. I was confident now that Aedan's inexperienced troopers could hold their own in a pitched battle, but they still needed more practice in scouting. Cavalry was supposed to act as an army's eyes and ears in unfamiliar territory—guarding against enemy ambush, finding the best march routes, and locating sources of supply and forage. This detour would give us another chance to exercise those skills.

But we found far more than I had bargained for.

The sun was far to the west by the time we rode out onto the heights overlooking the valley of Esdraelon. Several hundred feet below, a vast patchwork of wheat fields, ready for the plow and planting, spread before us. Off to the east, a thick forest of tall oak and pine trees grew up the steep slopes of Mount Tabor. Far to the right, almost at the edge of vision, another green swathe of trees marked the distant foothills of Mount Carmel.

The slope here was too steep to descend, so we followed the trail northwest toward a smaller valley separated from the larger Esdraelon by a spur of the main ridge.

Despite our best efforts, we hadn't yet made contact with the soldiers said to be operating in this area, but what we'd learned by questioning farmers and herdsmen met along the way seemed to confirm the shepherd's story. All of them had heard stories of Roman troops, though every account differed wildly as to their numbers, location, and purpose.

Some claimed there were dozens of soldiers, all in shining armor and wearing the finest cloaks. Others said there were only a handful. Some thought the man they were guarding was a high official from Caesarea. Others told us he was the procurator of all Judea. Still others were sure he must be someone even more important, perhaps the son of the emperor himself. One man said the soldiers had left three days before. Another assured us the Romans were still quartered in the area—though whether they were now in Garis, Gath-hepher, Japhia, or some other of a dozen different villages he couldn't say for certain.

It was maddening.

When I said as much to Aedan, he nodded sympathetically. "This is what we run into all the time, Prefect. Very few of these Jews will freely tell us what they know. More would send us chasing off in the wrong direction if they could do it safely. And the gods know they're all of them quite wonderfully ignorant."

He smiled wryly. "I think mostly they just want us to go away and leave them in peace, so they tell us whatever they think we want to hear."

I shook my head in disgust. We were on a fool's errand after all, and it was one I'd chosen myself.

The trail wound down off the heights and then ran west into the small valley I'd seen earlier. Surrounded by ridges and hills on three sides, it was almost a natural amphitheater. To the south, the ground was almost level, covered with olive orchards and small fields marked out by low stone walls. A jumble of ramshackle buildings spilled across the shallow ridge rising to the north. Terraced fields, vegetable gardens, and fruit tree orchards spread along the slope around the little cluster of houses.

I sighed. We were coming to yet another Galilean village full of stubborn, willfully blind, deaf, and dumb peasants. No doubt this time they would tell us Tiberius Caesar himself had been seen rumbling past in a chariot of gold drawn by elephants.

It was late afternoon. The shadows were lengthening, thrown toward us by the setting sun. Everything around—the birds, even the insects—fell strangely silent. The creak of saddle leather, our horses' hoofbeats on the stony path, and the low murmur of voices from the troopers riding behind me all seemed to linger in the air, fading slowly.

Suddenly, a bloodcurdling wail tore that eerie silence to shreds, echoing off the surrounding hillsides and boulders. In a flurry of madly flapping wings, dozens of carrion birds soared aloft, momentarily blackening the sky above a tangled clump of trees and brush not far ahead.

"Gods!" I reined in sharply. "What in Hades was that?"

Wide eyed, Aedan shook his head. "I don't know!" He drew his sword. "But nothing good, that's sure!"

Leaning forward, I soothed Dancer with a brief, gentle pat while peering into the woods for some sign of what had sparked that awful cry of horror. I couldn't make anything out. The trees were cloaked in shadow, and nothing seemed to be moving among them.

"There!"

I turned my head at Paulus' excited, boyish shout. He was pointing straight across the valley. He'd spotted a man running away from the woods—frantically scrambling uphill toward the village.

Without thinking further, I snapped an order to Aedan. "Bring him to me, Decurion! Alive, mind you!"

"Sir!" The tall Celt swung round in his saddle toward the pair of soldiers right behind him. "You two! With me!"

With a wild whoop, the three cavalrymen turned their horses off the track, splashed across a shallow stream, and then galloped up the slope, angling wide to cut the fugitive off from escape. One after another, they jumped their mounts over the stone walls separating fields. Swords flashed in the sun as they wheeled, closing in on the running man from three sides.

Trapped, their quarry fell to his knees. He threw his arms wide in surrender.

Aedan leaned over his horse's neck and roughly prodded the fellow to his feet with the point of his sword. Then the decurion and his troopers herded their prisoner back down the hill.

He dropped to his knees again before me, with tears running down his cheeks.

I studied the weeping man intently. He was about my height, but heavier-set, with a fleshy, sun-browned face and a prominent nose jutting above a full, unkempt beard. He wore only sandals and a plain white tunic. Thorns and low-hanging branches had ripped his clothing in several places. His arms and legs were scratched and still bleeding.

Without taking my eyes off him, I told Paulus, "Ask this fellow why he ran from those woods. What's frightened him so badly?"

The boy eagerly translated my questions into Aramaic, the chief language of these Galilean peasants.

Clasping his hands together, our prisoner stared up at me, terrified almost beyond his wits. With an effort, he managed to gasp out a few strangled, almost unintelligible words.

Paulus edged his mule closer to me. His face paled. "He says there are dead men among the trees." The boy swallowed hard. "Murdered men."

"Who are they and who killed them?" I demanded. "Ask him that!"

I caught a few more words this time, but not enough to really make sense of what they were saying.

Paulus shook his head. "He swears that he doesn't know. He says his name is Nahum and that he's only a poor farmer from that village up there."

I let that pass for the moment. "Is anyone else in those woods? Anyone alive, I mean?"

"Only the dead," Paulus translated. He shivered. "What is happening here, Aurelius Valens?"

I kept my eyes on the prisoner. "I don't know, boy. But I intend to find out." I drew my own sword. "Tell this Nahum he's going to take us to these bodies he discovered."

When Paulus relayed my order, the farmer shook his head vehemently, sending tears flying in all directions. Again, he held his clasped hands up to me, stammering out his plea.

"He begs you not to make him go in among those trees," Paulus said, his own voice shaking. "They are cursed now, corrupted by the horror within."

My jaw tightened. I didn't have the time or patience to waste on this nonsense. I leaned forward over Dancer's neck, bringing my sword close to the farmer's throat. His eyes widened farther.

"Tell this farmer the dead are dead," I commanded Paulus. "If he wants to join them, I can arrange it. If not, he'll obey my orders. The choice is his."

As I'd hoped, the threat persuaded our prisoner to set aside his professed fear of contamination. Trembling so badly that he could barely stand, he reluctantly agreed to guide us to the murdered men. Secretly relieved, I sheathed my sword.

Leaving several cavalrymen to guard our horses, pack animals, and servants, I took my soldiers into that shadowed patch of woods. The Galilean farmer Nahum went first. I followed close on his heels, with Aedan and another young trooper right behind me. Aristides and Paulus were next. The rest of the men trailed after them.

Dense thickets of thornbushes and briers lined the

banks of the small stream snaking down from the hills. There were several trails leading in. Most were narrow and overgrown—probably used only by wild animals coming for water. One was larger, wide enough for humans. Grim faced, we pushed in among the trees, brushing past low branches and trailing thorns that snagged and tore at our cloaks and tunics.

Nahum led us deep into that brush-choked copse of trees, straight to a small clearing somewhere near its heart.

And there we found what we sought.

Nine mutilated corpses covered the open patch of ground in a grotesque sprawl of arms and legs. They were naked, stripped of all clothing and possessions.

The oily, rancid stench of death and decay filled the clearing.

I swallowed hard, fighting the urge to vomit, digging my fingers hard into my palms. I would not disgrace myself, I swore silently.

Others weren't so proud. I could hear Paulus and several of the recruits retching helplessly behind me. The farmer Nahum sank to his knees, moaning in horror.

Aedan muttered, "This is a terrible sight, Prefect. The stuff of black dreams." He glanced at me. "What do we do now?"

I breathed out slowly and shallowly, trying to avoid the dreadful odor hanging in the air. "Keep the men back. Aristides and I will take a closer look first."

The decurion nodded grimly. "Better you than me. But there's not much either you or the doctor can do for these poor husks, I think."

"We can find out how they died," I answered shortly. "That's a start."

Aristides came forward, already pulling the pouch

with his medical kit off his shoulder. He sighed. "There are moments, Lucius, when I regret my profession."

The Greek physician knelt down at the edge of the clearing and began laying out items from his kit—two scraps of linen, a sealed jar, and a gleaming row of scalpels, probes, and other surgical instruments. Then he opened the jar and smeared a dab of strong-smelling ointment across each piece of cloth.

Aedan looked on curiously. "And what's that, if I may ask?"

The doctor handed one of the two pieces of linen to me. "A mixture of myrrh and frankincense blended with lanolin, a grease extracted from wool." He put the other scrap of cloth over his mouth and nose and tied it behind his head. "The fragrance will shield us from some of the putrid taint."

I followed his lead. The sharp smell of incense made my eyes water a bit, but anything was better than the awful odor emanating from that scene of slaughter.

Then Aristides and I walked into the clearing, carefully stepping over and around the sprawled corpses. We moved methodically from one to another, doing our best to learn what we could from the slaughter all around us.

Several had their throats cut, slashed from ear to ear. Others appeared to have been beaten to death. Their skulls were smashed in, leaving a splintered wreckage of bone and mangled brains strewn across the scuffed and gouged dirt. Wild beasts and the ravens and vultures now lazily circling overhead had been feasting on the dead, pecking at eyes and the other soft parts of flesh.

A fringe of blood-soaked white hair matted around the crushed skull of one of the bodies attracted my attention. I knelt beside it, staring intently into a ruined, ravaged face.

My heart stopped.

Despite the terrible wounds it bore, I recognized that lean, aristocratic profile. I'd last seen it in an elegant house in Antioch.

The dead man was Decimus Junius Silanus, a member of the Roman Senate, once a consul, and the friend and close political ally of Tiberius Caesar.

Aristides stared down at the body I'd identified as Silanus. He looked acutely worried. "You're sure about this, Lucius?"

I nodded grimly. "Certain."

"And these others?"

I ran my eyes over the corpse-strewn clearing. "Members of his personal household, I'd guess."

Strangely enough, now that I had recognized Silanus, it was easier to look past the sheer horror of shattered bone and gnawed flesh to see what lay beneath.

"There." I pointed toward another mutilated body, one with a full head of gray hair. "That was an old slave named Tiro."

For a brief instant I wondered whether or not poor Tiro had spent that denarius I'd slipped him so many days ago and so far away in Antioch—or whether it now jingled in the money pouch of one of his killers.

Something about the body closest to Silanus caught Aristides' attention. He showed me the dead man's right hand. "Look here, Lucius."

Though it had curled into a twisted claw, I could still make out black stains around the fingers and on what was left of the palm. "Ink?" I guessed.

The doctor nodded.

"The senator's private secretary?"

"Likely enough," Aristides agreed. He stood up again. "And where are Silanus' guards?" he asked softly. "You said he had a detachment of Tiberius' Praetorians with him."

"He did," I said. I walked back through the clearing, studying the sprawled corpses again. Even in death, something about a few of them—their sturdy build or old scars, perhaps—conjured up the image of tough veteran soldiers.

I nudged them gently with my foot, one after another. "This one. That one. And this big fellow here, the one with his throat cut."

"Three," the doctor observed. "Was that all of them?"

I shook my head. "I doubt it."

When I met with Silanus in Antioch, I'd seen two soldiers on duty at the front door of the house he'd rented. Nobody kept the same troops on watch all day, especially not the pampered Praetorians. As a rough rule of thumb, to keep two alert men on guard at any given moment, you needed at least six more backing them up. Based on that, I guessed Tiberius had loaned the senator at least eight of his personal troops as bodyguards for his mysterious trip through the eastern provinces. Three were dead. So where were the rest?

Chapter IX

After checking every corpse, the doctor and I walked back toward where Aedan, Paulus, and the others stood watching. The tall, fair-haired Celt came forward to meet us.

I gave him the bad news.

"A senator lies murdered?" Aedan repeated, astonished. "Here?"

I yanked the incense-laden cloth away from my mouth and nose. This far from the clearing, the stench was bearable.

Frowning, the decurion nodded toward the bodies. "The work of bandits, do you think?"

"It looks that way," I said flatly. "The killers stripped Silanus and the rest to the bone. They took everything of value — clothes, weapons, and money. Even their rings and personal jewelry."

"Bandits or not, this is an ugly business, Lucius," Aristides said. His mouth was set in a thin, grave line.

Now there's an understatement, I thought wryly.

This was a full-blown disaster. Roman senators weren't supposed to turn up dead in the middle of nowhere, especially a senator who was one of the emperor's most trusted friends. And most especially not a senator rumored to be prowling around the East on a secret mission for Tiberius.

"What will you do?" Aristides asked.

"My duty, I hope." I turned toward the clearing again. "I'll try to find whoever butchered Silanus and the others."

Now the doctor looked even more worried. "Is that wise, Lucius? This is Herod's territory. Shouldn't you let his officials investigate this crime?"

For a moment, I was tempted. The city of Sepphoris was close at hand, no more than one or two hours' ride away. Why not have the tetrarch's officers take this responsibility off my shoulders?

Then I shook my head. "No, Silanus was a citizen and a senator. Whoever killed him is subject to Roman laws, not to Herod's. And right now I'm the highest-ranking Roman soldier on the scene." That meant tracking down his murderers was my job—whether I wanted it or not.

Aristides sighed.

I knew what was bothering him. It was bothering me, too.

As a tribune of the Sixth Legion, I'd already stuck my hand into one adder's nest. And what had I gained by exposing Gnaeus Piso's support for corruption, extortion, and banditry? Capito was dead. My old legate Faustus was on his way home without a command. But Piso was still governor of Syria, and I'd come within a breath of ending up either disgraced or dead in an alley.

Now here I was staring at a situation that might be even more tangled—and with stakes that were infinitely higher. Germanicus had intervened to save me from Piso's wrath. No one would be able to help me if I failed this time.

The news of this massacre wouldn't reach Rome for weeks, maybe even months. But when it arrived, it would set the whole city ablaze. There would be a furor on the floor of the Senate. The emperor himself would demand answers. And a terrible vengeance.

I glanced at the ashen-faced farmer who'd led us to the bodies.

I knew the rules. When a Roman official is murdered by brigands, we strike back, hard and fast and fiercely. Wherever possible, we punish those responsible. If not, most soldiers follow a basic maxim: hit the nearest village. The principle is simple and sensible. Most bandit gangs rely on a base of support in the surrounding population—on farmers who provide them with food, on receivers who sell stolen goods for them, and on informers who point them toward rich pickings. Reprisals against the locals are intended to put pressure on these same people, persuading them to betray the bandits to us.

Various imperial edicts advise commanders to exercise restraint when conducting these reprisal raids. Again, the principle is sound. Using excessive force can easily backfire, turning the locals against us and not the bandits.

I frowned. Somehow I doubted anyone in Rome would approve of restraint in this case. Not when one of the dead men was a friend of Caesar's. Tiberius himself, every senator, and every leading man in Rome would expect me to pursue Silanus' killers to the limit—even if I had to leave a trail of burning villages and weeping widows in my wake.

All of which meant I held the lives of this frightened farmer, his family, and all of his neighbors in my own two hands. That wasn't a very comfortable realization.

I shook my head again impatiently. I'd taken the military oath of my own free will. No one ever promised me that living up to its obligations would be easy or trouble-free.

There were shouts in the distance.

I dropped my hand to the sword at my side. I'd been careless. Someone had attacked Silanus and his party and wiped them out. How could I assume they weren't still somewhere close by, waiting to ambush us in turn? One look at Aedan's face told me he shared the same worry.

A cavalry trooper came running up the trail. It was one of the men I'd left guarding our horses and the servants.

He skidded to a stop. "Prefect!"

"Report," I snapped.

"There are riders coming this way," the recruit said excitedly. "From the valley. They're armed, but we can't make out anything more yet."

I decided not to take any more chances.

I whirled toward Aristides. "Take Paulus and stay out of sight until I find out who these strangers are."

He nodded.

I grabbed one of the other young soldiers and pushed him toward the Galilean farmer we'd taken prisoner. "Litas! Keep an eye on that man. If he tries to escape, kill him. Understand?"

"Yes, Prefect!"

I spun back to Aedan. "You and the rest follow me!"

With the decurion and fourteen men, I hurried to the edge of the trees.

We got there in time to see a small band of horsemen trotting up the track from the valley of Esdraelon. I counted quickly. There were only six riders, five of them in armor.

They halted briefly some distance away, evidently

surprised to see so many strings of horses and pack animals grazing on the slope ahead of them. Then they came on.

Flanked by Aedan and my troopers, I moved out to intercept them.

Their leader was much older than I was—in his late thirties or early forties, I guessed. His stern, square-jawed face bore a tight-lipped frown. The greaves protecting his legs, the silver sheen on his armor, the vine staff slung at his flank, and the side-to-side scarlet horsehair crest on his helmet identified him as a centurion of the Praetorian Guard.

Four more guardsmen followed him. I eyed them carefully. At least now I knew where the rest of the senator's bodyguards were. A civilian—the tallest of them all, a man with a hooked nose and large dark eyes—brought up the rear of the small procession. He wore a red silk robe with long black sleeves.

I'd seen that strange-looking fellow before, I realized, in Antioch. I searched my memory and frowned. Silanus' slave Tiro had told me his name—Araneus. The old slave had also claimed he was a magus, a seer or sorcerer of real power. More to the point, he was another member of the senator's retinue who had somehow escaped the massacre we had discovered.

The centurion reined in his horse right in front of us.

He inspected Aedan first, then settled his gaze on me. "Just who in Hades are you?" he growled, leaning forward in his saddle. "And what are you doing here?"

My jaw tightened.

I'd never been very fond of the Praetorian Guard. Though many of the men in its nine cohorts were still veteran soldiers drawn from the regular legions, more and more of them were spoiled brats from the best fam-

ilies in Rome and the rest of Italy. Serving in the Guard
guaranteed them higher pay and more privileges—and
all with very little risk of real combat. There was a bitter joke among the troops fighting in Germany: Whoever saw a dead Praetorian?

Well, I thought grimly, remembering the carnage in
the clearing, now I had.

Anyway, this centurion looked tough enough to me.
The white scar left by a sword cut down his left cheek
and the puckered mark of an old arrow wound on his
right forearm proved that he'd seen his share of battles.

"I asked you a question, friend," he said coldly. "And
I don't like repeating myself."

Aedan's face flushed angrily. He took a step forward.
I waved him back. As the prefect of a cavalry regiment, I
outranked this Praetorian officer. But there wasn't any
point in getting into a pissing match with the arrogant
son of a bitch. Not yet anyway.

"My name is Aurelius Valens," I said mildly. "I command the Third Gallic Cavalry."

His eyes narrowed. "You're new in this area," he
said.

I nodded. "I'm on my way to Caesarea to take over
the regiment."

The centurion swung down off his horse and handed
the reins to one of the other guardsmen. "I'm Marcus
Aemilius Severus," he said, introducing himself. "Commanding an independent detachment of the Praetorian
Guard."

"What are you doing here in Galilee, Centurion?" I
asked—carefully emphasizing his lower rank.

For an instant, Severus bristled. I suspected he was a
man used to asking questions, not answering them.
Then he shrugged his shoulders. "I'm looking for a sen-

ator." He smiled thinly. "Sounds odd way out here, doesn't it? But that's the truth. This one's named Decimus Junius Silanus."

"I've seen Silanus," I said quietly. "Or rather, what's left of him."

That wiped the humorless smile right off the centurion's face. "What do you mean?"

"I mean that Decimus Silanus is dead," I said. "We found his corpse in those woods over there about an hour before you got here."

The Praetorian officer didn't flinch. "That's impossible," he snapped. "The senator had some of my best men with him."

"The best or not, they're dead now. Along with the servants. We've counted nine bodies so far, all of them stripped and mutilated."

"Nine?" Severus scowled. "I want to see this for myself." He shot me a suspicious glance. "If the bodies are mutilated, how do you know one of them was Silanus?"

"I met him once, in Antioch." I shrugged. "But judge for yourself."

"Don't worry," the centurion told me. "I will."

I led the way into the wooded hollow, motioning Aristides and the others back out of concealment.

The Praetorian declined the doctor's offer of a mask against the terrible stench in the clearing. I stood back, watching while he moved through the corpses, bending down now and again to peer more closely at one or another.

After several minutes, Severus came back to me. His face was hard and set. His eyes were angry. "You were right," he admitted. "That's the senator and his household."

"All of them?"

The centurion shook his head. "No. One of my men is missing. Silanus should have had four of them with him."

"Valens!" Paulus' voice piped up from behind us. "I think I've found something else!" When I'd ordered Aristides to stay out of sight with him, they'd taken shelter a few paces off the trail, deeper in the tangle of trees and brush. The boy was still there.

With Severus right behind me, I left the clearing and hurried back through the woods toward Paulus. He was kneeling down, peering into a patch of brambles and thorns.

"What is it?" I asked sharply.

"Someone's gone through there," Paulus said. He pointed toward one part of the thicket. "Do you see?"

I looked more closely and saw what he meant. Someone had crashed blindly through the undergrowth in one place, leaving a narrow trail of snapped branches and trampled brush.

The boy reached out carefully and held up one of the dangling pieces of branch for my inspection. "And see this?"

A length of scarlet thread hung from one of the razor-edged thorns. My eyes narrowed. It was impossible to be sure, but it looked like thread from a military cloak to me.

I turned my head. "Aedan!"

The decurion came up. "Sir?"

I drew my sword and nodded toward the wall of brambles and thorns. "You're with me. You take the left. I'll take the right."

Working together, Aedan and I slashed our way deeper into the thicket, clearing a rough path through the dense undergrowth. Though we were out of the sun, it was hot work. I could feel the sweat running down my face and back by the time we'd gone just a few paces.

We found another body several yards farther on, this

one lying facedown with the shaft of an arrow protruding from the torn links of his mail corselet. An empty scabbard hung at the dead man's right side. The decurion helped me roll him over onto his side.

I frowned. The ground where he'd been lying was spattered with dried blood. I pulled back a fold of the soldier's cloak and sucked in my breath at the sight of a wickedly sharp arrowhead sticking a finger's width out of the mail covering his chest. To penetrate two layers of armor, both front and back, that arrow had to have been fired at point-blank range.

"Another Praetorian," Aedan said.

Severus had followed us into the thorns. He nodded grimly. "That's Cassius Celer, all right."

Without saying anything more, he spun on his heel and stalked away, heading back along the path we'd hacked through the thorns. I ordered Aedan to have the dead guardsman carried out onto the main trail, and then I followed the Praetorian officer.

I caught up with him at the edge of the trees. He strode out into the open air. He stood breathing deeply for a long moment.

I waited.

"Cassius and I served together for more than twenty years," Severus at last said quietly. "With the old Sixteenth Legion, in the beginning. That was a good outfit. And we roared with the best of them, he and I."

I nodded. The Sixteenth had a lion as its emblem—a symbol of the god Jupiter. It was known army-wide as a tough, effective fighting force.

"When I came to the Guard, he moved up with me. We earned our promotions the hard way, I can tell you," the centurion said. "Not like some."

I nodded again. "And the others?"

"They were good soldiers," Severus said simply. He fell silent.

I supposed that was as fine an epitaph as any man could ask.

The wind shifted a bit, bringing with it a faint smell of death from the woods. I wrinkled my nose. The odor was an ugly reminder of the urgent problem we faced. I needed some answers from this man, and I needed them fast.

"What brought you here looking for Silanus?" I asked.

"He sent a dispatch asking for help," Severus said evenly. "It reached me late yesterday at Caesarea."

"May I see it?"

For an instant, I thought the Praetorian would refuse. But then he took a single sheet of papyrus out of his belt pouch and handed it to me.

I scanned the sheet rapidly. The hastily scrawled message it bore was brief—and dismayingly cryptic:

M. Aemilius Severus,

> *Bring a strong force as soon as possible to the village of Nazara in Galilee, south and east of Sepphoris. I may need your assistance.*

> *D. Junius Silanus, Senator and special envoy to the East for Tiberius Claudius Nero Caesar*

I looked up from the note. "Nazara?"

Severus indicated the village on the hill above us. "There it is. Or so I'm told."

I glanced at the four Praetorian guardsmen he'd brought with him. "And this is what you consider a 'strong force'?"

The centurion smiled, but again the smile didn't reach his wintry gray eyes. "No, Prefect, it is not. Which is why there are three troops of cavalry on their way here right now—from your own regiment, in fact. They should be less than an hour behind us."

That was good news.

I checked the position of the sun. With luck, those reinforcements would arrive well before nightfall. Of course, that still left the problem of just what I was supposed to do with them.

I looked back at Severus. "Do you know why the senator wanted soldiers here?"

"I do not."

The centurion's harsh, clipped reply surprised me. I raised an eyebrow. "You don't?"

Severus nodded at the dispatch in my hand. "I know what Silanus wrote there. Anything else is pure conjecture." He frowned. "And I don't like playing guessing games."

I gritted my teeth. This Praetorian and I were going to butt heads sooner than I had hoped.

"Prefect! More riders!"

I swung away, toward the shout. One of my troopers pointed to the west.

A long column of horsemen came into view, moving steadily toward us. Sunlight gleamed on helmets and mail shirts. Counting the scouts and flank guards I could see paralleling the main force—there were close to sixty men.

Severus nodded in satisfaction. He pointed to the gold-fringed green banner fluttering at the head of the column. "Those are your soldiers, Prefect. They made good time."

He faced me, with his hand resting on the hilt of his sword. "Now we can do what's necessary here."

"What do you propose?" I asked quietly.

For the first time, the Praetorian officer looked surprised. "Surely that's obvious?"

"Not to me."

Severus eyed me narrowly. Then he nodded toward the village on the hill above us. "It's simple. We take your troops to that dung heap up there. We crucify every Jew in the place. We take the women and children as slaves. We slaughter the livestock. And then we raze every house and barn to the ground."

"To what end?"

"To put the fear of Rome back among these Galileans, of course," Severus said. He looked at me. "You know the policy as well as I do. No one murders a Roman citizen—let alone a senator and consul—and walks away unscathed."

"I know the policy," I agreed. "But I don't know enough about what happened here to destroy that village. Not yet anyway."

The Praetorian officer snorted. "This massacre took place on their land. What more do you need?"

"Evidence of their guilt, for a start," I said.

"Evidence?" Severus shook his head. "Look around you, Prefect. This is the real world—not some marble-floored magistrate's court in Rome. Our hold out here rests on one foundation. Power. Nothing more. And nothing less. If we show weakness now, we're finished."

I shook my head. "What about justice, Centurion?"

"Justice?" Severus said with a hard edge in his voice. "What is justice? Did my men receive justice?"

I kept my mouth closed.

He stepped closer. "Now either you give the orders to smash that village—or I will."

I smiled crookedly. So much for Germanicus' attempt to give me a safe, out-of-the-way posting. I looked at Severus and calmly said, "I command here, Centurion. Not you."

His square-jawed face flushed a dull, dark red—emphasizing the old scar across his cheek.

"I intend to find and punish those who murdered Silanus, his servants, and your men," I continued. "And make no mistake. If these villagers played a part in those murders, they'll pay a high price. But I won't assume their guilt. And I will not punish the innocent simply to strike fear in the guilty."

Severus stared at me for a long moment. At last, he shook his head grimly. "You've got guts, boy. But no brains." He shrugged. "Remember this, Aurelius Valens. The emperor does not value those who set themselves against his will. And what Tiberius Caesar does not value, he soon discards."

Chapter X

We entered Nazara in force.

Counting the reinforcements summoned by Severus from Caesarea, I now had close to eighty cavalrymen on hand—the recruits I'd brought from Antioch and nearly sixty veterans organized in three troops, the First, Fifth, and Seventh. I put the recruits and their servants under Aristides' supervision. They had orders to collect the bodies and search the woods for any traces left by the killers.

Aedan and the veterans rode into the village with me. Paulus came along to translate. Severus, the astrologer Araneus, and the surviving four Praetorian guardsmen followed at the back of the column.

The streets were narrow, more unpaved alleys than anything else. They wound between crude houses built of dark, rough-hewn stones. Some were little more than caves that had been dug out of the hillside and then walled off to make a rude habitation or a stable for animals. The doors we passed were all shut tight. None of the locals could be seen outside their homes. Word of our approach had evidently traveled fast through the little hamlet.

Near the center of Nazara, the tightly packed labyrinth of houses spread out, opening up into a rough square around a small fountain. This fountain, fed by a spring rising on the slopes above, seemed to be the principal source of water for the village. A narrow channel carried the overflow downhill, toward the patch of woods where we'd found Silanus and his retainers.

I turned to Aedan. "We'll hold here."

He nodded appreciatively. "A good choice. With their water in our hands, these people will have to come out and talk to us."

It didn't take long.

Within minutes, I could see the doors facing the square begin to open. Throngs of silent men, women, and children peered out at us. They looked frightened.

An older man with a thick gray beard and long flowing hair left one of the larger houses and came slowly toward us. I walked Dancer out to meet him, followed closely by Paulus on his mule in case I needed a translator. Severus rode out from the end of the line to join us. I hid my irritation. Four of his men had been murdered, and the Praetorian centurion had a right to listen in.

I pulled up right in front of the villager. My horse seemed to make him nervous. He edged backward a bit. I urged Dancer forward again with a light touch of my heels, closing the gap. I wasn't here to make this Galilean comfortable.

This time the older man stood his ground.

"Do you speak Greek?" I asked.

He nodded warily. "Some." Deep furrows carved by care and toil surrounded his tired brown eyes. "Sir, my name is Mathias. I am one of Nazara's chief elders and the head of our assembly."

"My name is Lucius Aurelius Valens," I said quietly. "I command the Third Gallic Cavalry Regiment. We serve Tiberius Caesar and the Senate and people of Rome."

"Romans?" He seemed surprised, but not especially worried. "Please, why have you come to our village?"

"I'm here because of Decimus Junius Silanus," I said, watching closely to see how he would react.

Mathias only nodded calmly. "Of course."

I leaned forward in the saddle. "You know that name, then?"

"The Roman noble? Yes, naturally."

"How?"

"Because that man and his followers came to Nazara two days ago," Mathias said. "And before that, all the hills were alive with the rumors of his travels through our land." He lifted his shoulders. "We are a poor people. Our lives are simple. News of a Roman senator clad in rich garments, with proud soldiers and slaves at his disposal, spreads quickly."

I nodded my understanding, then asked, "How long were Silanus and his retainers in your village?"

Mathias didn't hesitate. "A single night. They left yesterday afternoon."

Startled by this claim, Paulus began to say something, but I silenced the boy with an angry glance.

I turned my attention back to the elder. "And where were they going next?" I asked.

Mathias shook his head. "They did not say. I saw the senator and his company take the track northwest toward Sepphoris, but there are several other villages in that direction." He spread his hands. "Perhaps they returned to the city."

"You haven't seen them since?"

"We have not."

This time Severus was the one who tried to interrupt. He edged his horse closer. "Enough," he growled. "This old Jew is lying and you know it."

I cut him off with a curt gesture. "Not now, Centurion!"

The Praetorian's face flushed red, but he remained silent.

I turned back to Mathias.

The elder looked from Severus to me with increasing concern. The confidence I'd seen earlier had largely evaporated.

"Why did Silanus come to Nazara?" I asked him.

Mathias tugged uneasily at his beard. "That I don't know. He didn't explain his presence to me or to any of the other elders. I can only tell you what he did while among us."

"Which was?" I demanded.

"He asked many questions," the older man said cautiously. "Strange questions. 'Who are the leading families in Nazara? Where did they come from? Were all those who live here born in the village?' And more of that kind."

I raised an eyebrow, reexamining the scattering of crude houses surrounding us. Though it was far tidier than some of the hamlets I'd seen in Germany or even parts of Italy, this place was tiny and clearly impoverished. Why would a wealthy, powerful man like Silanus even imagine this village — or the others in these hills — might harbor anyone of interest to him? One of his house slaves in Rome would lead a better life than would the most prosperous farmer in Nazara.

"And you gave him the information he sought?" I asked.

"To the best of our ability," Mathias said, clearly choosing his words with great care.

I doubted the senator had found many villagers who gave him complete answers. I'd seen this before among country people. They were too weak and too poor to openly defy the mighty, but they could always take refuge in apparently unshakable ignorance.

Of course, that same tactic could hamper my own investigation into Silanus' murder. Unsettled by that thought, I shifted in the saddle. If need be, I would have to cut my way to the truth in Nazara—no matter how much suffering I inflicted on its inhabitants.

"Why does this officer"—Mathias indicated Severus—"think I am lying when I say that the senator left us and has not returned?" He sounded apprehensive.

It was time to drop the mask, I decided.

I leaned forward over Dancer's neck, looking down into the elder's worried brown eyes. "For the best of reasons," I told him. "Decimus Junius Silanus, his soldiers, and his slaves are all dead—and their bodies lie heaped on your land."

The blood drained from his bearded face. Hoarsely, he asked, "Where?"

I pointed down the hill, toward the shadowed copse of trees several hundred paces away. "In there, among the trees and thorns."

Mathias shuddered. "I swear to you on the Most High that we did not kill those men! Nor did we know of their deaths!"

I stared back at him. "Do you seriously expect me to believe that? When I've found ten murdered men so close to your houses and fields?"

"But we never go there . . . to that place," the village

elder stammered. "It is wasteland, of no use to man or beast."

"Now you lie," I said bluntly. "We took a prisoner running from those trees. A man from Nazara who calls himself Nahum. He showed us the bodies."

Mathias appeared genuinely taken aback by this news. "Nahum?" Distressed, he shook his head. "Nahum is a respectable farmer, a man with four sons, and with daughters, too. Why should he go there—especially during the harvest?"

"That is just one of several things I intend to find out," I told him. "By whatever means I judge necessary."

I swung around in my saddle toward the horizon. The day was far advanced. I decided to finish searching the area before it grew any darker. Further interrogation of this man or the rest of the villagers could wait. Perhaps more time spent under the cold eyes of so many soldiers would loosen a few tongues.

I turned back to Mathias. "I'm requisitioning quarters for my officers and thirty troopers. Five houses should suffice. The rest of my soldiers will camp close by. Your village will provide food for us all, and fodder for our horses and pack animals."

"For how long?" he whispered.

"For as long as it takes me to discover the truth about these murders," I said grimly.

Though I wouldn't have thought it possible, Mathias turned even paler. He scanned the rows of horsemen behind me, counting rapidly under his breath. "We have barely enough to last through the winter months as it is. How can we feed so many?"

I understood his growing panic. Like so many poor farmers, these Jewish peasants probably lived from har-

vest to harvest, gathering just enough food to pay their
taxes and feed themselves—if they were lucky. With
some difficulty, I pushed aside my doubts. Severus was
wrong to want to slaughter these villagers without evidence of their guilt, but the centurion was right about
one thing. This wasn't a time to show weakness.

I kicked Dancer into motion, circling Mathias, forcing him to turn with me. "Understand me, Galilean," I
said. "My concern is with finding those who murdered
the senator and his men. If you and your people had
nothing to do with this crime, then I strongly suggest
you pray to your god that I succeed. Because if I fail,
starvation is the last thing you'll need to worry about. Is
that clear?"

He stared up at me in silence, tears welling up in his
eyes.

Suddenly, I felt ashamed.

Then, angry with myself for feeling pity for these
miserable provincials, I turned my horse away from him
and cantered back toward my waiting soldiers. I would
do my duty in this place, no matter how painful it
proved.

"Decurions and double-pay men, to me!" I shouted,
summoning the commanders and ranking subordinates
of the three troops I'd brought into the village.

They dismounted and gathered round in a tight circle.
I wished I'd had time to get to know these men better
before sending them into action, but that would have to
wait.

"Take your soldiers and search every house in the village. Every stable. Every silo and water cistern. And
every nook and cranny," I ordered. "First Troop starts
on the west. Fifth Troop moves in from the north. Sev-

enth Troop works its way inward from the east. You meet here in the middle. Clear?"

The decurions and rankers nodded.

"You all know the drill," I continued. "You're looking for rich clothing—for finely woven tunics, a toga, or a military cloak. For armor or weapons. For large sums of coin or for rings and other jewelry. For anything that could have belonged to the senator, his slaves, or the Praetorians. Right?"

There were murmured assents.

"Be thorough. But don't smash down doors or break the furniture unless you have to." I gave them a hard-eyed stare and then told them I wouldn't tolerate any looting. Any man caught stealing would earn a flogging.

A couple of the younger Celts looked disappointed. Many soldiers, especially tribal auxiliaries, saw punitive actions as a chance to supplement their pay. Trinkets, household goods, wine jars, and other small, valuable items had a tendency to "go missing" whenever troops conducted house-to-house searches.

The older men, though, nodded sagely. These villagers were already near panic. Pillaging their homes now would only spark trouble.

"If you find anything suspicious, arrest the house-holder," I said. "Then bring him to me. Understand?"

They nodded again.

"And if anyone tries to resist, I want them taken alive," I finished. "I need prisoners to question—not more corpses. Now, go to it!"

The decurions and double-pay men scattered back to their units, each bawling orders that sent small groups of soldiers into action. The troopers dispersed through the streets. I shut my ears to the sound of sword hilts hammering on doors and the sudden wailing of women and children being herded outside into the alleys.

The people of Nazara were in for a rough time. Part of me regretted that. But it could easily have been far worse. And it might yet be.

My gaze fell on Severus and his companions. The centurion had already dismounted. He and his soldiers were calmly watering their horses at the village fountain. Araneus, the astrologer, stood a little distance off by himself, apparently contemplating the sky.

I swung down out of the saddle and handed Dancer's reins to Commius, Aedan's groom. The decurion followed suit and so did Paulus. The three of us headed for the centurion.

Severus looked up at our approach.

"This search is a wasted effort, Valens," he said. "These Jews have had plenty of time to hide their plunder where even your light-fingered Gauls won't find it."

I ignored the dig. "I'm open to suggestions," I said evenly. "Where else should we be looking?"

Severus nodded toward the hillside north of the village. Several large whitewashed stones were visible, blocking the entrances to caves and other openings cut into the slope. "Up there for a start."

Paulus was outraged. "Those are tombs! Opening them would defile you and desecrate the dead."

The centurion smiled wryly. "What makes you think brigands and murderers share your superstitions, boy?" He turned his back on us, bending down to loosen the girth strap for his saddle.

I glanced at Aedan. "When we're finished here, take a patrol up among those caves and tombs. Report back if you find any that look as though they've been opened recently."

The tall Celt nodded. I knew I could trust him to be sensible. After a decade spent in Judea, he wouldn't recommend violating Jewish burial customs without good reason.

Severus glanced over his shoulder at me. "When you're finished here?" he said. "What does that mean? I've given you my advice. What more do you want?"

"Answers," I said firmly. "You heard what that Galilean elder said. Now I want to know what Silanus was doing here."

"And I told you I don't play guessing games," Severus snapped. He heaved the saddle off the back of his horse.

"You commanded his guard detachment," I said. "That makes it rather difficult to believe you didn't know his mission."

"Oh, I know why Tiberius Caesar sent him east," the centurion said, cooling down. He put the saddle down, then straightened up and turned to face me. "What I don't see is how this ridiculous jaunt of his to Galilee had anything to do with the orders he was given."

"Just what were those orders?" I asked.

Severus stared down at me from his full height. He kept his mouth shut.

"Decimus Junius Silanus is dead. His mission—secret or not—is over," I pointed out. I could feel my temper sliding close to the edge of control. "I'll ask you one more time, Centurion. What were the senator's orders?"

"First, send the boy away," the Praetorian said pointedly. "The emperor's directives were confidential."

I turned toward Paulus and asked him to wait for me at the entrance to Mathias' house. He glowered at me, but he obeyed, stomping angrily off on his short, ungainly legs.

I looked back at Severus. "Well?"

"Caesar is worried that there might be a rebellion brewing somewhere in the East," he said quietly. "Or, if not a rebellion, perhaps a political conspiracy of some kind aimed at him. The reports reaching Rome weren't specific."

"Reports from whom?"

Severus shook his head. "That I don't know. And if I did, I wouldn't tell you." He smiled thinly. "My commander, Aelius Sejanus, doesn't make a habit of flaunting the names of his agents far and wide."

That was probably true, I decided. Rumor said the Praetorian prefect Sejanus kept a web of spies and other paid informers busy ferreting out threats against Tiberius and the empire.

I understood the emperor's concern for his own safety. Augustus had died peacefully in his own bed, but he was the first great man in Rome to have managed the trick in nearly a century. Pompey the Great, Julius Caesar, and Marcus Antonius had all in turn met violent and bloody ends by murder, assassination, and suicide.

Still, I didn't much care for what I'd heard about the Praetorian prefect's activities. They smacked too much of the intrigue and underhanded dealing common during the old civil wars.

"So Silanus was investigating these reports of conspiracy or rebellion," I said slowly.

"That's right," Severus confirmed. "The senator was a powerful man—one with personal and political connections all over the East. I suspect he had his own agents in Antioch, Caesarea, and Jerusalem. The gods know we spent enough time sniffing about in those places."

That was logical enough, and it certainly fit the rumors I'd heard in Antioch. It also raised a troubling point. Both Piso and the lady Agrippina had been acutely concerned by the senator's refusal to explain his actions. How many others—whether in Syria or Judea or here in Galilee—had found whatever Silanus was up to deeply unnerving?

But right now something else was bothering me more.

"I have another question, Aemilius Severus," I said.

"Really?" The right side of his mouth twitched upward. "Just one? You surprise me, Valens."

I resisted the impulse to snap back at him.

I thought I was beginning to understand this Praetorian officer better. Severus was instinctively aggressive, both in war and in life. He'd come to Nazara fully expecting to be in charge of whatever was going on. But I outranked him and I'd used my rank to give orders he considered foolish. His constant verbal jabs were attempts to throw me off balance, to somehow regain the initiative.

There was only one practical way to deal with him. I had to hold my own temper in check—as difficult as that was.

"Go on, then," the centurion said impatiently.

"Why weren't you with the senator when he died?" I asked.

"Because I was obeying my instructions," Severus said flatly.

I stared at him. "Whose instructions?"

"The senator's."

"Explain that," I said.

Severus shrugged. "It's not complicated. Silanus sent me to Caesarea to confer with the procurator, his aides, and some of the tetrarch Herod's commanders. He wanted me to assemble a detailed report on the military situation in Judea and Galilee—on troop strengths, supplies, the status of fortifications, and the like."

That made sense. If Tiberius feared a possible revolt, he would need every piece of information he could gather to accurately assess the danger and to plan any response.

"The last I heard, Silanus and the others were still in Jerusalem," Severus went on. He frowned. "That's where I thought they were—right up until I received that dispatch asking for help."

That triggered a thought.

"Who carried the dispatch?" I asked.

"One of my men," the centurion said. He nodded at one of the four Praetorian guardsmen busy unsaddling their own mounts. "That one. Proclus."

I studied the soldier Severus had identified. Proclus struck me as the brawny sort who could hold his own in any fight, but his looks didn't inspire much confidence in his abilities as a thinker.

"Doesn't he have some idea of what Silanus was doing? Or why he wanted troops?"

"None," the centurion said. "I've asked. All he knows is that Silanus spent the better part of four days touring every dreary little village in this part of Galilee. Nazara didn't look much different than any of the other pigsties they'd already inspected."

I frowned.

"Talk to him yourself, if you must," Severus said. "If you hear anything I missed, I'll break my centurion's staff over my knee and retire to the farm Caesar has promised me."

I snorted. "You don't look much like a farmer to me."

The Praetorian officer bared his teeth in a tight, fierce grin. "I'm not."

I nodded. Most veteran legionaries looked forward to the grant of land they were promised after completing their service. A prosperous farm meant stability and security in old age. But this Praetorian, like many of his kind, had bigger dreams. Exemplary service in the Guard could open the doors to higher and higher military and political rank.

I stood thinking. Everything I'd heard fitted together. And yet nothing explained why a prominent and powerful Roman senator like Silanus would waste his time traipsing through Galilee asking odd questions of Jewish peasants.

I caught a flash of scarlet and black silk out the corner of my eye. Araneus, the astrologer and reputed magus, had finished his scrutiny of the heavens and was now pacing back and forth around the square, pausing now and then to peer intently at the surrounding houses.

"What about that black-eyed mystic over there?" I asked Severus. "Did you leave him in Jerusalem with the senator?"

"That weird creature?" Severus said. He scowled. "No. He came with me to Caesarea."

"Why?"

He shook his head. "You should ask him yourself. I have as little to do with his nonsense as I can."

With Severus and Aedan on my heels, I approached Araneus.

The seer looked at me in some amazement when I put my question to him. "With Decimus Junius Silanus? Why should I have stayed in his company?"

"You served him, didn't you?" I asked. "I would have

thought it customary for a servant to accompany his master."

"Serve him? That piece of common clay? Never." Araneus laughed harshly. "I serve Thrasyllus — and through him, your emperor."

Thrasyllus? I glanced at Severus.

"Tiberius Caesar's personal astrologer," the Praetorian said. His mouth tightened. "The fellow's been one of his hangers-on for at least fifteen years."

Which explained how this Araneus had evaded the legal decrees against astrology and magic, I realized. No doubt the legislation contained a small codicil exempting the emperor's private household.

"I came east to consult ancient records of wonders and portents for my master," Araneus said. "The old Jewish king Herod the Great collected valuable writings at his palace at Caesarea. I journeyed there to study them."

He sniffed. "It was convenient to attach myself to the senator's party. His petty political concerns were of no importance beside the mighty work I undertake."

"Those 'petty political concerns' may well have killed him," I pointed out grimly.

The magus gave an elaborate, uninterested shrug. "Silanus' eyes were blind before. Now they are blind forever. His soul was shriveled before. Now it is a mere speck of dust swirling in the winds of eternity. His fate was ordained a thousand years before his mother gave birth — and his death contains no more significance than an ant crushed beneath a small child's heel."

Despite myself, I shivered.

The tutors who'd tried to drum Stoic philosophy into my head as a boy had made great claims for the science of astrology. The fates to which we must conform can be read in the stars, they'd said. Influenced more by Aristides' skepticism than by my teachers' zeal, I'd had my doubts. But now, something of the absolute certainty in this man's voice made my flesh crawl.

I wasn't the only one affected. I glimpsed Aedan's hand dart to the amulet of Epona he wore around his neck.

Only Severus appeared unfazed. The centurion spat to one side. "The stars light the sky, nothing more," he said icily. "A man makes his own destiny—and mine, at least, lies in my own two hands."

His words broke the spell, if that was what it was.

Two spots of color appeared on the astrologer's high, pallid cheekbones. His black eyes glittered, but he kept his silence.

I breathed out. My hands were cold, but my grandfather's ring felt oddly warm.

Later, when we were well out of earshot, Aedan whistled softly. "What a pretty pair they are. The Praetorian and that tall stick of a sorcerer, I mean." He winced dramatically. "Can you imagine being forced to spend any great amount of time with either of them? It's almost enough to make me sorry for those big lummoxes over there, those parade-proud guardsmen—and that takes some doing, I tell you."

I smiled dutifully at that thought.

Severus and the astrologer. I mulled over what I had learned and what I had seen. Aedan was right. They were a strange duo. But three men had come east at Tiberius Caesar's command—not just two. The first, a proud, vengeful soldier. The second, an eerie mystic with a mind fixed more on the stars above than on the world below. And the last, Decimus Junius Silanus, a powerful, cynical politician charged by the emperor with hunting down would-be rebels or plotters against his life.

I stared at the tiny village around us and wondered again what could possibly have brought Silanus here — so far from anything of real importance.

Chapter XI

Our search of the village didn't turn up anything incriminating.

One by one the decurions reported in. Each brought a small collection of items their soldiers thought might be relevant. Among their finds were a number of belt knives, all of local manufacture; an intricately woven, tasseled garment that Paulus identified as a prayer shawl; and a few stacks of bronze and silver coins, all minted by Herod Antipas. The only weapons recovered were several spears, slings, and small bows, used by shepherds to fend off wolves. I studied the arrows with special care, but none matched the one we'd recovered from the Praetorian guardsman found dead in the thorns. And even Severus had to admit that he couldn't see anything that might have belonged to the senator or the other dead men.

When we finished checking through the confiscated goods, I ordered Aedan to lay them out on a blanket in the central square. "Let the villagers come and reclaim their own possessions," I said.

Severus laughed. "This will be amusing. We ought to

see one or two vicious little brawls between rival claimants."

Paulus frowned and shook his head. "That won't happen. You will see, Aemilius Severus. Our most basic laws — the Commandments given to us by the Most High — include a prohibition against theft. We Jews do not steal."

The Praetorian centurion only snorted and walked away.

Privately, I had my doubts. The boy from Tarsus had a high regard for his people and for their laws, but human nature is human nature. Some people cannot resist the temptation to enrich themselves at another's expense.

But events justified Paulus' faith. The Nazarenes came into the square by ones and twos, grave-faced and nervous around so many soldiers. Each man quickly and quietly gathered up his own possessions and took them away. If there were any quarrels or disputes over ownership they kept them well out of our view.

One thing was also clear. If these people had robbed Silanus and his men of their clothing, weapons, and jewelry, they hadn't hidden the loot within the confines of the little village.

Or anywhere else obvious close by.

As I'd ordered, Aedan took a patrol out to survey the tombs and caves beyond Nazara's boundaries. He came back empty-handed, reporting that all of them were sealed and none showed any signs of recent tampering.

Not much more turned up among the trees where Silanus and his men were butchered. Led by Aristides, my recruits combed that patch of woods from top to bottom before it grew too dark. Chief among their finds was a small heap of belongings dropped by the farmer

Nahum when he fled in panic: a cracked jar that once held wine, a round loaf of barley bread, and a coarse woolen blanket. Nothing belonging to Silanus or the other murdered men came to light.

We were still holding Nahum prisoner. He hadn't yet been able to offer a reasonable explanation for his strange visit to the woods. I wasn't sure what that meant, but I planned to find out. One thing I didn't want was the farmer concocting some plausible lie in concert with his neighbors or kinsmen. So I ordered him held at the camp my soldiers were busy erecting on the low rise just west of Nazara.

Neat rows of leather tents—each large enough to hold eight men and their equipment—were going up. Their horses were tethered to rope lines strung between stakes hammered in the ground. Sentries were posted at the corners of the camp and at points providing a commanding view of every likely approach. We could draw water for the men and animals from the stream at the bottom of the hill.

It wasn't perfect, but it would do.

Without a ditch or palisade, I knew the camp couldn't stand up to a determined attack. But my Celtic hotheads didn't have the temperament for much digging, not like their legionary counterparts anyway. Like most cavalry outfits, we would rely on mobility for our real defense, not field fortifications. With enough warning, we could run from more powerful enemies—and hope to hit weaker ones first.

The sun was almost down by the time I reached the camp.

I paid my first call on the senior decurion, a heavy-set, broad-shouldered officer. This man was a cousin of the Third Cavalry Regiment's old prefect, Sextus Gallus. He'd taken the Roman name Titus Marcius Taedifer. *Taedifer* means "torchbearer" and it suited him, both in looks and character. He was a red-haired firebrand of a soldier, a good man in battle, but rarely eager to think deeply in peace.

That much was plain from the moment the reinforcements from Caesarea joined up with the recruits I'd brought down from Antioch. When Taedifer spotted Aedan at my side, a huge grin flashed across his wide, freckled face. Nimble despite his great bulk, he slid out of the saddle and rushed forward to greet his old comrade, the taller, thinner, fair-haired Celt.

"Aedan!" The redhead clapped him on both shoulders. "You rogue! You're the last man I expected to run into out here! Weren't the women of Antioch pretty enough to hold your attention?"

Aedan laughed. "Oh, the women were fine, bright, bold-eyed girls, all of them. But stern duty called me back—whether I wished it or not."

Then he introduced me.

Before meeting him, I'd been worried that Taedifer might resent being superseded in command of the regiment. As the old prefect's closest living male relative he could easily have expected the promotion for himself. It was customary in many of the units we raised among allied or subject tribes. But the times and customs were changing. Germanicus and his uncle, Tiberius, both wanted tighter control over the empire's auxiliary troops.

If anything, however, the senior decurion looked relieved by the news that I was taking over.

"Better you than me, lad! I saw all the scroll-shuffling poor old Gallus had to do. Pay records. Hay allowance forms. Reports for this. Reports for that," Taedifer said, shaking his massive head slowly. "Sometimes I think you Romans would make us write down all our horses' bowel movements if you could." Then the big Gaul showed me that same toothy smile he'd given Aedan. "No, Prefect. I know when I'm well off. Command of a troop suits me. Point me at some enemy and I'll cut them up for you double-quick. But show me a stylus and a pot of ink and my marrow freezes solid!"

Now, several hours later, the regiment's senior decurion was showing me that despite his administrative deficiencies, he wasn't a fool when it came to tactics.

When I told him I wanted patrols out in every direction, Taedifer nodded. "Makes good sense, Prefect. Somebody jumped this senator and his people. If it was the locals, we've got them by the balls now. But if it was somebody else—brigands or rebels, say—I'd rather spot them before they sneak up and hand us our heads."

"Herod has a garrison at Sepphoris," I reminded him. "That's only a few miles away. They might know something about any bandit gangs in the area."

Taedifer shrugged. "The tetrarch's garrison is mostly infantry. I've been there a few times. I wouldn't trust half of Herod's boys to find their way out of a tavern in broad daylight." He clapped me on the shoulder. "Leave it to me, Prefect. I'll put the scouts out at first light."

Confident that I could rely on him, I headed for the tent holding Nahum and the soldiers assigned to guard him.

Severus was there ahead of me.

I sent the guards outside and began interrogating the farmer closely, hammering him with question after question in quick succession. The Praetorian centurion leaned casually against one of the tent supports with his

arms folded. He didn't say anything — just watched. For
now, he seemed content to allow me to handle matters.

Paulus was again serving as my interpreter. I didn't
like involving the boy from Tarsus so deeply in this ugly
affair, but there wasn't any real alternative. Nahum
didn't speak any Greek or Latin, and nobody else in
camp had enough knowledge of Aramaic.

"Why did you go to that grove of trees?" I demanded
again.

Nahum stumbled through the same answer he'd
given before. "I was hot and tired. I wanted to rest in the
shade."

"You could have found shade closer to your own
fields," I snapped back. "Why not rest there?"

The farmer swallowed. "It is the harvesttime," he
forced out. "There was too much noise. Too many other
people. I wanted quiet. I wanted to be away."

"Away from your own family?" I didn't hide my
skepticism. "What if your sons needed your help or advice?"

Nahum looked glum. "My sons are mostly grown,"
he said. "The oldest is almost a man. They don't need
me to hold their hands for them. They know the work."

I shook my head angrily. I was sure he was lying to
me. Like the other villagers, the Galilean and his family
depended on this harvest to avoid hunger through the
colder, wetter months. It had already rained once. If
the autumn rains began in earnest, any crops left in the
fields or fruit still hanging on the trees would soon
wither and rot. Would a farmer with that prospect staring him in the face just saunter off in the middle of the
day?

No. I was sure that something else had drawn Nahum
to those woods. Some other purpose. But what?

I began all over again—asking the same questions. And I got the same unsatisfactory answers. A soldier came in from outside and lit a hanging oil lamp against the gathering darkness.

At last, Severus lost his patience. The centurion stalked forward to glare down at the prisoner. "Have your men beat the truth out of this dim-witted peasant," he suggested. "Or let my lads sort him out." He looked up at me and smiled thinly. "They're quite good with the whip."

I looked at the Praetorian, trying hard to conceal my distaste. "This is a free man—not a slave, Centurion. Torture should be a last resort, not the first impulse."

Testimony from slaves is always taken under torture, on the grounds that a slave can't be trusted to tell the truth without coercion. But free men, even foreigners, have more protections against being beaten and whipped under interrogation. Though such fine distinctions were often ignored in the chaos of the civil wars, Augustus himself had worked hard to restrict the use of torture once peace was reestablished. Men were supposed to obey the law out of respect, not solely out of fear.

It was true that I had used force to question Domitius Capito's bandits, but those were soldiers I'd caught red-handed violating their military oaths, not just a poor foolish farmer whose story didn't satisfy me. The harsh discipline rightly imposed on the soldier is not appropriate to a civilian.

Severus gazed at me in some amazement. "You *have* been out in the provinces too long, Aurelius Valens. In Rome, we use the rack, fire, and scourge to break anyone who is guilty of a crime—no matter who they are."

I hid a grimace. The first years of Tiberius Caesar's

reign had been marked by a careful moderation and by his deference to the Senate, the consuls, and the law. My father had been especially pleased, citing Tiberius' qualities as proof of Augustus' divine wisdom in at last naming him his heir. But I'd heard rumors that the emperor was growing more violent toward those who opposed him. Now it appeared that those rumors were true.

O Divine Augustus, I thought bitterly, you brought an end to anarchy and civil war—and for that all Rome will be forever grateful. But what have you left us in your place?

I forced myself to speak civilly. Quarreling openly with a fellow officer would be bad for discipline. "Thank you for telling me of the latest practice in Rome, Aemilius Severus. But I think I will hold to the laws I have learned a while longer."

"As you wish." The Praetorian officer sketched an ironic salute. "You are in command here . . . for now." He moved to the tent flap. "I'll leave you to your gentler persuasion, Prefect, and look for my quarters for the night. One of these Jews who calls himself an elder has surrendered the use of his house to me." He frowned. "I only hope it proves cleaner than the rest of that flea-bitten nest of filth."

Once the flap closed behind him, Paulus blurted out a question. "You would not let this man be tortured, would you?"

I sighed. "Unless I can learn the truth in some other fashion, boy, I may be forced to it."

"But he's a Galilean and a subject of Herod Antipas!" Paulus protested. "You don't have any jurisdiction over him under your law."

"The tetrarch rules here by the consent of Rome. He knows that only too well," I explained gently. "And

Silanus was a senator—a confidant of Tiberius himself. Given that, I'm sure Antipas would be happy to let me crucify every man, woman, and child in this village if he thought that might turn aside Caesar's wrath."

The boy sat silent.

I spoke softly. "I'm walking close to a precipice here, Paulus. And I am walking in company with a man I suspect would be happy to hurl me over its edge."

Paulus shook his head stubbornly. "I don't understand."

"I think you do," I said. "That Praetorian is an ambitious man, a man who doesn't see limits in the stars or in his own future. And right now he's both angry and humiliated. Severus was sent east to protect the senator and he failed. More than that, his own men were slaughtered like sheep. If necessary, he'll try to cloak his failure in blood, even the blood of innocents—and I stand in his way."

I turned toward Nahum and growled, "I need the truth about these murders, and I don't have a lot of time to find it. If this farmer knows more about what really happened in those woods, I *will* have it—even if I have to break that knowledge out of him bone by bone." I stabbed a finger at the Galilean. "Tell him that. And this time make him believe it!"

Paulus didn't say anything. He just stared at me with that same mulish expression I saw every time he thought himself in the right.

I let it pass.

A quick glance at the farmer from Nazara convinced me that no translation of my threat was needed. The man was shivering uncontrollably. The sight turned my stomach. Was this why I had become a soldier? To terrorize peasants?

I turned back to Paulus and sighed. "Come on, boy. The sun's down. It's time you were in bed. We'll leave Nahum here overnight to contemplate the truth—and what he'll tell of it."

Before leaving, I issued orders to the two troopers assigned as guards. "I want one man with the prisoner at all times. Don't let him do anything stupid, like trying to escape or kill himself. Understood?"

They both nodded.

"And no one goes near him without my permission. No one! Not Caesar himself. Got it?"

They nodded again.

Still unsure of what I would do in the morning, I led Paulus back through the darkened camp, across the valley, and up the hill to Nazara.

Chapter XII

The sky was gray and hazy early the next morning when Aristides, Severus, and I met to go over what we had learned so far. We gathered in the front room of Mathias' house. I sat at the head of a wood plank table. The centurion and doctor occupied a bench running down one side of the same table. A platter of brown bread, a jug of wine, and three earthenware cups were set before us for breakfast. Paulus sat cross-legged on a woven mat in the far corner, close to a stack of shelves crowded with clay pots of various sizes.

I grinned. The boy had slipped in like a shadow, plainly hoping that if he stayed quiet, he wouldn't be sent away. I decided to let him be for now. At least here he was under my eye and not off raising havoc somewhere else in the village.

"Have you learned anything more from your prisoner?" Severus asked, toying with a small round loaf of bread.

"Not yet," I admitted.

"This investigation of yours is a dangerous waste of time," the centurion said. "By now the news that a Roman noble has been murdered and we're just sitting

on our backsides is racing through these hills." He
shook his head. "These Jews don't understand much,
but they know weakness when they see it."

"And so you still think I should destroy this village?
Just to demonstrate our power?" I said.

Severus nodded. "I do." He tore the loaf he was holding in half with a quick flick of his wrists. "It's the best
option. Keep that foolish farmer and the man Mathias
alive to question further if you must, but let's rid ourselves of this den of brigands or rebels before trouble
spreads."

"Brigands? Rebels?" I said skeptically. "There's no
real evidence of that."

"The senator sent for troops," the centurion pointed
out. "Why else would he do that?"

"I don't know," I said. "But then I still can't see why
the senator came here at all."

I nodded at the bare room around us. "Look, Severus.
This hovel is the house of the most important man in
Nazara. Is there anything here that's worth the attention
of a friend of Caesar's? These people are only poor
peasants."

"And Spartacus was only a slave," the centurion said
grimly, referring to the great slave revolt of nearly a
century before. It had taken three years of hard fighting
by several legions to crush the rebellious slaves.

"Spartacus was a gladiator," I corrected. "These
Galileans don't have any training in arms—or real
weapons either. Farmers using scythes and slings can't
stand up to well-equipped and well-trained soldiers.
How could they have overwhelmed your guardsmen?"

Severus shrugged irritably. "By stealth. By cunning."
He tossed the fragment of bread he'd been mauling to
one side and poured himself a cup of wine. "We know

Silanus and the others stayed here at Nazara," he continued. "But we've only the word of this Jew elder, Mathias, that they left."

"Go on," I said.

Severus stared moodily into his wine cup. "The villagers must have caught them off guard and unarmed," he said at last. "A pack of rats can pull down the finest hound—especially if they catch it alone and asleep."

"But the senator and your soldiers weren't caught asleep, at least not all of them," Paulus said from the corner.

The centurion wheeled round on him, plainly furious at being interrupted. "How do you know that, boy?" he asked. "You saw the bodies. They'd been stripped. There's no way to know whether they were attacked while armed or while in their bedclothes. Has your little Hebrew god given you some insight he hasn't shared with the rest of us?"

Paulus blushed scarlet, but he didn't retreat. "I saw the soldier in the thorns," he said stoutly.

I nodded, remembering the guardsman we'd found deep in the tangle of briers and thorns. "The boy is right, Severus. At least your comrade Cassius Celer was awake and armed."

The centurion scowled. "True." He set his cup down and shook his head. "Anyway, it doesn't matter who did the actual killing. You can't deny that these Jews were involved in some way. Those woods are too close to the village. They must have heard something when the senator and my men were being slaughtered."

Aristides spoke up for the first time. "Not necessarily."

"What does that mean?" Severus asked sharply.

"I took the time last night to examine the bodies more

closely," the doctor replied. He squinted through the open door. "And by now there should be enough light to show you what I found." The Greek smiled wryly. "If you're finished with breakfast, that is."

I looked down at the table. My appetite, never very strong in the morning, had vanished entirely.

Severus and I followed Aristides outside and down the hill to the single tent where we'd laid the mutilated remains of Silanus, his guards, and his slaves. At Paulus' urging, we'd kept the bodies some distance from Nazara to avoid inflicting ritual impurity on its inhabitants.

There were four sentries, one stationed at each corner of the tent. To ward off the stench, each man wore an incense-coated cloth over his nose and mouth. Though the nights were cool, the days up to now had been fairly hot, and the bodies were already beginning to decompose.

Aristides handed around more scraps of linen cloth and waited while Severus and I tied them in place. Then we followed the doctor inside.

I was glad my stomach was still empty. In the close confines of the tent, the sickly sweet smell of death was far worse than I remembered it from the clearing. Severus didn't shrink back. I nodded thoughtfully. I didn't like the Praetorian centurion, and doubted that I ever would, but his courage was undeniable.

Together, we watched Aristides kneel beside the ravaged corpse that had once been Decimus Junius Silanus. With the deft fingers of his left hand, he gently pried open the senator's mouth. Then, he used a small iron probe to work away at something caught between the dead man's teeth.

I craned my head, but I couldn't make out what it was. Despite the pale morning light streaming through the open flap and an oil lamp hanging from the roof beam, the tent was still only dimly lit.

"There!" Aristides said in satisfaction. He set the probe aside and held out what he'd extracted for our inspection.

It was a tiny fragment of cloth.

I whistled softly in sudden comprehension. "He was gagged!"

The doctor nodded. "They were. All except the soldier young Paulus found still in armor."

"Is that it?" Severus asked harshly, his voice strained.

Aristides shook his head. "No, Centurion, there's more." He held the senator's arms out for us to look at more closely. "You see?"

Squinting in the bad light, I noticed deep, raw abrasions on both wrists.

And then it happened . . .

Was it a waking dream? A vision? A scene conjured up by the vivid imagination I'd possessed since childhood?

Whatever their source, the images that rose before my eyes seemed so real, so immediate, that I could not move, could not speak, could not cry out. I stood frozen, forced to watch this vision in mounting horror.

It was night.

Panic-stricken, Decimus Silanus, his bodyguards, and his slaves stumbled blindly through the woods. They were bound and gagged. Men whose faces I could not see dragged them out into the clearing. Torches guttered beneath the trees, casting shadows that danced eerily across the small patch of open ground.

At a quick, muttered order, a club smashed into the

senator's face, splaying his nose into bloody ruin. A knife flashed across the upturned throat of the terrified slave pinioned next to him. It was the beginning of a scene of butchery made more horrible by the silence— a silence broken only by the soft, stifled moans of those dying and the hoarse, labored breathing of their murderers.

I shook my head frantically, trying to cast out the sickening images cascading before my eyes. They faded slowly, leaving me staring down at the twisted bodies lying in rows beneath the tent's leather roof.

A familiar voice broke in on my thoughts.

"No, I don't think there's anything more we can learn from them," Aristides was saying quietly to Severus. "Decay is too far advanced. The longer we leave these remains unburied or unburned, the greater the chance of a pestilence."

I breathed out slowly.

Neither the doctor nor the centurion had noticed anything amiss.

I considered what I had seen. Though shaken to the core of my being, I accepted the truth behind those images. That was how Silanus and the others had met their end. But this vision, if that was what it was, still left the most urgent questions I confronted unanswered.

Who had murdered them?

And why?

I left the mortuary tent and took deep breaths of the fresh, rain-scented air to clear my lungs and mind. Aristides' findings and the terrible vision they provoked raised more questions than they answered.

Silanus and eight others had been murdered while bound and gagged. That meant they had been captured first. But where had they been taken prisoner? In the village? In the woods where we'd found them? Or somewhere else? And what about Celer, the Praetorian guardsman we'd found among the thorns? He'd been stripped of his weapons, but his wrists showed no signs that he'd ever been trussed up like his comrades. Nor had he been gagged. Why not?

I shook my head, frustrated. This was like running blind through the twists and turns and dead ends of the Minotaur's labyrinth in the old Greek myth, knowing that the monster was right on my heels. I needed more information and I needed it quickly.

The doctor and Severus came out of the tent, and together we hiked back up the hill toward Nazara. Aedan joined us on the way.

The big, fair-haired Celt had two reports for me.

The first came from the scouts I'd sent out along the northwest track toward Sepphoris. If the senator and his party had come to grief along that route, I'd hoped my men might find traces of an ambush. My hopes were disappointed. The patrol had ridden all the way to Sepphoris and back—poring over every likely spot—without finding anything out of the ordinary.

"The rain?" I said.

"Heavy enough to wash away tracks," Aedan agreed. "Especially since there's a lot of bare rock along the way. Any ambush along that track would have left few signs—even without the bad weather last night."

"You should have scouted that route yesterday," Severus said. "Before the rains came."

I bit back a quick retort. The centurion must have known that his criticism was unreasonable. We hadn't found the bodies until late yesterday afternoon. Given enough men, I could have sent scouting parties willy-nilly across the Galilean countryside right away. But I didn't have enough men. As it was, I'd needed every available trooper just to search the village and its immediate surroundings before the sun went down.

The manpower situation was the focus of Aedan's second report.

Titus Marcius Taedifer had brought three cavalry troops with him from Caesarea—his own First, the Fifth, and the Seventh. Each troop should have had thirty-two soldiers in its ranks. But the Third Cavalry Regiment was so worn down by long service so far from Gaul that none mustered more than twenty men.

I didn't like that. You can only push a man so hard, and twenty cavalrymen can't do the work of more than thirty indefinitely. As a stopgap measure, I'd ordered Aedan to parcel out the twenty recruits I'd brought from Antioch among the three veteran formations.

"How'd it go?" I asked him.

"Not bad," Aedan assured me. He grinned. "To be sure, one of the hotheads groused more than a little."

"Durix?" I guessed. That young Celt had the biggest mouth of all the new troopers. But his willingness to take risks and his skills as a horseman and warrior almost made up for that.

The decurion nodded. "He told everyone who would listen that you should form the recruits into their own elite troop, that they shouldn't be paired up with a lot of broken-down old men and worn-out nags. And very eloquent Durix was, too—at least until he found himself assigned to dig latrines by one of those 'broken-down' old men."

Despite the horrors I'd seen over the past day, I smiled at the thought of the brash young recruit learning a much-needed lesson in humility.

Then something Aedan had said hit me like a hammer blow to the head. Something I'd overlooked. Something obvious.

I stopped and swore out loud. "The horses! Jupiter Best and Greatest, but I'm an idiot!"

The other three men stared at me in confusion. They looked at one another and then Aristides spoke for them all. "What exactly are you talking about, Lucius?"

"The horses!" I said again. "Where are the horses and other animals belonging to Silanus and his men?"

Their confusion cleared, replaced by dawning comprehension.

"By the Lady," Aedan said. "The prefect's right. Ten men are dead. That's ten animals missing."

"More," Severus said tersely. "The senator had two remounts for himself—very fine steeds he bought in Antioch. Plus another four or five mules to carry his personal baggage."

"That's sixteen or seventeen horses and mules," I said, adding them up. "So where are they?"

Aedan frowned. "Not in the village, that's sure. These people have a few oxen they share when plowing and a handful of donkeys. Nothing more."

"Then the Jews must have sold them," Severus said flatly, still stubbornly holding on to the belief that the villagers had ambushed and slaughtered his men. "And why not? More profit for them."

"Where could you sell so many animals all at once?" I wondered aloud. "Not in any of these hill towns. From what I've seen, they're all too poor and far too small."

The centurion scowled. "Sepphoris, then. It's a royal city and fairly large as things go out here."

"How large?"

Severus shrugged. "They say the amphitheater there

can seat five thousand. I suppose there might be twice that many living in the city as a whole."

I considered that. Sepphoris was sure to have a bustling marketplace. Even so, anyone trying to get rid of nearly twenty horses and mules in short order, some quite valuable, should have drawn attention. It was worth checking.

I turned to Aedan and told him to take a detachment to Sepphoris to make inquiries at the marketplace there. I wanted him back by the next afternoon at the latest.

Severus looked at me. "And what will you do in the meantime? Try to tickle more answers out of that lying farmer you're holding?"

I shook my head. I'd already decided to postpone interrogating Nahum for a while longer. I wanted the chance to talk to more of his friends and neighbors before tackling him again. And there were other questions I wanted to ask them. In the back of my mind, I was beginning to doubt that the villagers were guilty of serious involvement in Silanus' murder. Still, something in or around Nazara must have triggered the massacre.

The Praetorian officer frowned when he heard that. "Then, with your permission, I'd like to accompany the decurion."

I raised an eyebrow. "Oh? Why?"

"Some of the contacts I made with Herod's officials could prove useful," Severus said. "Someone trying to sell that many animals could have attracted the notice of his tax-gatherers."

That made sense, too.

"Any help you can give Aedan would be much appreciated, Aemilius Severus," I said, trying to conceal my surprise.

Did he really want to aid my efforts to find and punish the senator's murderers? Much as I wanted to believe that, it seemed unlikely. Severus was too ambitious—and probably too determined to erase any traces of his failure to protect Silanus. He must know that he couldn't dictate the contents of any report to Tiberius Caesar or the Praetorian prefect while I controlled the investigation.

Aristides echoed my thoughts later, while watching Aedan, Severus, and six cavalrymen trot out of Nazara, heading northwest toward the city. He looked worried. "That man is up to something, Lucius."

"I know," I said quietly. "I'm fairly certain our friend the centurion plans to try persuading one of the tetrarch's officers to put him in charge here."

"And you still let him go?"

"How could I stop him?" I shrugged. "At least this way, Aedan will have his help while tracking the senator's missing horses."

"What if Severus comes back with the mandate he's looking for," the doctor asked. "Would you just stand aside and let him destroy this village?"

That was the big question. I gained nothing from protecting these Galileans against Severus and his desire for revenge—nothing save a clear conscience. But if the centurion's worst fears were right, if my reluctance to conduct a reprisal for the senator's murder encouraged an open revolt against Herod and our authority, no one could save me. Not my father's influence. Not Germanicus. No one.

At last, I gave the doctor my answer. "No, Aristides, I will not stand aside," I said. "I gave my oath to the emperor and the Senate. But I won't take orders from Herod's petty officials."

*   *   *

"You plan to do what?" Paulus was incredulous.

"We're going to talk to the villagers," I told him again. "About the murders. About what Nahum might have been doing in those woods. And about the senator and his strange questions."

"Aurelius Valens," the boy said with exaggerated patience. "There are sixty or seventy separate households in Nazara. Do you have any idea of how long it would take us to interrogate them all?"

I resisted the urge to clout him in the ear. It was difficult. Very difficult. Every time I started to think favorably of Paulus, he found a new way to annoy me.

"I don't plan to talk to them all," I said. "Just the men most likely to have the answers I'm looking for."

"And who are they?" Paulus asked, not bothering to hide his belief that I was an idiot for even contemplating this course of action.

I ticked them off on my fingers. "The elders of the assembly. Nahum's closest neighbors. And anyone living on the edge of the village closest to those woods."

"Well, that makes sense, I suppose," the boy admitted, but he did it grudgingly.

"Your vote of confidence is duly noted," I said dryly.

"It's still ridiculous," he insisted. "These villagers understand the threat they're under. If they knew anything of value, surely you'd have heard it by now!"

Not hiding my anger now, I ran through the steps I was already taking. Besides sending Aedan off to Sepphoris, I'd ordered yet another search of the woods. Other patrols were out combing the neighboring towns and hills. And Aristides was going over every inch of every corpse one last time. "Can you add anything to that list, boy?" I said sharply. "Anything at all?"

For a moment, Paulus met my gaze head-on. At last, he sighed and lowered his eyes. "No."

I wasn't quite ready to let him off the hook. "Would you rather translate Nahum's screams while I have him whipped?"

He shook his head quickly.

I nodded. "Then come with me."

And so, with Paulus at my side, I began interrogating the other men of the village — moving from the highest, the elders of the assembly, to the farmers, and then to the lowest, the simple craftsmen.

One by one, they earnestly denied any involvement in the massacre. They couldn't tell me why the senator would spend so much time asking such odd questions in Nazara, or in any of the other hill towns. And no one, no matter how hard I pressed them, could offer a reasonable explanation for Nahum's strange behavior.

As evening drew near, it was beginning to look as though Paulus' pessimism was justified. More and more it appeared that I would be forced to have Nahum tortured into telling me the truth.

About two hours before sunset, we arrived at a run-down dwelling on the outskirts of the village. Several poor families shared the small, flat-roofed house. Dark volcanic stones were piled one on top of another, forming its outer walls. From the alley outside a narrow gate led into a tiny courtyard containing a common oven, a millstone for grinding wheat and barley, and a cistern.

Other doors opened into this courtyard, one from each family's pair of rooms. Three young women were at work there, preparing the evening meal. Four or five small children chased each other around and about their mothers, laughing and shrieking in delight. When they caught sight of my tunic and scarlet military cloak, they fell silent, staring up at me with wide, fearful eyes.

Despite our growing fatigue and irritation, Paulus and I moved from room to room, going over my list of questions with the oldest man in each family. Again and again we heard the same denials, the same protestations of innocence and ignorance.

I was tired and hungry and thirsty, and almost ready to admit defeat by the time we came to the last man in the house.

He was a young woodworker who lived in the smallest, shabbiest pair of rooms with his widowed mother. To my relief, he spoke a rough, plain form of Greek—a tongue I assumed he'd learned while working on one of the tetrarch's grandiose building projects in nearby Sepphoris.

His name, he told us, was Yeshua.

The Galilean craftsman was about my age, or at most a year or two older. He was about my height. His hair was brown and so were his eyes. I couldn't see much that would distinguish him from any one of a half dozen other young men in the village.

We interviewed him in the front room of his meager lodgings. A bench covered with a simple set of carpenter's tools—a couple of chisels, a saw, a mallet, and a plane for shaving wood—made it clear that he worked out of this tiny chamber. The thin straw pallet in one corner showed that he slept there, too.

Before I began, Yeshua handed me a battered clay cup of well-watered wine to quench my thirst. I thanked him and took a small sip, more as a courtesy than anything else. No one else we'd spoken to that whole day had dared to offer us as much. The wine, as I'd expected, wasn't very good. It was sour, probably the dregs of the last press, but I suspected it was the best vintage he had.

Paulus waved it away. He looked embarrassed. He was more used to offering alms to the poor than accepting hospitality from them. "My father's servants have better quarters, food, and drink than this," he muttered to me.

Except for a slight, sad smile, Yeshua ignored the boy's evident unease. I was grateful for that. Poor though this Galilean plainly was, that wasn't any reason to shame him.

But when I began asking him my questions, his answers didn't shed any more light on the massacre in the woods.

The Galilean just shook his head. "I'm afraid that I didn't see anything of what happened there with my own eyes. And I heard nothing with my own ears."

Nor would he make any guess about why Silanus had come to Nazara. "This senator of yours never spoke to me," he said simply.

Frustrated, I said pointedly, "You choose your words very carefully!"

Yeshua spread his hands. "What I say is the truth. Beyond that I may not yet go."

Stung by my failure to learn anything of use throughout the day, I replied more harshly than I intended. "You must know that I could have you questioned more rigorously. And far more painfully."

The Galilean nodded. "That is so." Then he smiled. "But you think yourself a just man, Lucius Aurelius Valens, do you not? What you've heard from my lips is the truth. If you believe that, why beat me?"

I was struck silent—staggered both by the self-

confidence of this simple craftsman and by the knowledge that he was right.

I was beginning to realize there was something unusual about this young carpenter after all. The other villagers I'd interrogated had been afraid of me. They
knew that my soldiers and I held their freedom, their
lands, and their lives in our hands. But Yeshua, though
one of the poorest men in Nazara, showed no fear—not
even the slightest apprehension.

Paulus stared at the two of us, surprised by my continuing silence. At last, he asked his own question. "If
you don't know why the senator came here or why he
was murdered, can you at least tell us why Nahum acted
so strangely? Why he left his own land during the harvest and rushed off to those woods?"

The carpenter shook his head. "Again, of my own
knowledge, I cannot tell you why Nahum would do such
a thing."

Paulus sighed. I realized that he hadn't expected
much from Yeshua and his low expectations were being
met.

The Galilean smiled, unfazed by the boy's disappointment. "But I think you'll learn that my mother
can."

I found my voice again. "Then I'd like to speak to
her."

Yeshua went to the doorway connecting their two
small rooms and invited his mother to join us.

She wore a long robe of faded blue, belted at the
waist. A simple shawl loosely confined her long, dark
hair. Despite the poverty of her surroundings, she had an
air of grace, of calm assurance, that would have been
envied by the most fashionable women of Rome.

Her name was Miryam.

When I asked her why Nahum had left his fields at harvest, she told me quietly, "The answer you seek is simple. Nahum went to the grove expecting to meet a woman and to find pleasure."

Puzzled, I asked, "An illicit tryst? Why didn't he just tell us that himself, and save himself from further peril?"

"Because the woman involved is the wife of another man," Miryam said.

I nodded slowly, at last understanding my prisoner's dilemma and the reason for his lies. Nahum could only prove that he wasn't connected to Silanus' murder by condemning himself for adultery. In Rome, such behavior would likely result in public shame and a disgraceful divorce. These Jews, however, adhered to a far more rigid code.

I looked at Yeshua and his mother. "I must speak to this woman."

Miryam shook her head. "I'm afraid that's not possible. She is no longer in Nazara."

"Where is she?"

"We sent her away to stay with her kinsmen in another village. She will not return until she is ready to resist Nahum's advances and live chastely."

"We?" I asked abruptly.

"The women of Nazara," Miryam answered softly, with the hint of a smile. "You would have done better, Prefect, to ask your questions about Nahum the Passionate, Nahum the Fool, of us—and not of the men."

Despite the irritation I felt at having been so far astray, I grinned crookedly, acknowledging the justice of her gentle criticism. I'd never thought to question Nazara's women. I'd jumped too easily to the common assumption that they were of no real account. My own mother would have been very quick to point out my error, I realized. And so would the lady Agrippina.

Paulus, however, wasn't so easily assuaged.

He frowned at Miryam. "You take too much on yourselves! If this woman is an adulteress, she should be tried by the assembly, condemned, and put to death!"

Yeshua turned toward the boy. "Should we stone her, Saul?"

Paulus flushed red. I remembered that was his cherished Hebrew name. How the carpenter guessed it, I cannot say.

"That is the Law," he answered stoutly.

"That is the Law," Yeshua agreed. He rose to his feet and left the room, returning a moment later with something held in his hands. He gave it to Paulus.

The boy stared down at the sharp, jagged edges of a rock evidently plucked from the courtyard just outside.

"Have you ever done anything that is wrong, Saul? Anything that is shameful?" Yeshua asked him.

Paulus clutched the rock tightly. "If I have, I have been punished!"

"For everything that you have done?" the carpenter said quietly. "And to the full measure of the Law?"

After a long pause, Paulus turned even redder. Then his fingers opened and the rock tumbled to the hard-packed dirt floor.

"Let the one who is without sin of his own cast the first stone," Miryam said, smiling in approval.

Angry and embarrassed, the boy rushed outside, leaving me behind to apologize for his rudeness — and to thank Yeshua and his mother for their help.

Considering what I'd just learned, I walked back toward Mathias' house. I stopped suddenly. I knew that I'd begun my interrogation of Yeshua in Greek. But now

I was seized by the strange conviction that he had been speaking to me all along in the purest Latin, and with the learning of a scholar. That was impossible, and I knew it, but I could not remember our conversation in any other way, no matter how hard I tried.

Later that evening, when I hesitantly asked Paulus for his impression of the carpenter's speech, the boy shook his head.

"Latin?" he snorted. "I heard none. Even the fellow's 'Greek' was barely fit for haggling in the marketplace." He frowned, clenching the fist that had held the rock. "And for all the air of wisdom and learning you claim to have seen, this Yeshua was of no real use. Nor were any of the other villagers we questioned."

I couldn't deny that.

I could cross Nahum off a list of suspects in Silanus' murder. But I didn't have anyone else to put in his place. The men my vision had shown me were still faceless. And I wasn't any closer to understanding why the senator had come to Nazara in the first place.

Chapter XIII

Aedan and Severus returned to Nazara around noon the next day.

I met them at the edge of the village. "Any luck?"

The Praetorian centurion shot me a dark look. Without replying, he swung down out of the saddle and tossed the reins of his horse to one of Aedan's troopers.

"Well?" I asked again.

"We found nothing!" he growled. "It was a fool's errand from beginning to end."

With that, Severus stalked off in the direction of the house he'd commandeered as his quarters. I watched the centurion go with some amusement. It appeared that my credit with him had fallen to a new low.

"Now there's a fellow I'm of two minds about," Aedan murmured from beside my shoulder.

I glanced at the decurion. "In what way?"

He frowned. "I don't know whether I'd rather wave farewell to that Praetorian bastard and see him off to Rome, or whether I'd feel safer with him up close and under my watchful eye."

I nodded. Aedan's thoughts paralleled my own. Severus' little jabs and criticisms and his insistence that

I should slaughter the villagers in immediate reprisal were a constant irritant and a continuing challenge to my authority. But when he was here at least I had some idea of what he was up to. His absence had proved more worrying. I'd slept poorly the night before, imagining him riding in from Sepphoris with orders from Herod Antipas to destroy Nazara and its people.

"He's right about one thing, though," Aedan continued. "We didn't pick up any trace of the senator's horses or other animals."

The Celt filled me in on what he'd managed to learn in a day spent trudging round the marketplace in Sepphoris. His inquiries among the several horse dealers hadn't yielded much more than a collection of negatives. No one had sold or even tried to sell so many animals recently. Officers from Herod's garrison had purchased two or three remounts in the past week, but none matched the descriptions Severus had provided.

"There's more," Aedan said. "I asked about Silanus and his party at the city gates. The sentries remembered them riding out into the hills several days before. But no one saw them return."

I winced. It was the same story wherever I seemed to turn. I had ten murdered men on my hands, but no witnesses and almost no real evidence. I was sure now that the senator, his slaves, and his bodyguards had left Nazara three days before. After that, they'd vanished without a trace—only to turn up dead a few hundred paces from where I stood.

So far, every patrol I'd sent out to probe the surrounding towns and countryside had come back empty-handed. Between the recent rains and the rocky ground, the scouts hadn't been able to find any traces of an ambush, or even the movement of a large band of men. Nor had they seen any signs of a bandit camp in the area.

"What about Severus?" I asked. "Did he turn up any news from the tetrarch's officials?"

Aedan snorted and shook his head. "Not a whisper. Not that he told to me at any rate. Oh, the centurion went scurrying to the palace fast enough. For a fact, he looked like a lovesick boy dashing off to meet a willing girl. But he soon came roaring back in a terrible, wicked temper."

"Herod's men wouldn't help him?"

The decurion smiled wryly. "Nobody important enough was there, it seems. The tetrarch has gone off to a new royal city he's building on the shores of the Sea of Galilee, and he's taken most of his court with him."

I raised an eyebrow. "When?"

"Three days ago."

Interesting, I thought. So Herod Antipas and his ranking officials had left Sepphoris on the same day Silanus left Nazara. Was there a connection beyond coincidence? Probably not. Their paths should not have crossed. Still, it was something to consider.

But there was something else to bear in mind first, I realized. I was fairly sure that Severus had rushed to the palace for his own purposes, and not for mine. He must have hoped to obtain an order from Herod giving him a free hand here. The tetrarch's absence would have thwarted that ambition, which explained why the centurion had come back in such a foul temper.

So how long would it be before Severus found some reason to follow Herod to the Sea of Galilee? Not long at all, I suspected.

*   *   *

Aristides, Aedan, and I met over the evening meal. Paulus joined us. To my relief, Severus did not.

The fare was very plain—a dish of stewed lentils and onions, bread, and a small plate of figs—yet it was filling. For a time the four of us ate in silence, intent on satisfying our hunger before turning our minds to more serious matters.

The doctor spoke first. He tapped the dish of lentils with his spoon. "We'll starve these people if we stay here much longer, Lucius. They don't have the surplus to feed a hundred extra mouths and more than a hundred animals for long. As it is, they'll be tightening their belts long before the winter's over."

I nodded. "I'm aware of that." I looked around the table before going on. "That's why I've decided to begin requisitioning the food and fodder we need from Herod's granaries and military storehouses in Sepphoris, starting tomorrow."

Aedan put his wine cup down. "Which means you've made up your mind that the villagers played no part in the murder of Silanus and his men," he said quietly.

I nodded again. "That's right. I said once that I wouldn't punish the innocent to deter the guilty. I meant it."

"Does the Praetorian know about this?" Aristides asked.

"Not yet."

"He won't like it," the doctor warned.

I shrugged. "I'm here to learn the truth, not to appease Marcus Aemilius Severus."

"Brave words, Lucius." Aristides looked worried. "But can you back them up? Can you prove that the people of Nazara didn't commit this crime?"

"Prove it? Beyond all doubt?" I shook my head and

then pushed my empty plate to the side. "But the facts we do have all point away from Nazara, and not toward it."

My three companions listened intently while I ran through my reasoning—perhaps as much to convince myself again as to persuade them. If the people of Nazara had murdered Silanus and the others, where were the senator's possessions? Where were the armor and weapons of his Praetorian bodyguards? And where were their horses and pack mules?

"Couldn't the animals have been turned loose to roam the hills?" Aristides wondered.

"Unlikely," I said. "Trained horses don't ordinarily wander very far afield. Even if murderers chased them off, they'd have stopped running somewhere close by. Our scouts would have found them."

No one disagreed.

"Then there are the bodies," I said. "If people in this village butchered the senator and the others, why were the corpses left without burial? Why take the chance that someone else might stumble across them—as Nahum, in fact, did?"

Aedan leaned forward. "Maybe they didn't have time," he suggested. "Digging graves isn't easy work."

The doctor shook his head. "There was time," he said. "Anyone living in the village could have finished the job. Silanus and the others were dead some hours before we found them."

"Nearly a full day," I commented, remembering my vision. "I think they were slaughtered the night before by torchlight."

Aristides gave me an odd look, but he let that pass. I realized I hadn't told him about the frightening vision that had flashed before my eyes in the mortuary tent.

"Or the villagers could have tumbled them into a tomb or a cave," I said. "We know there are several within easy reach."

Paulus spoke up excitedly. "Then the murderers were strangers, men who couldn't let themselves be seen by the villagers!"

He noticed our eyes on him, blushed, and stammered to a stop.

"Go on," I said gently. "Tell us what you mean, Paulus."

"Well, you see, that would explain why the bodies weren't buried," the boy said hesitantly. "Because the killers had to leave the area long before the sun came up, before the farmers here saw them and began asking awkward questions."

The rest of us nodded. What Paulus said made sense.

"And last," I argued, "could so terrible a deed be kept secret in a village so small? Most of these Galileans are related to one another in some fashion. Is it really possible that ten or fifteen or twenty of them could butcher a Roman noble, his slaves, and his guards and hope to keep the news from spreading among their kindred? From rippling outward from brother to father, from uncles to cousins?"

"No," Aedan said, rubbing his jaw. "Such a thing is not possible."

"You seem very sure of that," the doctor said skeptically.

Aedan shrugged. "I grew up in a place in Gaul that wasn't much bigger. And we had a saying there: 'Shout to the moon! Howl to the winds! But a whisper round the village well is louder than all such bellowing!'"

The tall, fair-haired Celt grinned. "By the Lady, that was true, too! When I was a boy of fourteen summers, I

kissed a girl betrothed to the old chief's son. In secret . . . or so I thought. The pity of it was, the news was
on the wing almost before our lips parted."

"What happened?" Paulus asked him, clearly interested.

"I decided it might be safer to take up the soldier's
trade," Aedan answered, grinning wider. "And so it was.
And so here I am."

"Fascinating," Aristides said dryly. He turned back to
me. "Very well, the villagers are innocent of this massacre. I accept your reasoning. But that still leaves us
with a rather serious problem, doesn't it?"

I nodded. "It does. If the people of Nazara didn't kill
Silanus and his followers, then who did?"

"Perhaps a band of rebels or brigands," Aedan said.
"This senator of yours was sniffing around Galilee for
signs of trouble. Well, maybe the man found more than
he bargained for."

"But our scouts haven't spotted anything that smacks
of a rebel movement in this area," I pointed out, thinking back over what I'd observed in my service along the
Rhine. "No hidden camps. No groups of armed men
drilling. No caches of weapons or armor."

"True enough," the decurion said seriously. "But
watch." He took a piece of bread, tore it into small
pieces, and scattered the resulting crumbs across the
table in front of him. "Nazara is only one of many towns
in these hills. Say only two or three men in each village
are involved. Most of the time, they're just simple farmers like all the rest of these Galileans. And when apart,
they're almost invisible . . ."

I nodded grimly. "Go on."

"But then a signal is given," Aedan said. He swept all
the crumbs back together into a mass. "They swarm

down from their separate places, strike, and then disperse again, leaving no real trace for us to find or follow."

I pondered that. It was possible. I said as much aloud.

Aristides grimaced. "I hope not. Rebellions are an ugly, useless business full of waste, butchery, and cruelty." His jaw tightened. "By the gods, that's a lesson these people should have learned only too well!"

When I asked what he meant, the doctor told us he'd spent some time during the day talking to Mathias and the other village elders. That didn't surprise me. Aristides made it his habit to question locals about the medicines and techniques used by their healers. He had often told me that his art grew by the slow and steady accumulation of knowledge. So he sought new cures wherever they could be found.

In this case, his inquiries had proved fruitless. The Jews in Nazara tended to rely on folk remedies that were already known to him, or on prayers to their god.

Once that was clear, his conversation with the elders had shifted to the history of their people and their village. Histories of all kinds also fascinated the Greek doctor, an interest I had long since learned to share.

Twenty-three years ago, he told us, somewhere around the time I was busy being born, Herod the Great died, leaving the region in turmoil. Tired of their old ruler's lavish building projects, his "impiety," and his excessive taxation, the people of Galilee and Judea rose in revolt against his three sons.

"The Galileans rallied around a man called Judas and named him their king," Aristides reported. "They say his father had fought earlier against Herod himself."

But Judas and his new "kingdom" hadn't survived for long.

Within a month, the governor of Syria had gathered a powerful force of legions and auxiliary troops and marched to crush the rebellion. Most of the soldiers headed for Judea, but a strong detachment burned its way across Galilee, wiping out villages and taking slaves wherever it went. Thousands of Jews were crucified and left hanging on crosses until they rotted. Thousands more, including many people from Nazara, fled deeper into the hills and hid. Some went even farther, to Egypt or the other provinces, spending years abroad before they dared to return. Every village and family in Galilee still bore the scars left by our terrible vengeance.

Listening to Aristides tell the story, Paulus looked sick.

I knew what he was feeling. So far, the boy from Tarsus had led a privileged life. He'd been born in a prosperous city in a favored province, one sheltered from some of the darker aspects of our rule. But now he was being forced to confront the harsh measures sometimes required to keep the Roman peace.

Unlike Paulus, I understood the need for those measures. War against the German tribes had taught me the need to hit hard and swiftly. Short, brutal, and victorious campaigns are kinder in the end than bloody, drawn-out stalemates. Even so, much of what Aristides described seemed senseless—pure viciousness and cruelty for its own sake.

"Who commanded this expedition?" I wondered.

"Quinctilius Varus was governor of Syria then," the doctor said coolly.

I snorted. "Varus the blockhead!"

That explained the unnecessary destruction. Quinctilius Varus had been the kind of incompetent general who relied on brute force to make up for his own shortcomings as a strategist and tactician. Ten years ago, long after Varus had laid waste to Galilee, Augustus had made the mistake of putting him in charge in Germany.

The idiot promptly led his troops into an ambush in the trackless, rain-soaked German forests. In a running battle, the barbarians slaughtered three full legions and several regiments of auxiliaries. More than twenty thousand men were lost. It was the worst disaster suffered by Rome in fifty years. I had gained my first military experience during Germanicus' attempts to restore the frontier and to retrieve some semblance of honor from the humiliation of Varus' defeat.

We all sat in silence for a time after Aristides finished his account, each thinking his own grim thoughts.

Paulus stirred. "Perhaps Silanus came hunting a successor to this Judas the rebel," he said reluctantly. "A son. Or a grandson. Someone who might take up the struggle again. Certainly, that would explain his strange interest in ancestry and bloodlines."

The doctor shrugged. "Mathias and the others claim Judas and his whole family were either killed in battle or captured and executed. But I suppose some of them might have escaped in all the chaos and carnage."

"It's still madness," Aedan said, frowning. "Herod Antipas has officials and soldiers in great numbers and all the reason in the world to secure his own throne. Even if there were whispers of a rebel heir abroad in the land, why send a senator all the way from Rome to seek him out?"

None of us had an answer for that.

I woke suddenly.

For a moment I lay still, my heart pounding. Something had roused me from a restless, troubled sleep. But what?

Was it only the vestige of a nightmare now dwindling to nothing? Or had I half heard a sound, some sign of danger, while drifting between slumber and consciousness? Was there an intruder standing close at hand, poised to strike me down? The image of Silanus' mutilated face rose in my mind. I shivered, chilled by the memory.

Moving carefully, with infinite patience, I felt along the floor beside the narrow cot. My fingers found and closed on the hilt of my sword. Reassured, I breathed out softly.

Then I waited, listening.

Nothing.

I opened my eyes. The room was empty.

My heart slowed, but it was too late—any thought of further sleep had fled. Whether mere nightmare or distant noise, something had tugged my mind fully awake.

I rolled out of the cot and stood up. Then I donned my tunic, cloak, and sandals, and slung the sheathed sword over my shoulder. Quietly, I stepped out into the common room of the house I shared with Aedan, Aristides, and Paulus. Snores from the other chambers told me that whatever had roused me had passed the others by.

Still moving lightly, I crossed to the outer door and eased it open. The sky outside was pitch-dark, speckled with stars. The moon was down. Only a faint hint of gray in the east signaled the coming dawn.

I stepped outside—startling the cavalryman Aedan had posted there as a sentry. He'd been dozing, leaning against the rough stone wall of the house.

The Gaul straightened up in a hurry. "Nothing to report, sir," he muttered nervously. "Everything's quiet."

The trooper had good reason to be worried. Falling asleep on watch was a serious offense, one that would subject him to harsh punishment if I chose to press charges.

I looked closely at the sentry. It was Litas, one of the young recruits I'd brought south from Antioch. Since he wasn't one of the veterans who should have known better, I decided to be lenient. This time. I made a mental note to have Aedan assign him extra duty. Maybe several days spent shoveling horse manure with the servants would remind him to take his duties as a soldier more seriously.

I nodded down the narrow alley leading deeper into the village. "I'm going for a walk." I eyed the young Gaul sharply. "Stay at your post. And this time stay awake!"

He swallowed hard. "Yes, Prefect."

With that, I strode off into the darkness. I'd tried telling myself that whatever had woken me wasn't important. But some intuition told me there was trouble abroad in Nazara this night. And my grandfather had always encouraged me to rely on my instincts, especially in the dark. "You're a Roman, Lucius. A child of the wolf," he would say. "The day is a time for the eyes and for reason. Once the sun is down, life is different. Like the wolf, you must trust your ears, your nose, and even the hairs on the back of your neck. Let them guide you."

I moved through the gaps between the houses, picking my way carefully over rough ground, pausing now and again to listen carefully. For a time, I heard nothing out of place, nothing unusual.

And then a noise came. At first, it was only a faint

whimper wafting on the breeze, so soft that it seemed more imagined than real.

I stopped, turning my head from side to side, listening intently.

I heard it again, louder this time. Now it was a low, terrified moan. I frowned. Something about that sound spoke of a woman in pain.

The muffled cry came again, emanating from a house not far away. I put my hand on the hilt of my sword and moved in that direction. I stopped outside a door faintly outlined by the flickering light of a lamp inside. My pulse accelerated. My instincts had led me to the right place. Someone else was awake in Nazara after all.

But who? And what were they doing?

I drew the sword out of the scabbard at my side and stood thinking for a moment. Should I call for help?

No, I decided. Rousing my men from their quarters across the village would take too much time and make too much noise. I didn't want to give whoever was behind that door a chance to slip away without being caught.

A voice spoke, snarling a command in a tone full of cold menace and unmistakable cruelty. Hearing it froze the blood in my veins.

It was time to move.

I reached out with my left hand and gently tested the door. It was latched from the inside.

I took a deep breath, nerving myself up. Then I aimed a swift, powerful kick at the door. It shuddered, sagging back against the shattered latch. I slammed the ball of my foot into it again. This time it crashed open.

Without hesitating, I threw myself through the opening and into the small room beyond, with my sword out and ready to deflect any blows aimed my way.

None came.

Instead, I found myself standing face-to-face with Araneus.

The tall, shaven-headed astrologer stared at me in shock. He held a long, thin-bladed dagger loosely in his right hand, very close to the flame of an oil lamp. A young girl sat huddled in a corner of the room beside a table piled high with scrolls. Tears stained her terror-stricken face. Her eyes were wild and unfocused. Her long black hair was a tangled mess. Several strands of it dangled from the clenched fingers of the astrologer's left hand.

For a moment I did nothing, resisting the battle fury roaring through me. I'd hurtled through the door expecting a fight, and now every fiber of my being urged me to hack Araneus down.

The astrologer's face darkened with rage. "Get out!" he hissed. "You have no business here!"

Recovering, I raised my sword, bringing the tip right up and under the astrologer's narrow, bony jaw. "You're wrong," I said flatly. "Now drop the dagger or we'll both find out how well you breathe with a gaping hole in your throat."

His eyes widened. He let the blade fall out of his hand. It tumbled to the floor.

Still holding the sword at his throat, I backed Araneus up against the wall. He stood pinned there, unable to move without spitting himself on my blade. The girl stared at us both, still shaking in fright.

Now I could summon help.

A shout brought soldiers running, first Litas, and then some of his comrades. I nodded toward the astrologer. "Tie him up!"

Araneus started to spit curses at me, vile incantations

naming dark goddesses and gods. "You interfering whelp! May Hecate drink your blood! Seth bind your tongue and soul! Anubis swallow you!"

The girl moaned.

I was too angry to feel frightened. "And gag the bastard as well," I snapped.

My troopers obeyed quickly, shutting off the astrologer's ugly flow of dire threats with a piece of cloth torn from his own robes. He writhed against the bonds holding him, but two of the Celts slammed him back against the wall and held him there. "Get him out of here!" I ordered. "Take him back to my quarters."

They hustled Araneus outside and into the darkness.

Awakened by the clamor, Aedan, Aristides, and then Paulus pushed into the small room. They listened in silence to my report of what I'd found, but anger and disgust were plain on their faces. I was glad to see them, especially the boy. From what I could make out through the girl's weeping, she spoke only Aramaic.

I sent the decurion back to our quarters with orders to make sure the astrologer was held under close guard. "Don't let him speak to anyone, Aedan," I said tightly. "Not a soldier. Not a villager. And not Severus. Right?"

The Celt nodded grimly and left.

"Paulus," I said next. "I need you to talk to the girl. Try to find out what's been happening here—what this so-called astrologer has been doing or demanding. But go easy, understand?"

His eyes huge in the lamplight, the boy swallowed convulsively. Then he nodded. He walked gingerly over to the crying girl and knelt beside her. She sat with her face buried in her knees, rocking back and forth, still clearly terrified almost out of her wits. He began speaking to her in a soft, urgent voice.

Aristides spread his hands. "And what of me, Lucius?"

I grinned at him, feeling myself relax for the first time since I'd come crashing through that locked door. "What about you, Doctor?"

He shrugged. "You seem in a fine mood for issuing orders. I thought you might have some for me."

It was true, I realized. After floundering through the morass of doubt and uncertainty surrounding the senator's murder, it was a relief to be able to act swiftly and decisively—though to what ultimate end I wasn't sure.

Severus, the Praetorian centurion, had told me that Araneus had his own powerful allies in Tiberius' inner circle. If that were true, I would have to watch my step in dealing with him. I knew one thing, though. By standing between Severus and the reprisal he demanded, I had essentially placed the village and all of its inhabitants under my protection. And friend of Caesar or not, I would not allow this so-called astrologer to play his weird sadistic games unchecked.

My eye fell on the scrolls heaped on the table. So Araneus had brought the fruits of his vaunted mystical research with him to Nazara. I decided it would be worth knowing a bit more about this mysterious quest he was on for his master Thrasyllus. I jerked a thumb in their direction. "If you want a task, Aristides, see if you can make some sense of those."

The Greek doctor picked up one of the scrolls and unrolled it. He whistled softly. "This isn't going to be easy." He held it out for me to examine.

I scanned it quickly and saw what he meant. The papyrus was filled with an almost illegible jumble of astrological symbols, different scripts, and odd drawings. I handed the scroll back to him.

"It's some kind of secret writing," Aristides said, more to himself than to me. He tapped a few lines. "A mixture of Greek and Latin here . . . some other language there . . . perhaps Chaldean?" His forehead wrinkled. "I make no promises, Lucius."

I nodded. "I understand. But do your best." I clapped him gently on the shoulder. "After all, you're the one who likes puzzles of all kinds, or so you claim."

Aristides nodded absentmindedly, already gathering up an armload of the astrologer's scrolls.

"Aurelius Valens?" Paulus said tentatively.

I turned back to him. He had taken off his own cloak and draped it over the shivering young girl's shoulders. She still sat huddled in the corner, but at least she looked calmer now. "What have you learned?" I asked.

"Her name is Sarah," Paulus said. "She's the daughter of one of the village elders. Araneus insisted that she act as his servant during his time here, and no one felt able to refuse him."

I nodded. It was a common enough arrangement.

"For the most part, her duties were bearable—fetching water, preparing his meals, and the like," Paulus reported. "She says the astrologer was harsh and quick to criticize, but no more than that. Until tonight."

"And what happened then?" I asked.

"He began hammering her for information about the village and the families in it," the boy answered. "He wanted to know about their ancestry. Were there any priestly families living here? Who had been born outside Galilee? What signs were they born under? And more in that same vein."

"Much the same information Silanus sought," I said.

Paulus nodded somberly.

"Did the girl have answers for him?"

The boy shook his head. "Not many. Sarah told him what little she could, but she says Araneus demanded still more. He threatened her with dire punishment and torture." He scowled. "His threats were serious. Her arms are covered with bruises, cuts, and burns."

I felt my face turn red with anger, both at Araneus and at myself. I'd been so busy probing Silanus' death that I'd paid no attention to whatever mischief that shaven-headed bastard might be up to behind my back. His strange looks and uncanny manner had so unnerved me that I'd been glad enough to let him go his own way. This poor girl had paid the price for my carelessness and fear.

"Take Sarah home to her father, Paulus," I said quietly. "Assure him that he will have compensation for the wrong done to his daughter, and that I will punish the malefactor myself. Tell him I swear all this on my honor as a Roman knight."

"What can you do? He's a citizen. Can you bring a case against him at Caesarea?" the boy asked uncertainly. "Will a Roman magistrate really care anything about a poor farmer's daughter?"

"Probably not," I admitted. "But our law forbids the vile use of magic, of spells and incantations. And Araneus tried to curse me earlier, in front of witnesses. If need be, I'll charge him with sorcery and prosecute him myself."

In the back of my mind I wondered whether or not I could fulfill that promise. In theory, the laws were applied impartially to all citizens. In practice, the emperor had tremendous power to see that courts accepted his interpretation of important cases. For a time after succeeding Augustus, Tiberius had scrupulously avoided interfering in the courts. But now? Would he really refrain from tipping the scales if the case involved a disciple of one of his closest cronies?

I did what I could to stave off those doubts. Rome and the emperor were a long way off. Right now, I had both the power and the responsibility to uphold the law as I understood it. That was enough.

I swung round on my heel and marched out the door. I had a few questions of my own for this so-called astrologer.

Unfortunately, it didn't take long for me to realize that I'd made a mistake in waiting to interrogate Araneus. He was made of stronger stuff than the farmer Nahum. The delay had only given him time to recover his wits and his balance.

"My master stands high in the emperor's favor. Who protects you?" he sneered as soon as Aedan yanked the gag out of his mouth.

I ignored the challenge. "Why are you here in Nazara?"

The astrologer drew himself up haughtily. "You have no right to ask me such a question."

"I have every right," I pointed out evenly. "A Roman senator lies murdered. It is my duty to capture and punish those responsible."

"You accuse me of this crime?" Araneus nodded toward his bound arms. "Do you see wings? I was in Caesarea Maritima when Silanus met his destined fate. A dozen men saw me there."

I shook my head. "I make no such accusation."

"Then release me at once!" the astrologer demanded. "My research is vital to the emperor and to Rome."

"Torturing a young woman?" I said, not bothering to hide my disdain. "You consider that important work?"

He shrugged. "I do what I must in Caesar's service. The girl had some of the answers I seek. The pain I inflicted extracted them from her, and thus was justified."

"I doubt Tiberius would take pleasure in hearing you say so," I said stiffly.

"You might be surprised," Araneus shot back. His black eyes gleamed. "The emperor takes his pleasure in any number of very unusual and interesting ways."

My jaw tightened, but I said nothing. I refused to dignify his salacious jibe with a response.

"Release me," the astrologer demanded again.

"I will not." I studied him coldly. "You lied to me once. Now I want the truth."

"I told you no lie!" Araneus snapped.

I folded my arms. "Earlier, you claimed your mission here had no connection to that of the senator. But now I learn that you've been seeking the same answers to the same bizarre questions. How do you explain that?"

Two spots of color appeared high on the astrologer's narrow, pallid face. He scowled, clearly irked by the implication that he and the senator had been pursuing the same mysterious goal.

Interesting, I thought. Silanus had been a senator and once a consul. He could have traced his ancestors back to the shining towers of Troy. And yet this clown thought himself the better man. Could I use his vanity against him?

"Admit it, all your mystical nonsense is a sham," I goaded him. "In the end, you're nothing but a jumped-up apprentice sent here on some trivial political errand."

"Not so!" Araneus seethed. "My master and I watch over the emperor's spirit, his *genius*. We are the guardians of Tiberius, and of Rome through him—a ward against all malignancies of the spirits of earth, wind, water, and fire." He glared at me. "The knowledge I seek for Thrasyllus is far beyond the comprehension of any simpleminded dolt—especially that of a greedy, grasping influence peddler like Decimus Junius Silanus."

I shook my head skeptically. "An eloquent speech, but unpersuasive."

The astrologer grimaced. "Pay heed, you fool! We stand on the brink of great and terrible events—of events that could shake the fabric of the world. Many will fall. A few will rise. This place might be the locus of those changes. There may be mysteries here that touch the realm of the infinite."

That was too much for me. I laughed in amazement. "In Nazara? In this little village?" I shook my head in disbelief. "Why not simply confess that you've come hunting a would-be Jewish rebel, just like the senator?"

"Silanus came hunting a rebel," Araneus hissed. "A blind and mortal man seeking another blind and mortal man."

So Paulus was right, I thought.

Then the astrologer's next words crashed in on my ears. "But I, Araneus, a magus of learning and power, I have come looking for a god!"

Chapter XIV

I wasn't surprised to see Severus appear early in the morning. The Praetorian centurion came to see me in full regalia, as finely dressed as though on parade before Tiberius himself. The sun glinted off rows of silver and gold embossed medals hanging from his highly polished mail corselet. Several gleaming armbands and a simple circlet of gold around his head offered more testimony to his acknowledged courage and good conduct. Clearly, he sought a formal interview to press his demands, probably in front of witnesses.

And that meant trouble.

I met him at the front door to Mathias' house. So the Praetorian wanted to overawe me with his decorations and awards for valor? Fair enough. But that didn't mean I had to play along. If I couldn't avoid a confrontation with Severus, I decided to make sure it took place on my own terms. If he can help it, a competent commander never fights on ground of the enemy's choosing.

"Come and walk with me, Aemilius," I said cheerfully, addressing him as a friend. "The sun is out, and I need a breath of good, clean air."

For an instant, Severus looked taken aback by my in-

formal manner. Then he recovered. With a slight frown
on his face, he followed me outside into the open square
at the center of Nazara. We began pacing slowly around
the village.

"I understand you've placed Araneus under close arrest," the Praetorian centurion said finally. He seemed
slightly more on edge than usual.

"That's right."

"On what charge?"

"Sorcery. Interference with a murder inquiry." I
shrugged. "I haven't settled on one just yet."

Severus frowned. "I advise you not to pursue a case
against him, Valens. That astrologer may be a fool, but
he's a vindictive fool, and one with a powerful patron."

"I'm aware of that," I said.

"You've interrogated him?" the centurion asked.

"Briefly," I said.

Severus studied my face intently. "And what have
you learned from him so far?"

I recounted the astrologer's strange claims.

He snorted. "Araneus thinks he's looking for a new
god? Here?" He shook his head. "The fellow's even
more demented than I first thought."

"I agree," I said. "But at least he confirms that
Silanus was searching for a rebel leader in hiding somewhere among these Galilean hill towns."

The centurion shrugged. He seemed calmer now. "A
so-called god or a damned rebel. It makes no difference." He tapped his vine staff against the stone wall of
a house. "If anything, that's just one more reason to strike
now. Wipe out this village and you destroy whatever
menace is brewing here."

"*Nazara delenda est?*" I said with a slight smile—
referring to Cato the Elder, a senator in the old Repub-

lic, who'd made a habit of ending every speech with the same stern demand that Carthage be destroyed, *Carthago delenda est.*

Severus frowned. "Mock me if you wish, but remember that Cato was right—and so am I."

I shook my head. "I will not order a reprisal on a whim."

"By the gods, Valens!" the centurion grumbled. "What will it take to satisfy you?"

"Evidence," I said. "Or at least some explanation of the murders that meets the test of logic."

"You want logic?" Severus said. "Then consider this proof. Fact: Silanus came to Nazara hunting rebels." He pointed down the hill toward that dark grove of trees. "Fact: Silanus and his followers were butchered there, within shouting distance of this village."

Severus then turned back toward me. "Conclusion: The senator found the rebels he was looking for. And they killed him for it."

I shook my head again. "Unfortunately, Aemilius, there are pieces of the puzzle which don't fit your theory, convenient though it is."

The centurion stared at me. "And what are those?"

To his credit, he didn't interrupt me while I ran through the arguments I'd made the night before to Aristides and the others. When I finished, though, it was clear that my reasoning didn't sway him.

He shrugged his shoulders. "I hear pure speculation, Valens. Not the evidence you prize so highly."

"What about the soldier we found dead among the thorns?" I reminded him.

"Cassius Celer?" the centurion said. "What about him?"

"Silanus and the others were stripped naked. Celer

was still in armor. They were bound and gagged. His hands were free. They were bludgeoned to death or had their throats cut. He was shot by an arrow."

"What of it?" Severus asked, puzzled. "Men may be murdered in different ways. They're still just as dead."

"But why are there so many differences?" I said. "If the senator's company was ambushed along the trail to Sepphoris and then brought back here at night, why weren't Celer's hands bound like the rest? Why wasn't his armor stripped off? Why wasn't he gagged? How did the killers know he wouldn't bolt and run, or call out for help?"

The centurion stiffened.

"Cassius Celer was one of the bravest men I've ever known," Severus said, forcing the words out through clenched teeth. He laid a hand on the hilt of his sword. "If you want to spit on his memory by implying that he turned coward or worse, I strongly suggest you reconsider."

"I'm not implying anything, Centurion," I said mildly. The strength of his reaction didn't really surprise me. Early on Severus had made it clear that Celer was one of his closest comrades. "I'm just trying to make some of the pieces fit."

Unbending slightly, the Praetorian officer took his hand off his sword. Then he shook his head. "You're making things too complicated, Valens. As usual. The answer's simple enough, and it proves these villagers were involved."

"Oh?"

"The senator and his men never left Nazara," Severus argued. "They must have been lured down to those woods by some ruse. Cassius stumbled across the ambush and made a break for it. The murderers got an arrow into him. He lived just long enough to struggle deep into those thorns, and none of them bothered to drag his body out. That's why he wasn't tied up or gagged, and that's why you found him in armor."

I thought that over. The centurion's outline made some sense on the surface — but only on the surface. It didn't explain the missing clothing, weapons, armor, and horses or the unburied bodies. And I still couldn't believe the villagers could keep so terrible a secret to themselves for long. I'd already questioned at least a quarter of the men in Nazara. All of them, except Yeshua, the young carpenter, had been frightened, but I'd never felt the slightest suspicion that anyone was lying to me.

"These Jews know the stakes," Severus said in reply. "Which of them would tell you the truth and put his life in peril?" He shook his head in disgust. "Accept the facts, Valens. You have nothing to show for your leniency. Instead, you've put the peace and our power at risk by being so dangerously softhearted."

Here we go, I thought.

"What are your intentions now?" the centurion asked, nodding toward the houses around us. "Will you waste more time lazing about among these hovels? Or spend your days prowling aimlessly around the nearby hills?"

With great difficulty, I controlled my temper. He was goading me. "Not exactly, no."

"What then?"

"I'm beginning to think we may be looking for the senator's murderers in the wrong place," I said slowly, putting words to thoughts that had been swirling in my brain for some time. "And asking the wrong questions."

Severus stared at me. "What do you mean by that?"

"We've all assumed the senator's death had some connection to Nazara or to one of the other villages he visited," I said. "But what if that's not true? You told me yourself that no one in Rome knew much about these rumors of conspiracy and rebellion he was sent to investigate. Just that they warned of a serious threat to the empire, or to Tiberius himself."

The centurion nodded, somewhat reluctantly, I thought.

"Well, look around you," I said patiently. "Do you really see anything here—or in the rest of Galilee—that could possibly be that serious of a threat? The last time these farmers made trouble, a single detachment of our troops crushed them without even breaking a sweat."

Severus said nothing. The sword scar on his left cheek twitched.

"But what if the real conspiracy was centered elsewhere—in Jerusalem or Sepphoris or Caesarea, or even Antioch?" I asked. "What if the real conspirators wanted to put an end to the senator's mission before he got too close to the truth? What better place to finish him off than out here, where no one would link his death to anyone but these peasants or bandits?"

Severus snorted. "And so now you think these unknown and unnamed 'conspirators' sent some band of assassins all the way to Galilee just to kill Junius Silanus?"

"It's a possibility," I said. I admit my sudden brainstorm sounded rather weak when put that way. But that's the peril of thinking out loud.

"Your own patrols haven't turned up evidence of any band of hired killers," the Praetorian pointed out.

"That's true," I admitted. "But my scouts have been mostly hunting for physical signs—for tracks, for camps, for hiding places. I'm afraid that too few of my men speak enough Aramaic to ask the right questions of the right Galileans."

"And who are they?" Severus asked. His voice revealed his growing impatience and irritation.

"There are shepherds scattered throughout these hills," I said slowly, remembering the man we'd met on the road to Sepphoris. It was his innocent comment about Roman soldiers among the hill towns that had led me to this place, to this new burden that weighed so heavily on my shoulders and my mind. That was just three days ago, I realized in some amazement. It felt like a lifetime.

The Praetorian officer shrugged. "So?"

I tried my best to explain my thoughts to him. I believed the people of Nazara were innocent of any part in the senator's murder. So we needed a witness, someone who had seen the real killers on the move, whether they were brigands or rebels or assassins from outside Galilee.

Anyone who was careful could avoid observation by the local farmers. The peasants tended their own fields by day, and by nightfall they were all safely abed. Their movements were regular, almost completely predictable. But the shepherds were different. This late in the year, their flocks roamed widely to find good grazing land. They camped in the open at night, usually on high ground with a good view over the surrounding countryside. And every shepherd kept a close watch for wolves and other predators.

So it was very possible that one or more of them could have seen something significant, perhaps even without realizing it.

"How will you win the confidence of these Jew

sheepherders?" the centurion asked sarcastically. "They've no love for us. And no reason to help — especially if any of their own kindred butchered Silanus."

"I'll take Gaius Julius Paulus up into the hills with me," I replied. "The boy is fluent in this people's tongue. And he worships the same god they do. He can speak to them in ways no soldier of mine ever could."

"This is madness," the centurion said abruptly. "You'll waste more days, even weeks, and achieve nothing. And all the time our hold on these people will weaken." He shook his head. "You leave me with no choice. I intend to appeal to Herod Antipas for full control over this matter."

"When?" I asked.

"Today."

I nodded as calmly as I could. I'd known this move was coming, but that didn't make it any easier to hear. "That is your prerogative. Naturally, I will oppose you."

"I would not advise it," Severus said. He lowered his voice. "You've made one great mistake already, boy. Don't compound your folly by making another."

For an instant, I felt myself waver. What did I have to gain by resisting Severus? The reprisal he wanted was in line with both our custom and with imperial policy. No one in Rome would thank me for protecting an obscure village full of stubborn, impoverished Jews. Far from it.

Tiberius Caesar had very few real friends. Decimus Junius Silanus had been one of them. The emperor was sure to demand blood and fire in revenge for the senator's murder. This grim-faced centurion of the Praetorian Guard would give him what he wanted.

Suddenly I felt weary and fed up. In Syria, I'd taken a stand against the corruption of my legion's legate,

Faustus, and of the governor, Gnaeus Piso. And I very nearly lost my life and reputation as a result. To be sure, Germanicus had intervened on my behalf. He'd even promoted me. But now I suspected he'd done that more as a salve for my wounded pride than as a ringing endorsement of my actions. In truth, he'd certainly wasted no time in shunting me off to the dreariest, least glorious region in the empire.

What punishment would I earn this time for opposing the emperor's will? Why should I put my military career and maybe even my life in jeopardy for the sake of a few peasant farmers and their families? And what could I really hope to gain by winning time to roam from flock to flock in search of answers that might not even exist?

Severus must have sensed my hesitation. He stepped closer. "You're a good soldier, Valens. But every good soldier knows when to fight and when to retreat. Now back away and leave Nazara's fate to me."

Those words burned like fire. I stared down at the gold band on the ring finger of my left hand. Honor and truth, I thought. A heavy burden. Once again, I faced a choice of two roads. Down one I would find safety, but safety purchased with the lives of innocents. The other offered only peril, and the dubious consolation of personal honor.

I knew which road my grandfather would want me to take.

I'd like to claim that was enough to make up my mind for me.

But it wasn't.

The faces of Mathias, the girl Sarah, the young carpenter Yeshua, and his mother Miryam rose in my memory. They were innocent of any crime. Was it just that they suffer death or be carried off into slavery to fulfill

Rome's appetite for vengeance? Or to strike terror into those who might rise against our power?

I looked up and caught the ghost of a satisfied smile on the Praetorian's face. Severus seemed sure now that I would back down and yield to his demands.

That faint, smug suggestion of a smile tipped the scales.

My shoulders stiffened. "I'll act according to my conscience, Centurion," I said. "I will not surrender this village to you."

The Praetorian officer sighed. "Then you are determined to fall on your own sword for these Jews. I'm truly sorry for that. They're not worth the risks you run for them." He eyed me coldly. "Very well. Herod can decide between us. My men and I ride out within the hour. Have your Gallic idlers ready to march with us. Or stay behind—we won't wait for you."

With that Severus stalked away, leaving me to contemplate the dangers of the coming day. Somehow I would have to persuade Herod Antipas to leave the investigation in my hands. If I failed, the people of Nazara would have only days left to live.

Chapter XV

The sun was high overhead when we rode down out of the hills and turned onto the road east to the Sea of Galilee.

I'd left Taedifer, the regiment's senior decurion, along with more than fifty soldiers in camp with orders to watch over Nazara. A troop of thirty cavalrymen, the Seventh, and a number of their servants came with me.

Aedan rode at my side, with Aristides and Paulus trailing close behind. The doctor had bundles tied to his mule containing the evidence we'd gathered—the arrow that had killed Cassius Celer, scraps of cloth used as gags, and oaths signed by Mathias and the other village elders denying any responsibility for the murders. He also carried the scrolls and notes we'd confiscated from Araneus. The astrologer himself was farther back in the column, still under guard. I didn't know how much of a hearing Herod Antipas would give me, but I wanted to be prepared for any eventuality.

"Make way there!" came a shout from behind.

I swung round in the saddle and saw Severus and his Praetorians moving up to take the lead, resplendent in their dress armor and billowing scarlet cloaks. Dancer whinnied in protest as they cantered past, but I pulled up slightly and let them go on by.

"That one thinks highly of himself," Aedan said, frowning at the centurion. "You command here, not Severus."

"I hope so," I said. Then I forced a wry grin. "We must forgive him. The gods themselves would surely tremble if a Praetorian had to swallow dust like other mortals."

The Celt turned round and saw the haze already enveloping the men and horses strung out behind us along the narrow road. Two more days without rain had again left the Galilean countryside bone dry. He spat to one side. "I suppose eating grit is all right for the rest of us?"

I shrugged. "To some, we're simple soldiers, fit only for duty in the muck and mire . . . and the dust."

Paulus had ridden his mule close enough to hear us talking. He frowned. "But the legions and auxiliaries guard the frontiers. You enforce the peace in every province. Surely Caesar values your service?"

I nodded. "He knows our value all right."

Then I lowered my voice, speaking just loudly enough for Aedan and the boy to hear me over the jangle of armor, the creak of riding harness, and the rhythmic thud of hooves on the hard-packed dirt road. "We guard the frontiers and we preserve the peace. But the Praetorians hold Tiberius' very life in their care. A province ravaged by barbarians or rebels can always be reclaimed and rebuilt. But who will push the emperor's guts back into his belly once an assassin's dagger opens it up? And, knowing that, which of us do you suppose Caesar truly holds more dear?"

Paulus fell silent. He slowed his mule and drifted back toward Aristides.

I rode on, feeling guilty at having shown so much cynicism in front of the boy. For all his pride in his own people and his god, Paulus had shown himself equally proud of his Roman citizenship. Was it my place to stamp so hard on his idealism—especially since I had shared it not so long ago?

I frowned. What was happening to me?

Once I'd believed there was no greater blessing for a foreign people than our benevolent rule. Everything I'd been taught had bolstered that fundamental certainty. All the histories I'd read. Every lesson imparted by my tutors. Every public speech and oration I'd heard. My experiences fighting along the Rhine had only reinforced the conviction that we had a right to impose order on the world. Outside the empire there was savagery and chaos. Inside it, peace and prosperity.

Now, though, I was being forced to face some unpleasant truths. Roman rule by men like Augustus or Germanicus could prove a blessing. But could I say the same for provinces dominated by the likes of Faustus or Piso, or for laws carried out by men like Severus?

I tapped my heels on Dancer's flanks, gently urging her into a slightly faster pace, and rode on.

It was nearly evening by the time we wound our way through a narrow pass and came down to the western shore of the Sea of Galilee. Tiberias, Herod's new royal capital, lay just ahead.

Named in honor of the emperor on his sixtieth birthday, Tiberias was scarcely a year old. Antipas had offered free land to some colonists and forcibly resettled others from nearby villages, but his new capital was still closer in size to a small town than a real city. Carpenters and stone masons were hard at work along the shore putting the finishing touches on several dozen houses and other buildings. Their white plastered walls and red roof tiles reminded me of home, of Italy.

Meanwhile, road gangs were busy laying stone slabs to pave the central colonnaded street. I also spotted a row of stakes hammered into the ground and piles of stone heaped at intervals. They marked the planned circuit of the city's walls. A thick-walled citadel already loomed on a spur of rock overlooking the rest of Tiberias.

I nodded to myself. The tetrarch had his priorities in order. He knew he wasn't loved, so he'd finished his fortified place of refuge before beginning work on the rest of the city.

Herod Antipas' new palace lay close to the citadel, high above the shore. The vaulted roof, covered in gold leaf, gleamed in the afternoon sun. Scaffolding and stacks of stones, bricks, and timber showed that parts of it were still under construction, but there were archers and spearmen standing sentry at its gates. The tetrarch of Galilee was in residence.

Severus and I had sent couriers ahead with the news of Silanus' murder and our dispute, ensuring us a clear path through the intricate maze of petty officials and bureaucrats surrounding Herod. The elaborate layers of protocol and hierarchy were a stark contrast to the careful simplicity of manner I'd seen in Augustus when I visited him with my father. Anyone from a far-off land visiting Rome might have marked Augustus down as a rather mild magistrate of middling rank. Yet the same foreigner entering this palace might reasonably assume that Herod governed the whole empire.

Aedan and the other cavalrymen stayed behind to

find quarters and stabling for our animals. For the time being, I left the astrologer Araneus with them.

Severus, Aristides, Paulus, and I were led deeper into the palace. Along the way we passed through a series of beautifully decorated rooms and hallways. Colorful frescoes adorned the walls. Superbly crafted mosaics were set in the marble floors. Some showed mythological beasts—winged rams, human-headed lions, and the like. Others were renditions of fantastic hunts. Tigers, lions, wolves, and stags were depicted being chased, speared, and shot by horsemen. A few scenes were plainly erotic, full of gods and human men and women cavorting and carousing with wild abandon.

Paulus stared at the walls and floors. His face darkened. "This is scandalous," he muttered.

I glanced at him, surprised. There was nothing here that would have been out of place in any wealthy villa across the empire. If anything, the decor gave the impression that Antipas wanted to be more Roman than a Roman and more Greek than a Greek. "Scandalous? In what way?"

"These images are strictly forbidden by our laws!" Paulus said angrily. His voice echoed off the high ceiling. "No man who calls himself a Jew could live here without being a hypocrite of the worst sort."

The elegantly robed official conducting us to the tetrarch glanced back. He raised a single immaculately plucked eyebrow and sniffed in disdain.

I winced. Like me, Paulus possessed a gift for saying exactly the wrong thing at exactly the wrong time. Whatever the truth about the tetrarch, this wasn't the moment to make enemies in his court.

"Lower your voice, boy!" I said through gritted teeth. "And keep your scruples to yourself. Antipas rules here.

A single angry word from his lips could annihilate the people of Nazara. Do you want their deaths on your head?"

Abashed, Paulus turned bright red. He dropped back and trailed well behind me all the rest of the way.

At last, our guide led us out into an elaborately landscaped garden deep in the heart of the palace. Palm trees towered over marble benches, beds of exotic flowers, sparkling fountains, and exquisite sculptures imported from the best workshops in Greece. At the center of the garden, courtiers in flowing, brightly colored robes surrounded Herod Antipas.

He was a paunchy, bearded little man reclining stiffly on the cushions of an ornate couch. Several golden dishes and jeweled cups laid out on a small table before him indicated that we had interrupted his evening meal. A handful of bodyguards stood close by, keeping a wary eye on the gathering.

I breathed in, preparing myself for the ordeal ahead. I planned to do my best with Herod, but I didn't have many illusions about the likely outcome. The Praetorian centurion had better connections in Rome than I did, and the tetrarch didn't strike me as a man who made a habit of thwarting what he thought was the emperor's will.

One of my grandfather's favorite maxims rose in my mind. "The good commander stays calm when all seems lost. He shows no fear and no uncertainty. He meets all ills, all setbacks, all disasters with a steady hand and a brave heart."

I stood straighter.

A robed courtier signaled Severus and me forward. "The tetrarch Herod, ruler of all Galilee and Perea, friend of Rome, and friend of Caesar, will hear your petitions."

The centurion and I saluted.

Herod's greeting was brief and formal. He welcomed us both, and he accepted the responsibility to judge between us, but he couldn't hide the enormous tension in his voice.

No surprise there, I thought. Hearing the news that a senator and close ally of Tiberius had been murdered in his lands must have come as a terrible shock.

Severus spoke first, seeking full control over the inquiry and the authority to take punitive action against Nazara. He strongly emphasized Silanus' intimate ties to the emperor. He also went to great lengths to make clear the influence wielded by his own superior, Aelius Sejanus, the prefect commanding the Praetorian Guard.

A telling argument, I conceded silently. The tetrarch knew very well that he ruled here at Tiberius' whim. What reason could I find to bend Herod's mind away from the swift, easy, and brutal measures proposed by Severus?

Herod turned toward me. "The centurion presents a compelling case for immediate action, Prefect. And yet you do not agree?"

There wasn't any more time for thought.

"No, sir. I do not," I said firmly. "If the people of Nazara were responsible in any way for Silanus' murder, I would lead the attack on them myself, and with a glad heart. But I haven't found any evidence to support such a conclusion. In fact, I believe them completely innocent of this crime."

"What does that matter?" Severus said, interrupting me. "Whether they're guilty or not is immaterial. A Roman senator is dead and practically within the bounds of that village. A village under your authority, most noble Herod. You must punish these people and do it soon, lest weakness breed rebellion against Rome . . . and against you."

"Justice is not weakness," I countered. "And rebellions are as easily bred by arbitrary cruelty as by refusal to act hastily or unwisely."

Herod's eyes slid away from mine. I was losing this fight, I realized. The tetrarch was not a man to take risks for an abstract ideal. He would take counsel of his fears. He would side with Severus and assure his own personal safety, no matter what it cost his subjects. I needed something that would make him more afraid of me than of the Praetorian and all his influence.

But what? Or rather, who?

Germanicus.

The name flared in my mind like a beacon in the night. Perhaps the moment had come to cast the dice and trust the Fates. I raised my voice slightly. "I do not believe Germanicus Caesar would approve a reprisal raid. Not without more proof."

Herod turned back to me. "You are closely acquainted with the esteemed Germanicus?"

"I am."

"How closely?" he asked, watching me carefully.

"I received the commission to command my regiment from his own hand," I answered truthfully. I would not lie to him, but I felt no obligation to disabuse the tetrarch of any mistaken impression he might form. With luck, he would understand my words as proof that I was one of Germanicus' favored subordinates. My grandfather might not have approved, but this was a time for subtlety, or at least as much of it as I could muster. Too many lives were at stake for any other course.

I only hoped that gossips hadn't yet spread the real reasons behind my sudden transfer to Judea.

As I'd hoped, Herod looked impressed. "And you don't believe Germanicus Caesar would approve of the centurion's plan?"

"I do not," I said flatly. "He has often said that our use of force must never be arbitrary—that it must always be justified both by law and by common sense."

That much was true, anyway. Dinner conversations during my stay at his home in Antioch had often centered on the best means to keep the peace in our possessions. "As the emperor's representative, he would seek the guilty first, certainly before punishing the innocent without good cause."

Herod sighed. His forehead wrinkled in worry.

I knew why.

He was torn between conflicting fears. Refusing Severus might anger Sejanus, and maybe even Tiberius himself. But Germanicus was the emperor's adopted son and he commanded all the eastern provinces. More to the point, messages would take many weeks to make the trip to Rome and back. Antioch, the center of Germanicus' power, was close at hand.

The tetrarch sat back on his cushions in silence. He looked acutely uncomfortable.

Severus and I watched in mounting impatience while he fiddled first with one dish and then with another, moving food from one place to another while he tried to decide what to do.

At last, Herod spoke. "This case is difficult. Very difficult. On the one hand, the centurion is quite right. The noble Decimus Junius Silanus is dead, and his death must be avenged. At the same time, I cannot deny the wisdom in the advice offered by Aurelius Valens. Certainly it is better, where possible, that vengeance should fall first on the guilty."

Neither Severus nor I moved a muscle.

He turned to me. "Therefore, I grant you more time, Prefect. Use it wisely. Use it well. I rely on you to identify and arrest those who murdered the senator."

I did my best not to smile in triumph. That was just as well, for Herod's next words showed plainly that he hoped to keep a foot in both camps.

"But you have seven days," he told me. "No more. At dawn on the eighth day, your authority over this inquiry ends."

The tetrarch turned toward Severus. "And then, Centurion, you have my permission to destroy Nazara utterly — along with all its people."

Severus called on me later that evening.

I'd been assigned rooms in the palace itself, as had Aristides and Paulus. Aedan and my troopers were allotted space in the barracks of Herod's Royal Guard, over in the adjoining citadel.

My quarters included an antechamber, a bedroom, and a small room for dressing and washing. The furnishings were extravagant, a celebration of the tetrarch's wealth rather than his good taste. The carpets, wall paintings, statuary, and furniture were all of the highest quality, but nothing was quite in the right color or style.

I was just washing the road dust off my head and hands when a servant brought the news that the centurion wished to see me. I toweled off quickly, threw on my tunic, and walked out into the antechamber.

There were a number of chairs around the room, but Severus had chosen to remain standing. With a disgusted expression on his face, he was examining one of the frescoes, a fairly overdone rendition of Dionysus leading a drunken revel.

He turned sharply at my entrance, characteristically abrupt. "We've crossed swords over this matter, Aurelius Valens."

"That is true," I said cautiously, wondering what ploy the Praetorian had in mind now.

"I won't pretend that I think that carping, vacillating fornicator Herod has made the right decision." Severus frowned. "But he has made a decision. And I will honor it."

"I'm grateful."

The centurion snorted. "Spare me your sarcasm." Then he shrugged. "What I'm trying to say is that you've won the argument—for now. And that makes it my duty to assist you in every way that I can."

It was your duty to help me before this, I thought, but I kept that to myself. I needed this Praetorian officer's cooperation more than I needed to score debating points at his expense.

"It's bad enough that Silanus is dead," Severus continued. "But whoever murdered him slaughtered four of my own men at the same time. So I want the bastards who killed Cassius Celer and the others crucified."

I nodded. "On that, at least, we are agreed."

The centurion folded his arms. "Do you still plan to traipse all over the hills around Nazara, hoping to find some shepherd who may have seen strangers riding in or out?"

I nodded again. "That's right."

Severus shook his head. "A bit chancy, isn't it? The

seven days you've been awarded will fly past swiftly. What if you fail? What if you don't manage to find this hypothetical witness in time? Or what if all those Jew shepherds were blind, or deliberately looking the other way?"

Those were all possibilities that haunted my thoughts. Because I had only Paulus to translate for me, it could easily take too long to scour the hills with any thoroughness. Given enough time, I had reason to think that we could turn up something useful. But the tetrarch's ultimatum had robbed me of that time, and turned my planned search into a desperate gamble.

"I've said before that I'm open to suggestions, Aemilius Severus," I said, trying my best to sound calm and unconcerned. Whether he really meant to help me or not, I knew the centurion well enough now to know that he would take advantage of any weakness I showed him.

"Do you still have that war arrow with you — the one your Greek doctor took out of Cassius?" he asked brusquely.

"Yes," I said. "Aristides has it in his care."

"Good." Severus smiled suddenly, a tight, humorless grin. "Because I have an idea. I may know someone who could tell us much about that little arrow."

I summoned Aristides while the Praetorian officer went off to fetch his expert. Shortly after the doctor arrived, Severus returned. He brought with him a man an inch or so above my height, strongly built and yet still lean and lithe.

I studied the newcomer carefully. A finely woven cloth band around his forehead kept a mass of long black hair away from his face and out of his deep-set brown eyes. A thick, carefully trimmed mustache offset a large, powerful nose and a firm jaw. His legs were slightly bowed by what I judged must be years spent in the saddle. Everything about him radiated decisiveness, authority, and an awareness of his own power.

A tough customer, I thought. And a born leader.

Severus made the introductions. "I present Vardanes, son of Bessas, a noble of the lands around Dara—and now a commander of one hundred horse archers in the service of Herod."

"Dara?" I asked. "Where exactly is that?"

"In Parthia," the centurion told me. "Far, far to the east. Beyond the Caspian Sea and Hyrcania."

I could scarcely conceal my astonishment. "A Parthian? In Herod's service?"

For nearly three generations, Parthia had been our most bitter and cunning adversary. Its fierce horse archers and tough armored lancers were a constant threat to the security of Syria and our other possessions in the East. We hadn't been openly at war with them for more than fifty years, but small-scale skirmishes and raids were fairly frequent along the frontier.

Vardanes smiled. "I am a Parthian, yes." His Greek was clear, though strongly accented. "But I am no enemy of Rome."

I raised an eyebrow. "Really? Then you are the first man of your country I've ever met who could say that."

The Parthian nobleman's smile slipped a bit. "Doubt me if you will, but I speak the truth. My followers and I have pledged ourselves to the service of Herod, the friend of your ruler. I keep my oaths."

My questions drew some of his story out of him in short order.

Parthia is a deeply alien land, the reverse in many respects of Rome. In principle, we have no king, but in practice one man, Tiberius, holds most of the reins of power. The Parthians have a king to rule over them, but he is a king in name only. Much of the real power in Parthia lies in the hands of the great noble families and of their strange priests, the Magi. Feuds and rivalries are common among these aristocratic families. Grudges are often held from generation to generation.

One such dispute had precipitated Vardanes' downfall.

Some years ago, he and a neighboring baron clashed over the control of some grazing lands between their respective fiefs. His rival was killed. Unfortunately, his enemy had powerful friends at the Parthian court, and they succeeded in having him outlawed. With his lands forfeit and facing certain death, Vardanes had no choice but to flee, bringing a company of his armed followers with him. Since then they'd earned their keep as mercenaries in Herod's army.

Severus had met him at one of the military conferences the centurion had convened in Caesarea.

"And your duties are?" I prompted, still wondering why Severus believed this Parthian soldier of fortune might be of some help to me.

"Unexciting." Vardanes smiled at his own jest.

I eyed him coolly. I didn't have the time to waste on a would-be comedian.

The Parthian shrugged, turning more serious. "We patrol the tetrarch's lands. We suppress brigands in an occasional skirmish. We keep a watchful eye on the Arabs to the east. We guard Herod on his journeys."

Much the same work as my own regiment in Judea, I realized. Perhaps he might be useful after all. "I'm told you may know something of an arrow we found near Nazara."

Vardanes nodded. "It is possible." He held out a hand. "May I see this arrow?"

Aristides offered it to him.

The Parthian held it up to the light of an oil lamp. He squinted along the shaft, studied the black-dyed feathers closely, and traced the shape of the arrowhead with a callused thumb. At last, he sighed. "I do know it. All too well. Arrows of this kind are used by a gang of bandits led by a man they call Gideon. A true villain — and one I have not yet been able to run to earth, to my regret."

"You're sure?" Aristides asked.

"Quite sure," Vardanes replied. He handed the arrow to Severus and turned back to the doctor. "I've plucked enough just like it out of my men and horses, or out of bodies we've found on the road."

So we might be chasing bandits after all! Some of the weight lifted off my shoulders. I knew that I'd speculated that the mysterious conspirators the senator had come east to track down might have killed him and his men, but all the same I'd been dreading the prospect of trying to prove it. Bandits were easier game.

"Where does this Gideon lurk?" I asked. "Somewhere in the hills around Sepphoris?"

Vardanes shook his head. "No. He and his robbers have their lair somewhere north of here, west of a lake village the Jews call Magdala. They prey mostly on travelers and caravans traveling between Tiberias and Caesarea Philippi." He frowned. "The country there is very rugged and broken. It's littered with boulders and honeycombed with caverns."

I nodded. That explained some of the Parthian mercenary's failure to eliminate Gideon and his bandits.

Vardanes' mounted archers were ill suited to close-quarters combat in rough terrain. They would fight best on level, open ground, where they could shoot, retire to reload, and then ride back to fire again.

Aristides looked skeptical. "Surely Nazara is too far afield for these brigands of yours," he told Vardanes. "It must be more than fifteen miles from the place you describe. That's a full day on foot. Why would bandits go all that way, and risk running into one of your patrols?"

The Parthian had a ready answer. "The lure of riches will prompt any man to risk his life, I think. This senator of yours had gold enough in his baggage to entice even the most cautious of thieves. From what I've heard, he spread enough coin around Jerusalem to send the news far and wide throughout all Judea and Galilee."

I turned toward Severus.

The Praetorian officer nodded sourly. "Vardanes speaks the truth. Silanus was very generous with the treasure entrusted to him by the emperor. He called it a 'form of practical diplomacy.' "

"How much treasure?" I snapped, angry with Severus for concealing yet another piece of important information from me. I was getting very tired of hearing constant surprises from him.

The centurion shrugged. "I don't know. Not precisely at any rate."

"Make a guess," I told him coldly.

"Perhaps the equivalent of a half-million denarii," Severus said quietly. "Mostly in gold."

Aristides whistled in shock. "Zeus! That's enough to buy an army."

The doctor was close. I did the sums as fast as I could. The money entrusted by Tiberius to the senator would have paid the salaries of five thousand soldiers for nearly six months. And the weight of it all—even in gold! At least now I understood why Silanus and his men had brought so many pack mules with them.

I frowned. "This is delightful news, Severus. If the senator was known to be carrying that much gold, my list of suspects expands to cover every group of greedy men in Galilee and Judea!"

The Praetorian held up the arrow that had killed his old friend and comrade, Cassius. "Not quite, I think."

"No," I agreed. "We'll see to this Gideon and his brigands, first."

After Severus and the Parthian were gone, Aristides looked at me carefully. "Do you believe all that, Lucius?"

"Can I afford not to?"

"It could be a ruse by that Praetorian bastard to send you chasing off in the wrong direction," the doctor warned. "He'd like nothing better than to see you fail so he can take over himself. That's the only way he can guarantee a report to Tiberius will absolve himself of any blame for the senator's death."

I nodded. "I know." Then I shrugged. "But this is the best lead we have right now. You saw the Parthian's face. There's no doubt that he recognized the arrow you took out of Celer. And he's right about a motive. The news of that much gold could draw bandits from a hundred miles away."

"True," Aristides admitted. "But I still don't like it."

"Nor do I," I said. "We'll chase these bandits for three days, and no more. If we catch them and they're guilty, well and good. If not, I'll still have four days to find the evidence I need to change Herod's mind."

Chapter XVI

Magdala lay just a few miles north of Tiberias. We arrived there early in the morning the next day, riding into town along a well-maintained road lined with tall palm trees. The highway ran straight through a narrow coastal plain bordering the Sea of Galilee. Beyond the palms on either side were vineyards and thick groves of fig, walnut, and olive trees. More grapevines and orchards covered the steep ridge rising to the west.

With me were Aristides, Paulus, Aedan, and the cavalry troopers and servants I'd brought from Nazara. Severus and his four guardsmen stayed behind. The centurion claimed he didn't want to "jostle" my elbow while I was busy hunting the bandit chieftain Gideon and his gang.

The doctor had snorted when he heard about that while we were assembling in the forecourt of the tetrarch's palace.

"And pigs can fly, Lucius," he said. Then he slapped his battered, wide-brimmed hat against one leg, beating the dust out of it before planting it back on his head. "I'll wager the Praetorian wants time alone with Herod to plant a dagger in your back."

"Probably so," I agreed. "But I can't do anything to stop him. And since that's the case, I can at least enjoy his absence."

I also left Araneus behind in Severus' custody. I didn't have much hope that the centurion would keep him in close confinement, but I'd kept all his scrolls and other notes. Aristides was still trying to decipher the astrologer's secret writings, though so far without any real success.

Magdala was bustling. The town was easily several times the size of Tiberias. Fishing boats of all sizes crowded its docks, bringing in the morning catch. The streets were full of people going about their daily business. Most were Galileans. A few were Greek. But all of them stopped to stare at us as we rode past.

I halted the column in the broad expanse of Magdala's central marketplace. We dismounted. The troopers took our horses to drink by sections.

Leaving them to it, Aedan and I strolled around the town, getting the feel of the place. My first priority was to find quarters for my men and animals, some building or group of buildings that we could use as a secure base while our scouts probed the countryside for signs of the brigand camp.

I wasn't very happy with what I saw.

The town was too busy, too crowded. Any movement we made from there would draw immediate attention from its inhabitants, and risk exposing our plans to Gideon and his gang of brigands. If the bandit chieftain were half as resourceful as Vardanes the Parthian claimed, he would have a network of spies among the townspeople. I couldn't hope to hide the fact that Roman troops were operating around Magdala, but that didn't mean I wanted Gideon getting a detailed briefing every time I blew my nose.

"We could camp in the open," Aedan suggested. "The nights are warmer this close to the lake. The lads won't mind roughing it a bit."

I shook my head. I had thirty soldiers with me—not enough to build and defend a fortified camp. Simply laying out a few tents and picket lines for our horses was just asking for trouble. With so many orchards and groves around for cover, a bold group of bandits could slip in close, knife our sentries, and catch us in our sleep. I'd come to Magdala to smash Gideon, not to be smashed by him.

After inspecting the limited number of public buildings we might requisition, the decurion and I turned and headed back through the crowded streets toward the marketplace. None met my minimum requirements. We were still trying to decide what to do when the solution found us.

It came in the form of a fussy, self-important little fellow, richly clad in a long, intricately embroidered robe. The bulky set of keys dangling from his belt, the rings on his plump fingers, and the fine silver chain of office around his neck all proclaimed him to be the steward of some wealthy household.

He walked straight up to me, bowed low, and then asked, "I beg your pardon, sir. My name is Ilasios. I am the chief steward of the lady Marah. She has heard that there are Roman soldiers in the town. Do I have the very great honor of addressing their most esteemed commander?"

I fought down a smile and instead nodded gravely. "You do."

The steward beamed. "And will you be staying long in Magdala? My lady bids me ask this," he explained.

"For a day or two," I said cautiously. The word of our arrival had spread faster than I'd anticipated.

The little man bowed again. "That is wonderful news. In that case, I bear an invitation from my mistress. She offers you and your soldiers the hospitality of her estate for the duration of your stay here. Her villa lies just outside the town, and it has every comfort you might desire."

Aedan grinned at me with a mischievous gleam in his green eyes. "The hospitality of a mistress, eh? Not a bad offer, Prefect. It'll do us all good to see a few pretty curves and hear a sweet, lilting voice."

Ilasios puffed himself up indignantly. "Have a care what you say! The lady Marah is a respectable woman. She is a person of the highest standing and dignity, the widow of one of our town's most prominent citizens."

Again I hid my own smile. The decurion's comment might have been impolitic, but it hit close to home. After so many weeks and months without the touch of a woman, my own pulse had quickened just at the prospect of staying under the same roof with one. Perhaps it was better for all concerned that our hostess was evidently an elderly woman of rigid propriety.

Acting quickly, I smoothed the steward's ruffled feathers with a few courteous words and gratefully accepted the invitation he offered.

The little man bowed a third time, and then bustled off to make everything ready for our arrival, leaving us staring after him.

Aedan laughed at last. "Now there's a fine thing, Aurelius Valens. It'll be just our luck if that little fellow proves to be more womanish than the old crone he serves."

"Well, if that's true, I hope you'll be able to restrain yourself."

The tall, fair-haired Celt grinned and thumped his chest in a quick salute. "Yes, Prefect. I'll behave."

The lady Marah's estate proved to be perfect for my purposes. It was just a short distance north of Magdala. Substantial orchards of fig trees, well-tended vineyards, and extensive fields surrounded a large walled villa built on a gentle rise overlooking the lake. It was a holding worthy of a Roman senator.

As we rode up the tree-lined drive and into the villa's courtyard, I was glad I'd taken the trouble to don my parade armor. Ordinarily I prefer wearing a corselet of well-made mail. The muscled bronze cuirass most officers wear on dress occasions looks impressive, but it won't turn the point of a sword or stop a spear thrust. On the other hand, it was just the sort of thing that would impress a wealthy widow generous enough to open her home to my troops and me.

Ilasios the steward stood there on steps leading up to a covered portico and the main door to the villa itself.

Aedan, Aristides, Paulus, and I swung down off our mounts and walked toward the steps.

The little man raised his voice. "My lady, I present the esteemed prefect of cavalry, Lucius Aurelius Valens, along with his officers, soldiers, and chosen companions!"

A woman came out of the shadowed portico and into the sunlight. She wore a robe of the finest emerald green silk, gathered in at the waist by a silver-trimmed belt. Her hair fell free in waves to her shoulders, unconfined

by shawl or headdress. Its color was the golden brown
of the most precious amber, and her eyes, lighter in hue
than most in the East, seemed to sparkle in the light.

I stared. This was no elderly widow, no aged crone.

The lady Marah of Magdala was young, no more
than a year or two older than I was, and she was strik-
ingly beautiful.

She stood at the top of the steps, appraising us with a
cool, collected expression. "Brave soldiers of Rome,"
she said crisply, "I welcome you to Magdala and to my
home."

Without thinking, Paulus exclaimed, "She is no
Galilean!"

Marah laughed, delighted. She clapped her hands together in approval. "Congratulations, Prefect! You have
a scholar—or a seer—among your following!"

She turned to the boy. Her eyes twinkled as he turned
beet red. "Now, tell me, teacher. How do you know I
was not born in this backward, rustic region?"

Paulus stammered out an answer. "Why, your
accent . . . your intonation . . . the words you use. They
carry the sound of Judea, not of Galilee."

Marah smiled at him, clearly impressed. "A teacher
indeed."

Then she turned her gaze on me. I felt warmer suddenly. It's the sun, I told myself resolutely. Only the sun.

"What this boy says is perfectly true, Prefect," Marah
said softly. "My family is from Judea. I was betrothed as
a young girl to my husband, and when we were married,
I came here to live in his native place." Her face tightened. "But now my husband is dead."

I fumbled for words, even more aware of the tiny
droplets of sweat on my temples. I had the sudden impression that I was treading on dangerous ground. I took

refuge in the banal, in the conventional formulations of polite society. "Please accept my sympathies on your loss."

Marah shrugged. "It was long ago." She hesitated briefly, then went on. "His death was not wholly unexpected. He was a much older man. *Much* older."

Something in her eyes and in her voice sent another wave of heat rippling through me.

"And all this estate is yours?" I heard myself asking. It was unusual for a woman in this region to own property of such value so openly, at least without a guardian.

Marah nodded. "Yes. This house and these lands belong to me. My husband had no close kin." Her eyes flashed angrily. "There were no other men bearing his name to rob me of what is mine by right."

Dangerous ground, indeed, I realized. Perhaps it was time to seek a safer subject. I cleared my throat. "You are from Judea, my lady. Do you still have family there?"

The fire in Marah's eyes dimmed. "Yes," she said. "I still have an older brother and sister in the land of the living. They reside near Jerusalem."

She stood on the steps a moment longer, still studying my face. I could not tell what she was looking for. Then she sighed. "But I'm sorry for boring you, Prefect. I'm sure I've kept you from your duties. And I, too, have work that must be done. For the duration of your stay here, I ask you to treat my home as if it were your own."

She turned to go.

On impulse, I took another step forward. "Lady Marah, a moment, please. Will we see you at dinner this evening?"

Marah looked back at me over one perfectly formed

shoulder. I thought I could discern the hint of a smile hovering on her lips. "Would you welcome my company, Prefect?"

I blushed. Say something, you idiot, I told myself angrily. You're not a schoolboy anymore. "I would, very much . . . I mean, yes, of course, we would . . ."

Her lips curved upward. "If that is so . . ." Her eyes twinkled again. "Perhaps."

And then she was gone, disappearing into the villa in a flash of green silk and graceful movement.

Aristides nudged me. "You may have caught a tigress there, Lucius." He chuckled. "Be careful or she'll have you combing her hair and managing her servants before your sword belt hits the ground."

I snorted and then darted a quick glance behind me, catching sight of the hurriedly suppressed grins on my troopers' faces. I felt myself turn red again.

I swung round on Aedan, sharpening my tone. "Decurion! Talk to the steward there and arrange quarters for these shiftless Gauls! But no man takes the weight off his own feet until his horse is groomed, watered, and fed. Understood?"

"Yes, Prefect!" Aedan snapped back clearly, quickly hiding the smile on his own face.

"Right." I eyed the sun. "And once you've done that, Decurion, come and find me—and bring two of your best trackers. We have work to do."

Aedan, two veteran scouts, and I moved off an hour or so later. We headed north, cutting across country and paralleling the high ridge that ran all along the western shore of the Sea of Galilee. This ridge grew steeper and steeper the farther we rode, until it reared more than a thousand feet above the shoreline in a great vertical mass of rock—a layered mix of gray- and red-tinted stone. Marah's steward had told us this peak was called Mount Arbela.

We halted some distance away, dismounted, and then walked forward to take a closer look.

I stared up and up, craning my neck until it ached. There were caves and fissures all along the face of that massive pile of rock. Most were up high, within two or three hundred feet of the summit.

Aedan looked at me. He raised an eyebrow. "What do you think? Could Gideon's band be lurking somewhere there?"

I shook my head. "I doubt it."

Those caves would offer a spectacular view of Galilee and of any traffic moving along the shore, but they were too high and too inaccessible to serve as practical bandit lairs. Any brigands hiding somewhere on that sheer slope would have to be part mountain goat or all bird.

We remounted.

A track ran along the cliff base, curving around to join a wider road that branched off from the highway beside the great lake and headed west, deeper into Galilee. There was another pass here, a narrow gap in the high ridge we'd been following.

I reined in.

I didn't like the looks of this defile, the Valley of the Doves. It ran southwest between sheer walls of rock that towered on either side. There were only a few patches of brush and even fewer trees, most of those scrub oaks. There was no real cover, no way to move up the road without being spotted by anyone watching from the cliffs above. The hair stirred on the back of my neck.

Aedan shared my misgivings. His fingers drummed

nervously on the hilt of the sword belted at his side. "That's a fine path to go in by, Valens," he warned. "Getting out again might be a bit trickier."

"I know," I said. Now that I'd seen more of the ground for myself, I could understand even better why Vardanes and his horse archers hadn't been able to catch the robbers infesting this region.

Dancer caught my unsettled mood. She whinnied softly and tossed her head. I settled her with a gentle pat, then glanced back at Aedan. "We'll go carefully, Decurion."

He nodded grimly.

I forced a quick grin. "Relax. We came here to find bandits. Don't be disappointed if we do."

The tall Celt snorted. "Fair enough, I suppose. If this were easy, that Parthian mercenary would long since have put Gideon and his men up on crosses."

We rode on into the Valley of the Doves. After a mile or so, the road took us up and out onto the plateau that ran west toward the Mediterranean. To our left, the ground was fairly level and open. A high, black, cone-shaped hill loomed some distance straight ahead. On our right, the landscape was a labyrinth of boulder-strewn ridges and brush-choked ravines.

Aedan, the scouts, and I turned off the road toward that rougher terrain, pausing frequently to dismount and search the ground more thoroughly. The sun was much lower in the sky before we found the first faint traces that might belong to our prey.

We were walking our horses along a trail that wound uphill through clumps of brush, thorns, and thistles. A scattering of sheep and goat droppings told us this was a path sometimes used by shepherds taking their flocks to pasture. But the droppings were old and dry. They crumbled at the touch. No flocks had come this way for many days or even weeks.

"Sir!" One of the scouts motioned me over to a patch of loose soil shaded by two large rocks. He pointed at the dirt. "You see?"

There were fresh tracks there. Two sets belonged to men wearing sandals. There were also four distinct hoofprints. So at least one man on horseback and two on foot had passed between those boulders sometime within the last day or two.

"Not shepherds," I said.

The cavalryman shook his head. "On horseback? And moving without their sheep? Not likely, Prefect."

I peered around the rocks. The tracks seemed to head directly for the mouth of a ravine that cut right through the ridge we were climbing. Despite the sun, I felt cold. We're close, I thought. But how close?

There was really only one way to find out.

I left one of the scouts behind to hold our horses and took Aedan and the other soldier in with me on foot. We moved cautiously, taking the time to study every inch of the ground ahead for anything out of place. Lizards, startled by our approach, skittered ahead, running lightly over heaps of jumbled, broken rock and steep slopes covered in loose gravel.

We moved on, heading farther up the cleft. We'd only gone a hundred paces or so when I stopped—suddenly aware of the silence. It was too quiet. Nothing stirred now. Not the lizards. Not any birds.

Aedan sidled closer. "We're not alone here," he muttered.

I nodded. "A lookout?"

"Yes."

"Where is he?"

"About fifty paces ahead. On the left, high up the slope," the decurion said, carefully looking away from the area he was describing. "In a big group of boulders."

I risked a quick, cautious glance. There, deep among the shadows, I spotted another shape, one that wasn't a shadow. Someone was concealed there, squatting motionless in the rocks. A sentry.

"Right. We've come far enough," I said softly. "We've seen one man. There could be a dozen more hidden farther on."

Aedan spat to one side. "For bandits, they keep a good watch."

I frowned. "True. I suppose a spy in the town could have carried the news ahead of us."

"Likely enough," the decurion agreed. He looked at me. "Now what, Valens? How do we back out without tipping our hand?"

That was a big problem. I was fairly sure that we'd found an entrance to the brigand camp. But if they realized that, Gideon and his robbers could easily slip off to another hideout before I could assemble a force to hit them. I didn't have the time to chase these criminals all over Galilee with Herod's deadline looming over my head. Somehow we had to persuade the man watching us that we'd learned nothing useful here.

"We become actors, Aedan," I said, finally. "And then we hope we fool our audience."

Taking action to match my words, I sat down on the nearest boulder and mopped theatrically at my forehead. I looked up at the tall, fair-haired decurion with a wide frown on my face. "Well," I said loudly so that my voice could be heard far up the ravine, "was this a wasted trip after all?"

Aedan blinked, taken off guard for an instant. Then

his face cleared and he shrugged broadly. "It seems so, sir." He turned in a wide circle and shrugged. "There's nothing here but rock. And dirt. And thorns."

I swore sharply and turned my attention to the trooper standing nearby with an uncertain grin on his face. "Idiot!" I groused. "If I wanted a long walk into the middle of nowhere, I'd have brought a willing girl with me—not some goat-loving, useless excuse for a soldier like you!"

The cavalryman hunched his shoulders, doing his best to look ashamed.

I didn't suppose that any of it would have fooled a sophisticated audience of Roman theatergoers for a moment. With a little luck, though, the bandit sentry up ahead wasn't that discerning. He certainly wouldn't understand our speech, but he'd pick up the tone clearly enough.

I was also counting on normal human mulishness. According to Vardanes, Gideon and his men had been operating undetected from this rough country for more than a year. If the brigand chieftain and his comrades had a snug, comfortable lair in this ravine, they might be reluctant to move without more proof that we'd found them.

"Let's push on west," I announced abruptly, standing up. "It's getting dark, and I've almost had my fill of this sun-blasted wasteland."

Aedan and the scout nodded.

Then, still grumbling loudly, we retraced our steps and walked out of that ravine. We didn't look back.

In case there were other unfriendly eyes on us, I led Aedan and the scouts on a couple of other half-hearted probes of other gulches and gullies farther west. We abandoned each in apparent disgust and then circled back toward the road leading down to the Sea of Galilee.

It was near sunset by the time we came down through the Valley of the Doves and saw the lake before us. The low, rolling hills on the distant shore were already cloaked in shadow and night.

Aedan rode silently at my side with a set, grim look on his face.

"What do you think?" I asked.

"Nothing good, that's sure," he said quietly. "That ravine is a death trap. Ten brave men with bows could hold it against the whole regiment, let alone just a single troop of thirty."

I nodded. The decurion was right. Any attack up that narrow, boulder-choked opening would be a blood-drenched disaster. Our march up the old shepherd's trail would be slow and noisy. Plus, we'd have to go in on foot. Even without the horses, I wouldn't have room to deploy more than four or five men in a fighting line. If the bandits were ready and waiting for us, we wouldn't stand a chance.

But what choice did I have? If I backed away from a fight here, if I retreated and left Gideon and his robbers alone, Herod's deadline would pass. The Praetorian centurion Severus would take command. And the people of Nazara would die.

Could I let that happen? Would my pride, my honor, allow it?

No, I thought. It would be better to die quickly in battle, even in defeat, than to die slowly over long years of shame. What I couldn't stomach was the thought of leading Aedan and the other soldiers who trusted me to certain annihilation.

Was there an alternative?

I pulled Dancer off the road and sat for a time, thinking hard. Around me, the last light faded fast. The tall cliffs of Mount Arbela glowed red and then blurred into a black, featureless mass against the sky.

The hint of an answer came. I turned to Aedan. "Tell me, Decurion. If you were a brigand, a robber, and a murderer, and hunted by half of Herod's army, would you ever leave yourself without a line of retreat?"

"No," the Celt said slowly. "I would not." His teeth flashed white in the darkness. "By the Lady, Valens, I begin to see what you mean. There must be another way in!"

"So there must," I agreed. "And we'll start hunting for it before first light tomorrow."

I tugged gently on the reins, urging my horse back onto the road. I felt more cheerful already. Dinner and the company of a beautiful woman lay ahead.

Chapter XVII

The faint smell of wood smoke hung in the air, blown our way by a light morning breeze. I held up my left hand, signaling Aedan and the two cavalrymen with me to halt. The ridge we were climbing leveled off just ahead and then fell away abruptly into the deep ravine we'd scouted the day before.

The four of us were out hunting for another approach to the bandit camp, this time from above. To avoid being spotted by any lookouts, we'd left Marah's estate well before sunup and taken a roundabout route into the rugged countryside beyond the Valley of the Doves.

Aedan sniffed the air and grinned wolfishly. "They're still here."

I nodded, relieved. Despite all our playacting yesterday, I'd been afraid that we might have frightened Gideon and his brigands into fleeing to another hideout, one I wouldn't have time to find.

We crept forward to the rim. I crawled the last few paces on my stomach. The smell of smoke grew stronger. Now it was tinged with the aroma of roasting meat.

I stripped off my helmet and peered cautiously over

the edge. At this point along the rim, the slope plunged at least forty feet straight down. This early in the day, the bottom of the ravine was still in shadow. My eyes took a few moments to adjust to the darkness, but already I could hear the soft murmur of voices from below.

Aedan crawled up beside me and took his own look.

We were right on top of what had to be Gideon's camp. Several men clad in drab, dirty robes were in view. Two sat cross-legged on the ground, cleaning a goatskin, scraping the hair off it with sharp knives. Three more brigands were perched on boulders, honing spearheads and daggers. The ravine ran roughly north and south here. I could just make out the still, silent shapes of sentries posted in both directions.

But where were the other bandits? Vardanes had told me that Gideon had at least thirty men in his band. From the Parthian mercenary's description of their past skirmishes and encounters, I saw no reason to doubt his estimate. And where was the fire I smelled?

Another man joined the others, appearing as suddenly as if he'd materialized right out of the sheer rock wall below me. He was older, with a full beard and long, matted hair streaked with gray. He spoke briefly to the pair scraping at the goatskin and then headed south down the gully to check the two guards on watch there, walking lightly despite his age.

One of the other men climbed to his feet, hefted the spear he'd been sharpening, and walked straight toward the side of the ravine. He vanished from our sight.

Now I understood.

The bandits had made their lair in a cave far beneath us.

I motioned to Aedan and we edged backward from the rim.

The decurion shook his head. "I don't like the look of it. Not at all. They've got a back door all right, but it's as deadly to us as the front." He gestured toward the ravine. "Whichever way we come, we'll be walking into trouble."

He was right. Mounting an attack straight up that narrow, boulder-strewn canyon from either direction would be pointless. If Gideon and his robbers stayed to fight, they might cut us to pieces. If they ran, I wouldn't be able to catch them. If they dispersed, I wouldn't be able to find them. This was their country. They would know every hidden trail and every bolt-hole for miles around. I only had thirty soldiers—not enough to launch an attack and safely block both exits.

Should I send for the fifty cavalrymen I'd left to garrison Nazara? For an instant I toyed with the notion. Then I rejected it. Summoning reinforcements would consume another two days of the handful left to me. If I could be sure these brigands were responsible for Silanus' death, the gamble might be worth it. The trouble was, I still couldn't be sure of anything.

No, I was going to have to go after those bandits in the ravine below with the troops on hand. Somehow we had to catch Gideon's men by surprise, and rob them of the choice to fight or flee, to bring them to battle on our terms.

But how? None of the readily apparent alternatives offered any real hope of success.

I crawled back to the rim and lay there for a time watching the activity below. I found myself making rough calculations of heights, distances, and angles. My mind flashed back to the fishing vessels crowding Magdala's docks and those of the other towns around the lake. A plan began to take shape—a plan so wild and so outlandish that any sensible soldier would have dismissed it out of hand.

Well, I decided, perhaps the time had come to stop thinking like a sensible soldier.

We were back at Marah's estate by midmorning.

Since I was fairly sure there were lookouts watching the pass, I dispatched more scouting parties into the hills as a ruse. My troopers had orders to make a great show of searching for brigands, but they also had orders to stay out of trouble and to stay well away from Gideon's camp. I wanted the bandits to believe they were still safely hidden.

I settled myself on a stone bench outside the villa, one with a view looking out across the Sea of Galilee. Dozens of fishing boats dotted the calm, sunlit waters of the great lake.

While I waited, my mind ran free. I tried to fix my thoughts on the questions surrounding Silanus' murder, but more and more I found myself thinking about Marah instead.

Her manner at dinner the night before had been perfectly civil, even cordial, but she had seemed somehow distant, almost withdrawn. And though her conversation touched on all the appropriate subjects in polite society—the food, the wine, and the weather—she revealed little or nothing of herself or her own opinions. Nor did she ask much about our business in Magdala. Though she knew we were hunting bandits, she sought no real details.

All the sharp wit and intelligence, all the passion, all the hidden fire of anger or joy I thought I had sensed on our first meeting, seemed to have vanished.

And yet . . .

And yet, I could have sworn there were moments when that look of desire or hunger of another kind flashed in her eyes again. But I could never be sure, never be certain.

I sighed. The lady Marah was a mystery to me, and one whose secrets I felt poorly equipped to discover. Like most young men of my age, I had already tasted the delights of physical lovemaking. Not in the brothels or taverns frequented by the common legionaries, of course. But even near the Rhine camps there were always a few women of better appearance who reserved their charms for the officers. If desired, their affection could be purchased discreetly.

This was not the same. Not at all.

Marah was not a citizen, but she had far more in common with a woman of my own circle than with the courtesans with whom I'd consorted in the past. They had been mistresses for a single night's release: a pleasurable roll among the cushions, a shared laugh or two, a cup of wine, and then a quick escape back out the door to the real world of soldiering on a dangerous frontier.

In contrast, Marah was a woman of wealth and education and good birth. Aristides had learned something of her family's history from Ilasios the steward. Before he died, her husband had served Herod Antipas as a high-ranking financial official here in Galilee. In Judea, her father had done the same sort of work first for the tetrarch Archelaus and later for the Roman procurator. Even her grandfather had been an important advisor to Herod the Great.

I frowned. In some ways, I'd been away from Rome, from civilization, too long. After so much time in the company of soldiers and the women of the camp, I wasn't sure how to talk to someone like Marah—how to delight her, how to spark her interest, how to bring her to life.

I heard footsteps on the gravel walk close by. I looked up, frankly glad of the interruption.

It was Aristides, with Paulus tagging along behind as usual. I felt a bit guilty seeing the boy. I should probably have sent him on to his teacher in Jerusalem by now, but the truth was I needed his skill with the language of the common people too much to let him go just yet.

The doctor looked weary and utterly frazzled. He dropped the satchel he was carrying on the walk and plopped himself down beside me with a stifled groan.

"A hard night chasing the serving girls?" I asked innocently.

Aristides winced. "Very funny, Lucius." He rubbed at his bloodshot eyes. "As a matter of fact, no. Would to Aphrodite that I had been. My time might have been better spent."

"Then you must have been working on the astrologer's drivel," I said.

He nodded.

"Any luck?"

Aristides shook his head in frustration. "Not much. I've gone through every scrap of writing and every drawing and star chart half a dozen times. As I feared, almost everything is in a strange form of secret writing. And look as I might, I can't find the key to this code." He shrugged. "What's left is virtually unintelligible— more the ravings of a madman than anything else."

"Such as?" I asked.

"One scroll contains references to an astrological sign of great significance—a new star in the heavens, I think—that is said to show the birth of a king," the doctor said. "Or perhaps a great man. Or possibly a god. The words are very confused."

I nodded. When I'd interrogated him, Araneus had claimed he was in Nazara searching for a god. Maybe this was a reference to some observation he'd made in the skies that had set him on his strange quest.

"Another appears to be a very complicated genealogy, though I could be mistaken. If I interpret his chicken scratches correctly, the astrologer was trying to trace the lineage of something called the 'House of David.'"

Paulus looked startled. He opened his mouth as if to speak. But then he shut it and shook his head quickly, as if firmly dismissing a possibility he found unthinkable. I glanced at the boy curiously. What had he heard and understood that Aristides and I had missed?

"And take a look at these," Aristides continued, pulling three small rolls out of his satchel. He handed one of them to me.

I unrolled it, holding it up to the sun to make out a faint tracing of characters and lines and star shapes. "What's this?"

"A horoscope," the doctor answered. "For a man born under the sign of Capricorn."

"And the others?" I asked.

"Two more charts. The second is for a different day in Capricorn, a later day. The third is for another birth, that one under Aries."

There was a strained note in Aristides' voice that I thought odd. There was nothing strange in finding a collection of horoscopes in Araneus' belongings. They were the basic stock in trade of any professional astrologer. I shrugged. "So?"

"As far as I can tell," the doctor said slowly, "they're all for the same person."

I stared at him. "A man born on three different days?"

Aristides nodded.

I whistled softly. The doctor was right. Araneus must be a madman.

"There's just one other piece of writing I can decipher," the Greek said reluctantly. "I think it's a prophecy—or rather the fragment of a prophecy. One I do not understand." He looked down at his hands and then recited it for me. " 'The Eagles will bow to the Dove. And the Sons of the Wolf will kneel before the Shepherd.' "

I considered that. The eagle and the wolf were symbols of Rome. But a dove? And a shepherd? What mystical significance could they possibly have? What meaning had the astrologer drawn from this cryptic saying?

Movement on the lake caught my eye. The fishing boats were hoisting sail or putting out their oars and drawing nearer to the shore. I tossed the scroll back to Aristides and rose to my feet. It was time to set my plans in motion.

It was an hour or so past noon.

I stood in the shelter of a doorway watching Aedan and four soldiers work their way along the waterfront of Capernaum, a prosperous town a few miles north from Magdala. The decurion and his men were inspecting each of the boats tied up at a stone pier extending out into the lake. From time to time, they paused to talk to some of the Galilean fishermen who were busy unloading their morning's catch and cleaning their nets.

Another cavalryman came up the street toward me,

leading his horse by the reins. It was one of the veteran scouts I'd taken up into the hills the day before.

I stepped out of the doorway. "Well?"

The scout shook his head. "You weren't followed here, Prefect. I'd stake my life on that."

That was good news. When I took Aedan and the others off to Capernaum a couple of hours before, I'd left this soldier behind with orders to watch for anyone coming after us. We had important business here, business I wanted to keep secret from those who might be spying for the bandits. The chances were good that Gideon and his band of robbers had friends in Magdala. With luck, Capernaum was far enough away to be free of their supporters.

When the decurion and his men finished their inspection, they rejoined us.

"I've found a likely pair," Aedan said. "They seem honest enough and both speak a little Greek."

"Good." I glanced down the street toward the pier. The fishermen were beginning to disperse, moving off toward their homes or the market carrying baskets of fresh-caught fish on their shoulders. "Wait a while longer and then pick them up. Do it quietly, if possible. We'll meet outside the town."

The decurion nodded.

I remounted Dancer and rode a short distance out of Capernaum. There I waited in the cool shade provided by a stand of walnut trees.

Sometime later, Aedan joined me there with a pair of plainly bewildered fishermen in tow. They were brothers.

The older brother, broad-shouldered and bearded, stepped forward. "Why have you summoned us, sir?" he asked nervously. "Do you want our day's catch for your soldiers?"

I shook my head. "No, I don't want your fish."

The fisherman, whose name I later learned was Simon, stared at me. "Then why are we here?"

"You're here," I told him quietly, "because I want your nets."

His mouth fell open. "Our nets?"

"That's right," I confirmed. "But I need to know one thing first." And then I told him just why I needed those nets.

The older brother slowly closed his mouth. He looked first at me and then at the cavalrymen surrounding us. At last, he nodded hesitantly. "They will serve, I think. But it would be better if we strengthened them first."

"Can you do that before first light tomorrow?"

Simon swallowed hard. Then he nodded. "We can."

"I sincerely hope so," I said softly. "Because you and your brother will be coming with us. And if your nets break at the wrong moment, the last thing you'll feel will be several inches of cold iron sliding into your back. Do we understand each other?"

Now deathly pale, both brothers nodded again.

I didn't especially like threatening these poor fishermen, but I didn't have the luxury of learning to trust them any other way. There wasn't time. The days Herod had allotted me were falling one by one.

Chapter XVIII

Dinner that evening passed like something out of a dream. My sense of time was distorted, cut loose from reality. Hours flew by in what seemed like minutes. And minutes stretched into hours. With action drawing nearer, I was keyed up—ready to take risks, to face danger, and yet all too aware that the gamble I planned could easily end in defeat and disgrace. Or in death. No matter what happened, I knew that I would not sleep that night.

The lady Marah's cook had gone to great lengths to prepare a banquet that could have graced the table of any patrician family in Rome. We were served grilled lake fish in a light saffron sauce. There were boiled eggs in small silver cups, and a salad of mint, coriander, green onions, and lettuce. Platters of fine cheeses, figs, dates, and pomegranates filled the center of the round table. Small, round loaves of fresh-baked bread were set at each place.

Aristides, Aedan, and Paulus ate with great gusto and every sign of enjoyment.

In contrast, I wasn't really very hungry. I ate more from habit and out of politeness. On some distant level

I was aware that each dish was perfectly seasoned and prepared. But I was desperately thirsty, and I drank deeply of the excellent wines that accompanied each course.

Should I blame what happened later on the wine?

No. I cannot. I will not.

It is true that I drank more than was my custom. But I was not drunk. My mind was my own. My thoughts and actions were my own.

I think I knew from the beginning what I wanted, no matter how hard I tried to hide it from myself.

I wanted Marah.

She reclined at table across from me. The glow from the oil lamps set around the room added a tinge of gold to her amber-colored hair. A circlet of sweet-smelling flowers around her brow gave her the dignity of a queen or a goddess. Tonight she wore a close-fitting gown of sapphire blue silk trimmed in silver. Her eyes shone brightly, enormous in the soft light.

Marah, too, ate sparingly, only nibbling delicately from the exquisite dishes set before her. But she was eager to hear my stories of service in distant lands and of my boyhood in Rome. And whether it was the wine coursing through my veins, or the sheer pleasure I found in seeing her smile and hearing her laugh, I rose to the occasion. My words came flowing more freely and with far greater eloquence than I usually command.

Despite that, whenever the conversation turned to her own life, she still maintained that air of caution I'd sensed earlier. Her reserve slipped only once near the end of the evening.

"Oh, I spend my days in comfort," she said in answer to a question from Paulus. "But each is much the same as any other. There is no excitement, no meaning, in Magdala."

Marah took a small sip of her wine and set the cup to one side. A servant refilled it instantly. "There is no one here of any learning or sensibility. These Galileans are a narrow people. They care little for anything beyond the price of fish, the rhythm of the seasons, and the strictures of the Law. No one really *lives* in this dull backwater. They simply exist."

I noticed Aedan and Aristides exchanging amused glances and frowned at them. The doctor winked back at me. I blushed.

"But Tiberias is just a short ride away," Paulus said. "Your husband was an official of the tetrarch. Surely, you would be welcome at his court. There must be people of education and good birth there."

"My husband was welcome at Herod's court," Marah replied. Her lips tightened for a moment. "But when his fat, greedy courtiers stare at me, they see very little beyond my villa, my orchards, and these fertile fields. To them, I am only the pretty widow of Eisakios. I'm the means to a great estate and nothing more."

I nodded slowly. It was an old story. Her father had made what must have seemed a good match for his daughter. Certainly, his family had gained a profitable alliance with a man high in the tetrarch's royal circle. Arranged marriages of that kind were the common fate of women from the upper reaches of any civilized society. Sometimes they worked well.

But not this time, I thought. Marah's marriage to the elderly Eisakios had clearly secured her fortune. Just as clearly, it had not brought her happiness. Now her first husband was dead and she wasn't willing to risk her freedom and her possessions to find another. This prison of wealth and luxury wasn't of her making—but her own pride and caution guarded its walls and barred its gates.

And she knew that.

Our eyes met across the table.

Aware suddenly that she had revealed more than she intended, Marah flushed a fiery red. Quickly, she urged me to give them all another tale of adventure in the German forests.

I obliged, telling her about the time that I'd been asked to escort a diplomatic mission deep into hostile tribal territory. It had been a journey full of misadventure, misunderstandings, some danger, and at a safe distance, even a little comedy. By the time we got back to our own lines, I hadn't been sure which was the greater threat to the safety of the frontier—the Germans, or the incompetent envoy I'd had to guide, a bumbling, puffed-up, very distant relative of Augustus himself.

The wine circulated twice more before I finished, "And to this day, I don't know whether or not I was really supposed to protect Servius Tullus, or lose him discreetly out in the wilds. But Germanicus promoted me to military tribune not long after that, so I suppose I got it right."

Marah laughed, delighted. By the time I'd fairly got my breath back, she was already asking more questions about other campaigns against the barbarians.

"If you please, my lady"—Aristides held up a hand, smiling broadly—"I'll bid you good night now. I've heard Lucius recite these tales on several occasions, and the Germans grow more numerous and fearsome each time." He rose from the table and clapped Paulus on the shoulder. "Also, this young man needs more tutoring in sound Greek philosophy if he truly wishes to consider himself learned."

"What?" Paulus said, surprised. He shook his head. "I don't need to study anymore. Not right now. And besides, *I* haven't heard all of the prefect's adventures."

His protests fell on deaf ears. Aristides bundled the boy out of the dining room in short order. No sooner had they disappeared out the door than Aedan also rose and made his own quiet farewell.

I was enjoying myself so much entertaining Marah that I scarcely noticed their departure. Her smiles, the pleasure she showed in hearing of strange places and peoples, the way her eyes lit up when she laughed— they were all intoxicating to me. I drank more wine without really noticing it. She matched me sip for sip while we talked on and on.

The servants came and went, clearing away the remnants of the food and discreetly refilling our cups. The oil lamps were turned down low, sending shadows dancing across the walls.

I fell silent, aware abruptly that we were alone.

The sun had long since set. Marah's servants were gone. The house was quiet.

At first, she seemed equally taken aback, but then she took a deep breath and rose gracefully off her couch. I got to my own feet and stood facing her, conscious now that only an empty table separated us.

Her eyes were bright in the dim half-light of the dining room. "It has grown late, Lucius," she said huskily. "And the servants seem to have gone to bed. Rather than disturb them, will you escort me to my room?"

"Of course, my lady . . . I mean, Marah," I stammered. "I would be very glad to."

I started to pick up one of the lamps to light our path,

but she shook her head gently. "We won't need that, Lucius. I am at home here and know the way."

Marah came to me then, took my hand in hers, and led me down the darkened corridor toward her bedchamber. Her very touch seemed to set me ablaze. The whole world narrowed down to her slender figure, shining face, and radiant eyes. She stopped at the door and turned toward me.

For a heartbeat, we stood close together, our faces only inches apart.

Time stopped. The future felt balanced on the edge of a knife.

Then her lips parted and I leaned forward and kissed her. Gently at first, and then with greater passion. Her mouth tasted sweet, mostly of honey and grapes blended with hints of other fruits, of raspberries, blackberries, and pomegranates.

I touched her soft cheek with trembling fingers and kissed her again.

Marah drew my hand down to her breasts. They were round and ripe beneath the smooth silk of her gown. I cupped one and felt the nipple grow beneath my palm.

She sighed in pleasure and whispered, "I am yours this night, Lucius." And then shyly, hesitantly, she said, "If you want me . . ."

Scarcely believing my good fortune and with my pulse pounding in my ears, I followed her into the room beyond and closed the door behind us.

One small lamp provided a fitful glow, casting its light across her bed. There were other furnishings in the chamber, but I paid no attention to them. My eyes were fixed on Marah.

She drew me close with her hands linked behind my neck. I put my arms around her slim waist. Our lips and tongues met and twined together a third time. I knew she could feel my manhood bulging beneath my tunic, brushing urgently against the silk covering her hips.

Marah broke our kiss with a low moan of pleasure. Then, smiling, she stepped back a pace. Her eyes were fixed on mine. With deft fingers she unclasped the silver belt at her waist. The belt fell to the floor. Her gown followed it, sliding first off one perfectly formed shoulder and then the other. The green silk cascaded down around her feet.

In an instant, Marah stood naked before me, openly delighting in the stunned admiration she saw on my face. Her soft, full breasts were crowned with nipples that rose proudly in the cool night air. My eyes traveled downward, past her taut stomach to the soft, curling tuft of golden brown hair between her legs.

Slowly, she lay back on the bed, with her arms spread wide. "Come to me," she whispered. "I am yours . . ."

My clothes fell beside hers in a rush and I joined Marah on the bed, hovering over her on outstretched arms. For a long instant, I held there, fascinated by the glow of the lamplight on her breasts, by the moistness of her lips, and by the growing hunger in her eyes.

Then her hand closed around me, pulling me down to her, guiding me deep inside.

We made love slowly at first, savoring each new movement, each new sensation. Our pleasure intensified, rising higher and higher. Drawn by it, we moved faster, finding a wild, fast, fierce rhythm that bore us onward to a shuddering, gasping, moaning moment of shared ecstasy.

Heart pounding, I lay locked in Marah's arms. My head rested between her sweat-slick breasts. For a long while we were still, breathing in unison in pure contentment. We did not speak. Words were pallid things before this glory, I thought.

I kissed one of her nipples, running my tongue over and around it. She tasted of salt and spice. I felt myself stir, rising again, and so did she. Marah laughed aloud in astonished joy. Then she drew me inside herself a second time.

Twice more that night we coupled, each time finding some new means of giving pleasure and satisfaction to each other.

And when at last we were spent, we lay together, entwined in one another's arms, gazing deeply into each other's eyes.

"Lucius," Marah said softly, running her fingers gently over my chest. "Tell me again of your home. Tell me about Rome."

I obeyed gladly, doing my best to paint a picture in words. I conjured up a portrait of Rome at its best—as a place of gleaming temples and public buildings, of graceful bridges, of statues and gardens, of flowing fountains, of elegant villas and orchards sprawling across the lush countryside on the city's outskirts.

Marah drank it all in. Her eyes shone. "Ah, Rome," she whispered. "It must be a city of wonders. It is the glorious center of all our world."

I reddened slightly, thinking of all that I had left unsaid. Of the darker side of my great city—the cramped, fetid tenements crammed full of the poor, the filth-laden alleys full of thieves and robbers, the slave pens, and the bloody spectacles of the games. I know that one can find the same squalid truths in any large city in the empire. And perhaps, after all, they are part of the universal human condition. But despite that, I hid those grim places from her. I was unwilling to tarnish the glittering illusion she cherished.

Marah sighed. Her eyes closed and she laid her head on my shoulder. "What a joy it will be to see your home, Lucius. To see it with you . . . to live there with you . . ." she murmured drowsily.

I stiffened, all at once realizing the magnitude of my folly. How could I have been so thoughtless, so callous? The possibility that she might expect me to marry her had never really crossed my mind. I had acted in the moment, driven on by lust and by longing. I had never stopped to consider the consequences of what I had wanted so very badly.

Whatever my heart might desire, the truth was that I was not free to choose my own path in love. Women are not the only ones who must contend with arranged marriages. My father had been planning alliances for me since the day I was born. One early betrothal, to the daughter of one of his fellow magnates, had already fallen through, shattered by my boyhood illness. But he had not abandoned the dream of linking our family with some other powerful clan in marriage.

For all her wealth, Marah was an alien, a woman of a subject people. I was a Roman officer and a member of the equestrian order. My father would never give me his consent to marry her. Even if I could overcome his objections, strict laws barred officers from marrying women of the provinces in which they served.

Could I bring her back with me to Rome despite all that? Could I ask her to live there in secret as my mistress? That, too, was beyond imagining. It would be a humiliation for her, a life of furtive meetings, of hidden shame. Such liaisons were common enough on duty in the provinces but they were unthinkable in the capital itself.

The sweetness I had savored so short a time ago now tasted only of ashes.

She looked up, plainly puzzled by my rigid silence. "Lucius? What is it? Is something wrong?"

What could I tell her? How could I explain the terrible thoughts raging in my brain? "Marah. My lady," I said hoarsely.

The smile faded first from her eyes and then from her lips. Her face, once flushed with joy and contentment, now seemed carved of stone. She pulled out of my arms and sat upright.

"Marah," I said again, still unsure of the words I might use. I reached out to her, but she pushed me away.

"Say nothing!" she snapped. Her eyes were alive again, but now they were filled with anger and contempt. "There is nothing to say. I know now how you must see me. And what you must think of me." Her mouth twisted downward. " 'The barren widow so desperate that she'll offer herself to any man,'" she said bitterly, mimicking a Roman accent. " 'The foreign whore. Pretty enough for sport, but not pretty enough for anything more.' "

I was horrified—both by her words and by the self-loathing they revealed. "No, Marah," I stammered. "That is not true."

She closed her eyes in pain. "Leave me, Prefect. Now." A single tear slid slowly down her anguished face. "Do not worry. I know this is my fault. It is my sin. You took only what I offered freely. You owe me nothing. You promised me nothing."

Another tear joined the first, rolling down the cheek I had caressed with such joy only moments before.

"Go," she said fiercely. "I ask nothing more. I only beg you to spare me further humiliation."

Aghast, both at my own selfish folly and at her rage and sorrow, I climbed out of her bed. Marah covered herself and then rolled away, hiding her face from me. She held herself rigid, as cold and unmoving as though she were made of marble and not flesh.

I stared at her for a long, painful moment, casting frantically about for anything I could say, for anything I could do. Could I find some words or deeds within me to undo the terrible damage I had caused?

But both my mind and my heart failed me—just as they had already failed Marah.

In shame, I dressed swiftly in silence. Grim-faced, I slipped out of her bedchamber and made my slow, sad way alone through the darkened villa to my own room.

For an hour or more I tossed and turned restlessly on my pallet, trying desperately to clear my mind enough to get some rest. At length, I realized that was impossible. Wherever I turned I saw Marah's anguished face before me. The thought that I had caused her so much pain tore and ripped at me like a dagger twisting in my gut.

I rose, donned my tunic and cloak again, and slipped quietly out of the house. If I could not sleep, at least I could try to regain some measure of peace in the clear, clean night air. Soon, I planned to lead my troops in a desperate attack on Gideon and his brigands. If nothing else, I owed Aedan and the others an unclouded mind.

I paced back and forth through the garden. The moon was rising, sending shadows flowing across flowerbeds, small knots of shade trees, and gravel paths winding between ornamental shrubs. I reached the chest-high outer wall and turned back toward the villa.

A door opened and then closed. Someone was coming, hurrying away from the house and heading for the wall. I froze in place. A spy? Was one of Marah's servants in the pay of the bandits and on his way to warn Gideon of our attack?

I frowned. It was possible. I'd kept my exact plans close to my chest, but one of my soldiers might have let something slip. My hand fell to my side. Nothing. In all my confusion and guilt and fatigue, I'd left my sword and dagger behind.

Sweating now despite the cold, I stepped back into the shadows of a nearby tree and stood still, waiting.

When the other figure was within arm's reach, I left the shadows and moved forward, blocking the path. "Hold!" I growled. "Stand and be recognized!"

Pale moonlight shone on the tears running unchecked down a woman's face. It was Marah, wrapped in a cloak.

I stepped closer. "My lady," I said tenderly. "Why are you here? Where are you going so late at night?"

There was silence for a moment. And then, at last, she answered me. "Will you deny me even this?" she asked bitterly. The anger and sorrow in her voice stabbed me to the heart. Another tear traced a silver, moonlit line down her cheek. "Will you deny me even the freedom to walk my own grounds?"

I hesitated for a moment. What right did I have to interfere, to badger her now? But I had a duty to my men. I could not take the chance, however slight, that the bandits might learn we were on the way to attack them. I nodded toward the wall. "Your grounds don't extend beyond that boundary. And so I ask this again only because I must: Where are you going?"

Marah slapped me across the face, a sharp, stinging blow that left my ears ringing.

I stood motionless.

She glared at me through tear-filled eyes. "Do you accuse me of treachery now, Roman? Do you think so little of me that you believe I would sell you to a criminal because you spurned me?"

Before I could say anything in reply, she slapped me again, harder still. My head rocked back. "Marah," I said softly. "Please—"

The sound of her own name on my lips seemed to trigger an explosion of pent-up rage. Marah's face contorted into a mask of almost inhuman fury. Despite that, she was still beautiful, but it was the beauty of an angry goddess—one determined to take a terrible vengeance. A shiver of superstitious dread ran down my spine.

She lunged at me, clawing at my face and eyes with her fingernails.

Appalled, I caught Marah's slim wrists and hung on desperately. It took all my strength just to keep her from hurting me or hurting herself. She writhed wildly in my grip, fighting like an animal caught in a trap. For a long, frantic moment she struggled in my arms.

But then, as quickly as it had come, her fury vanished. She fell forward against me, sobbing out loud. I held her close, saying nothing, feeling her hot tears falling on my chest. Slowly, gradually, her sobs faded, leaving only an empty, hopeless silence in their place.

Gently, very gently, I reached down and took her by the hand. She stiffened, but did not pull away. Her fingers and palm were freezing. "Come with me, I beg you. Come inside," I said quietly.

Numbly she allowed me to draw her back into the villa and down a corridor to the pair of rooms shared by Aristides and Paulus. Her tears had stopped falling, but she moved slowly, dragging her feet as though in a trance.

"Aristides!" I whispered hoarsely, through the closed outer door. "It's me, Lucius. I need your help!"

After a moment, I heard footsteps. The door swung open. The doctor stood there in an unbelted tunic, rubbing eyes that were heavy with sleep. Though he was clearly surprised to see us there, he didn't ask any questions.

He stood aside and let me bring Marah inside. I helped her into a chair. She sat without speaking, blankly staring at the wall. If she heard what we were saying, she showed no sign of it.

Aristides eyed her carefully and then turned back to me. "What help can I give you, Lucius?" he asked quietly.

I hesitated, choosing my words with great care. "The lady is . . . distraught. She needs sleep, a sleep without dreams. Can any of your foul-tasting concoctions grant her some ease?"

The doctor nodded slowly. "For a time, yes." He studied Marah again—plainly troubled by what he saw. "But heed me, Lucius. My medicines can do nothing to rid this gentle lady of any woes that haunt her waking mind. That is beyond my powers. When she stirs, when the drugs are spent, she must still face her life as it is."

I nodded grimly, bitterly angry with myself and with all the other men who had robbed her of the lasting love that should have been her birthright. First, her husband's age and then his death had denied her both passion and the consolation of children. Next, the open greed of

Herod's courtiers had driven her here to this lonely exile by the Sea of Galilee.

And then, when Marah turned to me—when she sought solace and comfort and rescue in my arms—I had failed her. I had proved myself a coward, both in her eyes and in my own. I felt sick, full of shame and barely suppressed rage. "Do what you can, Aristides!" I told the doctor harshly. "The gods know you have more to offer her now than I do."

He nodded somberly.

I turned away and my gaze fell on the muffled form of Paulus, snoring quietly on a straw pallet in the adjoining room. "Have the boy keep an eye on her while we're gone. Tell him she's ill. Tell him she must not be left unattended."

"You're leaving Paulus behind?" Aristides asked. The Greek shook his head. "He won't be happy about that."

"You know what my trade is, Doctor," I snapped coldly. "It is blood and agony and terror and death. Paulus is a mere stripling. He's already witnessed one field of murder and butchery. Do you want him to see another?"

Aristides wisely said nothing. He simply shook his head.

"Then here he stays!" I growled. I strode to the closest window and stared out. The sky in the east was lighter. The stars there were fading.

I swung away from the opening, suddenly anxious to be away from this place where I had brought such sorrow. "See to the lady Marah, Aristides. Treat her gently," I told him. "And when you've settled her to sleep, come find me. I'll be rousing Aedan and the rest of the men."

The doctor stared back at me. "It's time, then?"

"It's time," I said over my shoulder, already moving to the door. "The night wanes. The day approaches. The span allotted by Herod speeds past. And our stay at Magdala is at an end."

Chapter XIX

We were on the march soon after I left Marah in Aristides' capable hands. Aedan and the other troopers were already awake and readying their gear when I came to rouse them. I doubt the decurion had ever gone to sleep himself. Like me, he knew how narrow a margin we had in this venture. The difference between victory and ignominious defeat might easily be measured in a handful of minutes.

The sky to the east was faintly gray, but it was still full dark when we rode out through the gate of Marah's estate and turned onto the road heading for the Valley of the Doves. The moon high overhead lit our way, shedding an eerie, silver glow across the landscape.

Only that moonlight made this maneuver imaginable.

Night marches are rarely made by legionaries or auxiliary troops—and for good reason. There's a saying in the legions: Victory in war is made up of simple things. But in war, even the simplest things are hard. There is truth in that.

In the noise and confusion of battle, complicated plans and maneuvers often collapse. Orders are misheard or misunderstood or can't be carried out in the

time allotted. What seems easy in the mind of a commander proves impossible in the face of the enemy. Trying to move at night magnifies every one of those
difficulties a hundred times over.

Aristides joined the column before we'd gone far,
trotting up on his patient, long-suffering mule. He found
me at the head of my troops and drew close. "The lady
is sleeping now," he told me quietly. "And I left another
dose with Paulus should she wake too soon. The boy
knows what to do."

I nodded tightly. "Thank you."

"Lucius, I don't know what happened between you
two, but—" the doctor started to say.

"Not now, Aristides," I snapped, fighting the impulse
to kick Dancer into a gallop in order to put more distance between me and the scene of my failure. "Later."

If I lived through the coming battle, I would have to
face a reckoning for the anguish and sorrow and grief
I'd given Marah. I could not evade it. But this wasn't the
time or the place to indulge my feelings. Not with so
many other men's lives depending on my unclouded
judgment.

The doctor stared at me and saw the grim expression
on my face. Then he nodded. "Very well, Lucius. Later."
With that, he slowed the pace of his mule and drifted
back into position farther down the column.

We pressed on, moving as fast as possible through
the narrow pass and up onto the highlands beyond it.
The moon sank lower, sliding toward the horizon.

Soon we came to the landmarks I'd picked out the
morning before, an isolated pair of oak trees. From there
a path wound up the slopes to a point just above the
camp of Gideon and his brigands. The column turned
off the road onto that path.

I detached four troopers to scout ahead. I'd come this far to surprise the bandit chieftain, not to be surprised by him instead. Not counting Aedan and Aristides, that left me with twenty-six heavily armed horsemen. The two Galilean fishermen I'd pressed into service rode with us in a mule-drawn cart piled high with their stoutly woven nets.

The track was rough and steep in places. From time to time, the cart bogged down on the slope. Whenever that happened, we dismounted and manhandled it up the ridge by brute force. It was hard, backbreaking work, but I was always among the first to jump down and put a shoulder to one of the heavy wooden wheels. A good officer is always ready to lead by example. My grandfather used to say that any commander worth his salt wasn't above hauling on a rope if need be, no matter how elegant his dress or manners.

We were all sweat-soaked, dusty, and bruised by the time we reached the cliffs above the brigand cave. But we were there before first light.

I crawled to the rim and peered intently down into the darkness of the ravine. I could just make out the four lookout posts I'd noted the day before. There were men on watch, keeping both the north and south entrances to this ravine under observation.

My eyes narrowed. Gideon kept his gang of robbers under tighter control than I would have imagined possible. Standing sentry through the night wasn't work most bandits would relish. Well, with any luck, those watchers down there would be drowsy, lulled by long quiet hours of boredom and inactivity. More importantly, they shouldn't be looking our way.

I backed away from the edge and rejoined my soldiers. They were crouched about a hundred paces from the cliff face in a little hollow that would muffle the sounds of our preparations. We'd left the horses and mules tethered farther down the ridge, well out of earshot.

I strode into the middle of the hollow and stood there with my hands on my hips. "Here we go, lads," I said calmly. "We get one chance to do this right. One chance only. So listen closely!"

The Gallic cavalrymen rose and crowded around me. The two Galilean fishermen, Simon and his younger brother, stood in their midst, their bearded faces pale and set in the predawn gloom.

"First rule: No armor," I told them. "Swords and shields only." Setting my words to action, I took off my helmet and shrugged out of my mail hauberk. Then I looped my sword belt through the grips of my shield and slung them both over my back, leaving my hands free.

Without waiting for further orders, Aedan and the other troopers began following my example.

"Second rule: Only two men on the nets at a time," I said. "You wait until those ahead of you are down, before you go over the edge. Understand?"

Heads nodded.

"Third rule: Do *not* look down. Not until those feet of yours touch the ground." I grinned at them. "Trust your grip on the net. Don't worry about falling. You won't. And don't worry about your weight on the nets. They'll hold." I glanced at the fishermen. "Right?"

They nodded quickly and shifted nervously on their feet.

Most of the cavalrymen grinned back. I could sense their growing eagerness for action. They knew this was dangerous, but no man signs up to be a soldier without being willing to run some risks.

"Fourth rule: Once you're down, move quickly to cover . . ." Step by step, I ran through my plan of attack. When I was satisfied that every man understood exactly what I intended—and what part he would play in the assault—I led them quietly back to the rim of the ravine.

At my signal, a working party came forward, staggering under the weight of the heavy, linked fishing nets. Simon and his brother quickly lashed one end of each net around some nearby boulders. Then, guided by the two Galileans, my soldiers gingerly lowered them over the edge of the cliff, gently swinging the ends outward to keep clear of any obstructions.

The nets touched down.

We were ready.

I moved to the rim and looked over. Everything was still quiet, still peaceful.

Aedan laid a hand on my shoulder. "The Lady will look out for you, Valens," the tall, fair-haired Celt said. "She honors the brave."

I nodded my thanks, took a deep breath, and then swung myself over the edge of the cliff. Fighting off a wave of dizziness, I began the descent, climbing down slowly but surely. The skin at the back of my neck crawled, anticipating the sudden shout from one of the bandit sentries that would signal disaster. But I heard nothing. Nothing but the creak of the net under my weight and the harsh, labored sound of my own breathing.

My boots slapped on the ground and I turned around, already slipping the shield off my back and onto my left arm. Bending low, I dashed into the cover of a jumble of boulders not more than thirty paces from the mouth of the bandit cave. I could see a small flicker of light inside the cave's pitch-black entrance. Dry-mouthed, I drew my sword and laid the scabbard and belt against one of the rocks.

One by one, my troopers made the same descent safely and joined me in the shelter of the boulders. I counted them off silently. Thirteen . . . fourteen . . . fifteen.

And then the first rays of the rising sun broke across the eastern horizon above us, casting shadows far and wide.

One of the bandit sentries to the south stood up from his position and stretched. He turned toward us. Even at this distance, I could see the astonishment and horror on his face when he saw the long line of soldiers climbing down the sheer rock wall behind him.

The lookout's mouth fell open, but he seemed too shocked to call out.

Sword and shield out, I scrambled over the top of one of the boulders and dropped onto the gravel-strewn ground on the other side. "At them!" I shouted. "Get the bastards!"

Four of my troopers peeled off toward the stunned sentries, two heading north and two south.

The rest followed me along the ravine toward the cave mouth, shouting war cries at the top of their lungs. Yelling with them, I sprinted up the shallow slope toward the opening.

One of the brigands came out of the cave just as I reached it. He stared stupidly at me, blinking in the light. He wasn't armed.

I smashed the metal boss of my shield into his face. Blood spattered through the air. The blow knocked him sprawling, and I ran on inside the cave. Another bandit lunged at me out of the darkness, snarling, with a dagger in his hand. I stabbed him once in the stomach and shoved him aside with my shield. He shrieked, folded up, and fell backward out of my path.

The cave itself was not large—no more than twenty feet wide and another hundred feet or so deep. Its floor was mostly black rock, with a thin scattering of sand in some places. A small fire burning near the mouth sent huge shadows flickering across its walls. As I rushed inside, there was enough light to see that most of the bandits were still struggling out of their bedrolls. Some were frantically fumbling for their weapons. Others were simply staring in wide-eyed astonishment.

I grinned fiercely. We had caught Gideon and his robbers completely by surprise.

Just then a wickedly sharp spear point jabbed past my head, almost taking me in the right eye. I swore and got my shield up just in time to block the next thrust. The point slammed into the wood and stuck for an instant. Thrown off balance, the brigand staggered back, trying to tug his spear clear. One of the soldiers following on my heels hacked him down.

An arrow hissed past out of the darkness. It was followed by a thrown rock. I heard an oath somewhere behind me.

Another bandit scrambled to his feet and rushed forward, screaming foully. I ducked his first wild sword swipe and plunged my own blade into his chest. A second quick thrust finished him off.

More and more of my troopers poured into the cave. Anyone who resisted, anyone who got in their way, died swiftly—cut down by the wild, yelling, laughing Celts. A few brigands stood and fought. A few of those left alive threw down their weapons and cowered.

A handful managed to put their backs to one wall and face us. One of my battle-maddened cavalrymen charged them on his own, roaring a war cry. He killed two before he went down under their frantically stabbing swords and spears.

I grimaced. It was time to bring this action under control.

"Seventh Troop! Form line!" I snapped. My voice echoed weirdly in the confined space. "Shields together!"

For a heartbeat, I wasn't sure that the wild-eyed Celts would heed my orders. But then the discipline that had been hammered into them by years of training took hold. Shaking off their bloodlust, they obeyed, taking station on either side. I risked a quick glance behind me and saw Aedan leading another group of soldiers into the cave after us. Reassured, I swung round again.

The tiny knot of bandits against the wall drew closer together. None of them looked ready to surrender. The sound of the fighting in the rest of the cave died away, leaving only the low moans and gasps of the wounded in its wake.

"Soldiers of the Third Cavalry," I said quietly. "Advance."

We moved in slowly, steadily tramping over the bodies of those who'd already fallen, pressing ever closer to the brigands we'd trapped. This time each soldier stayed close to his comrades. From the front, our formation must have seemed a moving wall of interlocked shields.

Even in the darkness I could see the despair and fear rising in the faces of our foes. They weren't craven. If they were, they would already have surrendered to us. But even a brave man can feel his knees turn to jelly watching the silent, implacable advance of well-drilled troops.

We were within a few feet of them when their nerves snapped. The bandits threw themselves forward, attacking with wild cries and shrieks. Spear points and sword blades gleamed in the flickering shadows.

We slaughtered them.

A bearded robber lunged forward with a spear. Durix, one of my young recruits, deflected the attack with his shield. In that same instant, the trooper next to him leaned in and stabbed the Galilean in the throat. Another bandit charged, waving a sword over his head. Before he could bring it down, two of my Celts finished him off. One hacked the bandit's right arm off at the shoulder. The other thrust deep into his stomach.

I didn't have time to watch more of the fighting after that. I closed with an older man, one with a full beard and long graying hair. I felt sure this was Gideon himself. I'd seen him the day before, checking on the sentries outside.

The brigand chieftain was no coward. With his teeth bared, he threw himself at me, slashing wildly with a short-bladed sword. He had strength, but no real skill.

I parried one strike with my shield and then backed up, luring him away from the wall. He attacked a second time. Again, I caught his blow on my shield and then spun to the side.

Gideon stumbled forward. I leaned in and struck hard at his wrist with the flat of my sword. He groaned aloud. His own blade fell from his numbed and useless fingers. Before he could recover, I swung my shield around fast, slamming it squarely into his chest.

Half stunned, the bandit leader toppled backward. I stepped closer, with my sword at his throat. Gasping, he fumbled with his left hand for the dagger sheathed at his side.

I kicked his hand away and stamped hard on that wrist, too. I felt the bones break under my heel. His face turned pale, almost bloodless. His eyes rolled up in his head and he sagged back against the cavern wall. I eyed him warily—with good reason as it turned out.

Gideon made one last attempt to evade capture. With surprising speed, he threw himself forward, trying to spit himself on the sword I held at his throat.

But I stepped back before the point even drew blood. "No, you don't," I told him coolly. I wanted this man alive. Something was very wrong here—and I wanted to find out exactly what that was.

I looked up.

The battle was over. Most of the brigands were dead or dying, but we had a few as prisoners, five all told. Soldiers ringed them with drawn swords.

Our own losses were light. One man killed. Three more were wounded, though none very seriously.

"Bind this villain," I told two of the troopers closest to me. "And hold him apart from the rest."

They saluted with wide grins. "Yes, Prefect!"

I left them to it and joined Aedan. Together, the decurion and I began combing through the captured weapons and loot littering the cave. My face was grim when we began, and I'm sure it was grimmer still by the time we finished.

A handful of the bandits had owned bows. But not one of the arrows in their quivers matched the shaft we'd pulled out of the Praetorian guardsman we'd found near Nazara. And there was no sign of any armor or weapons or clothing that might once have belonged to Decimus Junius Silanus, his bodyguards, or his slaves and servants. Nor was there any trace of the thousands of gold coins the senator's pack mules were said to have been carrying. We did find a leather bag full of silver and bronze coins—several hundred at least—but they all seemed to carry inscriptions identifying them as having been minted for Herod Antipas.

I looked up from a row of wine jars that Gideon and his men must have looted from some passing merchant. Most were empty.

Aedan tossed an armful of swords and daggers to the ground with a loud, metallic clatter. He stared back at me, frowning. "We've been tricked by that Parthian snake, Vardanes."

"So it seems," I agreed. "But to what end?"

In a bid to find out, I had the man I'd taken captive dragged outside the cave. Our other prisoners had already confirmed that he was, as I'd suspected, their leader—Gideon.

Two soldiers propped him up against a boulder and left him there. The chieftain's burly arms were bound behind him. I wasn't taking any chances with this fellow. Behind the sweat and grime and pain, his face was that of a proud and defiant man, a man who would sooner die than accept defeat.

We looked at each other in silence for some time.

Gideon glared up at me. "Well, Roman," he growled at last. "You've beaten me, but only by some foul ruse! If you'd come charging up this ravine like honest men, we'd have knocked your heads about."

"Quite likely," I agreed, with some amusement.

"So what will you do to my men and me now?" the bandit leader jeered. "Slaughter us like sheep while we're trussed and helpless?"

"No," I told him. "I'll take you before Herod Antipas.

You'll be tried, and I'll testify against you. I expect that you'll be found guilty and condemned to death."

"For what crime?" the brigand demanded.

I shrugged. "The murder of the senator Decimus Junius Silanus and his followers, for one."

"Silanus?" Gideon screwed up his face in bewilderment. "Who is that?"

I kept a tight rein on my expression. The confusion in his voice was genuine. Whoever had killed Silanus, it wasn't this man, or any of his fellow thieves. No one could murder a Roman nobleman guarded by Praetorian troops and not know it.

Then why had Vardanes pointed me in his direction? Weary of chasing Gideon unsuccessfully for so long, had the Parthian mercenary simply seized the chance to have me do his work for him? Or was there a darker motive at work? I gritted my teeth. Wherever I turned in this maddening investigation, there were only more unanswered questions.

I looked down at the captive brigand leader. Could I learn anything useful from him at all?

"If not for the death of the senator, then any of your other crimes will serve to condemn you," I said coolly. "The penalty will be the same. Crucifixion."

Some of the defiance leached out of Gideon's bearded face. For the first time, I thought I saw a bit of fear creeping into his eyes. He swallowed. "Crucifixion . . ."

I nodded. "It's the usual penalty for murder, theft, and banditry."

He looked down at the ground. "The cross is an ugly way to die."

"Yes," I agreed. "It is. And slow."

Death on a cross is a gruesome and agonizing spec-

tacle. The condemned man is nailed or tied in place and
left to die, gradually strangled by his own weight. Exe-
cutioners who are exceptionally cruel provide a small
support for the dying man's feet, sometimes prolonging
the process for several days. We Romans view it as the
supreme penalty, the most wretched and shameful of all
deaths imaginable.

Gideon stared silently at the ground for some time. I
said nothing.

When he looked up again, most of his bravado was
gone. Beads of sweat ran down his dirt-stained forehead. "There are things I know . . . things I could tell
you . . ."

I leaned forward. "Go ahead."

The bandit swallowed. "If I do, will you set us free,
my men and I?"

"No," I said instantly. "I won't lie to you. I will not
set you loose to prey on travelers again. The crimes
you've already committed have earned you execution a
dozen times over."

Gideon sighed. He fell silent again, looking down at
his feet. Finally, he asked, "Then will you at least grant
us an easier death?"

"Give me a reason," I said softly. In truth, I had no
real desire to crucify these men. Even as a boy, I had
found the sight of a cross grotesque and evil. Nor was I
alone in my feelings. When Julius Caesar was a young
man, pirates had captured him near Rhodes. While a
prisoner he'd sworn to hunt them down and crucify
them once his ransom was paid. The pirates had laughed
at him. They should not have, for that is precisely what
he did. But Caesar was a merciful man—he hanged
them up on crosses only after cutting their throats first.

Gideon raised his eyes again, intently studying my

face. What he saw must have assured him I would keep
my end of any bargain, because he started talking—
slowly at first, and then faster as the secrets he'd kept
for so long poured out of him. "We were warned that
you Romans were coming, and we were offered a reward for your deaths," he began.

For the past year he and his gang had preyed on soli-
tary travelers and small caravans along both the Sea of
Galilee and the roads through these hills. Some of the
goods they stole were sold through a small network of
friends and supporters in Magdala. But the best items—
the finest wines and cloth, the most expensive spices,
and the like—were reserved for their patron, the man of
power and high rank who gave them his protection.

"What is this man's name?" I demanded harshly.

Gideon shook his head. "I don't know it."

I snorted. "I find that very difficult to believe."

"But it is true. On the Most High, I swear it," he insisted hurriedly. The sweat was rolling off him now.
Once he had been a reasonably prosperous fisherman, at
least until Herod's rising taxes broke him. When he
couldn't pay up, the tetrarch's officials confiscated his
boat and his house and left him penniless and starving.
For a short time, he'd earned a meager living by robbing
lone passersby of their possessions.

All too soon, though, he'd been caught, convicted,
and dragged off to one of Herod Antipas' dungeons to
await public execution. It was the usual sad, sordid run
of events for a man hounded into crime. But then something strange happened. A man, wearing a hooded cloak
to hide his features, came to his cell and struck a bargain
with him.

This man said he would arrange Gideon's escape and
supply him with weapons and a willing cadre of like-

minded men. More importantly, he would guarantee the new gang a safe hiding place in the hills and protection from Herod's roving patrols. In return, the bandits would give him half of all their loot and accept any new orders he chose to give them.

With nothing to lose, Gideon readily agreed.

The hooded man proved as good as his word. That night Gideon's cell door was left unlocked and unguarded. He fled up into the rough country to this cave, the one he'd been told about. In ones and twos, more recruits drifted in, swelling the ranks of his little band of robbers.

And so for months the brigands lived fat on the proceeds of rich merchants, lying low whenever they were warned of a close sweep by their mysterious patron. His share of the stolen goods was cached at one of several hiding places he designated and never seen again.

Then, near dawn two days ago, the hooded man himself came here on horseback to meet with Gideon in person—bearing both a warning of our plans to hunt him down and the offer of a large reward if we instead were trapped and killed.

"That sack of coins you found was the earnest money he offered us for the job," the bandit chieftain said wearily. "If it hadn't been for that, we'd have been up and out of here right after you and your patrol came sniffing around our front door."

I nodded absentmindedly, thinking of the hoofprints that we'd found so near the opening of this narrow ravine. This mysterious patron of his moved fast. I hadn't even decided to come after Gideon and his gang until late the evening before—not until after I'd talked to Vardanes.

Vardanes.

The memory of the Parthian's smirking face swam before my eyes. My hands curled into fists. "You say you never saw this man's appearance," I said, forcing myself to speak calmly.

Gideon nodded.

"Well, then," I asked, "would you recognize his voice?"

"I would," the grim-faced bandit said flatly. "I swear it."

"Good." I swung round and called for Aedan.

When the decurion arrived, I had Gideon repeat the story he'd told me. I watched quietly while the tall Celt's long face grew bleaker and bleaker. After the bandit finished his tale, I looked at Aedan. "Do you believe him?"

The cavalry officer considered that briefly. His mouth tightened. "I do," he said. "But I wish that I did not. It is an ugly and unlucky thing to hear of so much black treachery."

I turned toward Gideon. "All right. Hear me out. Your men die here—quickly and cleanly."

The brigand chief nodded. "And what of me?"

"You'll come with us to Herod's court," I said. "There you'll help me find this patron of yours. Once that's done, I promise you the same quick, clean end."

Gideon closed his eyes. His shoulders slumped.

Aedan and I moved away to arrange the swift and merciful execution of the five other bandits we'd captured. When all of them were dead, the decurion turned to me. "Now what do we do, Prefect?"

I stared out into the ravine. A band of clean, bright sunshine was already sliding down its sheer walls, chasing away shadows, pouring color back into the black and red rock and the yellow sand. I longed for a bath, for the chance to soak away the dirt on my skin and the blood on my hands. For the chance to rest and empty my troubled mind. But there was no time.

"You heard what I told Gideon," I told Aedan. "We'll finish tending our wounded and then we ride back to Tiberias."

"To track down this man who tried to buy our deaths?"

"That's right."

"And when we find this man?" the Celt asked. "What then?"

I shrugged. "I'll bring him to trial before Herod."

"And if the tetrarch will not agree?" Aedan persisted, speaking gently. "You heard that bandit's tale. Whoever he may be, this hooded man wields great power."

I swung back to face the Celt squarely. My mouth was set in a thin, determined line. "I'm a Roman officer, Decurion. I owe Herod respect, not obedience. If I have to, I'll kill this hooded bastard with my own sword."

Chapter XX

My Spanish mare, Dancer, plodded south along the shore road from Magdala to Tiberias. I slouched in the saddle, bone-weary after two full days without rest. Every part of my body felt sore.

It was late in the afternoon. The shadows of the evening were already drawing in. Reddish sunlight still touched the tops of the hills far across the Sea of Galilee, but the waters themselves were mostly dark, topped here and there by choppy, foam-flecked waves. The wind had swung round to the east, whipping across the lake in short gusts. There might be a storm brewing, I thought, somewhere far off in the deserts of the East.

Stiffly, I turned around to check the long line of men and animals strung out behind me. Aedan and Aristides were there, riding side by side in weary, companionable silence. The bandit chieftain Gideon came next, stumbling along with his hands tied behind him. Though he knew he was going to his death, he kept his head up proudly. The rest of my exhausted cavalrymen trailed after him in a straggling column of twos.

Paulus was somewhere behind the soldiers, moping along on his mule and maintaining a stiff-necked, scowling silence. The boy had rejoined us after relaying Aristides' instructions for Marah's care to her steward. But just as the doctor had predicted, he was still angry with me because I'd left him out of our raid on Gideon's camp.

I shrugged to myself and faced front again. Perhaps it was just as well that Paulus had refused to ride up here with the rest of us. One thing was certain: I didn't have the strength or the patience to deal with the boy's bad temper right now.

The road ahead wound along the shoreline, with the water on our left and steep tree-lined slopes rising off to our right. We were not far from the outskirts of Herod Antipas' new capital, less than a mile away.

I straightened up, willing myself to stay alert. It was increasingly difficult. The slow, steady rhythm of Dancer's hooves on the hard-packed dirt road lulled me from my sense of duty and set my tired mind adrift.

My thoughts wandered to Marah. Did I love her? I knew that I found everything about her intoxicating — her eyes, her voice, the softness of her skin, the quickness of her wit. But was that really love? Or was it only lust?

I sighed. What did that really matter? For good or ill, the hard truth was that Marah and I were cut off from each other by the competing claims of birth, of blood, and of duty. It was happening already. Much as I wanted to go to her, to comfort her, to beg for her forgiveness, I could not. We were miles apart and here I was — caught in the grip of my responsibilities and drawn on toward a confrontation at Herod's court.

In time, she would surely forget me, I thought. And someday I would find a way to forget her. For now, though, the memory of Marah's tearstained face haunted my thoughts. I rode on without speaking, wrapped in sadness. No matter how much I told myself it was folly to waste so much time regretting the mess I'd made of things, I couldn't help it.

Dozens of birds burst out of the nearest stand of trees, cawing and shrieking as they circled higher and higher overhead. Startled, I turned my head that way, peering into the thicket. Something had frightened the birds. But what?

I heard Aedan utter a sharp oath.

Horsemen appeared at the edge of the trees on our right flank. They were Parthians, clad in loose, tan-colored jackets and pale blue trousers. None wore armor, but they all carried powerful composite bows, with arrows notched and ready.

Their commander, Vardanes, walked his horse right out in front of me, no more than fifty paces away. Like his men, he bore a bow. Marcus Aemilius Severus followed him, resplendent in his dress armor and scarlet cloak. More mounted archers filed out of the woods and took station behind them both, completely blocking the road.

We were hemmed in on two sides. Swearing violently under my breath, I reined in hard. Dancer's head came up. Her nostrils flared and her eyes flicked back in alarm.

"Hold!" Vardanes commanded. He rose higher in the saddle, scanning the men and horses behind me. I saw his eyes narrow.

"What do you want, Parthian?" I said loudly.

"Only what is mine," Vardanes replied. Then, in one smooth, swift motion, he raised his bow, drew it back, and fired.

His arrow tore right past my ear. I heard a strangled,

choking cough behind me and spun around. The black-feathered shaft sprouted in Gideon's throat. For a long moment, the bandit chieftain stared back at me in horror. Then his eyes rolled up and he toppled in a gush of bright red blood.

I swung back to Vardanes, furious. "That man was my prisoner!"

The Parthian mercenary shrugged. "He was a criminal, Prefect. No one will mourn him. I've saved the tetrarch's judges a bit of time and trouble, that's all." He eyed me coldly. "Maybe you should worry more about yourself."

In that instant, I knew that my suspicions were correct. Vardanes was the hooded man, Gideon's secret patron. This smug villain was a traitor to Herod and to the rule of law. He was also the man who'd tried to buy our defeat and annihilation.

My temper exploded. I reacted instinctively. One part of my mind screamed that this was folly, but I ignored it — giving in to the fierce, wild urge to strike Vardanes down if I could. I kicked my heels into Dancer's flanks. She lowered her head and lunged forward, racing straight for the black-haired, black-hearted Parthian. I started to draw my sword.

The mercenary waited calmly, watching me come.

Two of the archers at the edge of the trees let fly. I felt the mare shudder as both arrows struck home, tearing deep into her vitals. She screamed — a horrible, high-pitched shriek that pierced my own heart. Writhing in agony, Dancer bucked and reared. Her hooves flailed madly, slashing at the air in all directions.

I threw myself out of the saddle and rolled off to one side.

Dancer crashed to the ground close by. She kicked

wildly a few more times. Then she shuddered once and lay still. My great steed was dead.

I lay pressed to the earth, staring at her crumpled form in shock. I'd bought Dancer when she was only three years old. I'd trained her myself, schooling her in the arts of war before we went off together to Germany. In all the years since, she'd proved a loyal companion, both in battle and on the road. I'd loved her for her speed, her agility, her unshakable good nature, and her courage.

Swallowing hard against the lump in my throat, I looked up. Through the tears welling up in my eyes, I saw that the Parthian archers had their bows up and drawn. They were ready to shoot again.

I glanced over my shoulder. Aedan and the other Gallic cavalrymen were still bunched up on the road. Some of them had drawn their swords, but a charge now would be madness. There was no room to deploy or maneuver. We were trapped in a killing ground between the woods and the water.

"Decurion!" I shouted. "Stand down! Now!"

Aedan stared at me for a moment. Then his shoulders slumped and he nodded. Grim-faced, he slid his own blade back into its scabbard. The soldiers behind him followed his example.

Seeing that, Vardanes yelled an order of his own. His men reluctantly lowered their weapons.

"Get up!" the mercenary commander told me. "But do it carefully."

I stood up slowly, keeping my hands well away from my sword or dagger. I blinked away the tears as best I could. I would not show any weakness to these butchers.

Severus walked his horse forward. He leaned down. "That was foolish, Valens. Very foolish." He shook his head. "You could easily have provoked the pointless massacre of your own soldiers."

Fighting to control my fury, both at him and my own stupidity, I forced out a question. "I know why Vardanes is here. What have you come for?"

"You," the Praetorian said calmly. "I've come to arrest you."

"On whose authority?" I demanded.

"My own."

I shook my head. "Impossible. You don't have any jurisdiction over me."

The centurion shrugged. "It is a bit irregular, I admit, but I feel certain my own commander, Aelius Sejanus, will confirm the order — if that should prove necessary."

"And on what charge am I to be arrested?"

"Interfering with the investigation of the murder of Decimus Junius Silanus."

"Herod Antipas himself gave me seven days to finish my inquiry," I snapped back. "Four of those days still remain. It seems strange that I should be arrested for interfering with my own investigation."

"Circumstances have changed, and your time is up, Valens," Severus said flatly. "The tetrarch has just received important news from Antioch."

"What kind of news?" I asked warily.

"Tragic news. All Rome will soon be in mourning," the Praetorian said. The sad look on his face did not reach his eyes. "Germanicus Julius Caesar is dead."

The world around me darkened immediately. Germanicus dead? I'd never known a healthier, stronger man. I knew he was ill when we left Antioch, but no one had believed it was a serious sickness. "How did it happen?" I croaked.

"They say Germanicus contracted a wasting disease, or a virulent fever of some kind," Severus said. He shrugged again. "That's the official word anyway. Of course, there are rumors of poison or black magic." His eyes glittered. "Having met that fat toad Gnaeus Piso and those in his immediate circle, I'm inclined to believe the rumors."

"Who rules in Antioch now?" I asked through gritted teeth. Germanicus had been too good, too trusting. Whatever the truth about his death, he should never have allowed Piso to stay in office.

"That's a matter of some dispute," Severus admitted. "Some say Piso. Others say Sertorius, the new commander of the Sixth Legion. I imagine a little blood may be spilled before we find out just who governs Syria and the East in Caesar's name." He leaned down from the saddle. "But what matters most to me, Aurelius Valens, is that you are out of my way at last. You no longer have a patron to support you."

I said nothing.

"As you can imagine, Herod is rather keenly aware of that," the centurion continued. "And so he's given me full authority to find and punish the senator's murderers in any way I see fit. As a first step in that process, I'm placing you under arrest." He nodded toward Aedan and Aristides, who were watching us with worried faces. "Along with the decurion and that Greek doctor there. I want all three of you safely under lock and key."

"And you have Herod's permission to do this?"

Severus shrugged. "I haven't bothered to ask him. I'm sure the tetrarch would prefer to remain ignorant of the details of my actions. It's much safer for him that way."

The Praetorian was probably right. With Germanicus

dead, Herod didn't have any reason to interfere any further. He could close his eyes to whatever Severus did, confident that it was now a strictly Roman affair—one for which he would bear no responsibility.

I raised an eyebrow. "If you control the investigation now, why arrest us?"

Severus smiled thinly. "Let's just say that I'm a cautious man, Aurelius Valens. I don't like taking unnecessary chances." He shook his head. "You strike me as a very determined young officer—certainly one too stupid to know when he's beaten. You've also shown a strange fondness for the Jews in that little rat's nest of a village. And I won't tolerate any more interference in my plans for them."

I stared up at him, knowing that my face must reflect the sick feeling in my heart.

The Praetorian nodded coolly. "That's right, boy." His smile grew colder still. "Nazara is finally mine to deal with as I see fit."

Then he wheeled his horse and cantered away without another word.

Vardanes snapped an order and his archers closed in. Two of them stripped me of my armor and weapons. Others signaled Aedan off his mount and did the same to him. Aristides quickly swung down off his mule without waiting to be told. He fumbled quickly with his saddlebags and then stood aside, nervously clutching his battered old hat in both hands. A Parthian hustled him over to my side.

I kept my face expressionless.

The rest of my soldiers were already filing past under close guard with their heads hung low. They were ashamed at having been ambushed so easily and then taken without a fight.

I looked away.

My eyes fell on Dancer's corpse. And I felt the breath catch in my throat when I looked more closely at one of the arrows buried deep in her chest. That pattern of black-dyed feathers was all too familiar. I'd last seen it on the shaft Aristides had dug out of Cassius Celer, the Praetorian guardsman we'd found dead in the thorns.

I looked up, still shocked, and found Vardanes watching me closely.

The exiled Parthian noble nodded to me, sketched a mock bow, and then rode off toward the head of the column, leaving several of his men to march Aedan, Aristides, and me toward Tiberias.

I watched the mounted men disappear around a bend in the road. One small figure on a mule was missing.

"Where is Paulus?" I asked the other two quietly.

"Gone," the doctor said. "He must have slipped off into the trees as soon as we were waylaid."

"The boy is well out of this," Aedan murmured. "I doubt these Parthian pigs plan to let us live long. That bastard Vardanes won't want to risk our wagging tongues."

"You saw the arrow, then?" I said.

The other two nodded bleakly.

Surrounded by our captors, we trudged on in silence toward Tiberias, each of us alone with our own grim thoughts.

Chapter XXI

When we reached Tiberias, Herod's new royal city, Aedan, Aristides, and I were shoved into a small, square stone hut once used by the workmen who built the tetrarch's palace. The floor was hard-packed earth. Narrow slits high up on the walls provided a very small amount of light, and even less fresh air.

There was a single stout, iron-framed door, but it was barred from the outside. Some of Vardanes' archers were on guard. From time to time, we could hear them talking idly to each other in their own native tongue.

Once the door was shut, Aedan hoisted me up on his shoulder to check the roof. It was made of wood timbers laid across the walls. The gaps were filled with a thick mixture of dried mud and straw. For a time, I poked and prodded at the beams and the spaces in between. Then I shook my head glumly and clambered down.

"No good?" Aedan asked.

"It's too well built," I told him. "The beams aren't more than six inches apart anywhere. We could pry out the mud easily enough, but none of us will fit through."

"We can't tunnel our way out either," Aristides said. "Look here."

While the decurion and I checked the roof for a means of escape, the doctor had been busy scrabbling with both hands at the hard-packed earth floor. He'd scraped away the dirt in several places along each wall, everywhere revealing the same solid layer of black basalt rock.

Aedan sighed. "They say the strongest houses are those craftsmen build for themselves. It seems a terrible pity that this is true." The tall, fair-haired Celt turned to me. "Well, now. We're boxed in. What do we do next, Prefect?"

I swung round, studying the walls, the roof, and the floor again, trying to see some weakness we could exploit to escape. Some other way out. There wasn't any. There was just the door — iron-framed, barred, and heavily guarded.

I looked back at him. "I'm afraid we wait, Decurion. We wait and we stay ready."

He nodded. The grim expression on his face mirrored my own thoughts. I didn't believe any of us had any illusions left about what the Parthians had planned for us.

On impulse, I stepped closer to the Celt. "One thing more, Aedan."

He looked down at me. "Yes, Prefect?"

"Please call me Lucius," I said quietly. This was the personal name reserved for use by my own family and by deeply trusted members of my household, like Aristides. It wasn't a privilege that I handed out lightly. Still, it wasn't much to offer the decurion. Not when obeying my orders had brought him here to this dark prison, to this likely killing house. No, it was not much at all.

But it was all that I had.

Aedan stared at me for a long moment. He stood there blinking in the dim light. Then he cleared his throat. "Thank you for this honor, Prefect . . . I mean, Lucius," the Celt said hoarsely at last.

We clasped forearms in friendship.

"I'm only sorry I've dragged you into this," I told him. "And you, too, Aristides."

The doctor shrugged. "I told you long ago, Lucius, where you go, I go." He smiled tightly. "Mind you, I'd much rather you didn't insist on putting your head in the lion's mouth so often."

"It's a bad position, to be sure," Aedan agreed. "But no soldier is ever promised safety and a long life. Besides," he said, "the Lady may not yet be finished with us. She prizes courage and daring—and those we three have in plenty."

I only nodded, silently envying the Celt his simple faith in the horse goddess of his people. For my part, I doubted that the gods paid much attention to the fate of any particular mortal. I'd seen too many good men die and too many bad men prosper to think anything else.

Before too long, the light coming through the narrow windows above us winked out. We were left in utter darkness. The sun was down. It was night.

Several hours passed with painful slowness.

I was sitting with my back against the wall when I heard voices on the other side of the door and the grating sound of the bar being lifted. "Aedan! Aristides!" I hissed.

We got to our feet.

The door swung open. A torch was thrust inside. I half closed my eyes against the blinding glare. Four archers came through the doorway one after another, moving easily with their bows ready.

Severus followed them in, accompanied by another Parthian holding a torch aloft. "Still awake, I see," he noted approvingly. "That's good, Valens. I like an officer who stays alert in the presence of his enemies."

My hands curled into fists, but I resisted the urge to go straight for his throat. The Parthian guards were too alert, too ready for trouble. Instead, I asked, "Why are you here?" My throat was parched and my voice sounded harsh and rasping.

"To keep you informed of my progress," Severus said, pretending to be surprised. He gave me a mocking smile. "I know how much you care for the Jews of Nazara—though why that is, I can't imagine. So I thought it only right that you should hear exactly what I have in store for them."

I said nothing. I didn't want to give him the satisfaction of knowing that his jibes were hitting home.

Unfortunately, my silence didn't deter the Praetorian from laying out his plan to destroy the little Galilean village. He spoke slowly, almost lovingly—and he was very thorough. Vardanes and his horse archers would do most of the cruel work. They would storm Nazara itself, with orders to butcher every adult male and anyone else who got in their way. Once the killing was done, they would seize any women and children left alive for sale as slaves. The proceeds, he commented offhandedly, should provide a tidy sum for the mercenary officer and for himself. My own fifty Gallic cavalrymen, the ones I'd left watching over the village, would act as a reserve—ready to ride down any fugitives who escaped the Parthian net.

"And once we've finished with the people, Vardanes and his archers will set fire to every field, every orchard, and every hovel," Severus said. He smiled. "By sunset tomorrow, Nazara in Galilee will cease to exist."

"For what purpose?" I asked bitterly.

The Praetorian centurion shrugged. "As reprisal for the murder of Decimus Junius Silanus, of course. Why else?"

"You're a liar," I snapped.

Severus' smile slipped. He raised an eyebrow. "In what way?"

"You know that Vardanes and his men murdered the senator and his retainers," I told him coldly. "It was one of their arrows that we found in your guardsman's back."

Severus stared at me. His face was now rigid, utterly expressionless. The sword scar on his left cheek gleamed white in the torchlight. "You noticed that then," he said at length. "The Parthian said you did. I had hoped he was wrong."

"Then you admit it," I said quietly, feeling suddenly ill.

I think I'd known that the centurion was somehow involved in the murders from the moment I'd realized Gideon and his bandits were innocent of them. Why else had he been so quick to rush the Parthian traitor to my room, to fill my ears with so many falsehoods?

Severus nodded calmly. "All right. I admit it."

"And how much did Vardanes pay you to look the other way?" I demanded. I could feel my anger growing, flaring hotter and hotter with every passing moment. "How much did he pay to buy your silence?"

"Buy *my* silence?" The stern-faced Praetorian officer was astonished. Then he gave a harsh, cruel, humorless laugh that sent a shiver down my spine. He shook his head. "By the gods, boy, you're a fool. You've got the wrong end of the stick."

Severus leaned closer, with one hand on the dagger at his side. "No one bought my silence, Valens. No one at all." He straightened up. His eyes were cold and very distant. "*I* gave the orders for the senator's death. No one else."

The centurion nodded at the archers on either side of him. "The Parthians were my instruments, my chosen weapons. Nothing more." He smiled grimly. "One could scarcely ask for a better band of hired killers. Only Vardanes speaks any real Greek, and I've never yet met another man so eager to get his hands on a little gold."

I stared at him, scarcely able to hear through the roaring in my ears. "You ordered the deaths of your own comrades?"

"It was necessary," Severus told me, frowning. "Regrettable, I suppose, but necessary. After all, it would have looked somewhat suspicious if the illustrious senator died and all his bodyguards lived."

My skin crawled. I was in the presence of an evil greater than I had yet imagined. I'd seen the centurion's face when he looked down at the body of Cassius Celer, his old comrade-in-arms. What kind of man could feign such surprise, such sorrow? What kind of man could arrange the cold-blooded murder of his own best friend? I wanted to back away from him, to press myself against the rough stones of the wall. I fought the urge. "Why?" I asked finally. "Why have you done this?"

Severus looked at me curiously. "For power, of course. What else is there of any real value in the world?"

"Power?"

The centurion laughed. "You are naive, Valens." He shook his head in mock wonder. "I'm amazed that you don't see it—even now. What do they teach you brave young officers these days?"

I held my tongue. He was baiting me, rubbing my

failure in my face. But the longer he talked, the more I learned. And the more he talked, the longer Aedan, Aristides, and I stayed alive.

Severus sighed. "Try to follow along, then—if you can." He folded his arms. "The equation is simple: Rome rules the world. The Senate rules Rome. And the emperor rules the Senate. Clear enough?"

I nodded.

"Ah," the centurion went on, "but who rules Tiberius? Who governs Caesar?" He shrugged. "Picture Rome as it was a few months ago. There are three factions competing for the emperor's favor. Three factions seeking power over his mind. One led by my commander, Aelius Sejanus—the prefect of the Praetorian Guard. Another in the Senate, dominated by Silanus. And a third bloc led by Thrasyllus, the master of that babbling mystic Araneus."

My jaw tightened. I would have known this if I hadn't been out of the city for so long. My father reveled in just this sort of filthy intrigue and gossip. I'd turned my back on it in a bid to serve Rome with clean hands, out on the distant frontier. And now I was paying the price for my own willful ignorance.

"And then Tiberius Caesar has a dream—a terrible dream," Severus mused. "He picks Decimus Junius Silanus to lead a mission to the East to quiet his fears. But the other factions persuade him to include their own representatives. Including me." The Praetorian smiled at me. "Don't you see, Valens? It was the perfect opportunity, the chance to winnow the field in complete safety. There were three evenly matched factions whispering in Tiberius' ear. Now, when I return to Rome, there will be only two."

"And you believe your commander will thank you

for arranging the senator's death?" I asked, forcing myself to speak.

Severus nodded. "I'm quite sure of it," he said confidently. "Aelius Sejanus is swift to punish failure. But he
is also generous with those who advance his interests."
He grinned at me, looking more wolf than man for a
fleeting instant. "I once told you I was an ambitious
man, Valens. I didn't lie."

"You want promotion. You want to become a tribune," I realized. "You want to command a cohort of the
Guard." There were nine cohorts in the Praetorian
Guard, each made up of a thousand soldiers, and each
commanded by a tribune. It was possible for a centurion
like Severus to rise to that rank, but it was exceedingly
rare.

The Praetorian nodded again. "That's right, Valens.
As a first step, at any rate." He chuckled. "After that,
who knows? Why should a man like me accept limits,
any limits at all?"

With an effort, I kept my voice steady. "If you've already achieved your aim by killing the senator, why destroy Nazara?"

"Araneus insists on it," Severus said. "And he still
speaks for Thrasyllus." He smiled wryly. "You've heard
the twitching fool. He swears there are strange prophecies swirling around that little place, prophecies that
could shake Rome to its foundations."

"But you don't believe that?"

The Praetorian snorted. "Of course not." Then he
bared his teeth in another wolfish grin. "Still, it is such
a tidy little package to hand to Caesar, don't you think?
His dream was true, I will tell him. Nazara was a dire
threat to his safety—as proved by the vicious murder of
his prized envoy, his close friend and ally."

I saw it indeed. Severus was right. He could make Tiberius believe the villagers were his enemies and then reap the rewards for having crushed them.

There was a long silence, broken only by the crackling of the torch that lit the hut.

"Don't you want to know what your own fate will be?" Severus said at last, growing weary of my restraint.

"You'll murder us, too, I suppose," I said, with as much disdain as I could muster. I saw Aedan and Aristides nodding somberly.

"I will," the Praetorian agreed. "Once I've finished my work at Nazara and reported to Herod." He shrugged. "I know you too well now to think I could ever trust you to keep silent—not even if I offered you all the treasure Silanus carried." Then he sighed. "You're growing wiser, boy. But it's too little, too late, I'm afraid. You've made too many mistakes, and now they're going to kill you."

He turned to go.

"I'm not the only one here who's made mistakes, Centurion," I told him, trying a shot almost at random. Something about what I'd heard still didn't jibe with the facts I'd found at Nazara. But what was it? "Your grand scheme has already veered off course, hasn't it?"

Severus looked back at me, plainly nettled that I'd spoiled his triumphant exit.

"Cassius Celer," I spoke my sudden thought aloud. "The Parthians weren't supposed to kill him, were they? Not your old friend."

His lips tightened.

"I saw your face," I reminded him. "You didn't expect to find Celer dead. You didn't expect to find him with an arrow in his back."

Now it was the centurion's turn to stay silent.

"Celer was supposed to survive the 'ambush,' wasn't he?" I pressed him. "I imagine he was supposed to swear that the Jews of Nazara had attacked them and murdered the senator."

Severus glared at me. He didn't say anything. He didn't have to. For once, I could read his thoughts almost as clearly as though they were my own.

"But something went wrong out there in the darkness, didn't it? Out there among the trees and thorns," I said. "Maybe Cassius Celer couldn't bring himself to betray the others at the end. Or maybe Vardanes decided it would be better if all the witnesses to his crime were safely dead."

The centurion said nothing. But the scar on his face was even paler now.

"How far can you really trust this Parthian murderer you've bought, Marcus Aemilius?" I taunted, doing my best to rattle him any way I could. "What will you do if Vardanes decides he's safer with you out of the way, too? One word from him and you'll find yourself lying in a ditch, with an arrow through your guts and the ravens pecking at your face. Just like your good friend Cassius Celer."

That was a solid thrust. I saw it strike home in his mind.

Severus grimaced. He spun around on his heel and plunged out through the open doorway. The Parthian archers and the torchbearer followed him out.

The heavy, iron-bound door clanged shut behind them, plunging the tiny hut back into absolute darkness.

Now that it was safe, now that no one else could see my own despair, I slid slowly back down the wall until I sat with my face buried in my hands. All my efforts had been in vain. I had accomplished nothing. I had won nothing. Severus would achieve his desired end. Nazara would be destroyed. And once that was done, there would be nothing to stop him from having the three of us dragged out to a sordid and meaningless death.

It was morning. Thin rays of sunlight streamed in through the high window slits. I raised my head, alarmed by the heavy tread of footsteps outside the door. Had Severus decided to finish us off first before riding on to Nazara?

I scrambled to my feet, motioning Aedan and Aristides to do the same. I looked them over. "Ready, comrades?"

They nodded, breathing deeply. The decurion appeared calm, the doctor less so. One of the things we'd all agreed during the long night was that we would go down fighting. We would not allow ourselves to be led meekly to execution, like lambs to the slaughter.

A ray of light fell on the gold band around the ring finger of my left hand. Honor and truth, I thought. A good way to live—and a good way to die, if need be. I squared my shoulders. Some of the terrible despair I'd felt in the darkness slid away, driven off by the prospect of action. Win or lose, I would do my best. No man could do more than that.

We didn't have much to fight back with—just our bare hands and the two small surgical instruments Aristides had managed to conceal inside his battered old hat. But they would be enough to make some of our enemies very sorry, I thought fiercely. If only we could get close enough.

I heard the bar being lifted.

It was time. I exhaled slowly. My thumb gingerly

tested the edge of the scalpel I held concealed in my right hand. It was razor-sharp.

The door swung open, revealing a small figure outlined in light. "Aurelius Valens! Aristides!" said a familiar voice. "It's me, Paulus."

"Paulus!" I exclaimed, completely astonished. "What are you doing here?"

The short, dark-haired boy from Tarsus stepped through the doorway with an impish grin on his face. "I'm rescuing you, Prefect."

I stared at him in amazement.

Two of the Parthian archers were visible behind Paulus. Their powerful compound bows were slung over their shoulders, but each wore a curved saber at his side. Their faces showed no clear, decipherable emotion—only cautious vigilance.

I nodded toward them. "You have strange allies in your rescue, Paulus."

The boy shrugged. "Don't worry about the guards," he said confidently. "I've bought their help."

My eyes narrowed. "You've done what?"

Paulus turned red under my gaze. "Well, actually, it wasn't me," he admitted. "Not exactly, anyway. It was the lady Marah."

Aristides moved eagerly toward the open door. I laid a hand on his arm, restraining him. "Wait, Doctor," I cautioned. "Before we risk an arrow in the back, let's hear what Paulus has to tell us."

Speaking rapidly, almost stuttering in his excitement, the boy recounted his adventures. When the Parthians ambushed us, he'd been lagging some distance behind the column—far enough away to let him disappear into the woods without being seen. He'd stayed hidden there, watching while the rest of us were rounded up and marched off. Then he'd followed along at a safe distance.

Once at Herod's palace, Paulus had been able to learn enough of what was going on by gossiping with the tetrarch's servants to convince him that we were in serious trouble. And so he'd turned right around and ridden back to Magdala as fast as he could persuade his balky mule to go.

When he told Marah what had happened, she had ordered her steward to give him a large sum of money to bribe our guards. "She's very worried about you, Prefect," the boy said earnestly. "She told me I should offer the Parthians whatever it took to buy your freedom. She said your life was worth all she possessed."

I swallowed hard. This was generosity beyond all measure. "The lady is kind," I said hoarsely.

Aedan glanced at me. I could see a sudden flash of merriment dance in the tall Celt's green eyes. "The lady is also beautiful," he murmured. "Don't forget that, Lucius."

Now it was my turn to blush.

"You can give her your thanks in person," Paulus said excitedly. "She came with me."

I swung toward him, even more surprised than before. "Marah is here?"

"Yes," Paulus said. "She's waiting close by, with a string of horses for the three of you." He puffed out his chest. "But I handled bribing the guards on my own. They wouldn't have listened to a woman."

Probably not, I decided. But why should I believe the Parthians would pay any more heed to the bargain they'd struck with this boy? I felt troubled suddenly. What was Marah doing here? Didn't she know how dangerous this was? She was sticking her hand into an adder's nest, a place of poison and fangs.

"Where is Severus?" I asked.

"Gone," Paulus told me. "And so is Vardanes. They took a strong force of soldiers and headed west at first light."

The two Parthian archers waiting outside the door were getting impatient. "Come. Come. You go," one said in guttural, broken Greek, motioning us out. "Hurry."

I glanced at Aedan and Aristides. "What do you think?" I said under my breath. "Does anyone believe they'll just let us go?"

"No," the decurion said, with a wry, wintry smile. "Why should those fine fellows out there risk the wrath of their commander when they can earn his praise— and keep the money, too?"

The Greek doctor looked troubled. "He's right, Lucius."

I nodded. Their thoughts mirrored my own. Once we were outside this prison, we were fair game. These Parthian guards could kill us all, claim they only shot us down when we tried to escape, and still pocket the gold they'd been paid to let us go free.

"Then we do this the hard way," I told them. "Understand?"

They nodded tightly.

Paulus stared at the three of us. "What are you talking about?" he asked.

"You'll see," I told him. My voice sounded strained and much harsher than I'd intended. Seeing his face crumple, I added, "But you have my deepest thanks for this chance, Paulus. Whatever happens, you've shown great courage and resourcefulness."

He turned red again.

I put a hand on the boy's shoulder. "Listen to me carefully, Paulus. Aedan and I are going outside now. But I want you and the doctor to stay here. No matter what the guards say or do, you two *will* stay put. Understand?"

"But, Aurelius Valens—I told you, I've paid them . . ." Paulus protested.

Aristides came up and guided Paulus toward the back of the hut. "Stay with me, lad. Lucius knows what he's doing."

I only hoped the doctor was right.

The Parthian at the door was getting angry now. "You must go! Now!" he growled. He laid a hand on the hilt of the saber at his side.

"Just a moment, friend," I told him, as casually as I could. "We're coming."

I turned and knelt down to pick my military cloak off the dirt floor. While my back blocked the guard's view, I gathered a handful of the loose soil and pebbles Aristides had scraped up earlier. I stood up and glanced at the decurion. "Are you with me, Aedan?" I asked quietly.

The fair-haired Celt nodded. "That I am, Lucius," he replied.

We walked out through the door. I took the lead.

The two Parthians backed away, staying just out of reach. They were cautious men, indeed. That was too bad.

Blinking against the bright sunlight, I looked around, getting my bearings. We were outside Tiberias itself, right below the massive spur of rock holding Herod's palace and his citadel, the place where the rest of my soldiers were confined to quarters. There were other buildings nearby, but all of them were being used only as storehouses for spare construction materials. Severus and Vardanes had chosen well. This was an ideal spot to hold a few inconvenient prisoners.

A slim, slight figure in a hooded cloak waited some distance away, holding the reins of four horses and a single mule. I caught a glimpse of a pale, determined face framed by golden brown hair beneath the cowl. It was Marah. My heart lifted.

Then it sank.

There were three Parthian archers on duty—not just two. The third guard stood watching Marah. He was too close to her for my comfort, and too far away from me.

And then, abruptly, there was no more time to worry.

Irked that Paulus and the doctor were still hanging back inside the hut, one of the Parthians muttered something to his companion. He moved closer to the door, peering into the dimly lit interior.

"You there! Come out!" the guard snapped. He started to draw the curved sword belted at his waist.

Now.

I lunged at the other Parthian, the one closest to me. Snarling, he backed up while feverishly unsheathing his own sword. I hurled the dirt and rocks in my left hand toward his eyes, and let the handle of the scalpel hidden in my cloak fall into my right hand.

The archer ducked his head to avoid being blinded.

I closed on him before he could recover, slamming into him hard enough to knock the sword out of his hand. My left arm locked around his neck in a wrestling hold and I yanked him off balance. The Parthian fell toward me, croaking in sudden alarm. I drew the scalpel across his exposed throat, opening it in a wide crimson slash. Blood pulsed through the air, in time with his failing heart.

I shoved the dying man away, snatched up the saber he'd dropped, and whirled around. The second guard was dead, too — lying faceup near the door with an iron surgical probe protruding from one bloodied eye socket. Aedan was already reaching for his sword.

But we were too late.

The third guard had his bow ready.

I stared at him across an infinity of space, twenty paces or more. The Parthian archer drew his bow back. His eyes narrowed. His arrow was aimed straight at my heart . . .

I froze.

And then I saw that slender cloaked figure appear seemingly out of nowhere, looming up right behind the guard. Her arm thrust forward, straight into his back.

The Parthian's eyes opened wide in shock and horror. His arrow flew wide, whirring off into the sky.

I started running.

The guard dropped the bow. He spun around, fumbling with his hand, trying desperately to grasp the hilt of the knife stuck right in the middle of his back. I reached him and slashed down with all my strength.

The Parthian screamed once, fell, and lay still.

I swung round, wildly searching for more enemies, for more men to fight and kill. There were none.

I slid to my knees, panting hard. The sky and earth seemed to be wheeling past me, spinning around and around through a dizzying, sickening arc.

I felt a delicate hand touch my arm. The world steadied.

"Lucius! Are you hurt?" Marah asked. Her voice shook. "Are you wounded?"

I looked up at her. The hood had fallen away from her

hair. Strands of it shone golden in the sun. There were tears in her eyes again. "No, no, I'm not hurt," I told her quietly. "I'm all right. Thanks to you."

With an effort, I levered myself upright, laying my own hand gently over hers. Her fingers were trembling. "I owe you my life," I said.

"As I owed you mine," she replied even more quietly. "You gave me joy at a time when I thought I would never know happiness again. That was no small gift, even if it was only for a fleeting moment. I understand that now."

"Then all our debts are paid," I said to her solemnly. "And we can begin again on an even footing."

Aristides and Paulus came blinking out of the hut and into the open air. The doctor paused just long enough to retrieve his bloodied scalpel and probe before hurrying over to us. The boy looked ill. He kept his head turned carefully away from the bodies.

Aedan came up, leading Paulus' mule and the horses Marah had brought with her. They whinnied and stamped their hooves, uneasy around the smell of so much blood. "What now?" he asked.

I shaded my eyes and found the sun in the sky. It was still early in the day, no more than an hour or so after dawn.

"We go to Herod's citadel and free our men," I told Aedan. "Severus and Vardanes are ahead of us, but they won't be riding fast. They'll want to keep their horses fresh for the attack on Nazara . . . and they won't know we're coming."

Aedan looked grimly pleased.

Marah stared at me in alarm. "Must you go after them, Lucius?" she whispered. "Haven't you done enough? Haven't you taken enough risks?"

"I don't have a choice," I told her. "While Severus and Vardanes live, none of us are safe. Not me. Not Aedan or Aristides. Not Paulus. Not even you."

"You could come away with me," Marah said softly. "We could run to any province in the empire. To the ends of the earth, if need be. I have money enough to keep us in comfort for the rest of our lives."

I took her aside, out of earshot of the others, and held her close. "Marah, you know that I can't do that. I can't flee my duty. I can't close my eyes to murder. I can't let innocents be slaughtered—not without a fight."

She looked at me for what seemed a long, long time. At last, she sighed. "No, Lucius. You can't. Not and remain true to yourself."

Slowly, regretfully, she pulled away, walked toward Aedan, and took the reins of one of the horses—a beautiful chestnut mare that reminded me painfully of Dancer. The Celt gave her a leg up, and she swung gracefully into her seat, riding sidesaddle.

I followed Marah and stood staring up into her face. "Will you ride back to your estate now?"

Marah nodded. She looked down at me gravely. The longing in her eyes pierced my heart. "And when you've fought your battle, will you come and see me, Lucius?" she murmured.

All thought of my father's disapproval, of the differences between us, vanished. I still didn't know what would happen between us, or what future we might have together. But I did know that I wanted very much to find out. "If I live, I will," I promised.

"Then live," she said simply. With that, she leaned far out of the saddle and kissed me fiercely.

I heard Paulus gasp. I ignored him.

When at length our lips parted, Marah took up the

reins and wheeled her horse away. Then she glanced back over her shoulder. Her face was alive, vibrant once more. "Until we meet again, Lucius," she said.

Aristides stood at my shoulder, watching her ride down the hill toward Tiberias. "A remarkable woman," he murmured. "But I do have one piece of advice."

"Yes?"

"If you ever make her angry with you, keep the knives away from her."

Chapter XXII

I lay flat on the crest line of a ridge, pressed close to the ground beside a massive boulder. From this concealed vantage point, I had a clear view all the way down the long, gentle slope and into the shallow valley beyond, a bowl with higher ground surrounding it on all sides. The main track from Tiberias to Nazara and the other nearby villages ran through there, winding past several small stands of trees, mostly scrub oaks.

Vardanes and his Parthians were down in that valley, a dark mass of men and horses slowly milling around on both sides of the trail. They were just outside of bow-shot, close enough so that I could hear the distant murmur of their voices. Most of the archers had dismounted, allowing their horses to graze. Severus and his four Praetorian guardsmen were there, too. I could see their red cloaks and the gleam of sunlight winking off their polished armor.

Beyond them, the track climbed up another slope, heading roughly west past a steep conical knoll strewn with jumbled rocks. Nazara was somewhere on the other side of that next rise, no more than a mile or so ahead.

"Lucius!"

I turned my head toward the source of the hoarse whisper and saw Aedan coming up the slope behind me. He stopped well below the skyline. Aristides and Paulus were trudging up the hill after him. I waved them on, signaling them to stay low. One by one, they slid into cover and crouched beside me.

"Any luck?" I asked Aedan.

The Celt shook his head. "None." He paused to take a quick swig from a leather water flask, then went on with his report. "All the scouts are back in. That sly snake Vardanes has pickets posted along every trail and goat path from here to the village. There's no chance of anyone slipping past them with a message for Taedifer and his men without being spotted."

I frowned. That was ugly news. I'd left the burly, red-haired decurion and fifty veteran cavalrymen watching over Nazara. I'd been counting on their aid in the coming fight. Without them, we would be heavily outnumbered.

I craned my head around, looking back at the small band of soldiers under my direct command. Together with a handful of their servants, they were waiting at the base of this low ridge resting their mounts after the hard, fast ride from Tiberias. I'd taken thirty cavalrymen into action against Gideon and his bandits. One had died. That left me with just twenty-nine trained troopers, three of whom were lightly wounded. But at least they were all eager to wipe away the shame of being caught off guard by the Parthians the day before.

Fortunately, winning their release from Herod's citadel had proved much easier than I'd first feared. With Aedan and me as his prisoners, Severus hadn't anticipated any real trouble from the rest of our men. He hadn't even bothered trying to disarm them. He'd simply ordered them confined to barracks inside the fortress and then bustled off with Vardanes to prepare the destruction of Nazara.

I smiled wryly to myself. For once, the Praetorian centurion had proved overconfident. He should have taken more precautions. At the very least he should have left more of Vardanes' archers behind to keep an eye on his prisoners. There wasn't any love lost between the Parthian exile and his rival captains—a common problem for armies made up of hired warriors, each jealous of his own prerogatives, pay, and reputation. And not a single one of them owed any loyalty at all to Severus, whom they viewed as an arrogant Roman interloper.

In the end, none of Herod's other mercenaries wanted to entangle themselves in what appeared to be a private fight between the Praetorian officer and me. By acting against me without the tetrarch's explicit orders, Severus had given them an out. The guards had stood aside when Aedan and I rode into the citadel, and they'd stood aside again when we brought our troopers out, along with all our weapons, armor, and other gear.

Herod ran a sloppy, slipshod army—fortunately for me and for the people of Nazara.

"Why are the Parthians just sitting there? They were at least an hour or two ahead of us," Paulus said impatiently. "Why haven't they attacked already?"

Aedan checked the position of the sun with a practiced eye. "They're waiting for the farmers to come in from their fields."

I agreed with the decurion's assessment.

"Vardanes isn't a fool," I told the boy. "If he attacked now, he'd have to disperse his horsemen through the maze of fields and orchards around Nazara. He doesn't have enough men to do that and make sure that none of the villagers escapes. He won't take that risk." I shook my head grimly. "No, Vardanes and Severus will let those poor people put themselves all the way into the noose before they draw it shut."

Paulus scowled down at the horse archers massed below us. "So what can we do to stop them?"

I frowned. "*You* will do nothing, boy. A battle's no place for someone your age—especially someone who's never handled a sword in his life. If I could spare the men, I'd have you on your way to Jerusalem right now."

Paulus stiffened. Angry and ashamed, he stared down at the ground, refusing to meet my eyes. I could tell he was tired of being dismissed, left behind, and generally ignored.

I sighed. I hadn't meant to speak so coldly, but the truth was I was feeling very guilty about the boy. His father had trusted Germanicus to arrange a safe passage for him from Antioch to Jerusalem. In turn, Germanicus had put him in my care. And what had I done? Dragged him from one scene of bloodshed and carnage to another. The battle that was coming was bound to be a desperate and bloody affair. It was also a battle I knew we were far more likely to lose than to win, though I buried that knowledge deeply within myself.

"The boy has a good question, Lucius," Aristides said quietly. "You command fewer than thirty men, armed only with javelins and swords. Severus and Vardanes must have close to a hundred horsemen down there. And all the Parthians carry bows powerful enough to bring a man or horse down at more than two hundred paces." He hesitated for a heartbeat, then went on. "Forgive me for saying so, but the odds seem a bit steep."

Somehow I found the strength to give him a lopsided smile. "Your years with the legions have done you some good after all, Aristides. You've summed up the tactical situation as neatly as though you were a commander of thousands."

"When I smell horseshit, I know there's usually a horse around somewhere," the Greek doctor said dryly, quoting an old country proverb that had been a favorite of my grandfather's.

I accepted the reproof with as much good grace as I could muster. "We are outmatched," I agreed, thinking out loud. "We don't have superiority in numbers. Or in weapons. But we do have one great edge: surprise. Vardanes and that Praetorian bastard don't have the faintest idea we're on the loose and within striking distance."

I stared down at the Parthian horses placidly grazing in the tall grass lining the trail to Nazara. "And we must make the most of it."

The faint wisp of a scheme began taking shape in my mind. It was still a desperate gamble. But it was the best of the various alternatives. I ran my gaze over that valley and the surrounding heights one more time, memorizing the terrain and estimating distances and ranges. My tactics soon took on solid form. I knew what we had to do.

I looked back at the others. They were watching me closely.

"Listen!" I told them. "Here's how we're going to win this fight . . ." Then, using the point of my dagger, I sketched out my battle plan in the sun-baked dirt of the hillside.

*   *   *

Within the hour, Aedan and I were on horseback, trotting steadily toward the mouth of the little valley occupied by the Parthians. My troopers followed in a column of threes. To screen our movements, we were riding parallel to the ridge, keeping the high ground between our quarry and us for as long as possible. I was astride a gray stallion, once the property of the lone soldier killed in our clash with Gideon's bandits. He was a big brute, but fleet of foot and trained for war.

I looked back over my shoulder.

Aristides and Paulus stood watching us go. They were surrounded by the cavalrymen's servants, who had strict instructions to get them to safety in Jerusalem if this attack went badly. Before we moved out, Commius, Aedan's servant, and the other grooms had all volunteered to join the attack. Though they knew how long the odds were against victory, none of them wanted to be left behind. I'd thanked them quietly for their courage and their devotion, and then repeated my orders. The servants weren't equipped with armor or trained for close-quarters battle. Taking them into combat would only get them killed, without serving any useful purpose.

My soldiers and I were paid to run risks. But I had no intention of dragging anyone else—especially not my old friend and the boy—down with us.

Aristides saw me looking at him and solemnly lifted his old battered hat high over his head in a salute. I knew he wasn't happy seeing me ride off, but he'd contented himself with a gruff warning. "Watch yourself, Lucius. And please try not to get hurt this time. I'm tired of bandaging you up after every battle."

After a moment's hesitation, Paulus waved his own hand in farewell.

I hid a smile. The boy from Tarsus was still irked that I wouldn't even let him watch the upcoming fight with the Parthians. Somehow I expected him to find a way to flout my orders, probably with the willing aid of those I'd set to keep him safe.

We pulled up a short distance from the entrance to the valley, but still well out of sight of Vardanes and his men. Ahead of us, the trail to Nazara swung wide through a gap in the ridge we were paralleling.

Aedan and I trotted up and down the formation, making one last inspection. Each soldier wore a mail corselet and an iron helmet. Each bore a long sword sheathed at his right side and carried a large oval shield on his left arm. And every cavalryman had three javelins in a quiver slung from the right rear horn of his saddle.

Satisfied by what I saw, I rode back to the head of the assault column. Aedan fell in five ranks behind.

I wheeled my horse around and plucked a javelin out of my own quiver. Then I stood higher in the saddle so that the silent waiting soldiers could see me clearly. "I'm not going to waste my breath making a fancy speech," I told them, pitching my voice to carry all the way to the back of the formation. "You all know your trade. Keep your ranks. Stay close to your comrades. Watch and listen for my orders. If I fall, look to Aedan. Is that clear?"

Heads nodded down the length of the column.

"Good." I forced a confident grin onto my face. "Then let's go give those goat-loving Parthian bastards a swift kick in the ass!"

That drew a deep, appreciative laugh. My men were keyed up and ready to fight.

I wheeled again and held the javelin aloft. Then I

brought it down abruptly, signaling the advance. "Soldiers of the Third Gallic Cavalry! Forward!"

We moved off at a slow walk, riding steadily toward the bend in the trail. The Parthians were close, just around that corner.

Two hundred paces from the mouth of the valley, I kicked my horse into a trot. Behind me, the column sped up, moving faster now. I glanced backward. Every trooper had a javelin out and ready.

One hundred paces. We were cantering now. I could feel my pulse hammering faster and faster, my breath quickening. Soon, I thought. Very soon.

My horse strode smoothly through an arc, following the curve of the trail to Nazara. We came up and over a low rise and thundered down into the valley.

There were men and horses up ahead. The Parthians! A few were in the saddle. Most were still on foot, holding the reins of their mounts. I saw heads turning, mouths opening in shock.

I took a deep breath, filled my lungs, and roared, "Charge!"

The troopers behind me took up the shout. We broke into a gallop and raced up the trail, flying straight toward the stunned enemy.

My focus narrowed to the ground ahead of me. To the feel of the horse between my knees. To its mane streaming in the wind. To the horrified face of the nearest Parthian, frantically trying to string his bow.

Too late, I thought coolly, swinging my left shoulder forward while drawing my right arm back. The point of my javelin wavered, then centered on his chest. Now! I rose higher in the saddle and hurled the spear with all my might.

It flashed through the air in the blink of an eye and

struck home, tearing deep into the Parthian's stomach. He folded over and toppled off his horse.

I raced past, already pulling another javelin from the quiver slung behind me. Another man loomed up out of the dust, this one on foot. He had a saber out. I threw hard. I don't know whether or not I hit him. We galloped on, pounding up the track.

I swung round in the saddle. Most of the Parthians were fleeing, scattering away from the trail like a flock of frightened geese before a pack of snarling dogs. Others were down, crumpled in the dirt.

My hand closed on the last javelin in my quiver. I leaned forward, found a target in range, and threw again. A horse shrieked and crashed to the ground, spilling its screaming rider and then crushing the life out of him.

The trail ahead was clear. We were through!

Gripped by a feeling of triumph, by a sense of exultation close to madness, I laughed aloud. "Swords!" I shouted.

My troopers obeyed, still yelling their war cries. Like me, they were caught up in bloodlust, in the wild urge to kill and kill and kill again. To slash and hack and stab our way to victory.

I drew my own sword. It flew out of the scabbard, whirling in a gleaming arc through the sunlight. I turned again in the saddle. Should we turn back and charge again? The Parthians weren't any match for us at close quarters.

Dead and dying men and horses littered the trail and the open slopes on either side. But I could see a mass of mounted men gathering a few hundred paces away. My exultation faded. The Parthians were already re-forming, recovering fast from their initial panic.

An arrow hissed past my face, burying itself in the ground in front of my horse. I swore viciously and leaned forward over my horse's neck. We passed a small copse of scrub oaks. More shafts screamed toward me. Some skittered off rocks in a shower of sparks. Others thwacked into bark or tore through the undergrowth.

The trooper riding on my left went down suddenly, caught by an arrow through the throat. Sanity came rushing back. Our charge had killed or wounded many of the Parthians, but we were still heavily outnumbered. I wheeled out of the column, looking for Aedan.

He saw me and shouted a question: "What orders, Lucius?"

I pointed up the trail to Nazara. "Stick to the plan! Go now! Ride hard!" Then I swung my sword toward the rocky knoll rising south of the track. "The rest of us will hold them there!"

Aedan nodded tightly. He threw me a quick salute with his blade. "Good fortune!" Then he turned and roared a command to the troopers closest to him. "With me! At the gallop!"

Six troopers broke out of the column and followed the tall Celt in a mad dash west up the track. The rest of the cavalrymen followed me in a wide arc to the south, forcing our horses up the slope of that cone-shaped hill. Our once-tight formation was breaking apart as the faster horses outpaced the slower ones, and as we threaded our way between boulders and trees.

I glanced over my shoulder. Vardanes' archers were coming after us, firing their powerful compound bows from the saddle. Another flight of arrows arced through the air and hammered down all around us. A soldier close to me screamed as an arrowhead punched through his armor and into his back. He fell forward, then slid off his horse and disappeared beneath its hooves.

I swore again as another trooper grabbed at my arm, pointing wildly down the slope. "Prefect, look! The decurion!"

I stared over my shoulder, still urging my mount up the slope. I could see a tangle of men and horses writhing in the middle of the track, hit by a dense volley. Some of the archers were peeling off from the Parthian force, swinging wide to cut us off from Nazara.

The sour taste of bile rose in my throat. Had Aedan or any of his men escaped that slaughter? Or were they all caught in that arrow-torn heap? For a fleeting moment, despair closed in—all blackness and fear and mounting panic.

With an effort, I shook it off. Whether this battle was won or lost, my soldiers were looking to me. If we were going to die, it was my job to make sure Vardanes and Severus paid dearly for their triumph.

I tore my eyes away and focused on the hill ahead. The knoll was steeper here and my horse was laboring, fighting its way up toward a pile of boulders crowning the summit. Come on, boy, come on, I told the stallion silently, using my knees to urge him to one last effort.

The horse forced its way higher, finally stopping only a short distance from the top, unable to go farther. White foam flecked its flaring nostrils and streaked its heaving flanks. I swung down out of the saddle. "Dismount!"

Then I swatted my exhausted mount on the rump, sending it stumbling back down the slope. "To me! To me!" I shouted. "Up shields!"

The men left to me, fewer than twenty now, obeyed—sliding to the ground in a jangle of armor.

They chased their own horses off and closed around me. We raised our shields, trying to lock them together.

More Parthian arrows hissed through the sky, clattering off of shields or thudding into the hillside at our feet. One of my cavalrymen fell, hit in the chest. He rolled down the slope, tumbling over and over in an awkward tangle of arms and legs.

Step by step, I led the others backward up the hill and into the partial cover provided by the jumble of rocks covering its rounded peak. "Stay low, lads," I called. "Keep your shields up! Make these bastards come to us!"

We crouched, holding the high ground under a storm of arrows. More shafts shattered on the rocks or lodged deep in our shields. Another trooper went down, struck in the shoulder. He lay tight-lipped, bleeding profusely, but he still held on to his sword.

Minutes went by and our losses rose with them, slowly but steadily. Of the men I'd brought with me to the top of the hill, already three were dead and another three too seriously wounded to fight.

I could make out Vardanes below us, still on horseback. The Parthian noble was urging a thin skirmish line of dismounted archers up the slope. He'd kept most of his men in the saddle. They were massed at the base of the knoll, ready to ride us down if we broke and ran.

Five men in gleaming mail and scarlet cloaks were moving up behind the skirmishers. My eyes narrowed. Severus and his Praetorians had joined the fight. I couldn't fault their tactics. At close range, the archers advancing on foot could cut us to pieces. If we charged them, the skirmishers would fall back and we'd be caught out on the open hillside, exposed to murderous fire from the mounted men below.

The dismounted archers and the guardsmen drew nearer. I tensed. They were almost in reach.

The arrows were coming faster now, hissing down in volley after volley. The Parthians on horseback were aiming high. Their shafts soared into the sky and then plunged down onto us, falling with tremendous force.

More of the men around me were hit. Some stayed up, trying to ignore the pain from their wounds. Others slumped, dead or dying. I bit my lip. My little band of soldiers was dwindling fast. Soon, I'd have to make a terrible decision: stay in among these rocks and watch my troopers fall one by one . . . or make a last desperate charge in the hope that we could kill a few of the enemy—perhaps even Severus himself—before we were killed in turn.

I felt sick. My wild-eyed gamble had failed. I'd led these men into a slaughter pen, and all for nothing. We would die, and so would the innocents of Nazara.

Better to attack now, I decided grimly. Better to go down that open slope and die fighting than to crouch here and be butchered. I moved a little way out in front of my troops, ready to lead them down.

Then I stopped, staring past Vardanes and his mounted archers. Was that movement beyond the nearest copse of trees?

An arrow ripped through the mail bunched up over my right arm. The point missed me, but the force of its passage drove the metal links deep into my flesh. My eyes blurred. Two more shafts slammed into my shield, rocking me back.

I heard a voice shouting orders and saw Vardanes up near his skirmish line, pointing straight at me. He was ordering his dismounted men to concentrate their fire on me. Severus was at his elbow, yelling something.

I took a deep breath . . .

And a trumpet blared suddenly, loud and shrill.

I peered over the edge of my shield again and felt my
heart soar. Two ranks of Gallic cavalrymen charged out
from behind the trees, smashing headlong into the
Parthian flank. I recognized Aedan in the lead and found
myself half laughing, half crying in sheer joy. The tall,
fair-haired Celt was alive. He'd followed my orders.
And he'd brought Taedifer and the soldiers I'd left
guarding Nazara into the battle at the best possible moment.

Horse archers toppled to the ground screaming,
skewered by hurled javelins. Others went down under
fierce sword strokes. The cavalrymen tore a huge hole
in the enemy formation, driving deep. Swords and
sabers flashed in the sun.

The Parthians were forced back in disorder. I could
see them wavering, right on the edge of panic. One by
one, they were peeling away from the melee, drifting
away out of the fight, ready to run.

Down the slope below me, I saw Vardanes swing
around, plainly stunned. He shook his head once in disbelief, spat a curse at Severus, and wheeled his horse
downhill. Saber held high, he rode straight into the
press.

Aedan went to meet him.

Their blades clashed, fell back, and met again. Vardanes cut viciously at the Celt's head. Aedan ducked
under it and thrust. For a long moment, the Parthian
noble stared down at the sword buried deep in his chest.
He shook his head again, slumped wearily, and then he
fell—disappearing among the hacking, slashing mass
of horsemen.

The Parthians broke. They scattered in all directions,

throwing away their sabers and bows in panic. Aedan and Taedifer's men charged after the fugitives with their bloodied swords held aloft, shouting in exultation.

I looked down the slope. The dismounted archers were standing thunderstruck, staring back over their shoulders at the slaughter in the valley below them. One solid blow would break them, too.

I whirled toward my little band, a wild grin on my face. They saw it and roared. "Up!" I shouted, waving my sword down the hill. "Up and at them!"

My men, the handful who could still move, rose from among the bloodstained, arrow-scarred boulders and charged after me, plunging toward the Parthian skirmish line. Panicked, the archers threw their bows aside and fled in terror.

Only Severus and his guardsmen stood firm.

I headed straight for the grim-faced centurion. He was mine.

Severus saw me coming. One corner of his mouth lifted in a wry smile. Then he attacked—lunging forward with startling speed. I threw my shield up just in time, driving his short, stabbing blade off target. He took my riposte on his own shield.

Again and again, our swords flickered in and out—slashing, thrusting, and parrying. We circled each other, now attacking, now defending. Both of us ignored the larger battle still raging around us, intent only on killing each other.

The Praetorian was fresh, barely winded. I was exhausted, already worn down by nights without sleep and days full of hard riding and even harder fighting. He was taller than I was. And stronger. He was also incredibly skilled. Three times in quick succession I narrowly dodged lightning-fast strikes that could have finished me.

The last one, a wicked thrust that slid past the bottom of my shield, stabbed my right calf.

I fell back out of reach. The wound didn't hurt yet, but I could feel blood trickling down my leg. Droplets of sweat fell into my eyes. They stung, blurring my vision. I shook them away impatiently. Somehow I had to find a way to finish this fight before he wore me down.

"Run away, boy," Severus said quietly. "You're no match for me. Run away and live."

I shook my head stubbornly. "Never."

The Praetorian shrugged coolly. "So be it."

And then he attacked again, pushing in with a series of powerful thrusts and slashes that forced me back up the hill step by step. I never got the chance to counter-attack. It was all I could do to defend myself.

Severus was smiling openly now. He held the initiative and he knew it.

My wounded leg throbbed painfully now whenever I had to put my weight on it. The centurion drove me back another few paces and the pain grew with every step.

I winced. And then I saw his eyes flicker downward. In that instant, I knew what Severus would do next. He moved forward with his blade held high. But that was just a feint.

I threw myself toward him, trying to get inside his reach before he could ram his sword down into my injured leg again.

It almost worked.

My sword deflected his thrust and threw it aside. Our shields slammed together and locked. I stared into the centurion's cold, angry eyes. We were only inches apart.

Grunting with effort, he shoved me backward with one powerful heave. My right foot came down on a loose stone and the leg buckled. I lost my balance and stumbled forward again.

Right onto Severus' sword thrust.

I felt the blade smash through my armor and tear deep into my stomach, right under my ribs. It stopped there, buried halfway up to the hilt. He tugged it out with a cruel grin. I staggered back up the slope, suddenly engulfed in agony.

The Praetorian laughed aloud. He moved forward, drawing his own shield aside to give himself room for another deadly thrust—the one that would finish me.

Bastard.

Desperately, I summoned up every ounce of my fading strength and lashed out with my own shield, trying to smash the metal boss into his grinning face. Caught by surprise, Severus fell back down the hill.

His sandal came down on a slick patch of my blood and he slipped. Swearing in sudden panic, he teetered there, fighting to regain his balance on the steep slope.

Now, Lucius, I thought. Strike now. Or die alone.

I swung my sword as hard and as fast as I could. It slashed through the air, aimed straight at his face. He saw it coming. But too late. Much too late. His eyes opened wide.

The blade bit deep and stuck.

Severus was thrown to his knees by the impact. His shattered face was a ghastly mask of blood and broken bone. Only one of his eyes was left intact. It stared back at me for a brief moment, full of pain and utter incredulity—and then the life in it flickered out. The centurion toppled to the side, tearing the sword out of my hand. He writhed once, quivered, and then died.

I fell to my own knees, swaying as the pain worsened. It was a fire now, an inferno blazing deep inside me. I could feel the blood pouring out through the great wound in my stomach. I did not look down. I knew the horror I would see there. No man could take such an injury and live long. The fire burned higher.

I was dying.

I don't know how long I knelt there, bleeding my life out into the dirt of that barren hillside in Galilee. Time drifted past. It no longer had any meaning for me.

"Curse you," I heard someone say hoarsely, drawing nearer.

Wearily, I lifted my head and saw Araneus climbing toward me, reeling past the corpses heaped here and there across the slope. The astrologer's robes were torn and bloodied. His eyes were wild—full of madness and hate and rage.

He raised a dagger, staggering closer. "Interfering fool," he gasped. "You've ruined everything. You've destroyed everything . . ."

I stared at him, noticing a huge gash in the side of his head. One arm hung limp at his side. I thought I could see the white of broken bone poking through a ragged tear in his sleeve. The magus must have been caught up in the final melee, hacked down, and left for dead.

Araneus saw the Praetorian centurion's corpse and hesitated. His face was haggard and ashen. He shook his head bitterly. "So Severus failed, too. Now he is spinning away into the void, into nothingness. And I am lost. And all is lost." He looked up. His jaw tightened. "Well, then, I'll take you with me. I'll kill you myself."

Despite the agony, I felt my mouth twist into a contorted smile. "You're too late," I forced out through the pain.

The astrologer snarled, and moved toward me. He raised the dagger high.

"No!" The high-pitched, boyish shout rang out across the hillside.

Araneus turned, still snarling. A rock crashed into his forehead, gashing it to the bone. He groaned, trying to focus on this new threat through the blood pouring into his eyes.

Paulus was there, just a few feet away.

Araneus grimaced. He staggered toward the boy, still holding the knife.

Paulus stood his ground. He bent down and picked up another rock. Then he hurled it with all his might.

The smooth stone flew straight, smashing into the astrologer's head with a dull, heavy sound. It crushed his skull. Scarlet streams of blood gushed from his nose, ears, and eyes. Araneus swayed once and then fell. His dagger buried itself in the ground.

Paulus stood mute and horrified, looking down at the man he'd just killed. His right hand, the hand that had thrown the stone, clenched and unclenched. After a moment, he turned to me. I saw the shock on his face when he first saw the terrible sword wound in my stomach. He gasped. Tears rolled down his cheeks.

I tried to speak. No words came. I made a new effort, straining against a mounting tide of anguish. "Paulus," I panted. "Bring the doctor. Bring Aristides . . ."

And then the pain roared higher still, consuming everything around me. The world faded and was gone.

I regained consciousness sometime later. I was lying propped up against a boulder. My eyes focused on an ant crawling across the blood-drenched soil toward my torn right leg. I could not move.

The pain from my wounds was still present, but now
I felt it at a great distance. I looked away from the ant.
All color, all life, was draining out of my surroundings,
leaving only shades of gray. The world was growing
colder. I shivered.

A shadow fell across me.

Weakly, I raised my eyes. A man stood there, looking
down. I could not make out his face. "Aristides?" I
whispered.

The man knelt beside me. It was Yeshua, the young
carpenter from Nazara. His face was full of sorrow, full
of pain.

I looked away, unable to bear the sight of so much
sadness. I looked down the slope, seeing the dead men
and horses strewn all across the hillside and the little
valley. There were dozens, some lying together, others
alone.

My gaze fell on a body not far away. It was Durix, the
bravest and most boastful of the recruits I'd brought
from Antioch. He lay curled up against a rock, still
clutching the shaft of the arrow that had killed him.

I swallowed hard.

The Galilean followed my gaze. He sighed. "This
battle was not my wish, Aurelius Valens. Too many
men—good and bad alike—have died here."

I turned back to Yeshua in confusion. Not his wish?
What did he mean by that? But now the pain was coming closer again, growing in intensity. It was robbing me
of breath. I fought for the strength to speak and found to
my amazement that I wanted to comfort him, this man
who was alive and unhurt. "Don't mourn us," I said finally, gasping out the words in short spurts. "We did our
duty as soldiers. We fought to protect your village from
evil."

"Not my village," Yeshua said softly. "Me."

I stared up at him, blinking back sudden tears. The Galilean was silhouetted against the sun.

He turned his face upward toward the clouds, toward the sky. "Father, hear my prayer," he said quietly. "I know the hour is not yet upon me. But still I ask this in your name."

A new wave of pain rippled upward through me, driving the breath from my torn and bleeding body. I closed my eyes—but not before I saw a flickering, dancing tongue of fire hover over the young Galilean's head. In that instant, too, I heard the sound of mighty wings fluttering close by.

And then I felt Yeshua's hands press down hard on my stomach. I stiffened, arching my back, expecting unspeakable torment. But there was no terrible agony, no searing pain.

None.

I felt only warmth and comfort and happiness. I drifted at peace, not caring suddenly whether I lived or died. The voices of those I loved most in the world came to me in the darkness: my mother, my grandfather, Aristides, Marah, Aedan . . . even that of my father.

Then I heard a new voice, that of the Galilean. He leaned forward and whispered in my ear, "You will live, Lucius. But no longer solely for yourself." He touched my forehead gently. "When the time is right, come and follow me."

And though my eyes were closed, still I saw a great blaze of blinding light shining before me. It grew and grew, ever larger, ever nearer, and ever brighter, illuminating every part of my being. The darkness around me vanished, leaving only this great light.

Trembling, I stretched out my hand . . . straining to touch the wonder I beheld.

And then I fell away, tumbling down and down, falling all the way from the heavens to the earth.

Epilogue

It feels strange to read again something I wrote in such frantic haste so many years ago. So much has happened, so much has changed—both in my own life and in that of the world—that some might see a great distance between the young, fiery soldier who penned that narrative and the man I am now.

And yet there is not really that wide a gulf between us—between Lucius Aurelius Valens, that impatient, intemperate soldier, and me. I think now that much of what I have since become was there already, waiting only to be called, when Yeshua of Nazara first laid his hands on me.

But it is true that that young carpenter—for such I then believed him to be—set my feet on a different road, on a path I might never have followed of my own accord.

"Come and follow me," he said.

Such a simple thing—and yet so difficult.

I did not know then what that quiet command would really mean, or how it would take shape in my life. My road here to Antioch was longer and full of more twists and turns than I could ever have imagined. Some of those I have written of here, Aristides and Aedan and Paulus and Marah among them, walked this journey with me—though in very different ways and often at different times.

Those days have left me with many other tales I long to tell. They were full of great joys and terrible sorrows. I have found true friends and encountered bitter enemies. I have witnessed heroism and cowardice, malice and love, foul murder and noble self-sacrifice. I have seen emperors take the stage in glory and then depart into the shadows—Tiberius, Caligula, Claudius, Nero, and more besides. And I have lived long enough to see those who were thought mighty brought low, and those who were thought worthless raised high.

But only now—at long last—do I begin to understand the true work for which I am intended. For years I have traveled far and wide throughout Judea and Galilee, through Syria and Asia, and even to Rome itself, gathering the stories, the witness, of many different people.

I have begun weaving those stories into an ordered account—a faithful account—of all that I have learned. I will write this narrative in Greek, for now I bear a Greek name, the counterpart of Lucius. With the passage of time, most of my Latin has all fallen away, along with those parts of my early life that no longer have meaning. Here is how I shall begin:

"In the days of King Herod of Judea there lived a priest called Zechariah who belonged to the Abijah section of the priesthood, and he had a wife, Elizabeth by name, who was a descendant of Aaron. Both were worthy in the sight of the Most High, and scrupulously observed all the commandments and observances of the Lord. But they were childless: Elizabeth was barren and they were both getting on in years . . ."

—LUKE

Acknowledgments

Many people have helped me tell this story.

Thomas T. Thomas, Greta Rosenberger, John Gee, Pam McKinney-Peckinpaugh, Bill and Bridget Paley, and Jeff Pluhar all provided support and helped me across a number of hurdles. Many of the members of the ConsimWorld Discussion Board also provided encouragement and good advice, especially Goran Semb, Ken Schultz, William Terdoslavich, Austin Lange, Mark Perry, and Walter Zaagman.

My agent, Robert Gottlieb, chairman of Trident Media Group, L.L.C., first turned my eye toward the remarkable possibilities of the Roman era—and then stood by me from start to finish. My editor at New American Library, Dan Slater, shepherded the book to publication with a mix of encouragement, insight, and sound counsel.

Most important of all, I want to thank my wife, Mennette Masser Larkin. Her keen ear for language, sharp sense of character and plot, and near-infinite patience made *The Tribune* a far better book.